CELINE L.A. SIMPSON

MUSIC TO MY EARS

THE DUOLOGY

LADY LUCK

Rip Rey

xoxo Nugatt

Luke xD

Angus Dravin

Aspen

CELINE L.A. SIMPSON

Music to my Ears

(MTME Book 1)

First edition

ISBN: 978-1-7635659-2-0

Editing by Joeli Woodrow
Cover art by Celine L.A. Simpson

This book was professionally typeset on Reedsy.
Find out more at reedsy.com

for everyone who was convinced
that the band on stage
made direct eye contact with them

...

They did. they absolutely did.

Dax & Allie

1

Allie

I was 100% one of those people that insisted that the more I pressed the button that illuminated the little walking man, letting me know I could safely cross the road, the faster the light would change. I thought the world was separated into two types of people. There were those like me, who believed in the power of the speedy tapping of the crosswalk button, and there were those who believed it wasn't connected to anything and thus, didn't do anything.

I loved December, but holy cannoli, the wind was so cold I could almost feel the snot I was consistently sniffling up turn into little icicles in my nose.

Rapidly pressing the crosswalk button, I was hopping from foot to foot, eager to make my way towards the light. The heavenly light of the iridescent 'Open-24-Hours' corner store that was a blissful 1-minute walk from my apartment.

I had a shitty day, a *really* shitty day. The kind of day that almost had me thinking that maybe the crosswalk button didn't do anything. Maybe it was all a lie and I really was just your run-of-the-mill idiot who pressed it too much and too quickly. But then the light changed, and I was instantly reaffirmed that that was complete baloney. It might have been the only win I had for the day, and you better believe I was grabbing it with both hands.

Today was another 'I need something so sweet my teeth will fall straight out of my head' kind of day. So, after working late and receiving far too many, and completely unsubtle, ass-pats from my knob of a boss for a congratulations on yet another successful marketing campaign execution, it was all I could do not to crawl into the corner store.

As the light got brighter and my frozen feet brought me closer to the haven I'd been yearning for, I tried to appreciate the quiet calm that was the inner city. The type of quiet that you didn't get often but when it happened, the silence seemed to be too loud.

The melody of Mozart's *Rondo Alla Turca* trickled into my mind. My fingers trilled the air in front of me as if my hands were gliding over the ivory keys of my beloved piano. I could hear the build of my favourite moment, the perfect crescendo, that I almost let my eyes shut, to completely immerse myself into its bliss.

The warm air that so abruptly opposed the frigid wind outside the small corner store hit me, or rather I hit it, and it shook me from the only moment of peace I had found all day. The immediate contrast made my nose sting to the point of making my eyes water, causing my face to scrunch up and look like something I was confident resembled a raisin.

So, it would appear to anyone around me that I was caught in that dreadful in-between moment where you needed to sneeze, but you couldn't. And the sneeze itself has yet to decide whether to just flutter away or come back with vengeance.

In an effort to recollect myself, I quickly unwound my *skeenie* (it was both a scarf and a beanie – a *skeenie*), took off my gloves and threw them both into the tote bag I had slung over my shoulder.

To add onto the almost-sneezing face scrunch, I also felt myself immediately start to perspire thanks to the sudden temperature drop and the ridiculous number of layers I had on.

Running my hand through my hair to give it a bit of life after its own slumber beneath my *skeenie*, I made a beeline for the baking aisle. Throwing a casual wave to the cashier who saw me here so often, and always at the same time buying the same thing, I should've really tried to find another corner store to alternate between. But as I said, this one was a 1-minute walk from my apartment, so, fat chance.

There was only one other person in the baking aisle, unusual, but it had happened before.

The loud whispers from the figure that was bundled behind the upturned collar of his thick, black, almost floor length coat – very *Sherlock Holmes* – was not something that I would've usually concerned myself with.

The guy was keeping to his own business and I was more than happy not to have a witness when I carried more than my body weight of do-it-yourself brownie packs to the checkout. But my completely unabashed admiration for his bright, red hair - long enough to be tucked behind his ears and fashioned in a sort of messy-but-on-purpose way - had me gaping like an opened mouth trout.

There were some people who could just *do* that with their hair, and I was so envious it made me want to hurl. Don't get me wrong, I loved my hair - it fell just to the top of my bum and cascaded in long, light brown waves. I'd never *not* grown it, and it had only ever been short once and it wasn't an experience I wanted to have again. Ever.

I just wished that sometimes I could've been that person, the one who bleached the living daylights out of their hair and then poured on a colour dye, all in the safety of their own bathroom and with complete disregard for all the YouTube 'hairdresser reacts' videos that assured you that you would 100% end up with spaghetti hair if you did the above.

Regardless, the tall guy with the red hair and cool jacket was in the baking aisle, same as me and I understood that, it resonated. Clearly.

Maybe it was the day I had, or that fact that at the end of it all I could admit to myself that I was feeling a little, okay *a lot*, lonelier than usual, but I turned to face him.

"Everything literally looks the fucking same, how are there so many versions of the same thing?" he whisper-shouted to whoever was on the other end of the phone plastered to his ear.

I took a deep breath and popped my best 'hello, I know we're strangers but I swear I'm not weird despite my socks and gross greasy hair. I actually shower often and have a great shampoo and conditioner regime' smile and walked over to help him out.

2

Allie

I lifted my hand up in a half-hearted wave, "Hey," and then dropped it immediately.

I was confident that my smile was the most inviting thing in the world until the tall guy with the red hair whipped his head towards me so fast, I thought I heard his neck crack.

His face was a mask of both shock and horror and made me feel like I had something green in my teeth. It felt like it was a freeze-frame of a moment that held for too long and immediately regretted.

The single second it took for his phone to fall from his face to the ground snapped both of us out of it and had me taking a small step back from what was already a respectable distance from a stranger to start with, while he bent down to snatch it up.

I cleared my throat and tried again, my smile probably looked a bit more forced than before. Because it *absolutely* was.

"I don't usually eavesdrop, but I heard your conversation and thought I could help. I love to bake. Not, like, every day, but I bake sometimes. Maybe, like, once a week and not always on weeknights like tonight. I bake on the weekends too. You know, if I'm not busy," I trailed off.

The confident flow of my explanation fizzled off into a whisper as it became very clear I was rambling, feeding him information he did *not* need to know.

I would've loved to have just wrapped my *skeenie* over my face and waited for this dude to walk away because not only was that completely the opposite of what I wanted to say, but this guy was gorgeous. Like, woah, I didn't realise people like him existed in real life, much less in a simple little corner store by my apartment.

He managed to school his features from what I could only assume for him was the unpleasant view of my 'world's most inviting and I swear I'm not a weirdo' smile, to something that looked like worry.

His head whipped to the other side, leaning back to get a good view of the whole aisle behind him. Then he did the same to the side behind me before his eyes - eyes that were a hazel-green and had me, again, looking sort of like a trout - landed right back on me. His gaze was heavy to the point that any lingering chill from outside disappeared very, very fast.

Gulp.

"What?" he said. Not really a question.

He just kept looking at me as if this entire interaction was the strangest thing to ever happen to him. Who knew? Maybe it was. I didn't know this guy from a bar of soap. For all I knew, I could have interrupted one of the most important conversations of his life.

I pointed to the shelf in front of him but I couldn't follow it with my gaze. I mean, when I told you that he was a sight to behold, a sight like I'd never beheld myself before, I meant it, "I thought I might be able to help you, you know, find what you needed."

10 points to Allie for pumping out coherent sentences.

He looked between me and where I was pointing, and his features softened. A guarded expression still held firm, but it was almost like he had decided I wasn't all that much of a threat, or at least not a threat that could kick his ass. Awesome.

The person on his phone was shouting something which caught his attention and he quickly lifted it to his ear again, but his eyes didn't leave mine.

What the shit is happening right now?

"Yeah, no, I'm still here. Sorry, I dropped my phone—No, it's fine. You don't need to come in, I'll just ask for help. Aspen, it's fine, I'll be out in a minute."

His girlfriend? Or boyfriend? *Aspen.* A name that could apply to any person or gender. Bugger.

He shoved the phone into the front pocket of his black skinny jeans. My eyes tracked the movement with no attempt at being subtle whatsoever. I'll admit, it wasn't my best moment, but it *had* been a long day and let's be honest, that was the closest to stimulating-male interaction I'd had in a very long time. If you know what I mean.

I cleared my throat again and plastered on my smile despite my racing heart and asked again, "So, what were you after?"

He still held onto the bemused expression before he answered, and not with what I thought he was going to say, "Do you know who I am?"

Alrighty. What a giant asshole.

As far as first impressions went, that was not a winner.

I could feel my face scrunching up again but this time it was sort of like what would happen to your expression when you walked through someone else's fart while shopping. Yep, almost exactly like that.

"Didn't we just meet here, just now, in the baking aisle?" I clarified to him, but also half to myself because I *swear* I'd never seen this guy before.

His eyebrows shot up at that like this was incredibly surreal, "Oh, right. Sorry, I thought—," he paused, then shook his head, "Nothing."

His hand moved up to push his red hair away from his face.

Ah, very good, so it was just the straight up messy-hair look, not the messy-on-purpose look.

I had taken another step back, suddenly eager to remove myself from the situation as fast as possible regardless of the fact that I had just stumbled upon the most attractive man I'd ever seen in my life.

"Baking powder," he finally said. He looked from me to the shelf in front of him. I think I preferred shock-and-horror to unsure-and-awkward if I was being honest, "I'm supposed to get baking powder. My brother likes to bake."

Ah, brother.

My face softened and a genuine smile ghosted over my lips. He didn't need to explain what the baking powder was for, but I took it for what it was; an olive branch between strangers who found themselves in an incredibly awkward first encounter. Maybe he wasn't such an ass.

Maybe.

"Well, you won't find it there, that's all the decorative baking stuff like food dye. The baking powder is down the other end with the flour," I gestured with my thumb behind my shoulder as I started to walk backwards.

Once he had taken his first step towards me, I turned my back and walked as casually as I could down what had just become the longest aisle I had ever been in. It was probably not obvious to the untrained eye, but this was very out of character for me. To talk to random hot dudes and help them find their runaway baking ingredients.

I had never been more aware of my walking style in my whole entire life.

Again, what in the world is going on? It's like, midnight on a weekday.

The soft tapping of his boots behind me was the only indication that he was actually following and hadn't done a 'fakey' and sprinted the other way.

I grabbed the brand I used and handed it to him, making sure not to let my hand touch his, as much as I would have loved to have 'accidentally' touched his hand.

"Thanks. I was never going to find that," he laughed lightly.

Oh, God. Could this get any worse? He had one of those side, half smiles that you always read about, and I'll be damned if it didn't make my insides scream and knot up. I always thought that was absolute nonsense - no single smile could make you want to cry out for mercy, but there you had it. I did manage to, however, maintain enough of my dignity and cry on the inside.

Dare I say, another 5 points?

He looked up only to have the sexy side smile fall from his face, which then had me realising that the good old trout mouth expression I tended to adorn was up, front and centre. Closing my mouth with an audible snap, I cleared my throat – again – and offered a smile. I was 80% sure it looked natural and not at all offensive or creepy.

"I'm Dax," his hand shot out between us and I looked at it for probably a second too long before I reached out and slid my hand into his.

Yep, *definitely* glad I was touching his hand.

It was large and completely swallowed mine, and it was coarse and callused like someone who used their hands in life. Not like mine, which I knew were soft and small.

I looked back up to meet his gaze, "Allie. Alice—I'm Alice."

"Alice. Nice to meet you," his side smile reappeared and my day suddenly felt a whole lot better, "I have to admit, I didn't actually think anyone else would be here at this time," he let out a breathy laugh as he let go of my hand and moved to rub the back of his neck.

Instinctively, I tucked both hands behind my back, but this felt good. This felt like we'd levelled up. That our conversation had gone from horrid to awkward to now normal.

I was going to tally this with another 5 points and not expect anything else from the evening. Quit while I was ahead.

Pointing behind him back the way we'd come down the aisle, I explained my purpose for being present before I thought better of it, "The only place to get a brownie mix box at this time."

"Ahh," he nodded in sincere understanding. It made my smile widen and my hands fall from behind my back to my sides.

He started to walk backwards until I stepped towards him. He turned around and headed straight for the pre-mixed cakes. Grabbing one from the shelf – not my usual brand – and handed it to me.

"Those," he pointed to the box I now held, "are my favourite."

Another olive branch.

So, he liked brownies too.

"I thought your brother was the baker?" I smiled and flicked my eyes to the baking powder he was holding.

He looked down at it and then back up at me. His eyes were brighter than before, like he was completely content to be right in that moment with me.

"Oh, he is most definitely the baker, hence his use of baking powder instead of just a ready-to-go box. You're more my kind of person, Alice."

My stomach felt like it encompassed an entire lightning storm. Every wave and jolt made my body very hot and then very cold.

I laughed in response, my face stretching into a smile that felt far too wide.

"Does your brother dress like you? I don't think I could picture boots like those," I point to his all-ties-and-buckles combat boots, "baking in a kitchen." I lift my eyebrows at him for some extra sass.

"Would you believe me if I said that this is exactly what he bakes in, but also with eyeliner and his hair spiked up in every direction?" His face looked so serious I couldn't help but burst out laughing.

A shuffling sound came from the end of the aisle behind Dax, where the cashier stuck his head around the corner. I slapped a hand over my mouth to muffle the rest of my cackling.

I yelled an apology just as he snapped a photo of us.

That was weird, I really hope the next time I came here my photo wasn't plastered to the sliding doors with a notice declaring me a public nuisance due to my disruptive sound levels.

When Dax turned back around to face me, any humour that was lighting his features before had all but disappeared and was instead replaced with a deep frown.

"Craig, the check-out guy, doesn't get out much. He probably just took a photo for the purpose of memorising our faces," I laughed again, trying to lift the mood.

For some reason his frown *bugged* me. It didn't have a place in our conversation. A conversation I was really, really happy to be having.

The frown eased a bit, "That is entirely creepy if that's actually what Craig spends his time doing."

"Oh, he's harmless. I think," now it was my turn to frown and Dax's turn to laugh.

I thought that the conversation was going to end there. It felt like if it was going to naturally dwindle, it would've been then. I was, however, pleasantly surprised when Dax asked me another question.

"So, do you always help random guys in the baking aisle?" he enquired.

"Oh, all the time," I nodded in complete sincerity.

I didn't, I never did.

"Really?" he said, eyebrows raised in a mocking show of shock.

"That's actually the only reason I'm here. I don't really even like brownies," I went on, sagging my shoulders in a mocking reply of being found out.

"I knew it," he said while snapping his fingers like he'd just solved a crime.

"You did not!" I gasped.

"Oh, I absolutely did," Dax might be wittier than I was. He didn't stop there, "Especially with that winter get-up you had on coming in here, it *screamed* 'I hit on guys in 24-hour corner stores to pass the time.'"

My own eyebrows hit my hairline and I reached out and tapped him lightly with the brownie box I held, "I was *not* hitting on you!" my face heated up immediately, "Oh my god!" Never mind that he had seen me walk in here wearing my *skeenie.*

"Honestly, I'm just glad you made the first move and not me. I was wondering how I was going to keep away from you with that beanie-scarf contraption you had on."

"It's called a *skeenie,* thank you very much, and it's the most convenient article of clothing I own."

"I 100% believe that," he laughed and I joined in.

I had just thought of a good reply and barely opened my mouth when a loud *hooonk,* that dragged on for longer than necessary, sounded rather abruptly from outside, causing me to jump and my heart rate to spike.

Dax turned to look behind him where you could vaguely make out a black car with someone waving out the back-passenger window. He looked back to me and lifted his hand in a stoic wave as he started to move backwards.

"Thanks again, Alice," he held up the baking powder in my direction in a sort of 'toast' style.

The only thing I could think of to yell after him was, "It's Allie. Just Allie is fine!"

That sexy side smirk made an appearance one more time before he dropped a note onto the counter to pay for his item and hurried outside into the car.

I stood there like an idiot for another minute before I grabbed a second box of brownie mix - this time in the brand I usually got, just in case his choice wasn't up to scratch - and made my way to the check out.

Not an asshole then.

Definitely not.

3

"Dude, I thought you got absorbed into the aisle or something," Aspen leaned over and shoved me as he sped off down the street.

The rest of the band - Angus, Luke and Rip - were all crammed into the back of the sedan.

It was probably important to point out that this was a small car, and we were five fully grown men. It was also not the only - nor the biggest - car that was owned between the five of us. But since the very beginning, we would always pile into this sedan and head to gigs, sound checks, anything.

So, for fear of breaking tradition, as we left the soundcheck for our show tomorrow night, here we were crammed into the same sedan that took us to our very first gig.

We had wanted to end the tour in our home city, so we were doing one quick show before heading off to do a couple more across the country and then back here for the final shebang.

It felt good to be home, to be in the city that not only we grew up in but that we could stay in our own places and not in hotels or tour buses.

Angus and Rip lived together and were the first to be dropped off. None of us lived particularly close to one another, but if we did a big loop from where we left at the stadium, it worked out.

Sticking my hand out the window we all shook in our standard half-hand shake-half-hand-slap manner, really it just looked like a lazy handshake, and set off again.

Luke was next; he hopped out at his building where he shared an apartment with his girlfriend, and I stuck my hand out for the same slap-shake. It didn't really warrant words which suited me fine just now.

Aspen sped off again, circling back around the inner city to our place.

I tore my gaze from the window, looking but not really seeing a whole lot. I let out an exasperated sigh and moved my hand through my hair, pushing it off my face, "There was a girl. She was buying brownie mix," I explained with a mumble, turning my attention back towards the window, "Alice—Allie."

His eyebrows lifted as he cast his gaze at me briefly, "Oh, yeah? She get a picture?"

"Mm. No, she didn't know who I was."

Aspen's laugh was traced with both bewilderment and disbelief, "Ha! Are you kidding?"

See, I wasn't an asshole, and I was entirely aware that she thought I was the world's biggest bellend when I asked her if she knew who I was.

Taken out of the context of my life, I knew how that looked. To assume that everyone was just magically aware of your presence, I mean, I got it, but everyone, *everyone,* knew who I was. I hadn't met anyone in my adult life who didn't. Until tonight.

"Mmm," it was the only response my brain could manage.

"Could it have been the hair? It's never been that colour before," Aspen went on, clearly still shocked that it was possible.

I mean, I understood that this still sounded like we thought an awful lot of ourselves but no matter where we went, or who we were with, everyone knew. The check-out guy from the 24-hour corner store even snapped a photo with me when I walked in. I just asked him not to post it online 'til I left. There was no reprieve, and we weren't complaining. We didn't mind it. Sometimes.

"No, Ap. I'm telling you. I looked her right in the face for a very long time and she had no idea. It was like she'd never met a bigger asshole in her whole life. You should have seen her face when I asked," I had to laugh.

I couldn't *not* laugh. It was sort of like the face you'd make when you stepped barefoot into dog-poop on your lawn, first thing in the morning when you were grabbing the paper. But after that, it went well. Really well.

It was silent between us for a while longer while Ap sped a bit too fast through the too-quiet city.

"I shook her hand," I spoke it out loud for the sake of saying it, just to see how it felt rolling off my tongue.

"Oh?"

"She was funny, too."

"Funny's good, Dax," I could hear the smile in his voice.

Allie. Alice.

I liked Allie better. She just *looked* more like an Allie. The long, dishevelled hair. The seafoam green eyes. Definitely an Allie.

Aspen had a small smile I would have loved to wipe right off his face but I'll tell you, the man had a flare for baking, and there was little that could come between me and one of his chocolate chip cookies tonight.

We pulled into the underground parking lot of our building. Jumping out of the car, a small but loud *beep* sounded as Ap locked it and we made our way to the elevator.

I pressed the call button for the lift continuously until it arrived. There was no doubt in my mind that it made it arrive faster and I'd go to the mat with anyone who said different. We shuffled into the small square space. I scanned my card on the reader and punched the number at the very top; floor 37.

The trip to our apartment could have lasted an hour or five seconds. I was so in-my-own-head I couldn't stop thinking.

She had no idea who I was.

"Dax?" Aspen waved his hand in front of my face. I swatted it away as the elevator doors pinged, opening to our home.

"Did you get her number at least?" he called after me as I headed straight for a hot shower and him, straight for the kitchen.

"Nope. No, I didn't."

Why didn't I just ask her for her number?

4

Allie

"No, Savannah, I'm saying that he looked me right in my face and asked me if I knew who he was. Can you imagine the *cajones* on this guy? I couldn't believe it. I thought he was the world's biggest asshole. No one has a face like his and also struts around being a gentleman."

Or at least in my experience.

I took a long swig of my wine as Sav, my best friend and ride-or-die, looked on while absentmindedly fiddling with the many pieces of metal she had decorating her ears.

"But…" she prompted, hopeful.

"*But...*" I went on, "it did turn out that he was not an asshole. Not at all. I wasn't even sure why he asked, maybe he had thought we met or something. And he was *funny*. And I could have kept talking to him if he didn't have to leave so fast. And he was nice too, not just 'hello, how are you?' nice, but 'buys his brother baking powder in the wee hours of the morning, nice'. Also, he had excellent taste in brownie mix. *Yum.*"

A small, amused *humph* sound left my friend as she tended to her own wine glass, "His name, you said?"

I squinted at her. I'd definitely 'said' it already. She was only asking to gauge my reaction, my expression.

Savannah was one of those 'people readers' who could do so with annoying accuracy. *Insert eye-roll here*. I had no secrets from Savannah, I also had no say in whether I did or not, she just knew.

"Dax, he said," I looked down while my finger idly circled the rim of my wine glass that was being drained far too fast.

Another *hmm* sounded from her direction and I could feel her eyes on me. I dared a look up and a small smile played on her lips that had my hand twitching to chuck my wine at her. In a loving way, of course.

Savannah had been my best friend since we were little more than excreting machines waddling between our parents' apartments. Apartments that were placed directly across the hall from one another. The doors were always open, and we were always going back and forth.

Same school and same after-school tutor – old and barely alive – but where Sav's extracurricular was dance, mine was hours and hours spent playing the piano.

If I had a spare anything, it was spent on the piano. Any time not spent sitting directly at the piano, with Sav or poking our heavy breathing tutor with a stick fashioned from three pencils expertly taped together, was spent listening to all the music I was learning.

Anything classical called to me like a moth to a flame. The peace of it, the complex simplicity that I felt from both playing and listening was one of the few joys of my youth. My life.

My main dudes *Beethoven, Mozart* and *Bach* were my closest companions besides Savannah, egging me on to conquer my self-doubt and become the world class pianist I dreamt of being, or at the very least – because we all needed a backup plan – to be someone who fiddled the keys for a living.

I passed all eight grades with flying colours (internal fist pump), and then all of a sudden found myself alone, in the very same apartment across the hall from Savannah's family – who were still there though mine had disappeared – faced with an eviction notice and completely broke.

The pet shop I had worked at part-time had an opening in their head office for a Marketing Manager, a position that had been open for a long time and they found themselves eager to fill it. So, I pleaded my case, lied a little on my CV, and four years later I was working the same job.

There you have it. Alice Charlotte Jamison summed up in a matter of minutes. Probably less.

Savannah clapped her hands then rubbed them together after setting down her glass of wine. That meant only one thing - she had hyped herself up enough to voice something to me she knew I wouldn't want to hear, see or do. Great.

"Alright—," she started to say before I, with a mouth full of wine and an empty glass in hand, jumped off the couch in her living room and headed straight for the kitchen to refill, all the while furiously shaking my head.

I swallowed, "Nope. No, no, no. No Sav, I'm sorry I won't."

"But you haven't even *heard* what I was going to say!"

She eyed me with a singular, daunting, dark and perfectly shaped brow as I plopped back on the couch, full wine glass in one hand and in the other I held the bottle. The latter I passed to my friend for her own refill.

"Give me 20 seconds to say it. I swear it's not bad. It's something fun."

"Yes, but it's *your* fun. You did the hand-clap-rub thing. I know, Savannah," I might not be a people-reader, but I was a Sav-reader.

"Allie!" she dragged out the last syllable of my name with an infantile whine.

We just stared at each other then. Fighting a battle that was being waged by the severity of our intense gazes. I folded with a mighty exhale.

"Fine. 20 seconds," her responding smile was so big I smiled too. Dammit. Another massive gulp of wine down, she started to plead her case.

"I have two tickets to see *Lady Luck* in a couple weeks for their second last show in the city and my plus one dropped out. I need you to come with me—"

10 seconds to go.

"—They're mosh tickets, right up the front and I LOVE THEM. PLEASE COME. I DON'T WANT TO GO ALONE. PLEASE!" she made it with three seconds to spare. Impressive.

"*Lady Luck* is punk?"

"Rock," she corrected me. "Well, like rock, punk-rock," the smile on her face was so blindingly hopeful that she knew I had to say yes.

"I have something on though, Sav," I said as I picked invisible lint off my jeans. I never have anything on, everybody knew that.

"No, you're going to hole up in your apartment with string-bean-Dean and play your piano in your room that only has one sad little window."

"Hey!" I swatted the air between us, "Dean is—well he pays the rent and keeps to his space. Plus, he's never late with rent and always lets me have his leftovers." Yes, I was aware that I mentioned the rent thing twice but really, Dean didn't have too much else going for him in my books.

Savannah's face scrunched up at the last point. The very same 'I just walked through someone's fart at the shops' look I had worn myself the night before during my interaction with Dax.

Dax. I wonder what that's short for?

"I don't know Sav. Rock concerts are *loud.* And the lights..." I trailed off.

Her eyes took on a sad, protective look which she dropped almost immediately, but her features did soften from ecstatic to understanding -yet-hopeful.

"Allie, it will be fine. I swear. We will be so close to the stage you won't even be able to see the big lights over the audience and you can wear your earplugs to help," she sat there waiting.

No matter how many times I declined, she'd never stop asking. Even if she found other people to ask. I just *couldn't.* I was working through it, be it slowly, but still. I knew if I said no, she wouldn't push it but doing more of this kind of *stuff* would help me. It's what I needed to do.

I nodded. Folding again, "Okay. Fine."

Her answering *whoop* was enough to make me feel a kernel of excitement over the frantic pounding of my heart.

"Awesome, Al! We'll have to leave for it early, like, maybe around 4PM. But I'll message you again closer, don't worry. The concert won't start 'til 7 but we need to make sure we're one of the first in line so we can be right up front."

"Don't you get your tickets from your work though? Can't we just get, you know, *escorted* to the very front?"

Savannah worked for one of those massive business enterprises that owned all the music venues in the city. When I said all, I meant *all* of them. From the little 'indie' holes-in-the-wall to the stadiums. Same company but hitting every single niche. Brilliant, I tell you. It was safe to assume that Sav had tens of thousands of dollars' worth of free admission under her belt.

"We get to go backstage after the concert, but I got the mosh tickets, which effectively means first come first served. I am determined to make direct eye contact with Wyatt or at least Angus. Maybe get Aspen to wave at me. *De-ter-mined.*"

And when she sets her mind to something, there was little that could stand in her way, I'll tell you that for free.

Groaning as I stood up from the couch on relatively unsteady legs, I grabbed my tote bag, slung it over my shoulder, slipped into my Chucks without even casting a second thought to doing up my laces, and wound on my *skeenie*. Sav's was a 15-minute walk from my apartment.

Bundled up, I looked back and tried to channel the same confidence from the night before, urging it to light up my face like a supernova.

"See you later. It will be fun. I can't wait!" I gave her my most enthusiastic wave. Maybe she was at least semi-convinced by it. Maybe.

Her answering yell was much louder than before and laced with excitable profanities that followed me all the way out of her building and onto the street below.

5

Allie

Like most days when I made my way back from work, I thought about how much I really needed to start cooking more meals at home, and the amount of money I would save if I did meal prep like every other responsible adult my age.

The idea lingered for as long as it usually did – about 3 seconds – before it melted away with the rest of the things I knew I needed to do but would probably never act upon.

I pushed open the door to my favourite Chinese restaurant and waved at Wendy who promptly brought my food over from the kitchen at the back.

"Hey, sweetheart. How are you?" Wendy walked right up to me and gave me a big squeezing hug.

She smelt like sugar. Just way too sweet that it made you wonder what her home would smell like if the scent followed her around so aggressively.

Wendy herself was wonderful though.

"Hey, Wendy. I'm good, just a quiet one," I smiled back at her.

"Alright. Well, you eat up. Go on, I'll see you again soon."

I nodded and said my thanks on my way back out, waving to the guys in the kitchen as I left. It was about a 7-minute walk from my apartment which again, suited me fine.

All I could think about was heading home, changing into my comfies and smashing a bowl of Chinese takeaway that was about a-portion-and-a-half too much for what I needed and then playing my piano for a very, very long time.

I was in the process of relearning *Prelude in C Major*, a composition by *Bach* I played relentlessly as a younger teen, and then, like so many things that were once important and special, I forgot about it. I was quite close to finishing it and my fingers ached to run along the keys.

My apartment building was old, and so were their attempts at safety and security. The door heading into the building itself didn't have one of those things you needed to tap a card on to get in, not even a lock. Even better, you didn't need anything beyond the ability to press an elevator call button to reach any of the floors. I was impressed that they had locks on the apartment doors, to be honest.

I kept tapping my finger on the button for the elevator until it arrived. Much like my philosophy with the crosswalk button, it made the elevator arrive faster than if I had only pressed it once and then just stood there. The thought of doing that actually made me all tingly with anxiety.

Insert entire body shiver, and not the good kind, here.

The elevator carried three scents depending on which corner you stood at; an old gym bag, yeast and, the least offensive and thus my favourite even though it had made my eyes water on more than one occasion, onions. But, for all the poor qualities of the apartment building, the apartments themselves were nice. Well, mine and Dean's was, at least.

Unlocking the door, I kicked off my work boots before heading to the kitchen still with all my winter wear on. By the time I walked the small distance down the hall, I was too hungry to even care, so I set about making myself a bowl of food - *skeenie* and all.

I had just sat down when string-bean-Dean got in from work.

"Hi, Allie," he said while he took off his coat, hat and scarf.

"Hey, Dean," I gave him a floppy wrist wave.

Seeing Dean in his coat reminded me that I still had mine on. I took it off, along with my *skeenie,* and let them both drop directly onto the floor behind me.

Dean constantly smelled like packet Mac and Cheese and wore only one colour in varying shades. That colour was orange.

If you're imagining a peach coloured shirt and terracotta pants that zipped off into shorts, then you're imaging Dean to a T.

I asked him about it once. He said that he tried a minimalist lifestyle for a year, but it never stuck. One of the points was to have multiples of the same thing and to only wear that. To remove any dependency on material items so as to fully embrace life.

I got it. I even thought there was some truth in it, but what I didn't get was how Dean looked at that aspect and thought 'yes, the colour I'd like to wear every day for the rest of my life is just a range of different shades of orange', but there you had it. He was particularly proud of the zip option that converted his pants into shorts because 'they were versatile', he said.

Now you see, this was why he was called string-bean-Dean. He was the ultimate string bean.

"I got some Chinese, want some? Pay back for your leftovers the other day," I motioned to the selection of meals in front of me with my fork.

"Yeah, sure. Thanks, Allie."

"Sure, sure," I said.

Honestly, I didn't know why I even thought about it but, I assumed he would sit at the kitchen island with me. Don't get me wrong, Dean and I weren't really friends, but it wouldn't kill him to step out of his bubble while he was eating the food I bought. When I ate his leftovers, at least I did it in the common space.

He shouted a thanks down the hallway as he headed to his room and sealed himself inside with a loud bang of the door. It caught me off guard making my breath catch in my throat. My heart rate immediately spiked, and my stomach turned.

I squeezed my eyes shut, gripping the sides of the island for support and just breathed. Breathed and breathed and breathed through it like I always did.

In for 10 seconds, out for 10.

I did that 10 times until my stomach stopped rolling like I was on a ship at sea.

That was good, I got control faster than last time.

I sat at the kitchen island just staring at the half-eaten food in my bowl but not really seeing it. My appetite had vanished completely. Damn it.

I huffed a disappointed breath and closed all the containers of food I had fully intended to eat and put them in the fridge. Just as I was placing my bowl in the sink to wash, a knock sounded from the front door.

I frowned to myself. I hadn't invited Savannah over and she never came up unannounced and Dean, well, he never had friends over.

Picking up my clothes from the floor of the kitchen, I hung them up as another far less patient knock came again. I opened the door and my heartbeat spiked again for the second time and I instinctively closed the door between us a bit more, hiding behind it slightly.

"Ben," I had intended for his name to sound more like an insult rolling off my tongue, but it was barely audible.

He had the audacity to smile at me like we were old friends, "Hey, Al. Just came to pick up my things."

His things? I hadn't seen Ben in 8 months and all of sudden, there he was at my door wanting his *things?*

"Your what?" I said. The anger that was now certainly making my face flushed pushed any meekness away from my demeanour.

"You messaged to tell me about my stuff you had put in a box? I haven't had time until today to come and get it."

Ah, this 'message' was sent the night we broke up. *8 months ago.*

"Are you *kidding* me, Ben? I sent you that message when we broke up. What makes you think I haven't thrown it out?"

"Have you?" he asked, his eyebrows knitted together as if the thought had genuinely not crossed his mind.

That even though he cheated on me for the better part of our almost 3-year relationship and then, once he was found out, explained that it was in fact *my fault*. That each one of his unfaithful encounters was because of something I had said or done, and that perhaps it was high time that I took a good look in the mirror at the kind of person I was. To have made someone I 'loved' feel like they needed to seek that 'love' somewhere else.

I found it hard to remember any of the good times we had now that it was over. I had considered moving out of the city and moving in with him come the end of the year. He knew I didn't drive but he refused, and I mean *refused,* to move in with me. Dean had even been open to finding somewhere else to live.

All I could say was that I counted my lucky stars that none of that ever happened. I counted them double time that I listened to the little niggly voice in my head that kept on saying *not yet, not yet, not yet* whenever a conversation came to pass about taking the 'next step'. To 'growing' in our relationship.

I was going to puke. I could feel the emotion pulsing behind my eyes and my throat started to constrict. I hadn't thrown out his stuff, it sat under my bed.

I rolled my eyes, closed the door and locked it.

"What the hell, Allie?!" his shout was dampened by the door between us, but it was still very much a shout.

"I'll get your box of shit, Ben, but there is no way in *hell* that you're stepping foot into my apartment," I huffed back at him as I walked down the hall to my room.

I grabbed the box from under my bed making sure that everything was in there. It was. I had made sure the first 5 times I opened the box after I'd initially packed it; I just didn't want to leave anything to chance because I really, *really* didn't want to see him ever again. Ever.

Grabbing the box, I had resolved not to say another thing to Ben when I handed him his shit and watched him leave my life forever. In the 10 seconds it took to walk from my room to the front door, I had once again found strength in the anger that was coiled in the centre of my stomach.

I stopped short, almost dropping the box.

Dean was leaning against the kitchen island talking to Ben. Dean had let Ben *in* and was talking to him in the kitchen.

"What the actual fuck Dean?!" They both turned to look at me like my reaction was completely unwarranted, "Why did you let him in? Did you not think my locking him in the hallway was a clear sign that I didn't want

Ben in this apartment?!" my voice was rising with every word that left my mouth and it was but mere minutes before I began to cry, I could feel it.

I wouldn't give Ben the satisfaction. Nope, over my dead body, Ben.

I walked over to him and shoved the box at him.

"There, now please leave."

"Are you sure this is all of it?" he gave me a quizzical look like he wouldn't put it past me to keep a thing or two as a memento. You have *got* to be kidding me.

"Oh, bite me, Ben. That box of crap has been under my bed for the last 8 months. If I hadn't forgotten about it altogether, I would have tossed it out. Now, you have your stuff, and I won't say it again, you are not welcome in this apartment. Now *leave*."

He just looked at me like he couldn't fathom the disrespect I was hurling at him, like the end of the relationship had taught me nothing. Oh, believe me Ben, it had. I could've written a freaking book on all the things I'd learned.

With one more look down his nose at me, he glanced at Dean and reached a hand out around the box, balancing it on one of his knees.

"It was good to see you, Dean. Let's grab a drink sometime," he offered him a warm smile that I had never been on the receiving end of. Not once.

"Yeah, sounds chill, dude. Let's do it," Dean shook his hand and flashed him a smile in return. I could have popped right out of existence in that moment and neither of them would have noticed.

Ben left my apartment without another word and I walked right up and locked the door, pressing my weight against it until I was sure I could make it all the way to my room before falling apart.

I pushed away from the door and kept my eyes on the floor as I walked back down the hall to head to my room.

"Hey, Allie, you really shouldn't—"

I whirled on the spot, "No!" I yelled, my voice cracking in the process. Well, I clearly didn't make it back to my room before losing my cool as I stood there, a finger pointed directly at Dean, who had never heard me yell in the whole time we had shared an apartment.

"No, Dean," I collected myself and lowered my voice. I didn't yell, I wasn't a yeller, "You had no right to let him in here. This is *my home* too. If I lock someone out in the hallway, you don't let them in. Not without at least asking me first. It is none of your business what has gone on between Ben and I."

"Allie—," Dean tried to start back up, but if I knew Dean – and I did – it would've just been a reworded version of what he was going to try and say to me the first time, which was that I really shouldn't be so rude, and that Ben was a nice guy.

I walked away completely ignoring him, and when he called my name one more time, I called back down the hall, "Poor form, Dean!" before sealing myself inside my room to sit at my piano and play.

And play and play and play.

I didn't sleep well. I didn't sleep at all really, until the sun came up and I dozed off for about ten minutes before my alarm rang.

I dragged my feet all the way to the kitchen where I sorted out the drip coffee machine to do its thing while I scaulded myself in the shower. I stood there for so long that I thought I actually fell asleep and then I ended up with no time to wash my hair. Yay.

Tying my robe around me, I made my way back to the kitchen and grabbed the largest mug I owned, filling it all the way up before going back to the bathroom to dry my hair and apply a small amount of makeup. I didn't usually wear make-up, but the bags under my eyes were large enough to store a small fortune so today was an exception. The thought had me looking at the expiration date of a lot of the things I had in my makeup bag. Most of which I had owned since I was 18. Now being 25, let me verbalise your exact thoughts: *Nasty*.

Did I put it on my face anyway? Of course.

I drained my coffee and threw on some black stockings and a blue dress before running out the door, still hopping into my boots and wrapping on my *skeenie*. I was late. I blamed the shower-snooze moment I had. Well, really, I blamed Ben.

3 years of my life. I had made peace with it now, but mostly when I looked back on that time and saw everything I so stupidly looked over, I got angry. Angry at myself, angry at him, angry at Dean (just because he was there). Everyone, really.

The world was my enemy when I reflected on those 3 years of my life and it took a long time to stop blaming myself for his endeavours. Because I had believed him, I had thought there was something wrong with *me.* I didn't think about Ben anymore.

It was colder this morning than usual, and a fine mist hung in the air like a big cloud had fallen all the way from the sky overnight and fell asleep along the city streets. I gripped my tote over my shoulder a little tighter than usual, hoping that the tightness in my muscles would warm me up.

The reality that there was a coffee machine at work that was, most importantly, free for staff members was the only thing powering my steps. Darting in between the other busy on-foot commuters, I tried to get from point A (my apartment) to point B (my office) as fast as possible without rubbing shoulders with too many strangers as possible. I hated it, walking in a crowd and having person after person rub *their* shoulder on *yours.* A shiver of repulsion went through me at the thought.

I was about to cross the road, consistently tapping the button for the little man to light up, ignoring the stares of everyone around me who thought I was a lunatic, when I saw him across the street.

The shoes were different, the pants and jacket were different too and his collar was down. But there was a guy walking the way I had just come on the other side of the street with red hair and my stomach flip-flopped. It flip-flopped and started doing the tango with the rest of my organs.

I started pressing the crosswalk button so fast that my arm began to cramp. And before you ask, no, I didn't cross the street unless the man illuminated. I was a law abiding citizen.

I was going to run after him like a crazy person. I really, *really* didn't want to. I even tried to make a pros and cons list in my head to try and work through it, but I just felt like this was my chance, you know? Maybe it was meant to be that I saw him again.

Dax, from the baking aisle.

The light changed and I sped walked across the street back the way I had come from, away from my office. That's when he stopped and turned to speak to the person who was walking just behind him. I hadn't even noticed he had been walking with someone. As he turned, I saw his face.

I felt my whole-body droop, just totally deflate like a balloon.

I turned myself back around and walked the last couple minutes to my office building.

I was absolutely losing it.

I was just about to run after a *complete stranger* who I thought was someone I literally didn't even know. Someone I met for 20 minutes and that was it, story over. What would I have even said?

It didn't matter anyway. It wasn't him.

6

I could see every single person in the crowd.

I was looking for her. I was looking before I even *realised* I was looking.

Anyone with hair a similar shade, or really anyone at all. I looked and looked, in between every single song, and I had absolutely no idea why. She didn't know who I was.

I feel like a massive french fry.

The boys were insane tonight. As a unit, we always complemented one another. But everything, *everything* went so right tonight. It was the perfect way to kick off the end of our last leg.

After the show, as usual, we all packed up in Aspen's black sedan, and at this point I was honestly surprised the car hadn't died - it was over 20 years old. So old that it shouldn't even be on the road, but no matter how many times we piled in and the ancient suspension let out a back-cracking groan, we always arrived safely and in one piece wherever we were headed.

Ap called the car his lucky charm, which I thought was kind of nice. It had been my car first, before I passed it down to him when I left home for college. Needless to say, that was an experience that was short lived.

Dropping the boys off at their houses, we all had to be packed and at the airport in two hours. We were flying across the country for two shows back to back before we got to come back home, decompress for a couple days and then finish off the tour here.

This had been our biggest tour yet, and it felt like it too. We had been to more places than ever before, played more shows – bigger shows – and were on the road for longer.

When they asked us if we wanted to start or end the tour at home, we all said 'end' without hesitation.

I shoved enough clothes for a few nights into my duffle bag, chucking in my essentials and then packed my backpack with things for the plane. It was going to be a long flight and I couldn't sleep on planes. I wished I could, but I always liked to look out the window. To see it all.

In a life that was as loud as mine – a life I loved – but one that was overwhelming, it reminded me that it could end at any time, that I was so *small* in the grand scheme of things. It gave me perspective. It reminded me that I was lucky. So, I could never sleep because I was always looking.

Aspen yelled for me from where he was waiting in the living room.

"Coming!" I called back, then grabbed a notebook and pen to throw in my backpack for any last minute lyrical inspiration that flew my way.

When I say that it happened anywhere, I seriously mean it. My notes section on my phone was full of lyrics, but when I could, I preferred pen and paper. And let's not even approach the voice memo app. If anyone were to play them all one after the other, they would have a hard time believing what I did for a living.

"We're gonna be late, Dax," Aspen said, giving me an exasperated sigh as I walked into the living room.

Aspen was always on time. He was the reliable, planned, scheduled, responsible person in the band. So, being even a minute behind schedule was like a deflated soufflé to him. Those were his exact words.

We walked out to the front of our building where a car waited for us. Our driver was new, so we didn't know his name, but he seemed like a nice guy. He complimented our music and mentioned his daughters were big fans then requested a photo op before we boarded our flight.

Ap and I talked about a few things from the show that we thought were especially good, like Rip throwing in a random new riff into one of our songs and how it had elevated the entire pre-chorus. Aspen thought we could re-release the song as a single with the altered guitar, and as usual, my kid brother was on the nose. His ideas were always amazing, and I made it a point to tell him exactly that as often as I could.

Ap and I had snapped a photo with the driver before we grabbed our bags from the boot of the car and walked inside the terminal.

We were dropped at a different part of the terminal than the main entry, a bit more private where we were also taken through a private security screening room. Even though we tended to fly late to avoid the bigger crowds, there were always concerns for everybody's safety anytime we moved from one place to another, so we got used to the precautions that were put into place. I don't think I even remembered what the regular front of an airport looked like anymore.

We walked into a private room where we waited until our plane was ready, and we'd be seated after all the other passengers had boarded.

Also, I'd like to clarify that no, private jets weren't always ideal or economically sound ideas, regardless of what our profession was. So, we took regular commercial planes the same as everyone else.

Angus was sitting down, on his phone. In front of him was a pile of bags that Ap and I added to. There was a lot of space in the room they had put us in but we tended to huddle, hence the pile of bags.

Rip and Luke left to get something for us to eat - my request for just a packet of chips - while I sat down in the chair next to Angus and waved at a rest of the crew. Some of the team had already left on a previous flight.

I pulled out my phone and scrolled through Twitter. I sent out a message letting everyone know that we were heading out for the following final shows and we couldn't wait to see them. I settled in and fully intended on spending the rest of our waiting time to board responding to fans who were commenting on my tweet.

I was so absorbed that I didn't even notice Jenna come into the room and sit right next to me. Not until she bumped her shoulder into mine. Angus, the not-so-subtle prick, pretended he got a call and walked out of the room. Aspen said he saw something out the window that he needed to get a closer look at from outside of our waiting room. There was literally nothing to look at except for an empty tarmac, dickhead.

"Hey, stranger. You're a hard guy to get alone!" she said, holding her cold beverage in both hands and sipping it through a metal travel straw.

I gave her a small smile and put my phone away. I didn't particularly want to speak to Jenna, but I also wasn't a jerk.

"Ha, yeah," I reached up to rub the back of my neck before pushing the hair out of my face. I really wanted to just pull it all forward and count to a hundred until she left but, again, not a jerk, "It's been crazy these last few weeks with the end of the tour," I responded, leaning forward in the chair resting my elbows on my knees.

"Yeah, absolutely! Oh, that reminds me. You still have something at your place that you wore on stage, Phoebe keeps asking me to get you to bring it, but I keep forgetting. Next time you remember, bring it, 'kay?" she took another sip of her drink.

"Sure, sorry," I said and silently hoped that was the end of the conversation.

Jenna had been my girlfriend. A very long time ago.

She'd come onboard in the hair and makeup department to help Marco out when things took off for us and, well, Jenna was attention grabbing. That was really the perfect way to put it. You couldn't walk into a room and not look directly to her first, she just *commanded* any space she was in. Something I had experience with too, so I guess I gravitated to her because I thought we stood on common ground.

I tried to stand on that common ground with her for 10 months and then she just called it off. I wasn't surprised at all if I was being honest.

I tried; I really did. I had liked her a lot at the time, but even though she toured with the band, our relationship just fell by the wayside. When we had a break over Christmas time, things were fun. We had a great winter together, but the rest of the relationship just muddled into itself and before I knew it, she had packed her things, called it quits, and went to stay with Phoebe from the outfit department.

Jenna and Phoebe had been in a relationship now for the last three years and I was, and I seriously did mean this, so stoked for them. Phoebe was great, and just because Jenna wasn't for me, didn't mean she didn't have good qualities too.

When Jenna told me she and Phoebe were exclusive, she had really turned up the pity party. I kind of just sat there and stared at her as she assured me that it wasn't my fault and I didn't turn her off men so 'don't think that for a second'. And ever since, she hadn't really stopped with that attitude, as if her relationship continued to wreak havoc on my heart. That she was the reason I was alone. I assure you; she wasn't.

All the above being considered, I still tried to be her friend, but Jenna was *a lot*.

"So, how *are* you, Dax?" she asked.

Her use of my nickname bothered me. It was saved just for family and the guys. It sounded *off* coming out of her mouth more than anything. She alternated though, when she wanted to get deep and meaningful, she called me Dax. When she had no interest in talking beyond your standard 'hi' and 'bye', she used my first name, Wyatt. So, I knew exactly the sort of conversation this was going to be.

"I'm good, Jenna. Thanks. You?" I replied, turning my head to look at her from my position, still hunched over my knees.

"Yeah, I'm good, hun. Really, really good! Excited for some down time with Phoebs, it will be a proper dream." She smiled and then frowned a bit, as if mentioning her girlfriend was a no-no in front of me.

Before I could even reply she leaned closer to me and spoke a bit softer, "How are you *really*, Dax? Is everything okay?"

Please, no. Not this again.

"Yes, Jenna I'm good. I'm keen for some downtime too. Maybe sleep in for once," I laughed lightly to try and emphasise how okay I was, anything to avoid this conversation.

"You know," she went on, not picking up anything I was putting down, "I was thinking, I have a friend who you would really, really like! She also really loves your music, so that's a great icebreaker!"

Here we go.

"Thanks Jenna, but I'm actually pretty good on the whole dating thing."

"Dax," she gave me a pointed look, "You haven't had a girlfriend since we broke up, you know, and that's over 3 years ago now," she put her hand on my shoulder and it literally took all my strength not to shrug it off.

"What are you talking about? I've seen plenty of people since we broke up, Jenna. I've told you before I have no internal squabble about you and Phoebe, I'm happy for you. For you both," I said and offered her another warm smile to show her I meant it.

"Mmm," she said, frowning to herself a bit. Her eyes scanned my face like she was reading me. I wasn't sure what she was reading because there was literally nothing beyond the words I had already spoken to her, "I know you *say* that, but I just don't *feel* like you're being completely honest, you know?"

"Jenna—," I started, but she was committed to the conversation.

"Sleeping with someone is not the same as seeing someone, Dax."

I huffed a breath and leaned back in my seat, scooting all the way down so that my head was leaning on the backrest, "That's really none of your business, Jenna," I mumbled.

I really didn't want to be speaking to her about this. Like, at all.

"Of course, it's my business, silly! We're friends, and when you're worried about your friends you try and fix it."

"Fix it?" I was stunned, the bite in my voice was hard to keep at bay. I knew she didn't do this to crawl under my skin, but I had told her and *told* her so many times.

She didn't let up, "You're so emotionally unavailable and you weren't like that when we started dating. But towards the end and all the way up until now, it's like you just turned off all your feelings. I'm sure that if you get out into the world and date, you'll see that things don't have to be this way."

"What way?" I asked back.

"You don't have to be so...I don't want to say the wrong thing here, but finding someone might make you better."

"Make me better?" I felt like a parrot.

"Yes! Exactly, oh, I'm so glad you're getting it. Carly is *so fun.* You will absolutely love her," Jenna pulled out her phone, presumably to text her friend that I'd agreed to a date. I was sure I was not the only one here who could clearly see I'd not done that in any capacity at all.

"Jenna, I don't want to go on a date with your friend," I said, trying to sound firm, but still trying my hardest to be civil.

She looked up from her phone wearing a mask of confusion, "But you *just said—*,"

"I said nothing Jenna, nothing," I stood up, not really wanting to be next to her anymore, "I am *fine.* I literally tell you the same thing every time you have these conversations with me. Conversations, by the way, that are not your place to have with me at all. It's been *years,* Jenna, since we dated—"

She cut me off, "That's *exactly* what I'm saying!"

"Then stop talking for a second and just listen to me," I'll admit that my voice raised a little higher than I would have liked, but she just *pushed and pushed.*

She sat there, and leaned into the back of the chair, showing me clearly that the floor was mine with a little head tilt to the side and raised one of her eyebrows like I was delusional and she could humour me if she had to.

"I am not *broken,* Jenna. You do not need to fix me. And even if I was broken, it's not your job, or your place, to try and do it. I am fine, I have been fine since we broke up. We dated for 10 months, not years. It was great, yes, it was a nice time, but it ended and that's fine. I am not mad, or sad, or crushed about it. I feel nothing but actual happiness for you and Phoebs, she's awesome and that's great. It is. But I don't need you constantly, and I mean *constantly,* talking to me and about me – because I know that you do – to other people about the state of my emotions and my personal life. This might come as a shock to you, but our breakup was not the end of the world, for either of us. So, I need you to stop, because I can be your friend, but not like this. You cross a line every damn time you do this Jenna."

"But—," she went to cut in again.

"No, I'm sorry, but no. I'm not having this conversation with you, now or ever again. I'm done, leave it alone. Okay?" I looked at her, hands at my sides just waiting for her to reply.

I was breathing heavily, and it took everything to just keep the anger out of this conversation. I hated how she spoke to me, *hated* it.

She just nodded. That was good enough for me.

I turned to leave the room needing to walk off the ball of restless energy that now sat in the pit of my stomach. I came up short when the guys and the two security guards that were travelling with us were standing in the doorway just watching it all happen like it was a live theatre performance.

Great. I just put my head back down and kept walking. They got the hint, and all shuffled to the side to let me pass.

"Flight boards soon!" Ap yelled out to me as I walked away.

I raised my hand in confirmation that I wouldn't be long.

Emotionally unavailable.

I wasn't emotionally unavailable. Things worked well when I focused on one thing at a time.

My mind was sort of set up like a storage locker, or maybe like a house where everything was still packed away in boxes, but everything was labelled clearly.

Jenna was packed away tight in one of the boxes that was further towards the back, so to speak. That time of my life wasn't something I thought of or reached for, but it was there, nonetheless. Everything was. Every birthday, every holiday, every girlfriend or break up or studio session.

It was all there. Compartmentalised. I only unpacked a box if there was something in it I needed. I'd always been that way and it always worked. Always. I'd never needed more than that, never *wanted* more than that. The stuff I never reached for? It never came up and I never thought about it.

Some people had journals; some people meditated.

I had my life packed up into boxes, and it worked for me just fine.

The guys had already boarded the plane, Luke, Angus and Rip in one aisle and then I was supposed to be by the window, as I always asked to be, with Aspen in the middle and Jake, the security guy, was next to him.

I had to step awkwardly over their knees to get to my seat. I wasn't late but in standard Aspen style, he had everyone board as soon as we were told it was our time, so even though we had another 10 minutes before the doors closed, here they all were.

"Hey, sorry," I said after I had sat down, shoving my backpack under the seat in front of me where more of the tour crew were buckling in for the flight.

I didn't see Jenna, but I also didn't look for her. I didn't feel bad about anything I said, I didn't.

"All good," Aspen said, giving me a smile. He didn't mention anything about what had happened with Jenna, and I'd wager he passed on that advice to the other guys too. They wouldn't have said anything though. They all knew how she was with me and no one particularly appreciated it.

Eventually the captain came on the overhead speaker and gave us more information about himself and the type of plane we were on, how long the trip would be and the flight path they chose while the plane taxied to our runway. And then, just like that, we were off. The lights of the city below were beautiful. That was another reason I loved to fly at night. You could see all the lights that weren't visible in the day.

The seat belt sign turned off when we reached altitude and the cabin crew let us know that food and drinks were coming by soon, and that they would do that twice. I took off my seatbelt and reached in my bag for my headphones and my book. I was reading a mystery-thriller and it was just getting good. I grabbed my chips too, always preferring to bring a snack than buy a snack.

I put down the food tray in front of me to lean my book on and I was scrolling on my phone to find a playlist to listen to when I unintentionally tuned in to the guys' conversation they were having behind me.

"—alley. I've heard so many good things, bro!" Rip said with a hefty amount of enthusiasm.

I yanked my headphones out of my ears and turned around in my seat. Not ideal, as the move caught the attention of most of the other passengers on the plane and since I had started sporting the red hair, people saw me very quickly and recognised me just as fast. A few very audible gasps sounded as those who might not have known we shared their flight now became painfully aware. I offered a small smile to the rest of the plane, but it wasn't at the top of my lists of concerns. Not when Allie's name had just been plucked from my mind and thrown out into the world like that.

"Did you just say Allie? You know Allie?" I asked. My heart was going so fast. The girl from the baking aisle found her way back into my head. How did Rip know Allie?

"What?" he said. He looked incredibly lost.

"You just said you knew Allie," I replied, expectantly.

"I was just saying that there's a huge river and *valley* you can see from a lookout where we're going. It's supposed to be pretty cool and I thought we could all go for a hike while we were there."

I just stared at him while my brain caught up to what my mouth had done. Aspen was definitely going to be telling them about Allie now.

I slid back down into my seat, slouching down as far as I could go and put my headphones back in. My face felt as red as my hair. I was trying to find a song to put on as quickly as possible, but not before I heard Aspen start to sing quite loudly, "Wyatt and Allie, sitting in a tree. K-I-S-S-I-N-G..."

7

Allie

Sav and I had met at our usual Italian place that was right between our apartments. It was just around the corner from work, so I ended up staying a bit longer to tie up some loose ends for the day.

Work had been non-stop for the last few days with the end of our campaigns on the birdseed coming up, and a last minute effort to optimise our ads to surpass our targets meant all hands on deck. Needless to say, I was ready to be swept off my feet by the weekend. Dean was meant to be out of the house which was just an added bonus.

I had ignored him for the better part of the week after his less than impressive foot-in-mouth situation regarding the whole Ben thing. I finally said hello to him yesterday after he greeted me first, then he told me he was heading out of town for the weekend. Maybe he did it on purpose to give me some space, but I doubted it. Unfortunately, string-bean-Dean was a bit too dense to have thoughts like that on his own.

Regardless, I wouldn't be sharing my takeaway with him any time soon.

I got to the restaurant before Savannah so when they seated me at our table, I ordered two glasses of our favourite wine and scrolled on my phone until she arrived. I was so deep in thought that I didn't realise she was there until she grabbed my face in her hands.

"You spend too much time on your phone," she said by way of greeting, and leant down to kiss my cheek.

I waved away her comment. She said it to me all the time and I definitely agreed but, being on my phone for *work* and being on my phone for *me time* were two completely different things. If only my eyes knew that and only generated migraines when it was the work portion of the screen time.

Sav sat down and took a grateful sip of her wine, making an *ahh* sound after that made me smile. She'd had an intense day. One of the things with working at a music venue was that they were constantly battling the rip-off tickets game.

There was a matinée on today and they had over 200 people arrive who had purchased their tickets off a reseller who botched up all the tickets and disappeared from existence. To say that was a shitstorm was an understatement.

"The saving grace and light at the end of the tunnel is seeing *Lady Luck* next weekend. It's what's pulling me through the hard times right now," she said dramatically as she took another sip of wine.

Before I responded back with some news that she was going to find absolutely thrilling, the waiter arrived for our order. We only ever got the same thing, so I ordered two plates of mushroom and truffle ravioli and some garlic bread, as well as a second glass of wine for Sav, which she shot me a grateful look for.

Sipping from my own glass, I set free my declaration, "I have been listening to some of *Lady Luck's* music this week," I said proudly, smiling from behind my glass as I took a second swig and set it down.

"No!" The smile on Savannah's face was striking.

"Mmhm, I have," I said, matching her smile with my own.

"Which album? Hold the phone, *Allie*!" she gave me a face that translated to 'I can't believe you're listening to music from my favourite band just so you might be able to sing along at the concert with me' then reached over and squeezed my hand.

For Sav, it was always the little things that made her feel loved.

I squeezed her hand back before playfully tapping the back of it to lighten the mood and my sappy friend, "The one with the rose and thorns on the front. There are maybe three or four songs I really like on that one. Though,

I have to be honest, the names are confusing because they don't match any of the lyrics," I knew I was frowning at my own thoughts.

Savannah laughed, "I know! What ones?" she prompted.

"Oh, uhm, I like the song *Run.* I also like *I'm leaving with the money whether you give it to me, or I take it right out of your hands,* that's the one that stumped me a bit. And the last two are *Anything to Take You Home,* and one that says something about a cemetery."

"Ooo! *Carve This on My Headstone?* That's my favourite too!" she squeaked.

"Yep! That's the one. I haven't listened to their other albums yet, but I figured a few off the newest one was better than none at all," I said.

Our food arrived on the table and I picked up my fork to dive in. I was starving.

"How did you even get the songs?" Savannah asked over a mouthful of pasta as she shoved some garlic bread in her mouth. She was not a graceful eater, I loved it.

"I bought their CD," I said around an equally large mouthful of my own food. I was not a graceful eater either.

"You bought a *CD?!"* she was baffled.

I nodded my head with high eyebrows, "Mmhmm," I said as I reached for my glass of wine.

My eyes caught on a figure at the front of the restaurant. Savannah was still talking about something to do with how CD's were a dead technology but all I could do was stare.

A man, a tall man, stood facing away from the main dining area and he was wearing a long black coat that reached all the way to the floor. The collar was turned up and he was wearing a black beanie.

I stopped chewing with my mouth still full of food, and it was like my whole body was in a trance.

After my experience at the start of the week, I had pretty much given up hope of running into Dax again. I had convinced myself that it was one of those missed opportunities that you always see people making movies about, the dwelling on the *what if,* but I took in the figure facing away from me, his clothing and his height. I was convinced all over again that it was him.

Maybe fate heard my pathetic inner monologue and the rapid tapping of the crosswalk button when I thought I saw him on my way to work.

The blood was rushing in my ears and I was breathing heavily through my nose thanks to the gob-full of pasta and bread that now resided in between my pearly-whites. I just couldn't look away from him.

Savannah moved her head in front of my view, obviously catching on that I wasn't present in whatever conversations she was having with herself. I moved to look around her as she started waving her hand in front of my face, but absolutely nothing could break my stare.

The guy reached up his hand moving to pull off his beanie. As his hand got closer to his head, my ass lifted higher off my seat. I was going to run for it.

He tugged off the winter hat and I landed painfully loud back in my chair. His hair was blonde under the beanie. Any of the bits sticking out were hidden by his upturned collar.

I was actually going insane.

"Earth to Allie," Savannah was now lazily waving her fork with a piece of speared pasta on the end in front of me. Like she had given up using her hand to wave because she'd been doing for so long and it was too much effort.

I quickly chewed and swallowed the food in my mouth and took a quick sip of wine.

"Sorry," I mumbled, my head dropping down a bit as colour no doubt filled my face.

"What was that?" she asked.

"What was what?"

She gave me a look that said, 'it's written all over your face so spill.'

I cleared my throat, "I thought I saw the guy from the baking aisle. He looked the same from the back with the hat on," I said, I winced a bit at the memory of my first episode of thinking I'd run into him again, knowing I was about to tell that to Savannah too.

She knew something else was up, *"And..."*

"And I thought I saw him on my way to work at the start of the week too," I said it very fast and with my eyes closed before shoving more food into my mouth.

Her inhaled gasp was incredibly loud, and what was then followed by a whispered shout, "Allie!"

I rolled my eyes at her, "It's nothing."

"Oh, it's not *nothing.* Someone's caught your eye! This is good, Al! I think it's high time you jumped back on the horse; you've been off it long enough."

"It's not like I decided to jump off the horse myself, Savannah. It reared up, I fell off and then it kicked me in the face as it ran away only to come back every 8 months to steal my damn apples."

She frowned at the last bit; her mouth opened to enquire but I shut down that line of conversation toot sweet, "It's nothing, don't worry. Just being dramatic."

"And you didn't get his number?" she asked, though she knew I didn't.

"Nope," I replied, popping the 'p' at the end.

"Well, you know what you should do?" she points her fork at me again, this time, pasta free. I had just taken the last bite of my own meal, "You should periodically check the corner store! You said his brother bakes, right?" I nodded and she continued, "Well, he will need something else baking related eventually."

She had a point.

"It's whatever, it was just a conversation. I'm just, I don't know, tired, I guess."

Savannah gave me one of her looks again but, mercifully, let it pass. She pushed me, *a lot,* but she also knew when to let it go.

I was eternally grateful for the walk home if only to try and burn off some of the food. What could I say? I loved having big dinners, it was just so satisfying. So, the 10-minute walk home was welcomed especially as the streets were near empty.

I was happy to walk. Anywhere and everywhere. Driving? Not so much for me anymore. I could be *driven* places, which surprised me too. But driving myself? No.

Three years ago, I was doing just that. I was driving home from work.

As I was merging onto a freeway, I had my classical musical blaring through my car speakers – I knew it wasn't the standard thing to blare but, whatever - and I was loud-humming along to all of it. Every single note I heard was branded into my brain. I noted every dip, every drag and hold. Every rise and fall. It was wonderful and no, I didn't listen to that song anymore.

The drive wasn't too far, 20 minutes to the apartment I lived in just outside the city, all on my lonesome and not too far from where Sav and I grew up. I knew the drive so well that I could've told you the seconds and minutes between every merge, every turn, every stop sign I came to, and whether the road I was getting onto tended to be bumper-to-bumper or not-so-bad at the time of my commute.

I was probably a minute from exiting the freeway when a truck was merging onto the very same road. The breaks had been faulty, and it was a merge from a decline. I didn't see the truck fast enough, didn't hear the loud blaring horn that rang for far too long until I caught the big, massive lights in my mirror. The impact caused my car to flip five times.

The driver of the truck was fine; bruised ribs and a tender face from his seatbelt and airbag, and the impact of his truck hitting my car managed to slow him down. I didn't remember anything after the sound and the lights, but I could tell you that my car was very small, and very old.

I spent 6 months in the hospital and was labelled with so many injuries that it went over two pages. Broken ribs, internal bleeding, whiplash, soft tissue damage, a compressed spine and my whole face was purple from bruising and swelling. My right leg was broken in three different places and I needed surgery on my right hip (yes, every time I went through a body scanner, it beeped). My arm was also fractured. There was more but, you got the picture.

I was very, very lucky. It was weird that I could say that now. That I could feel that way about the accident now.

It was just after I had met Ben, too. The relationship was so new when everything happened. Maybe it was the honeymoon phase or maybe it was that he might have been a totally different person at the start, but he stuck around. I guess for a long time I felt like I owed him something for that, too.

Anyway, after I was discharged, Sav helped me move into the city where I had organised to share an apartment with string-bean-Dean from work. He messaged hoping I was okay, I messaged back saying thanks and asked him what he was up to. One thing led to another and I mentioned I wanted to move into the city ASAP, and he mentioned he was looking for a roommate. The place was only a 10-minute walk to my office. Sav's place was a 15-minute walk away and the corner store was only a minute down the street. So, yes, walking was good, I loved to walk.

There was some trauma that lingered from the experience. Bright lights and loud sounds sometimes triggered my PTSD. It was like an out of body experience but also like being trapped in your own mind with no doors or windows.

Every time an episode hits me, I see two bright lights behind my eyelids and I hear the aggressive honk of the truck's horn like I'm standing right in front of a semi-trailer. Then I get shooting pains; in my face, my back, my leg, my hip. The anxiety attack that follows makes me feel like I'm shrivelling up like a piece of dehydrated fruit. My hands tingle and go numb and then I can't breathe.

I had learned to manage it, different techniques to calm myself down. Crossing my legs and placing my hands on my chest. To breathe. Sometimes tapping my collar bones helped too, it grounded me. All the things I'd learnt from therapy – western and holistic. I hadn't been in a long time though, things just got to a point and then stopped going anywhere. Stopped helping.

The memory of the accident drifted as the soft melody of *Prelude in C Major* moved through my mind keeping me company, as music often did on my walks. So, when the sign for the 24-hour corner store came into view, it took me a little by surprise.

Savannah's suggestion echoed in my head and I soon found myself standing in front of the automatic double doors which kept opening and closing, sensing me standing out front.

He's not in there.

But he could be. He might be.

He might walk in as I walked out.

What would I even do if I saw him again? 'Hey! I've been trying to find you.' That's not weird at all.

The doors slid open once again and my feet moved of their own volition into the corner store. Craig was there, as usual. I didn't stop to speak to him, but he did stare at me the whole time which wasn't normal for Craig. I walked around and stood at the start of the baking aisle.

It was empty.

The memory bubbled to the surface and I could see him hunched over and looking for something that was nowhere in front of him, and I could see me, going straight for the brownie section. This was a waste of time, what was I even doing?

I turned to leave, giving Craig a small smile on my way out. That's when he spoke to me for the first time ever saying more than the word 'hi'.

"I didn't know you knew Wyatt Smith, Allie," Craig said. Craig was also apparently from New Zealand. I had been coming into this corner store for over 3 years and I just realised that the only words he's spoken to me were 'hi' and 'Craig' after I introduced myself one time.

I processed that little nugget of information as I answered him, "I don't know anyone by that name, Craig."

"Yes, you do. I saw you talking to him last week," Craig looked at me very intently and I instinctively took a step back because it occurred to me that though I waved at Craig on average twice a week whenever I'd come in for brownie mix for the past three years, I didn't even know he was from New Zealand until tonight. I didn't know Craig at all.

Stranger danger, Allie.

"I think you've been working too many shifts in a row Craig. I have never spoken to a Wyatt Smith in my life," I said, giving him a stern look in return.

"I took a photo of you two in the aisle speaking. I know people get funny when they have famous friends, but you don't have to lie about it," he scoffed like he was genuinely offended.

"I'm not lying Craig, I mean it—," the words got caught in my throat as Craig thrust his iPhone into my face showing me a photo he had uploaded to Instagram with a caption that said, 'Wyatt Smith just came into my work!'.

It was a photo of him and Dax. His red hair was unmistakable.

My insides did a weird thing seeing his face again. My mind had not done it justice.

Craig then swiped to the next photo in the post and it was Dax and I. Me with my hand over my mouth muffling a laugh and Dax looking over his shoulder with a frown.

"Craig, that guy's name is Dax," I said, but my voice wasn't convincing.

"Allie, I think you're the one who's losing it, mate. You spent 20 minutes speaking to the lead singer of *Lady Luck* and you're telling me you didn't know? Yeah, right!" that was apparently the end of the conversation for Craig as he turned around and promptly ignored me.

My brain wasn't working but my body managed to walk me out of the store and plant me in front of my apartment building. I stood outside in the cold just staring at the front door because it had just occurred to me that I had spent 20 minutes in the baking aisle with the frontman of the most popular rock band in modern rock and not only did I have no idea who he was, but I was seeing him live in a week and I was supposed to be right at the front of the stage.

Holy applesauce.

If fate was real and had taken pity on my inner monologue, this was an absolute doozy of a situation.

I pulled out my phone and typed the band name into google. A small gasp left my mouth as thousands of photos of *Lady Luck* popped up. Usually Dax had black hair, but holy guacamole, that was him.

I shoved my phone away and finally took a step into my apartment building.

Holy shit, Dax was Wyatt Smith.

8

Allie

I couldn't feel my hands and it had nothing to do with the weather. I was so nervous I might've actually puked. Lovely.

I couldn't believe I was here. The last week, as one could imagine, consisted of me mapping out how this was going to go down. I couldn't sleep, my brain was so overloaded with plans I might as well have been the blueprint section at your state library.

I was pathetic, which was new for me. I had finally reached the level that I so closely teetered on and usually edged more on the side of quirky, where most people just gave me sympathetic looks and immediately classified me as 'socially awkward'.

One realisation quickly morphed into another as it was never more blatantly clear to me than in that moment of being three hours early for a concert, yet somehow still late, that I just did not get out enough.

The line was already wound around the side of the stadium with easily about a hundred people in front of us. Savannah, however, looked incredibly pleased with the situation and assured me, though I needed absolutely no assurance, that battling them all to the very front of the mosh pit was no problem at all. So close that when Wyatt – who I now knew was Dax – apparently did his signature head shake halfway through their show that we would 'be majestically hit with his sweat'. I mean I really shouldn't have to say this, but ew? Gross.

The hours spent waiting had Sav and I alternating between who would run to the café – not across the street like everybody and their mother was doing – but the one a block over and completely empty, for refreshments and toilet breaks.

Every time it was my turn to duck off it was as if I had never felt such intense relief before in my life. I knew Savannah knew that I was keeping something from her, but I just, I wanted to keep this to myself for a bit, just in case. Just to *see.*

I wasn't sure what I was expecting to find out, but I just wanted to see him first, then I'd tell her. I was sweating so bad, but in saying that, I felt calmer than I could have been. It was either that or I had settled myself so far into delusion that I was now comfortably living in a reality that was no longer my own. Either way, I was fine.

The sun was setting, and the bitter winter wind picked up, making me incredibly grateful for my *skeenie* and my gloves, even though when I met Sav at the base of my apartment building, her face fell with quiet disapproval. I got it, I mean this was a rock concert and I was wearing a *skeenie,* but I'd take it off, of course, and I was wearing something black and ripped under my massive coat, so, I would fit in when the time was right.

Not a second too soon, the doors to the stadium lobby opened and people were being let inside. Tickets were authenticated and scanned, and bags were checked no matter how small they were. Any food and drink purchased outside the stadium was taken and thrown away as contraband, standard, and within 20 minutes we were inside.

My arm being violently tugged by Sav-on-a-mission who went straight for the correct door – perks of working at the venue – and down the stairs, through the gates that sectioned off the mosh area – needing only to wave at the security guard there, Dave, apparently, and used her bony elbows to land us straight at the front of the pit. If I had had my pencil-tower-poking-stick from our tutoring days, I would have been able to touch the stage.

Holy moly, okay. I wasn't beyond being able to admit that I was a bit excited. I hadn't been to a concert since *Michael Bublé's* Christmas concert in 2011, and at that point, it was riveting. I knew for a fact that I wasn't the only one who claimed that as the 'traditional album of Christmas'.

I tried picturing him up there, the guy I had met in the baking aisle, and I guess I could imagine it, but he didn't seem like a rock star, he was normal? Not that rock stars *weren't* normal, I just meant…I honestly didn't know. This felt very much not like my life.

Out of habit or nervousness, or both, I ran a hand through my hair, fluffing it up and letting the long waves fall to my front. He probably wouldn't even remember me.

The mosh area started to fill up and I really should have known that the 7PM starting time was in fact *not* the starting time, but the 'stage doors open' time, where we would then wait for an extra hour for the lights to dim, and then another 30 for the support band to come on.

The support band was called *Watch Them Burn* – charming – and I didn't really mind them. Savannah sang along with every single one of their songs. Halfway through their set, I took off my *skeenie*, gloves and coat and shoved them into my tote. As predicted, Savannah's approval for my outfit underneath all the layers made up for her initial disapproval, and I did my best to dutifully bounce around with her.

The lights were not flashing nor were they completely turned on but set to cast a medium-lit haze over the audience. The big light show was usually reserved only for the headlining band, and my ear plugs – effective and discrete under my long hair – were completely apt in muffling the sound to where it was completely enjoyable.

I was living in the moment, not thinking about anything else – trying my best not to acknowledge that Dax was in the venue and would be within spitting distance in a matter of moments. Nope. My mind was clear. Very, very clear.

And you know what? I was having *fun.* This was *fun.* An honest to God revelation and the amount of inner pride I felt for myself in that moment was enough to clog my throat with emotion (internal shimmy of celebration).

This wasn't a big thing for everyone, and it never used to be a big thing for me, but it was now. I knew from the glint in Savannah's eyes that it was a big thing for her too. My victories were her victories, and vice versa. The bone crushing hug she dragged me into pushed all the air from my lungs and had me laughing at the same time. It was then followed by my face being squished between her hands and having her yell the lyrics to the song that was being performed right into my face.

I was mind-blowingly stoked, it made me start to get a bit emotional, that was until Sav grabbed my shoulders and mouthed over the music, *"Are you okay?"*

I nodded back to her enthusiastically just as the song came to an end. *Watch Them Burn* took their bow and thanked everyone for their time. They then gave a big, warm, rock-n-roll welcome to *Lady Luck.*

I was crouched down in front of the stage when I *felt* the screams of the stadium reverberate through the floor. A clear sign that the band had walked on stage. My heart was in my throat and I honestly needed to do a nervous-pee so bad that the idea of standing up from my crouch was almost more frightening because of the potential pant-wetting situation that could happen rather than seeing Dax.

I shoved my tote bag just under the gate in front of us and stuffed yet another layer of clothing I was wearing into it. I came to find that mosh pits got very, very, warm. I was now left with my skinny jeans and oversized *'Your face is a work of Moz-Art'* shirt.

I gave myself the world's worst and shortest pep talk. Everything I was going to do and all I had planned went right out the window when I popped up. It was all I could do to slap on my biggest smile and show Savannah I was indeed ready to rock. I probably looked insane.

How was this actually happening though? And why was it so important? If felt important. I shook the thought from my head and tried to convince myself that he would see me and that would be it. No spark of recognition and everything I thought up or perhaps imagined during our meet-cute was just more of me edging towards that 'pathetic' tier I usually lingered just below.

My smile lasted all of a second before morphing into the very same opened mouth trout look that I seemed to have modelled more in the last 2 weeks than in the entire year prior. Savannah, bless her soul, was screaming so loud I could hear the scars forming on her vocal cords despite my ear plugs.

I really wished I could take in her excitement, but my eyes had locked with the frontman of the band. His black boots were laced and buckled halfway up his shins, the skin-tight black jeans that were tucked into them and sat just below the line of his boxers. Seamlessly moving into the faded *Iron Maiden* band-T that he wore and complemented by the weathered – so cool I could choke – leather jacket that also sported a few too many unnecessary buckles (not complaining).

Topping it all off was his face - the very same face that was far too sexy to be in the 24-hour corner store that was a 1-minute walk from my apartment - and the messy, bright red hair.

Dax was on stage and he was looking right at me.

9

Allie was in the front row.

I was just staring at her, genuinely trying to understand if I was looking at the same person from 2 weeks ago, and how that was possible.

The front row of *my* concert. For the band that *I* was in. The very same Allie that did not know who I was. The same Allie that despite that very real and true statement, I had looked for continuously in every show we had played since we met, since I saw her.

What the hell is happening right now?

She honestly looked like she was in shock, but then her face softened a bit and she smiled, giving me the same quick wave she did in the baking aisle. I might have been on stage, but I could have been anywhere in the world as I gave her a smile and wave back.

My tongue felt like a weight in my mouth and suddenly the probability of my being able to sing and perform seemed entirely out of the question. Allie was in the front row of my concert; I was literally looking right at her.

And then I realised, she'd figured out who I was.

The stadium had erupted with screams so loud the stage beneath my boots rumbled, but my eyes were on Allie, and her eyes were on me. Okay, so, maybe being on stage was a bit of an issue. She without a doubt knew I was Wyatt.

The daze of our intense eye contact was broken when the girl next to Allie grabbed her face in both hands and turned it towards her own before proceeding to scream directly into her face. If I wasn't so shocked, I would have laughed.

It was moments like this where years and *years* of stage persona, performance training and knowledge came into play and without a second to spare or collect my fractured attention, I screamed into the microphone I held, honestly relieved that any sounds came out of my mouth at all.

"ARE YOU READY TO ROCK TONIGHT?!" I held the mic out to the crowd and cupped my ear to show I was waiting for their reply. It was deafening. Even so, and though it was completely untrue, I followed it up with, "I CAN'T HEAR YOU!" and I was certain my teeth shook in my gums from the sheer volume of the crowd, "You might know this one, it's called *Run.*"

Song after song and the crowd kept getting louder. This was why we loved our home city. We were one of them, and they knew it too. My fingers danced along the frets of my guitar as me and the guys got lost on stage, in the electric buzz that filled the air every time we played live.

I ran up to the back of the stage, many times, and stood facing Aspen as he played the drums as I always did, but this time I used it to help keep my attention on the music, to make sure I remembered I was performing live in front of tens of thousands of people.

I tried my best *not* to look at Allie because I desperately, *desperately* needed to focus on the show. But I did, I peeked, and one moment she was there and the next she was gone. Her friend looked worried and dazed, but she stayed put.

After the whole 65 minutes of the concert, the very moment the music ended and the screams from the stadium burst into life, the blonde-haired girl that was standing with Allie, the one that screamed right into her face, made a beeline for the exit. I had never seen someone move through a mosh pit so quickly and with such little friction in my life.

* * *

We set up a meet-and-greet after the show, smiling and signing things from different people, taking photos and asking for names, but I was wholeheartedly thinking the entire time that I had *broken* Allie. Or somehow upset her to the point where she left the concert and it made me *sick.* If she had figured out who I was and then she had run away, well that wasn't saying too much, was it?

Was it because I was trying not to look at her? Maybe I made her feel unimportant. No, surely not, I was playing a show, I was *working.*

Guilt rushed through me then. I didn't lie, but I also didn't really tell her who I was. I mean, I could have but it didn't really feel like baking aisle conversation, and now I had no way to even message her, to find out why she ran out. I had wanted to tell her who I was, what I did for a living, of course I did, but it was 20 minutes in the baking aisle. An easy, effortless, *enjoyable* 20 minutes.

The blonde-haired girl, who had bulldozed out of the mosh pit and standing to the side with a security guard named Dave, caught my attention.

I stood up abruptly. The kind of stand-up moment where you took everyone off guard, including yourself and all of a sudden everyone stops talking and they're all just *looking* at you, waiting for you to do something.

What is happening? Did I have stage fright? Was that what was happening right now?

Aspen jumped to his feet next to me and leaned in.

"Dax, what are you doing?" he whispered and then leaned around to try and look at my face.

I knew my mouth was opening and closing like a fish out of water. I turned my head between Ap and the girl who was talking to Dave, who was now also looking at me. I managed to convey to my brother in the most incoherent way possible that the girl from the store had been in the front row, and then she disappeared but she was there with *that* girl. At least, that's what I wanted to say, I was almost positive none of it came out except for maybe 'Allie' and 'friend'.

Aspen got the point and asked the security guard to our back, Philip? Peter? Something that started with a 'P' for sure, to grab the girl talking to

Dave and see if she could come for a chat after the signing.

With a firm hand on my shoulder pushing me back down to my seat, Aspen patted my back and apologised to the fans waiting in line.

Get a grip, Dax.

The last thing I wanted was for the fans in front of us to think we didn't want to be right where we were, because there was little else that brought me joy like meeting the people that made what we did possible. So, I got my shit together and for the next hour we made every single person who came up to see us feel like they were the most important person in the world, because it was true. They were.

I'd never had to juggle more than one point of concentration at a time. It was probably more accurate to say that I *couldn't.* I *didn't.* I'd always been able to compartmentalise, and probably to a fault. When it was band time, it was band time and I had no problem ignoring everything, and *everyone* else.

Ap was the same and the rest of the guys could split their attention and still got the job done. I guess that's multitasking for you. It's why every relationship besides the one with my brother – and my parents I guess – had never made it to the year mark. Sure, I could have fallen in love plenty of times. When the band was having a break between tours or we were in one spot recording, I was more than capable of being a good boyfriend; loving, doting, spontaneous. But when the band was on, well, it was the only thing that was on.

We all stood up as a unit and waved to everyone before heading back into our dressing room. It was more of a mini apartment with no bedrooms. Just a basic kitchen, lots of couches and to my great pleasure, the blonde-haired girl tagged along with Dave and…Patrick?

Luke howled as we entered our little back room and was soon joined by the rest of us. Screaming, yelling, making weird noises pretty much just to be loud. You name it, we did it. We met in the middle of the room for our ritual end-of-show huddle, chanted the name of our band three times and then screamed again, and that was that.

We thought as youngsters just starting our band that we needed to do it before and after every show. Now, we just did it because it was tradition and thought it was so stupid that it made us laugh. We tried to drop it a while ago and even though nothing went wrong, the performance felt unfinished until we did it.

I walked over to the girl who was standing next to Dave. “Hi.” I lifted my hand in a half-hearted wave.

“Hello!” her responding smile and enthusiasm were very reminiscent of someone who might have met higher profile personnel semi-regularly and held herself together well.

This was a good start.

“I’m Wyatt, and this is Aspen, Luke, Rip and Angus,” I motioned behind me to my band mates lounging on the couches.

They all replied with different variations of the same greeting at the same time. The blonde-haired girl leaned around me to wave at the rest of the band.

“Hey guys! I’m Savannah. It’s so nice to meet you all, I’m a massive fan,” her smile was infectious and bright.

I smiled back with a small nod of my head in thanks. Her own smile dampened a bit as she leaned forward. I leaned forward in reply.

“So, I’m a bit confused as to why I’m back here. Don’t get me wrong, I’m stoked and have pinched myself a few times already but, I’m curious,” ah, we have a no-shit-Sherlock sort of woman here. Perfect.

This was going very, very well. What were the chances!

“Alright. No beating around the bush then. How do you know Allie?”

Savannah’s eyes locked with mine and her hand slowly lifted to cover her mouth as her eyes widened.

“Oh, my, *God. Oh my god, oh my god, OHMYGOD,*” she began to pace immediately. Okay, so I could deduce that she knew about the baking aisle.

“Savannah—” there was no hope of stopping the inner spiral I could see unfolding before me. All the pieces of this moment, and the moments most likely recounted to Savannah by Allie, were falling into place.

She spun to face me and expertly yelled, "The hair!" right into my face. I will admit I flinched because I knew, *I knew.*

"Wait. Hold up. Who the fuck is *Dax?*"

"Well, I'm Dax," I offered her my least predatory smile. The one that said, 'sure! You can kick my ass if you want to and I won't fight back.'

This was not going well.

Savannah looked at me like I'd grown a pair of boobs right before her eyes.

"It's my middle name. Well, it's a nickname of my middle name. Maddox. Dax, my parents and Ap call me Dax. And the guys too sometimes, but that's just in private. No one knows about that, so…" I pushed my hair back from my face.

I'd not only broken Allie but I'd broken her friend too. She just sort of, stopped. Her eyes got a far-off look and she may or may not have been breathing.

I waved a hand in front of her face but certainly did not go any closer, "Savannah, are you okay?"

"I think I need to sit down," Savannah placed a hand on her forehead.

Dave, the security guard, walked over to help support Savannah as he led her to one of the free couches. I walked behind them and sat down next to Ap. We all just looked at her. Okay, stared.

This couldn't get any worse.

"So, you were at the 24-hour corner store getting *baking powder* for Aspen?"

"Yes, I was. And then Allie showed up and, well, I'm assuming she told you the rest."

A perfect eyebrow rose at that, confirming to me that the whole 'do you know who I am' thing absolutely came up in conversation and Allie thought I was a giant asshole.

Oh, look! How about that, I was wrong. It just got worse. Great.

"I thought she was a *fan*! I didn't know she didn't know me; everyone knows me. Us. It had gone so well after that though. The talking, you know. And I wanted to tell her, of course, but it just didn't come up," I explained to both Savannah and the rest of the guys, all the quizzical looks I got back confirmed that I sounded as stupid as I felt.

Why was this so important? It felt important.

Savannah waved off my explanation, "Yeah, yeah *Wyatt.* I'm not the one that needs that explanation, bucko. Oh my *god,* this makes so much *sense* now. Oh, and she was doing *so well.* Damn. *Shite.*"

"Doing well with what?" I asked, confused. The rest of the guys were still watching this all go down like it was a ping pong tournament.

Savannah waved off my question again.

"Savannah—"

"Sav is good," she interrupted, though her smile was kind.

"Right, *Sav,* well I was hoping for a way to speak to her. Maybe grab her number. I wanted to explain..." I reached up to rub the back of my neck, I was at a loss for words. That had never really happened before.

It was totally the wrong moment, but Aspen reached out and smacked me in the chest with the world's stupidest smile on his face. I shot him a look that promised so much pain he had no idea, but his attempt to muffle his smile had me rolling my eyes. His smile was clearly catching because the rest of the guys were suddenly sitting there with shit-eating grins on their faces too.

Sav looked between us, "*You* want Allie's number?" her expression was pretty locked down, but I could see the similarities to boys' smiles ghosting her face.

"Yes, absolutely. I mean, it would be nice to see her again. Maybe see if she'd want to go out. When we met it was nice—"

Aspen chose that moment to lean over and start to make kissy noises in my ear. I gave him a solid punch in the arm that had him howling out. I offered Sav a pleasant smile and absolutely no explanation. I knew anything that happened here was probably getting relayed to Allie and, so far, I was coming off as the most awkward person ever.

An awkward rock star who doesn't know how to talk to girls. Wonderful. Nice, Dax.

Sav sent over Allie's number with the disclaimer that she was going to, "100% let her know what the name of sweet-baby-Jesus happened, because this was *insane* and not real life and just didn't happen to anyone, like, ever," and wished me good luck. Then proceeded to pass on a direct warning and clear series of events of what would happen to my balls should I do anything wrong by her best friend.

I honestly would have been disappointed had she left without issuing one. Sav seemed like the 'squish my friend's heart and I'll squish your face' sort.

She shot a wink off to Angus and patted Dave the security guard on the shoulder and headed out, but not before thanking us for the invite to chat over her shoulder and that she'd hoped to see us around. I decided immediately that I liked Sav.

I released the world's longest breath that I didn't even realise I was holding, and let my head fall into my hands. Aspen walked over and stopped before me. His boots, which were pretty much the same as mine, were the only thing in my line of sight and I couldn't be arsed to lift my head from my hands.

"Good luck, *bucko.*"

I lifted my middle finger up to my four band mates who were all happily laughing at what was going to be a very interesting conversation. Even so, there was still one underlying thought that kept coming to the surface of my mind, and that was I couldn't believe my luck.

10

Allie

Work was usually a drag, but today, it was dragging super hard. My phone buzzed for the first time all day and if there was a world record for 'fastest time to pick up a phone from a desk', I just beat it.

It was Sav.

Savvy: *Hey doll how are you?*

Allie: *Hey, I'm good.*
Just work, you know.
What's up?

Savvy: *Okay, so I have news...*

Allie: *Are you okay?*

Savvy: *yep I'm fine*
it's about the concert.

Allie: *Oh, yeah*

I'm sorry I left early.
I was feeling a bit...
overwhelmed.

Savvy: *No babes, that's fine.*
I understand, but I think you'll
be awfully interested in what I
have to say.

Allie: *Okay, now I'm worried?*

Savvy: *You should come by after work.*

Allie: *Come round to mine?*
I'll be home by 6.

Savvy: *Ugh...but Dean?*

Allie: *...*
Fine
but you're buying me dinner.

Savvy: *Deal. Anything is better*
*than Dean's leftovers. *gag**
Love ya xxx

Allie: *Me too xx*

Well, there was no chance in hell I was going to be able to focus on work now, because I had some pretty massive news for her too, like, 'hey Sav, I randomly met Wyatt Smith at the 24-hour corner store and had *no idea* he was a famous singer and I'm pretty sure he thinks I live under a rock because I was oblivious and then we waved at each other when he was on stage at *his* band's concert and remember when I thought he was an asshole for asking me if I knew him? Well, turns out I was the asshole who not only didn't recognise his life's work and success but also insulted his shoes in reference to baking.'

And then I realised. *Holy fuck knuckle,* she knows. *She knows.*

She knew that I knew that Dax was Wyatt, and that I knew and didn't tell her.

I was going to throw up. This was *a lot.*

I sat with my head wedged between my knees until I calmed down and found something to distract myself with at work.

The pet store Head Office had a relatively large staff base. They rented an entire floor of a fairly new building and I was in the corner for the marketing team. With all our most recent campaigns launched, now we were just monitoring. Seeing how they were performing, making any necessary optimisations to our ads and observing customer feedback and interest. The usual things. We had a lovely large budget for the campaign, so we were just letting it go crazy and I was pretty much free with my time for the week.

I did the tasks that I had to do daily. It was enough to take my mind off the Dax-Wyatt-Savvy situation for exactly 4 seconds.

Emails, social curation for the following day's posts on social media, scheduled those to go up automatically, found a couple of influencers online who would be interested in showcasing a new type of dog shampoo we were selling to their followers.

If you're wondering if people could really be influenced to buy dog shampoo, the answer was yes. People could be influenced to do and buy just about anything and such was the nature of my job.

The best part about living with Dean was that I didn't have to see him at work either. He worked in the I.T. department which lived happily on the other end of the floor. We didn't even commute together. Our whole life-schedules were completely non-conflicting that it practically felt like I lived by myself *except* when Savannah came over.

You would've assumed it was just the leftovers situation and his incredibly vanilla demeanour, maybe even the fact that his voice had never ventured beyond the single tone he used to speak and laugh in. No, I wasn't not kidding. He reminded me 100% of *Squidward* from *SpongeBob SquarePants.* It was also because he had a very unhealthy attachment to my best friend, and he hung around like a bad smell (on top of his usual odour) the moment she set foot in the apartment.

By the time 5PM rolled around, I was so ready to leave that I had been sitting at my desk chair with my coat, gloves and *skeenie* on for 15 minutes already.

I headed home first to change quickly. My apartment was, well it was very *Allie.*

There was lots of wood and all the carpets were beige. As far as a colour went it was incredibly neutral and it balanced out the ridiculous amounts of colour that was splattered everywhere else.

The living room was blues and greens and yellows, but all in moderation, and it also housed a secondhand sofa that I found on Facebook Marketplace for $15. Sure, I had to have it professionally steam cleaned four times but now it was practically brand new. It was a lovely light blue sectional, so I was impressed by that particular save.

The rest of the colour came from chairs in different shapes and lots and lots and *lots* of blankets and pillows. Then there were the plants and the plant pots.

It was full, but not overcrowded and it wasn't dusty either. It was astoundingly clean, and Dean had no issues whatsoever that I took charge of the interior decoration. He got the massive bedroom with the en suite and we halve the rent so, I suppose that was our compromise.

I chucked my keys in the bowl on the hallway table and dumped the rest of my stuff on the chair right next to it. Yanked off my boots and headed straight for the bathroom. I showered, shampooing my hair twice (if you haven't tried it you should and I'll accept your thanks later), then waddled to my room in my towel.

My standard clothing of skinny jeans and big sweater were adorned and after a quick blow dry of my hair, I was wrapped securely once again in all my winter wear. Yes, of course including my *skeenie,* and I headed to

Savannah's, where I had to walk by the 24-hour corner store.

A pang of unease went through me as I walked by the automatic doors and a rush of the warm air from inside wafted out to me.

I had absolutely refused to think about Dax since I had run hell for leather from the concert last night (except for just now at work, evidently). I was so convinced I was going to be able to see him up there. This guy I met at the baking aisle, this cool and really nice and *funny* guy, and be able to wave and enjoy the show and then go backstage and see him, fall in love and Bob's your uncle! But then, there he was, and there *I* was, and I had thought about it *so much* that I just, well, I ran. Obviously.

It had occupied my thoughts so much that when the stadium went dark and the big flashing lights turned on that nothing else had pierced my mind. No accident or anxiety beyond seeing him, Dax, *Wyatt,* on stage and trying to convey my coolness in the short seconds our eyes met.

This guy I had thought of nonstop since the awkward first encounter, who I was hoping I might find there again and be brave enough to get his number. But nope, Dax was not normal. He was… whatever he was. He was the frontman to the biggest band in rock and when we met, *I didn't even know who he was.* Not only did that reinforce my loner-loser status but, I felt like an idiot. Like it was all an inside joke everyone knew but me.

All his sexy side smiles became mocking as I looked back at them through my memory bank, and the brownie mix he had claimed to be his favourite didn't quite hold the same amazing taste in my mind as I had originally thought. I felt stupid, which was in itself stupid.

I call this one the 'classic Allie-over-thinker'. It's a move I make often in the comfort of my own mind.

I hit the buzzer for Savannah's apartment and a second later, the electric crunching sound notified me that she had granted me access to the building. She was on the second floor and the door was already open, letting me walk right in. I took off my shoes and winter wear and plopped on the couch where a glass of wine waited for me.

I. Love. Her.

The sounds of the oven door closing shut echoed my way from the kitchen and Sav rounded the corner not a second later, planting a kiss on my head.

"Hey, Al."

I leaned back and smiled at her, "Hey, yourself. What's for dinner?"

"Frozen pizzas," she sent me a wink.

Hmm. Something was up.

"With garlic bread?"

"Of course," she smiled at me over the rim of her own wine glass.

Definitely up.

I made sure to find my own beverage incredibly interesting while Sav found a way to explain to me what was so important that she'd go as far as to put pizzas *and* garlic bread in the oven for me. It may not look it but that was a lot of effort for Miss T.V. dinner over there.

"I met Wyatt," she looked like a stunned deer, but it got my attention and my eyes flashed up to hers so fast that I knew that she knew I knew that Dax was Wyatt.

"Oh?" I was going to need to know exactly where the bottle of wine was to refill my glass in about 5 seconds. My ears were already burning from embarrassment.

"Mmm. It was crazy. When I went backstage, I was asked if I wanted to meet the band. Naturally I thought it was because of my incredible makeup and, let's be honest, I looked very good in my outfit of choice."

I nodded my head in agreement. Savannah was bangin'. Her platinum blonde hair darkened at the roots and ended in a bob around her chin. I'd never seen anyone able to pull off that haircut but her. She always had her lips painted red, the lipstick was called 'heartbreaker', and it made her blue eyes brighter.

Sav sported an entire sleeve of tattoos that she added to whenever, wherever. She had more that dotted her legs, too. And as if the universe owed her or something, despite this badass exterior, she was also the nicest person to ever exist.

"That's so cool! You met your favourite band," and before you ask, yes, it would have killed me to exude anymore enthusiasm than that.

"Mmm, yes that was very cool," she took a deep breath, "And, so I asked why they'd invited me and that's when Wyatt Smith said that he saw me with you and wanted to know how I knew you. He said, 'how do you know Allie?'"

Savannah took another sip of her wine and the hold she had over her expression was good, impressive even, but it was a telling sign that inside she was bursting with so much excitement she could probably pass out.

"That's so weird. Maybe my name was on my shirt or something," it wasn't. I didn't even know why it would have been.

"Maybe. Could have been, or..."

"*Or...*," I mimicked her, there was no way I was moving this conversation forward. Jeepers, it was so *hot* in this apartment. Why did she keep it so hot in here?

She took another deep breath, "Or it might have been that after I realised who he was, he realised that I already knew who he was and he was the tall, sexy guy with the red hair from the corner store with the baking powder and that's why you ran out of the concert like a headless chicken," it all left her mouth so quickly, if I hadn't lived the events myself, I would have needed her to repeat it with a lot more information.

I let out a long breath. I was caught out, but that was a new record on time taken to figure me out on Sav's end.

I'm getting better. 5 points to Allie.

"Yes, okay, that's all correct. I saw Dax, *Wyatt*, whichever his name is and I had never felt more stupid in my whole life and so I left. Are you happy now?"

Savannah's face fell in a bit of surprise, "Allie, what are you even talking about. This is so exciting!" her face lifted again, and she clutched her wine glass with both hands.

"How is this exciting? I made a complete fool of myself, Savannah! In front of someone who I've only met once and thought I had made a connection with. Who I'd actually begun *looking* for when I was walking on the street? Did you know I went into the corner store once more to see if maybe he was there? Thinking he was my *neighbour*. My neighbour!" I repeated to make sure I got the ridiculousness of this situation across.

"Only to have Craig, the check-out guy, break the news to me like the hermit-living wiener I was. And then I had built it up in my head I was going to be *so cool,* and then there he was in his leather jacket with all the buckles and it was me and *gah,* I felt like such a phoney. I don't *go* to concerts and *rock out.* I was wearing earplugs, for crying out loud!" it all came out in a huff and all of a sudden, I wanted to cry.

"Ahh," she said. Nodding her head like she was picking up what I was putting down. I knew she wasn't. She did that any time she thought I was being ridiculous, then eventually I came to the same conclusion as her and we just moved on. Yeah, well, not this time lady.

"So, that's the end of that," I nodded my head in finality. I would not think about Wyatt Smith anymore. I wouldn't think about Dax either. Because in my mind they were two different people.

One was someone who I got on with and related to – as much as you could relate to a stranger in 20 minutes – and laughed at my jokes and told me I was his *kind of person,* and the other was a buckled up, leather wearing sex-god who sang with the voice of an angel to thousands and thousands of people.

I'm not even going to acknowledge where that thought train came from. We are going to wash right over that like a river flowing around a rock.

"Yep. Sounds good," Savannah said. I was just about to sigh in relief when she dropped the next bombshell, "Except it's not because he has your number and I can tell you that he's already whipped."

"What?! Savannah!" I set my wine glass down softly but firmly. And then my next words to her even shocked myself, "He said that to you?"

Get a grip, Allie.

The smirk she wore was infuriating. She hopped off the sofa to go and tend to the pizzas as she said, "Nope. But I know how to read people and I have never been so confident in something as I am of *that.*"

11

"I'm still getting some feedback in my left earpiece," I noted to our sound guy, Noah, who was set up to the left of the stage. He held up a finger, motioned for me to first wait a second and then followed it up with a thumbs-up to try again.

I headed straight into the chorus of one of our songs. The feedback from my guitar had stopped and it all sounded perfect. I motioned back to him with my own hand gesture for 'perfect' just in case he couldn't hear me properly.

"Thank you!" I removed the earpieces and let them hang around my neck, lifting off the strap of my guitar, I set it in its stand. I made my way off stage and handed Noah the earpieces, thanked him with a pat on the back before I headed towards the back little apartment-slash-dressing-room where the rest of the guys were waiting. All their individual sound checks were done, and we'd play a few songs as a band later before the main show.

This was the last night of our stadium tour for the album. It was bittersweet but being able to stay where we were for the next few months was a relief too. We had finished recording our next album in the summer and it was coming out soon.

Once it was out, we'd set out to do some press for it and then shortly after we'd pick up and head out on our next tour for the new album. It felt exhausting just to think about it, but I knew after a few months of downtime, the itch to travel and play live would hit us all and it would be nothing but good times ahead.

I opened the door and leaned on the frame, knocking lightly. They all stood up together and we walked out to the parking lot to head home and chill before the show. Aspen drove us all to our apartment. We tended to hang out together especially before the shows. If we split off, sometimes we weren't on the same level and, well, things just always *gelled* better when we were.

I found myself flopped on a chair in our living room. Rip was in the kitchen making a sandwich when he called out to see if anyone else wanted one. Of course, we all responded with a yes to which a disgruntled "lazy assholes" was replied.

Aspen and Angus were playing Call of Duty and Luke was out on our balcony having a cigarette. I was staring at the number in my phone that was sitting under the only name I was thinking of for the past several days: Allie.

"Are you going to invite her to tonight's show?" Aspen asked while his attention remained firmly placed on the T.V.

"Why would I invite her back to the same show she bolted from? Also, she probably has work or something," took a shot in the dark with that excuse.

"Mmm," Aspen replied. I flipped him off even though he wasn't looking.

"Saw that."

But how?

"Dude you're being such a baby about it. Just call her or message her first *then* call her," Aspen went on, his attention on the TV.

"She won't reply."

"Oh, she'll reply," he was incredibly confident for someone who was constantly losing against Angus.

"She won't," I replied.

"She will," he shot back.

"Aspen," God, he was relentless sometimes.

"Dax," he said back, just as sternly.

"Okay! Fine, *fine.* I'll message her."

One text, that was all.

And if she didn't reply?

Then that was that matter settled.

Dax: *Hey, Allie.*
It's Dax, from the baking aisle.
Savannah gave me your number.

The bubble with the 3 dots popped up and vanished 3…no, 4 times.

Allie: *Hello*

Okay. I suddenly had the undeniable and overwhelming need to throw my phone out the window and pace around the apartment.

She replied.

Dax: *So, this is crazy, huh!*

Why…?

Allie: *This is...well yes, it's crazy lol*

The bubbles popped up again. Once. Twice.

Allie: *So, Dax isn't your name then?*

Dax: *No, Dax is definitely my name. Or else my mum has had it wrong for the last 27 years...*

Why can't I *unsend* a text message?

Dax: *I was hoping to explain after the show...but you left.*

Allie: *I did. I know. Sorry. I wasn't feeling that great. It gets really hot in the mosh pit. Did you know that? You probably did. The music was great though, you were great.*

Dax: *That's good. That's awesome, thanks, I mean. Yeah it does get pretty hot down there in the mosh!*

Allie: *Yeah haha*

Dax: *Would you like to grab a bite?*

Allie: *With you?*

Dax: *I mean...*

Allie: *Yes, I'd like that.*

She said yes. I needed to go for a run or something.

Dax: *You could come over*
to mine if you wanted?

Allie: *Yes, I mean, I would.*
I don't have a car, though.
I don't drive.

Dax: *Maybe yours, then?*

Allie: *We can do mine.*

Dax: *Okay, cool! What time*
suits you best?

I waited.

I waited and waited, and she just didn't reply.

Rip handed me my sandwich and I ate it staring at my black phone screen. I finished the sandwich and she still hadn't replied.

Aspen came and got me when it was time to head back to the stadium for our last show. I didn't want to play. I had never *not* wanted to play. Ever.

We got to the stadium and jumped straight on stage to run through a few songs as a band before heading back into the back room to get ready.

"Dax, are you with us?" Aspen had his hand on my shoulder as we walked off the stage.

"Mm. Yeah, no, I'm good."

"Sure you are, bud," he left it at that, obviously not believing me.

Jenna and Marco were waiting for us to start getting ready while Phoebe and Lilly, our outfit coordinators, were on the other side of the room sorting out our clothes for the stage.

I had left my phone in the room needing to be away from it for a while. I wasn't really attached to my phone, but it could have been an extra limb after the past few hours. I picked it up and turned it over to unlock it.

Allie: *Tomorrow?*
Is 6pm okay with you?
56 Collin Street.
Apartment number 20.

My smile was stupid. It was stupidly big. I knew it and I didn't care at all.

Everyone else knew it too.

Luke who was first in the chair being airbrushed by Jenna whooped and yelled, "Yeah, baby, she replied!"

"Who replied?" asked Jenna.

"Wyatt's new girlfriend," Aspen chimed in, wagging his eyebrows up and down. I held up my middle finger to them all as I stared at my phone.

She replied.

"Oh my gosh, Wyatt! That's so exciting!" Jenna looked at me with so much excitement she was giving Aspen a run for his money. Her eyes also held this warm sympathy dashed with a bit of pity for me. It made me sick.

I sent her a tight-lipped smile before I moved my attention back to my phone.

This was good. This was really, really good.

Dax: *6pm is perfect.*

12

Allie

"Yeah, hi. Wendy, it's Allie," I said through the crackly line of the phone to my local Chinese restaurant.

"Allie! Oh, it's so good to hear from you, how are you?" she replied enthusiastically. It made me smile every time, she reminded me a lot of my mom.

"Wendy, I spoke to you last week," I corrected her. I could almost *feel* her swatting my comment away as complete nonsense.

"You should just call to say hello, Allie. Maybe even come *in* to eat one of these times."

"Yeah, yeah, I know. I'll come in soon," I wouldn't.

The restaurant had a terrible atmosphere and because it was a 'family restaurant', there were always crying babies. I loved kids, I loved babies, hopefully be lucky enough to have some of my own one day, but for now, I preferred to eat in the silence of my apartment.

"Mmhm," she replied, she also knew I wouldn't be coming in, "Alright honey, what am I getting you? The usual today?" she asked.

"Uhm, yes please. Could I also get an extra of the number 5 and number 19?" Wendy's silence was an indication that she was jotting down the order for the kitchen.

"Company tonight? Is it Savannah? Oh, she's so darling you know how much I love her. Put her on for a hello!" that also made me smile. Sav and

Wendy probably got on better than her and I did. Savannah actually *went in* to eat.

"Actually no, not Savannah tonight. It's a friend," that was not the right word but I couldn't exactly tell her that it was the lead singer to *Lady Luck,* who was also the most beautiful person I'd ever met, and he was coming to my apartment, "His name is Dax. He's new."

"Oh Allie!" I had to move the phone away from my ear because if not, her ear-piercing squeal would have been the last thing I'd have ever heard from that side.

"Yes, yes. Very exciting."

Please don't mention Ben, please don't mention Ben.

"Yes, that certainly is! The last time you had a guy was that Ben fella!"

Awesome.

"Oh wonderful, you remember," I couldn't keep the disdain from my voice.

"Of course, I remember. I get so sad every time he comes in here to eat with his new girlfriend. It's just such a shame," she went on 'tutting' at the situation.

"He cheated on me Wendy; it was a blessing not a shame," I piped up. His visit from the other day still lingered.

"Oh, of course, honey. You're absolutely right. Did you want the fortune cookies?" she, thankfully, changed the subject.

"Yeah, I'll take extra if you can sneak them in," I said, the annoyance I felt already simmering away. Wendy didn't mean to; she was just a bit... oblivious.

"Sure can, sweetheart. Have fun! Can't wait to hear all about it!" she chimed.

Yeah, fat chance Wendy. I was never telling her about another romantic endeavour of mine ever again. Not that this was a romantic endeavour. I was just...dipping a toe in.

I ordered the food at 5:30PM and it arrived exactly 30-minutes later. Perfect. The food would still be hot by the time Dax arrived. That was 5 points for me in the hostess department.

I took two bowls out of the cupboard and then grabbed a couple spoons and forks. I assembled everything on the kitchen island in one big tower. It looked incredibly stupid. Just as I was dismantling the leaning-tower-o f-bowls-and-Chinese-food, a knock came at my door that caught me so off guard I threw the spoons I was holding. This was going to go terribly; I could feel it in my bones.

I ran quickly to pick up the fly-away spoons, chucking them in the sink before flinging myself at my front door. I smoothed out my dress and ran a hand through my hair. I was so nervous. Why was I so nervous? Why did this feel so *important?*

I opened my front door and there he was. I was still nervous, yes, but I also felt relief. Contentment? Weird.

His hands were tucked into the front of his jeans. He wore some all black chucks with another band shirt that said *'Smashing Pumpkins'* – whoever they were – on it and the same long, thick black coat from the baking aisle.

I was just taking it all in when he spoke. He was gentle and unsure and completely like the guy I had met in the 24-hour corner store. Maybe there was hope for this yet.

Maybe.

"Hi," he said, offering an effortless smile that made his eyes sparkle.

Oh, get a grip Allie you're drooling all over the welcome mat.

"Hey!" I shouted right at him. I yelled right into his face. I cleared my throat, "Hey. Hi, sorry, Hi. Please, come in. The food just got here so you've got great timing," I offered him a smile.

"Shoes?" he asked, pointing to his feet.

"Off is good," I said over my shoulder as I made my way back to the kitchen.

You could see the kitchen from the front door, so I knew I wasn't leaving him blind and unaware of where to go in my apartment.

I grabbed a couple more spoons from the drawer and proceeded to take the lids off the food.

Dax strode into my kitchen after having left his shoes and his coat by the door. His bright red hair and dark clothes oddly fit into the colour around him, not like he absorbed it but like he reflected it back.

I grabbed the bowls and cutlery and took them to the living area where I set them on the coffee table.

This last-minute location change was completely unintentional, but it was better than explaining that while I waited for him, I was fashioning the food and crockery into a tower on my kitchen island. I didn't have to say any of that to him, but I 100% knew that I would.

"Do you want some help?" he asked.

"Uhm, yeah you can grab some of the food, I just thought maybe the living room would be more comfortable," I said as I grabbed as many of the food containers as I could after putting all the lids back on.

This was just going so great, he probably thought I was insane with the word 'idiot' stamped on my forehead.

He smiled at me like he didn't think I was an idiot at all and grabbed the rest of the food before following me to the living room. I sat down on the couch, grabbing a pillow onto my lap as he dropped down with a big exhale. Dax rubbed his hands up and down his thighs before he ran a hand through his hair and looked around, taking in the living room.

"I feel like this room was entirely decorated by you," he offered as a conversation starter.

I smiled, "You would be absolutely correct. String-bean-Dean has absolutely no sense of interior flare, so it was left in my capable hands."

His eyebrows shot up at the mention of my roommate. I thought I slid that in there quite well, actually.

"*String-bean-Dean*?" he repeated back to me with a breathy laugh.

"Yeah. He's okay. We work together and he lets me have his leftovers but he's kind of a...well, he's sort of a jock-strap," my face was scrunched up like I just downed some sour milk.

Dax's head tipped back, hitting the back of the sofa as he let out a proper belly-laugh. It was incredibly contagious, and I was laughing along with him to the point where my eyes were watering and my cheeks ached.

This was *nice.*

I grabbed a bowl and handed it to him along with a spoon and fork. I didn't know if he was the kind of person who ate his noodles with a fork or a spoon, so I kept with my top tier hostess vibe and gave him options.

He took the bowl and the cutlery – opting for the fork primarily – from me as the laughter died down on both our lips.

It might have been the instant feeling of being relaxed and comfortable that overcame me after our joined laughter at Dean's expense, but I felt bold, so I ran with it.

"What's Dax short for?" he looked straight at me then, the smile on his face faltering a little bit, like he had forgotten why he was here. That we didn't know each other, like, at all.

"Maddox. My full name is Wyatt Maddox Smith, my mum has always called me Dax and it kind of just stuck with family. To everyone else I am Wyatt. To the entire *world* I am Wyatt Smith, the frontman of *Lady Luck.* But to the people I care about, the people closest to me, I'm just Dax," he explained this all as he was shovelling food into his bowl, but my eyes were glued to his face and my entire body was frozen.

"So why didn't you tell me your name was Wyatt? I might've known who you were if you had. Instead I've babbled about meeting *Dax* at the corner store, but I didn't even really meet *you.*"

"You've been babbling about meeting me?" his mouth quirked to the side in his sexy smile, still filling his bowl with food.

"Don't change the subject," I countered immediately. His smile grew more at that and then his face became very, very serious. He brought his focus back to me.

"You did really meet me. I am more Dax than I am Wyatt. Don't get me wrong, I love being both," he added, quickly, "I love being on stage and music and the stadiums and the tours, I love it. I *live* for it. But Dax is me without all those pressures, those responsibilities."

Dax's shoulders relaxed, "I guess that's why I introduced myself like that. Meeting you, speaking to you. It felt easy. Like I'd known you already even though I know I put my foot in it when I asked you if you knew who I was."

I gave him a knowing look that had him letting out a small laugh and rubbing a hand over his face.

"I thought so," his face was squished in a wince like remembering that part of the interaction was hard for him to do.

"Only for a second though. I changed my mind on that pretty much straight away," and then before he could say anything else, I jumped in again, "You thought talking to me was easy?"

I was bewildered. That didn't happen to me. I was always facing the *Ben's* of the world, a little too weird to be *easy*.

"It was a relief. To speak to you, someone who didn't know me and have you talk back to me like an actual person. Not because you were related to me or liked my music. When you spoke to me, you were looking at *me*. It was normal, and you were...," Dax seemed to retreat into his own mind for a second before he turned to look me in the eyes, "You completely surprised me Allie, and I freaked out because if I told you my first name, the way you looked at me might've changed."

I was not expecting that. I was also not expecting to lean forward and press my lips to his without any warning on either part, especially not with keeping my eyes completely open.

Oh fuck.

I pulled back, setting my empty bowl on the coffee table and stood up. I took a step back from the couch – and Dax. My hand came up, my finger moving across my lips that still felt warm and tingly from touching his.

"Oh, I'm so sorry, I...oh, *god*—" I said. I could feel the emotion building behind my eyes, not because I was sad or angry but because that was entirely embarrassing.

Minus 5 points, minus 10 points, MINUS 10 POINTS.

Dax set his bowl down and stood. His chest rising and falling as fast as mine as he stepped closer, only stopping an inch from me. He was so close that every time I breathed in; my chest touched his. His eyes looked over my face as if he was searching for something, something he shortly thereafter found.

His hand reached out to hold the side of my face, "Is this okay?" he asked. His voice was whispered, and I was eternally grateful that neither of us had started to eat the Chinese food if he was really about to kiss me.

I nodded my head, probably a bit too frantically, but it was good enough for him.

His lips met mine much softer than when I had gone the distance, and I remembered to also close my eyes this time around. I melted into him straight away and was more than happy for him to take the lead. His other hand came up as both of mine landed on his chest. A small throaty sound I didn't even know I could make left me as I felt the definition of his chest beneath his shirt.

The pace picked up and his hands drifted, roaming over my curves hidden beneath my flowy dress like he had imagined every dip and was going through them all just to see if his mental map was right. It wasn't just him; I had thought about this more than I would have ever admitted as I lifted my hands and gripped fistfuls of his bright red hair, earning a throaty groan from him.

Holy shit, this was so hot. *Was this really happening? Mmhm, yep. Yep, this was happening.*

He moved us backwards the way we had come, settling us back on the couch. The Chinese food was completely forgotten on the table. At that point it just seemed like just a bad idea to have ordered such an aromatic food in the first place, but with this whole glorious liplocking moment, that was seriously not even on the horizon of my mind.

He broke away, his eyes hooded with lust and his lips edging towards swollen from the out-of-this-world smooching we were doing. I had no doubt I looked the same and I was totally present for it. He looked over me again before he asked one more time, "Is this okay?"

Translation: 'Is this too fast?' Absolutely not.

"No, no, this is— this is good. This is perfect," the smile my jumble of words earned was enough to have me pulling his face back to mine.

How did anyone know how to kiss like this? I'd never been kissed like this before in my life.

His tongue swept against my bottom lip and I'll be damned if that wasn't the sexiest thing in the whole world.

His hands continued their voyage of my body and I was burning through and through. The sounds that were starting to erupt from me were dangerously close to moans and my hands weren't nearly as satisfied with holding his shirt and gripping his hair like they were just a minute before.

Things were moving very quickly in the direction where there very well might be no clothes involved at all, and then he slowed down the rhythm. Instead of hot and heavy, his mouth on mine became slow and sweet, and then it ended in the most beautiful decrescendo I'd ever witnessed.

The only sounds in my apartment were our heavy breathing as we remained as we were on the couch, him lingering above me and me below, just taking each other in. It was almost more intimate than anything I think we could have done.

I reached up and straightened his shirt before trying to organise his hair back in the effortless pushed back mess he had come in with. His smile was small and did incredibly sinister things to my hormones.

He leaned back and brought me up with him, and just as I had done for him, he did for me - fixing my dress so it sat properly on my shoulders and sorting out my hair. His touch was so gentle. No one had ever touched me like that before.

The pads of his fingers that held proof of his musical talent, lingered across my cheek sending another shiver through my body before he dropped it back into his lap.

We were still staring, just looking. *Really* looking. He was quite beautiful, I thought.

"Chinese?" he asked, his voice still heavy with the rasp of emotion from our meet and greet just now.

"Chinese," I replied and turned to start filling up my bowl.

13

ALLIE

I learned something valuable during my Chinese takeaway dinner date with Dax: a good, smokin' hot make out session was the best icebreaker ever.

There was heat and want and so much need I could have sworn I was morphing into a damn butterfly. But then he was kind, and tender and a gentleman, and all I kept thinking was that no one had ever been that way with me before. Did that make me the anomaly, or did that make *him* the anomaly?

Just like our laughter at the expense of Dean before all the lip action, our... *moment* lifted any type of veil that had unintentionally settled over us when he walked into my apartment.

I wasn't sure what I expected. If you had asked me if I thought it was going to go well when I shouted my greeting right into his face as he stood in the threshold of my home, the answer would have been no, without a doubt.

The time between meeting Dax and then finding him sitting on my $15 Facebook Marketplace couch was not how any other male had ever come to find themselves there. Not that there were really many men before Dax. There was Ben, but I didn't count him, the three years of my life he wasted, or how much of that time he insulted my couch by sitting on it with his ass. There were a couple more when I was still living out of the city before my accident but, they hadn't sat on *this* couch, and none of them had ever come with a story quite like Dax's.

He'd said that I surprised him, well, Wyatt Smith surprised me right back and he paid with interest.

The date – because it was absolutely a date (squeals like a teenage girl on the inside but offers a casual smirk with hair-flip on the outside) – went about as perfectly as it could have gone.

After Dax matched me bite for bite of the mammoth serving size I gave myself (5 points for Dax on consumption support), he helped me ferry the bowls into the sink and the leftover Chinese food I would not be sharing with Dean into the fridge before we plopped back down onto the couch.

Dax chose to sit in the middle while I had taken the corner - everyone knew that the corner spot on a sectional was the place you wanted to be. He lifted my feet up and put them over his lap like he had done it a hundred times before and it made my heart do a weird little flip.

We sat for a moment and digested our food before he turned to look at me.

"How did you find out?" he asked, a small smirk playing on his lips.

"Find out what?" I asked back, even though I knew what he meant, I just wanted to hear him talk.

Allie, you're ridiculous.

"How did you know I was going to be on stage at the concert?" he elaborated.

"Oh, you'll love this," I said, though it was bold of me to assume I knew what he'd love after being in his company for a total of an hour and fifteen minutes.

"Mmm," he waited.

"It was Craig from the corner store," I said with a grin.

Dax burst into another belly laugh, he said he had a suspicion it might've been Craig, based on the fact he had taken a photo of us like a little creeper.

When I mentioned I had then followed up the shocking revelation with a Google search, Dax dove for the pillows on the other end of the couch and groaned.

"The poses where we all fold our arms, that's never our idea, I just want that to be known," he defended his band.

"There are thousands of photos of you all like that, it sure looks like it's your idea," I laughed in response, hugging a pillow to my chest.

I moved my feet off his lap thinking he was probably over it and was too polite to move them, but then he reached back down to swoop them up into the same position before giving me a look that made it impossible to keep his eye contact. I looked down and felt my cheeks pinken immediately.

I swallowed and I was pretty sure he heard it.

He pulled out his phone quickly, tapped away for a second and then pocketed it again.

"Is everything okay?" I asked.

He gave me an easy smile back, "Perfect," he rested his hands back on my ankles.

"Okay, I have a question," I said, playing with the frilly bits that framed the pillow I held.

"Shoot," he replied.

"What inspired the red hair?" I looked up at him.

"Ah, well, I figured it was time to try something new," he said, as if that was all the explanation that was required for such a drastic colour change.

"Yes, but most people add highlights, when they 'want something new'," I did the quotation marks in the air and everything, "You went from black to blonde to red. I don't even want to know how long it took you to get it blonde enough that the red would come out as bright as it looks now." I pointed to his hair.

He looked down at his hands as he was picking at his nails and he barked a laugh, "It was actually an incredibly long process. No one has wondered that before."

"Sweet lord, how could no one wonder that?!" I exclaimed, "I've seen enough of those 'hairdresser reacts' videos to know that you would've been fighting an uphill battle."

"What videos?" he stopped fiddling with his hands and looked at me.

My inhaled gasp almost made me choke on my own spit, "Stop it! Are you saying you've never seen them?" I was already up and off the couch and making a run for my room to grab my laptop, "You're gonna *die!*" I yelled from down the hallway.

Dax had, in fact, not seen any hairdresser react videos which was shocking to me in and of itself. He sat next to me and unquestioningly watched about four videos in a row before I looked at him with what I knew was a ridiculous smile on my face. It wasn't hard to note that I loved those videos.

"I think if I had seen those, I wouldn't have ever tried to do it," he cringed a bit, "In my defence though, it was done by the hair and makeup team on the crew."

"I think you escaped unscathed. I can attest to the fact that it is still very soft. It seems pretty strong too given all the bleach," I went on before I realised I was referencing the fact that I had *tugged* at his hair. I was going to deduct 5 points from myself for that one.

Good one, Allie.

Dax, bless him, just laughed and thanked me for the compliment with a wink that came way too naturally to him.

We moved on and he told me about how he and Aspen, his younger brother and the drummer for *Lady Luck,* had gotten into music as kids and started their first two-man rock-and-roll band when he was ten and Aspen was eight.

"What was your band name?" I asked.

"Nope," he made a motion of sealing his lips, locking them and throwing away the key.

"Holy smokes, so it was bad, huh?" I got way too excited about finding out, that I moved to kneeling next to him on the couch. He just shrugged, crossed his arms and kept looking straight.

"No, that's not fair, you have to say! The suspense will truly kill me Dax, I'm not kidding, I need to know," I started bouncing. I figured if I was as annoying as possible, he would eventually relent.

He made the motion of *unzipping his lips* before he said, "Don't forget I have a younger brother. Your tactics are completely ineffective," he then rezipped his lips again, making me laugh and tip my head back.

"Dax come on. This isn't fair," I grabbed his face with both hands and turned it towards me. He looked at me with such a mischievous glint in his eyes that I knew I'd have to play dirty to get the answer.

I was gambling that this would work, but I looked him dead in the eyes and said as seriously as I could, "Please, forgive me for this," then, I attacked him.

My nimble fingers went straight for the danger zone of his unprotected rib cage because he had, so foolishly, crossed his arms. He immediately let out a howling scream-laugh that made me laugh even harder. He was yelling out my name in a hoarse voice that had my heart do another little flip while making me laugh so hard I snorted and thought I was going to get a stitch on my side.

"Just tell me Dax, and this will all end," I said over his laughter.

He relented. My gamble paid off. I sat back on the balls of my feet as Dax's laughter faded and he was slouched, breathing heavily with his face in a pillow.

Once he managed to compose himself, he sat up and pushed his hair back.

"Okay, okay, you win," he said, his sexy side smile made a show and it was by pure will-power alone that I remained where I was.

"If you ever tell Aspen that I told you this, he will kill me, Allie," he pleaded for secrecy.

"I will take it to the grave," I placed my hand over my heart to show him just how serious I was.

"Our band was called *Socks and Sandals.*" he scrunched his eyes up tightly as he said it.

I had never cackled so loudly in my life. I fell off the couch.

I had tears in my eyes by the time I managed to confirm that the genre of their band was rock. He nodded, laughing too. It took me a good ten minutes to compose myself.

Dax told me about the rest of the guys and how they all met. They'd all gone to the same high school but were in different year groups. Dax and Rip were in the same year, Angus and Luke in the year below, and Aspen was in the year below that. They didn't all connect until they had unintentionally run into one another at a *Warp Tour,* and the rest was history.

"Do you play anything?" he asked me after we had settled back on the couch, my feet back on his lap.

I smiled, "I do," I said, "I play the piano."

"How good are you?" he said, wagging his eyebrows at me.

"I've done all eight grades. It's what I wanted to do. I wanted to join an orchestra, travel and play the piano," I said. I had never said that out loud to anyone except for Savannah.

"Why didn't you?" he asked, like it would have been the simplest thing in the world to do. I suppose it might have been.

"It's not a happy story, Dax," I said, fiddling once again with the edges of the pillow in my lap.

"Not all stories are happy, Allie," he replied, his voice not holding a single ounce of mocking or disdain for a heavy topic on a first date.

I looked at him and he looked back at me. I searched his face, trying to find anything that would tell me sharing this would backfire. I didn't see anything.

I took a deep breath, "I studied piano all through high school. If I wasn't with Sav, I was playing the piano or listening to songs that I was trying to learn," Dax smiled at that, like he knew exactly what that was like.

"It was just me and my mom growing up. Savvy and I had grown up across the hall in the same apartment building just outside the city. My mom got sick when I was sixteen. She died just before I graduated," I said. My voice wasn't more than a whisper by the time I had gotten the sentence out of my mouth.

"Allie—," Dax started.

I looked up at him and gave him a small smile, "It's okay, it was a while ago now. She deteriorated fast. I was so focused on my music through it all that I don't remember it affecting me until she was gone. I knew she was going to be gone and I just clung to my music. It was stable, it was constant, you know?" I asked. He nodded. I knew that he knew what I meant.

"Anyway, she passed away and I was left on my own, in the same apartment I grew up in and with not much else. I stayed with Savannah for a bit and then I got the job I have now."

"What do you do?" Dax asked, and I realised I hadn't even mentioned it.

"I work in the marketing department of a pet store. Nothing exciting, but it's fun sometimes."

He smiled at me like he knew that was a lie.

We were quiet again for a while. It was the most comfortable silence I'd ever been in besides being with Savannah.

"Will you play something for me?" he asked.

I looked at him again, trying to see if I could share this with him. I wasn't sure. This was mine. No one touched this part of my life except for Savannah and even then, I didn't play in front of her.

He let me look, as if he knew I was looking for a reason to say no. The truth was that I couldn't find one. I nodded my head and stood up. I took his hand in mine and led him down the hallway to my room. He sat on my bed and I sat at the piano and played for him.

I started with my favourite, the *Rondo Alla Turca.* It was loud, and lively and it pulsed through you, giving no other option but to sit and listen. I slowed it down and moved into the *Prelude in C Major.* It was a softer tune, more delicate.

I finished, lifting my hands off the piano and I turned to look at Dax.

My heart was pumping so loudly I could feel it in my fingertips, but he just sat there and looked at me with such blatant awe on his face.

"I'll make you a deal. If you teach me how to play the piano, I'll teach you how to play the guitar," his throat bobbed as he swallowed.

I looked at him, really looked at him, as I released a breath I didn't know I had been holding.

"Deal," I said.

Dax left shortly after we struck our deal. He gave me a kiss on the cheek and said he'd message me. I walked back into my apartment with the stupidest grin on my face.

I headed to the kitchen and cleaned the bowls we'd eaten out of when my phone pinged from the living room.

I turned off the water, dried my hands and walked over to pick it up.

Dax: *Is it too soon for me to text you?*

I smiled and plopped down into my regular position in the corner of the couch and responded straight away.

Allie: *Sorry, who is this?*

Dax: *Just wanted to let you know that you're the lucky winner of a brand new car!*

Allie: *You're kidding! I didn't even enter a competition. That's fate for you.*

Dax: *If you just send through your card number, the expiry and whatever that number is on the back I'll have your free car sent right over.*

Allie: *Woah, just like that? You don't need my address?*

Dax: *Nope!*

I was laughing so hard I thought I was going to pee.

My phone rang.

"Hey," I said, trying to calm down from my laughing fit.

"Just wanted to clarify that if someone contacts you for winning anything for free, please don't give away your card details," Dax said, equally as breathless from laughing on the other end as I was.

"Okay, perfect. Thank you for that clarification," I said, still wiping the tears from my eyes.

"Okay, I'm going to text you again now. Just wanted to make sure you knew it was me," he sounded… shy.

"I knew," I said quietly.

The phone call ended, and my phone pinged a second later.

Dax: *Hey*

Allie: *Sorry, who is this?*

Dax: *Oh my god, Allie!*

14

Allie

It felt like it wasn't fair to still have an almost full week of work ahead of me, not after the world's best first date.

I groaned as I got out of bed but, surprisingly, I felt spritely.

Dax and I hadn't made any plans to see one another again, but we had talked the entire evening until I had eventually passed out. Maybe it was a rock star thing, but I would have wagered he could have kept talking all night had I not lost consciousness.

I walked back into my room after my shower, snuggled into my fuzzy robe, a hot cup of coffee in my hand and picked up my phone to check what the weather would be like.

Winter was still very much upon the world, but I wanted to be prepared for the 10-minute walk to my office.

I had a message from Dax waiting to be read that must've come through when I was in the shower.

Dax: *Question. Are you a morning person?*

He had started doing that last night, firing off questions to me rapidly like we were on a speed dating show. I had begun firing them right back, catching on quickly. Another wonderful ice-breaker tip.

I had to admit, hearing from him at almost the same time that I took my first sip of coffee for the day released so much serotonin into my body, it should have been illegal.

I replied, my face already wearing a smile.

It was probably an accurate assumption to be made that for the last 9 hours, I had been smiling continuously. I wasn't putting it past myself to have continued to smile through my sleep either, hence the collective 9 hours.

Allie: *Mornings are a good time for me, as long as I have a big cup of coffee.*

I sent it off and quickly threw on a pair of work pants and a blouse. The weather app said that it was going to be a bit overcast and windy. I didn't want to have to hold down my dress the entire walk to work for fear of showcasing my nether regions to the world.

I shot back another message before rushing out the door.

Allie: *Tea or coffee? And then to follow on from that, white or black?*

The weather app had been correct. It was a hit or miss sometimes, but it was definitely windy. My *skeenie* was wrapped around me tight and my jacket was buttoned all the way down.

I was the sort of person that genuinely loved winter. The fashion, the weather, the everything. But I found myself wishing that the warmer weather would hurry up just a little on my way into work.

I got to work and peeled off my layers as I sat at my desk. The immediate contrast in temperature between outside and inside made me immediately start to sweat as per usual and also made me eternally grateful that most of my work wardrobe consisted of dark colours.

My phone pinged.

Dax: *Coffee. Black as my heart baby.*

I snorted, actually *snorted* out a laugh that grabbed all the attention of the marketing team that worked around me. I mumbled an apology.

Allie: *You made me snort-laugh and the people I work with are not impressed.*

Dax: *Haha. If it was anything like the snort-laugh from last night I can absolutely see how someone might report you to H.R. for disrupting the work environment.*

My mouth dropped open like, yep, you guessed it, a bloody trout. The sass of this guy!

I was definitely not complaining.

Allie: *Watch it Mr. Socks and Sandals.*

Dax: *That information was not given voluntarily. I would like the jury to be aware that was quite literally* *tortured out of me.*

My laugh was much more controlled, my body shaking to keep it contained. I was not going to get any work done, I could just tell.

Allie: *Ladies and Gentlemen*
we're Socks and Sandals
are you ready to rock tonight?!

Dax: *You win.*
What about you? Tea or Coffee?
Black or White?

Allie: *Coffee.*
Black as my heart baby.

Dax: *You're my kind of person, Allie.*

My heart fluttered like it had the night before. I took a leap and assumed that that was something I needed to get used to.

I put my phone away and made a point to get all the work I needed to get done as fast as possible.

The rest of my week went much the same.

Dax and I spoke through the whole day, every day, and we asked lots of questions.

His favourite colour was red. I thought if I had to, I could've guessed that one. Mine was blue, like midnight blue.

He said he could have guessed that too, but I didn't see how.

His favourite day of the week was Tuesday because the pressure of the Monday was over, and the rest of the days offered ample possibilities.

I thought that was a wonderful answer.

My favourite day was Thursday. When he asked me why, I answered honestly. It was because that was when I usually got Chinese take away. I could feel through the airwaves that he was having a good ol' belly-laugh at that. This proceeded with me sharing with Dax the fact that as a grown woman of 25 years old, I had probably cooked myself a meal once. And that was years ago, and I didn't really count it.

He was shocked, of course, but went on to assure me that 'cooking wasn't for everyone' and that Aspen was the real kitchen-goer in their household.

I knew he was just being nice.

The week was coming to a close and I felt like I was on cloud nine. I was so *happy*. It seemed weird to me that I could acknowledge the presence of that emotion only now, when I had thought I was happy every day before that.

If this was what it was like to 'get back on the horse' like Savannah had so gracefully put it, it made me seriously wonder why I hadn't done it sooner.

It was Thursday and as I walked by the corner store on my way home from work, the ingenious idea that I had semi-regularly flowed back into my mind.

Tonight was the night. I was saying *au revoir* to the below-average leftovers from string-bean-Dean, and *adios* to weekly Thursday night Chinese takeaway deals. The conversation I had with Dax had turned on the metaphorical stove within me.

I was going to cook myself a meal. A real life, adult meal. And of course, when one thinks of real life adult meals, what do you think of?

Spaghetti and meatballs. Naturally.

The trip in and out of the 24-hour corner store was uneventful. It wasn't Craig who checked me out and I sent out a massive thank you into the world for sparing me. I knew if it had been Craig, he would have asked more about Dax, and the idea of him pawing at my personal life, *Dax's* personal life like that, made my skin crawl.

This was a good meal to start off with, it literally had three ingredients; spaghetti, meatballs and a tomato-based pasta sauce. Plus some salt and pepper, because, c'mon, I'm not a monster.

Dean got home just as I had put the kettle on to boil for the pasta. I murmured a hello back to him after he greeted me first. He asked about my week and I gave him as broad an answer as possible, then I asked about his.

I was more than happy to keep this level of distance from Dean. Until he apologised for being such a jerk, he was going to be hard pressed to get anything out of me. I just hoped for his sake that he did that before I divulged the situation to Savannah. There would be no hope for him then.

It took me ten minutes to figure out how to turn on the stove top. My mind went to fire and gas, but what was before me was, in fact, electric. Imagine my surprise.

The pasta was in the water, I even added a bit of salt like that packet said to do, to make sure that the noodles didn't stick together.

I was going to be generous. 10 points to Allie. This was a milestone.

The pan was on the biggest burner because that just felt right, and I turned the little illuminated digital heat settings up to level 5. Whatever that meant.

The oil was hot and by the time all the pre-rolled meatballs were on the pan, it was not going well. The oil was spitting and every time I leaned over the pan to try and stir the noodles, the oil hit me, and I squealed.

Then, amidst the chaos, the last thing I wanted to happen, happened.

My phone started to ring. Not just any ring but the unmistakable diddle that was a FaceTime call.

It was Dax.

I shouldn't have. The pasta was probably over cooked and there was oil flying everywhere, but I picked it up.

He was grinning like a buffoon when I answered his call and because I could see my own face in the front camera, I could tell that I looked terrified.

His face dropped.

"What's wrong?" he said straight away. Concern laced in his voice.

"I'm going to burn down my apartment," I announced. This was ridiculous.

He smiled at my dramatic answer before he asked another question, "And how will you do that?"

"No, I can't tell you," I said, shaking my head.

He was really trying to hold his laugh in then.

"Allie, maybe I can help," he said, being the voice of reason.

"You'll laugh at me," I said, my mouth turning into a little pout.

"Oh, absolutely, I will," he said, his face incredibly serious.

I rolled my eyes but relented, tapping the little icon to flip the camera around.

"I'm trying to cook a meal," I said.

Though Dax couldn't see me, I could see him, and his face lit up into the most beautiful smile. I stuck my tongue out at the screen.

"Dax! This is not funny. There's oil flying everywhere, and the spaghetti is going to be all mushy," I whined.

That finally broke his control and he let out a throaty laugh, "No, this is okay. I can help you. What number have you got the stove on? Is it electric?" he asked. Okay, so he was just being nice when he said cooking wasn't for everyone.

"It's at a 5," I said.

"Oh my god, Allie," he was enjoying this way too much. I flipped the camera around so he could see me and stuck my tongue out at him again, which just made him laugh even more.

"Turn it down to 3, it's too hot," he said.

I did as he instructed.

"Also, now would probably be a good time to flip the meatballs," he said.

I went ahead and did that too, breathing a sigh of relief when they weren't burnt on the other side.

Dax talked me through the rest of the cooking experience. And by the end of it, it wasn't that much of a disaster.

I drained the noodles and added the meatballs to the pot before pouring in the sauce. And taadaa! Allie's homemade spag-and-meatballs. I bounced around the kitchen clapping so loudly that Dean stuck his head out to see what was going on. That sobered me up real quick. I apologised and went about my business pretending to clean something until he disappeared.

"Okay, make yourself a bowl, but don't eat it yet," Dax said when I relayed that the coast was clear.

I mean, that was a weird request, but I obliged. He hadn't steered me wrong yet.

I sat down at the kitchen island with my bowl in front of me and leaned my phone on a vase with some flowers in it that usually lived in the centre of the island.

5-minutes later and Dax was sitting down like he really was across from me, except he was smaller and obviously in my phone.

"What was that?" I asked, a smile tugging at my lips at his mysteriousness.

He lifted the plate in front of him that showed peanut butter on toast.

"I thought we could eat together," he said.

There went the little flip flop movement of my heart.

"Okay, now you can take a bite."

I cut through a meatball and stabbed it with my fork before twirling some spaghetti around it too. I was just about to lift it into my mouth when he abruptly yelled, "Wait!"

"For crying out loud, Dax, I'm going to die of starvation," I said.

He shook his head, "Hold your fork down a bit and give me your biggest look-what-I-made smile."

"What? Why?"

Dax just smirked, "Please with a cherry on top."

How could I say no to that? So I humoured him, giving him the most natural smile I could manage on an empty stomach.

"Okay, go ahead," he said, finally.

"Don't need to tell me twice!" I replied and took a bite.

He watched me chew, leaning towards the screen to the point where almost his whole face was in the picture, and his face alone.

"So?" he prompted, "how is it?"

I chewed a little more and then swallowed.

"I'll give it a 6 out of 10," I said, giving him a tight lipped smile.

"That's a pretty decent score!" he said as he took a bite of his toast.

We ate together in a comfortable silence for a bit, but I had to ask, "Why did you make me smile holding my food?" I'm pretty sure I knew.

"I took a screenshot," he said, like it was no biggy.

"Dax!" I said.

"Allie!" he mimicked me.

"Do I look like I'm camera ready?" I replied, "My hair is basically a birds nest, pretty sure I have oil all over my shirt—"

"You look beautiful, Allie," he cut in.

I almost dropped my fork. I was glad we were phones apart because my face went so red, I could have been mistaken for the sauce on my plate.

"This was a big moment, I had to document it. I'm proud of you."

"For cooking a meal that required only 3 ingredients?" I scoffed, taking the last few bites.

"Yes, for cooking a meal. Will you make me this 6 out of 10 dinner sometime?" he sounded so hopeful, like he was asking to be more than just *nice*.

I picked up my phone and put it at an angle where I could move around the kitchen and Dax could still see me.

"Really?" I asked, looking at him.

"I have never been more real in my whole life," he said, the seriousness in his face and voice both a game and completely real, just like he said.

"Okay, I'll cook it for you. Thank you for your help," I said.

Dax hung out with me while I cleaned up the kitchen and put away the leftovers into the fridge. He came with me into my room and, ever the gentleman, didn't complain once as he dutifully looked at the ceiling of my bedroom because I had tipped the phone away as I got changed into my jammies.

We hung out like that for the rest of the night, until Dax was settled into his own bed and the last thing I remembered was him telling me that the first four chords he would teach me on the guitar were G, D, E Minor and

C because those were his favourite notes. He also added that they were the prettiest ones.

15

Allie

My alarm woke me up and the realisation that I had fallen asleep on the phone to Dax was like being doused with cold water.

Honestly, Allie! He's going to think you have narcolepsy.

That was not exactly the look I was going for; snoring and drooling on my pillow.

I grabbed my phone and saw that I had a message from late last night.

Dax: *Good night.*
I wish I could say you snore,
but you don't.

It was becoming quite apparent to me that Dax might just be my kind of person too.

I rolled out of bed and straight into the shower. Fuzzy robe on and I was making my way to the kitchen to get my coffee when someone knocked on my front door.

Keeping in mind it was 7AM on a Friday morning, I was not expecting anyone.

I walked over and opened the door a bit, completely aware that I was in my robe and naked as the day I was born beneath it all.

For the time of morning, he looked far too put together.

Instead of his long coat, he sported a leather jacket that was different to the one he wore on stage. More lived in. Used.

His red hair was still wet, making it look darker than normal as he looked at me and held up a brown paper bag and two takeaways with a terribly handsome grin.

"Breakfast?" he asked.

It took me a minute to process what was happening, but as soon as my brain caught up with the situation, I enthusiastically opened the door wide and waved him in.

"You're my hero, Dax," I said as I shut the door and followed him to the kitchen.

"I know," He quipped over his shoulder.

We got to the centre island and I sat down as he put the stuff on the counter before he made a full 180 and headed back towards the front door.

"Where are you going?" I frowned. Was he just dropping it off? My heart sank a bit.

He looked back at me and pointed to his feet.

"Shoes off," he said with a wink.

He remembered.

That was the best send off to work I'd ever had. Not only did he bring me a chocolate croissant for breakfast and a black coffee, but he walked me to work.

Yes, you heard me correctly. He walked me to work.

I cannot be the only person who was baffled by what was going on.

I mean, this could only be compared to hitting a hole-in-one, twice in a row. I didn't play golf but I was using my imagination here. Clearly.

Firstly, it was one of my favourite crisp January days where the sky was blue, the sun was out and the air was chilly. Secondly, he walked me right to the door and kissed me on the cheek before asking if I wanted to hang out on Saturday. Talk about starting the day with a double whammy.

I gave him my most controlled nod, as to not look like a bobble-head, and waved goodbye as I walked into my building. I was still dazed by the whole morning, and then my phone pinged, and my face adopted a smile for the rest of the day. It was my most used expression as of the last week.

The day was full of more speed-dating questions.

Favourite Olympic sport to watch, would I prefer the beach or the mountains, if I had to – in a life and death situation, he made sure to clarify – choose between socks or a blanket, what would I pick?

For every answer I gave, he gave one back. I didn't think I could get sick of that. The openness. The honesty. It was so *new* to me and it was all consuming.

What we were going to do on the weekend had me stumped a bit. I knew that Dax was famous, for lack of a better word, even though he didn't seem famous when he was eating peanut butter toast with me on FaceTime and explaining with incredible passion that, no matter what anyone said, Female Ice Skating was the best Olympic sport to watch. Hands down.

So, when I asked him what we were going to do, he suggested grabbing some takeaway coffee and heading out of the city. There was a park he went to that was about 30 minutes from where he lived that wasn't very busy. He said if he sat away from the path and wore a beanie, then no one recognised him.

So that's exactly what we did.

16

Aspen let me borrow his car for the day.

I breathed into my hands as I waited for Allie to meet me at the bottom of her apartment building.

I had suggested we head out of the city. I usually went to the place we were going to alone. Sometimes Ap came with me but it was nice to get away, be surrounded by quiet.

I had been once, earlier in the week, for the first time in months. Now that we were finished with the tour, we had some down time. We had just over a month before we started our album press tour, but that still gave us plenty of time to live a little out of the limelight. Time to recharge.

Allie walked out of her apartment, wrapped in her *skeenie* as she had called it in the 24-hour corner store.

How was that only 3 weeks ago?

Her face lit up when she saw me, and my heart did something stupid.

"Hey," she said quietly. Her bag over her shoulder and a blanket clutched to her chest.

"Hey," I echoed, opening the car door for her.

She stepped in and I walked around and got into my side.

The drive was quiet, but it was pleasant. I liked that I could be quiet with Allie. That she didn't need to talk all the time and that she seemed just as comfortable to sit in the silence with me.

"Cats or dogs?" I asked her.

"Dogs," she said, not having to think about that one for a moment, "I'm allergic to cats." She elaborated, scrunching her nose up like the very thought made her need to sneeze.

"Okay, so no cats," I nodded.

"Sweet or savoury?" she asked me back.

"Both," I said, "If I have one, I need to have the other."

She nodded in complete understanding and looked over to me, her seafoam eyes sparkling as her mouth formed into her prettiest smile yet, "You're my kind of person, Dax."

The urge to reach over and hold her hand was there, but I held off. Allie was ringing her fingers and averted her eyes to her hands, so I figured that to grab one would be interrupting something.

The drive was only 30 minutes and by the time we got to the park, not only was it practically empty but the spot I had wanted was under a few trees was free of people, and to top it off, the sky was starting to dot bits of blue amongst the heavy grey.

Allie had brought two blankets, one to sit on and one to put over our legs. It made me smile and felt like a very *Allie* thing to think of.

Sitting with her in person and speaking to her over the phone were almost the same. The only difference being that if I wanted to, I could reach out and touch her. She was *right there.* So I did just that. Often.

I leant forward and grabbed her hand, entwining my fingers with hers. Allie's lips tugged into a small smile as her cheeks took on a rosy hue.

"Is it nice to have some time off?" she asked.

I nodded, "Yeah. When you're on the move so much sometimes you forget what it's like to sit still."

"I can imagine," she said, offering me a small smile.

Allie also never asked me about the band. Not because I thought she was uninterested, but because maybe there was more that she wanted to know. That's what it felt like, at least. That was new for me.

"We head off in about a month for the press tour for the new album though, then some more down time before we head to tour for the shows," I went on, feeling like telling her about my life plans for the immediate future was kind of necessary.

My heart started to speed up as I thought about what her reply could be. We weren't even dating, really. We were just hanging out, you know, casually.

"A month is still a long time," she replied softly, like she knew that I was worried about her answer, that for some reason it was important.

"Yeah, I guess it could be considered a long time," I replied, my eyes were glued to our entwined hands.

"It all depends on what you fill it with though, doesn't it?" she asked.

"What would you fill that time with?" it was hypothetical, but at the same time it wasn't. I knew the question was loaded.

"Well, I like this park, so I would probably spend some time here," her thumb started moving in circles on mine, "I also like my apartment and playing the piano, so I would spend some time there. I also just discovered that I have this urge to learn the guitar, so I would fill it with that too." Her smile turned mischievous and it reached all the way to her eyes, making them crinkle. She was beautiful.

"That sounds pretty good to me. You've got it all planned out," I said, a wash of relief passing over me.

"Cooking too," she went on.

"Ahh," I nodded my head, "Of course, your newest and possibly your greatest talent?" I enquired, teasing her a bit.

"Hey, you just wait until you have my 6 out of 10 meatballs, you'll be grovelling for seconds."

I tipped my head back and laughed, causing Allie to shove my shoulder and say my name in a whining way. It only made me laugh harder.

We were at the park until after lunch time. It went by way too fast and I didn't think I'd ever been hit with so many promising lyrics for some new songs in a long while, all of which I had dutifully listed into my notes.

I pulled my phone out so often, I had practically written a song by the end.

I caught Allie frowning, trying to lean over and sneak a look but when she asked, I told her not to worry, that it was nothing.

And it *was* nothing. At the moment. Nothing but ideas and words and phrases.

When I told her, I wanted there to be something to show.

I had a small collection of notes from almost every time I saw her or spoke to her, all safely tucked away on my phone. There was always something that came to mind that I had to get down. Every time.

She asked then too but, no, not yet. I'd show her soon. I wanted it to mean something when she read the lyrics, heard the songs.

It wasn't until Allie's stomach let out the loudest, and I mean *loudest,* growl I'd ever heard that we made any move to leave.

We packed up and headed back to her apartment.

"Would you like to stay for dinner?" she asked. She sounded nervous, "Even though I know it's still technically mid-afternoon." She frowned a bit, in a way that I was coming to learn was another very *Allie* thing to do.

I looked over at her and smiled, as if she didn't know I had been waiting all day for her to ask, "Dinner at mid-afternoon is how I hoped today would wrap up," I said.

"What a relief," she said, her hand going to her chest sarcastically, "There is one thing, though," she went on.

"Mmm?" I asked, keeping my eyes on the road, perfectly happy and content.

"Well, string-bean-Dean will be home. We're not on good terms. Don't ask, it's a long story. So maybe we could chill in my room and watch a movie or something?"

"Do I need to have a word with string-bean-Dean?" I asked, sneaking a look at her. She was smiling down at her hands and it did another stupid thing to my heart.

"Not quite yet, but I'll let you know," she said.

"Alright, I'll be on call," I said, "And pizza and a movie sound perfect to me," I finished.

"Cheese?" she asked.

"Only my favourite dairy product," I answered.

She rolled her eyes and pulled out her phone to call the pizza place, ordering one large cheese pizza and making sure she mentioned that one of the people who would be consuming their creation claimed that cheese was a favourite and that if it could be the best cheese they had, that would be appreciated.

I realised that I'd never want to put this into a box.

I never wanted to take any of the time I spent with Allie and tuck it away. I thought about everything in my life that was tucked away and organised, about the house in my mind where everything was still packed up, and I wanted there to be *more.*

I wanted Allie's throw pillows and weirdly shaped chairs. I wanted her shoes by the front door and her jacket on a hook.

It was the first time I looked at all the other boxes in my mind and thought they would all be better off if Allie went through them.

17

Allie

I finally got to see Dax's apartment.

Well, he called it an apartment, but I was going to be real, it was a freaking penthouse. It was at the very top of an incredibly intimidating building and when he came to pick me up on Monday night after work, he assured me that it was nothing extravagant.

It seemed that Dax wouldn't know what 'nothing extravagant' was if it sat on his face.

He had made sure that Aspen was out for when we got there.

"I don't want you to feel like you're being pulled in all directions. Aspen is very excited about the fact we're hanging out," Dax had said as we walked up to his massively pristine white and very expensive looking kitchen.

My eyebrows lifted at that, "Why?"

Dax went ahead and busied himself in the kitchen, pulling lots of different things out of the fridge. He was going to make me a stir-fry, since he knew of my preference for Asian cuisine.

"Aspen is enthusiastic about my happiness, to put it lightly," Dax went on, still with his head in the fridge.

My chest panged with something that told me there was a lot more to what that meant, that there was more than just a surface deep understanding.

He went on, "So, the idea that we've been hanging out, and that I have been happier than usual… Let's just say he's walking around the house yelling our 'couple name' out in the form of song."

I let out a laugh and the tightness that had formed in my chest released a little. "He has given us a 'couple name'?" I asked, "What is it?" I couldn't help myself.

"I don't think you want to know," he said, though his mouth was pulling up at the side while he started to wash the vegetables in the sink that was in the kitchen island I was sitting at.

"Oh, come on! I need to know. I will tickle you again, I'm not above it, Dax," I said. I got to my feet and moved around the island.

He moved away from the sink with the water still running. His hands held up in front of him and dripping with water, "Okay, okay! I'll tell you."

I squinted my eyes at him, so he knew I meant business before moving back to my spot.

"He's been calling us *Wallie*," Dax's face told me that even saying the word out loud was painful for him.

"You're kidding me," I said, a bubble of laughter erupting out of me until I was hanging over the side of the island, trying to catch my breath, "That's the worst ship name I've ever heard!" I wiped the tears from my eyes.

Dax was still cleaning the vegetables, "Well, I implore you not to tell him that. He was very pleased with himself," he smirked.

Dax loved his brother. That was very clear to me, it made me smile. It reminded me of the way I loved Savannah.

I started moving my head to get a look at the penthouse.

"You can take a look around if you want," Dax said, his eyes were on me while simultaneously chopping the washed vegetables.

Cooking wasn't for everyone, my ass, Dax!

"Okay," my voice was already far away with the wonder of what I might find. I hopped off the stool and made my way through the living room.

The ceilings were high. Like, very high. And the place was decked out with fancy lights and modern looking furniture. It felt like they had gotten someone to come in and decorate it the way they imagined all rock stars lived.

The only bit of Dax, or maybe his brother, that I saw was a faded beanbag in the corner that had the Green Day *American Idiot* Album cover on it. The one that was clenching the bleeding-heart shaped grenade. That screamed 'Dax' to me.

I walked through the living room, up some stairs to another sitting area where there was a long hallway that stretched on farther than you would have thought for a living space at the top of a building.

I walked down the hallway and all the doors were open. I walked by the first and it was a room that was just filled, and I mean *filled* with guitars, so many guitars that it would have taken me a long time to count them. They were all organised neatly in stands, except one fancy looking black one that was on display facing front on to anyone who walked in, or past, the room.

"Wow," I said softly, before I hurried onto the next room.

I kind of felt like I was illegally poking around their things, but did that stop me? Nope.

The next room was a bathroom then the following door was on the other side of the hallway. It was much the same as the guitar room but this one was clearly Aspen's, as it held a set of drums. The walls and floors were all carpeted, I imagine that was for soundproofing. The walls surrounding the drums in the middle reminded me of floor to ceiling bookshelves, but instead of holding books, they held drums. Lots and lots of different drums and cymbals.

It was freaking cool.

On my way out there was a sign on the door that said 'Warning', but under that word someone had written in a Sharpie that said, 'if I'm rocking don't come knocking', it earned one of my snort-laughs.

I continued my snooping of the rest of their home. There were a few more doors but the next one held a king size bed. The walls were all black and so was the bedding. There was a whole rack of guitars set up in this room too and one was plugged into an amp and just resting on top of it, a notebook beside it.

I knew I shouldn't, but I walked in.

This was Dax's room.

His bed was made, which earned a smile from me. I'd thought he'd have been the sort to make his bed.

On the right bedside table was a book, I didn't recognise the title, but the back made it out to be some kind of memoir of a guitarist in a band. That seemed very apt too.

I learned two more things. That Dax liked to read, and he also slept on the right side of the bed.

There was a door that led off into what I assumed was a closet. I was just about to walk in when he called my name from the kitchen.

My heart sped up so fast, like I'd been caught doing something wrong.

I rushed out of his room and walked back down the hallway. As I was making my way through the living room, I stopped for a second and just *looked.* Took him in.

He was standing at the stove, stirring something around in one pot and then checking on something else by lifting a lid.

He was… well, I hadn't quite made my mind up on what exactly he was. But I just knew that I liked to be around him. Watching him in the kitchen making us dinner made my heart do its signature flip. Every push back of his bright red hair, every comment he said to himself about the quality of his own cooking.

He reached up to grab a couple of bowls out of a cupboard before he turned, taking a breath as if he was about to yell my name again.

As he spun, he saw me, and his face lit up. I'd never seen anyone's face light up like that just for seeing me.

"Allie," He said softly, with a smile. He cleared his throat, "Did you get a good amount of snooping in?" He enquired, quirking a brow.

I kept my face neutral as I made my way over to him. I hadn't responded yet and his expression took on a nervous sheen that made me wonder what he might have been worried that I found.

I walked right up to him, reached up and put my arms around his neck before I leaned in and gave him a kiss.

His lips were soft, and they kissed me back straight away. He put the bowls he still held down on the counter behind me and his arms circled around my waist, pulling me to him.

We hadn't kissed again like we had on my couch. Most of the lip action had been simple, and far too appropriate, lip touches or a gentle peck on my cheek.

But when he pulled me against him, I felt a rush just like I had from our first date in my apartment.

I pulled away to look at him, but he spoke first.

"What was that for?" he asked, smiling down at me.

I reached up to move some of the hair that had fallen into his face out of the way. It probably wasn't necessary, but I wanted, *needed,* to touch him.

"You make your bed." I said, as if that was the reason.

"Is that bad?" He asked, smirking a little.

"No, not bad." I leaned in to give him another kiss.

"Thank you for cooking dinner." I said, as I released him and tried to step away.

He grabbed one of my wrists as it was unlocking from my other and moved it back around his neck where it had been. He crouched down to lift me up by my waist, setting me on the kitchen island. The movement earned a squeak of surprise from me.

"Will you come over to dinner tomorrow?" Dax asked. His voice, a mere whisper as he leaned in and gave me another soft peck on the lips. My stomach burst into butterflies and I suddenly got very, very hot.

"I haven't had any food yet, what if you're a bad cook?" I returned his kiss with one of my own. I lifted my hand up, entwined my fingers into his wild, red hair.

"If my cooking is terrible then I'll improve and keep trying until I find a meal that's at least a 6 out of 10," he placed a kiss on my jaw as I tilted my head back in a laugh. I looked back down at him, still smiling wide.

"Deal," I said, "I'll come to dinner tomorrow."

Dax pulled me closer again until I was almost not sitting on the island at all but being held up by him. My hands were frantic in his hair and there wasn't one part of me that didn't absolutely acknowledge that Dax's hands were on my ass.

A loud pop came from the stove that jolted us both out of what was a make-out session that rivalled the first in every way. The stir-fry was still on the stove and it had just spat a piece of onion at us like it would have preferred us to be doing… whatever it was we were doing, away from the kitchen.

I turned back to Dax as he turned to me and I even surprised myself by going in for one more kiss, it lingered, and it was not at all light or soft.

He looked a little stunned but not in any way that could be considered bad. Like, at all.

“Stir-fry?” I croaked.

“Stir-fry,” he said, letting me down gently and popping a kiss on my temple before turning back towards the stove.

Every night for the rest of the week was just like that. Dinner at Dax’s, me always giving him a 5 out of 10 rating so that he would insist I come back the next night to try again for the winning number 6 out of 10.

The food was a 10 out of 10 every time, and the lip action sessions got better with every meal. Every time I saw him, I wanted him more. It was building up and driving me insane, I just wanted to scream. Scream at the people I passed on my way to work. Scream at string-bean-Dean every time I saw him walk into our shared apartment. I even want to scream right into Dax’s face, because how could he not know that I was drowning in my own hormones.

Dax dropped me back off at my apartment every night after dinner, each time no matter how heated our non-verbal interaction became, he’d always leave me with a kiss on the cheek and usually after about a minute I’d received another speed-dating question.

Tonight was no different.

“What are you doing tomorrow?” he asked, as we walked into my building and he called the elevator button. He pressed it the entire time until it arrived.

Was it weird that that turned me on more than anything I’ve ever seen in my life?

"Tomorrow is reserved for Savannah," I said.

He gave me a little pout.

"I've not seen her in two whole weeks. I think that's a record for us. You're taking all my time," I teased.

"I won't apologise," he said back.

"Even if you did, I wouldn't accept it."

We walked up to my door and I could hear string-bean-Dean inside whipping something up in the kitchen.

"When will I meet your roommate?" Dax tried to pass it off as a nonchalant question, but I knew he was itching for an introduction.

"When you want to lose your appetite," I scrunched my nose up and frowned at the same time, earning a laugh from Dax as he reached up and tried to smooth the lines between my eyes.

"He can't be that bad," he said, leaning in to give me a kiss on the cheek.

"Trust me, he is that bad," I leaned in and gave him a kiss on the lips as a thank you for my kiss on the cheek. It veered from our standard routine, but who said the girl couldn't go in for some lip action?

Dax leaned in as I was leaning away, capturing my lips in another kiss that had my blood heating instantly.

We pulled away but he left his forehead resting on mine.

"Night, Allie," his voice was all sorts of sexy, and soft and rough and...

"Night, Dax," I said, stealing one more kiss before slipping into my apartment.

I walked straight into my room, saying hello to Dean as I walked by. I closed the door quietly and landed with an un-lady like *humph* on my bed.

My phone pinged.

Dax: *Will you go out on a date with me Sunday night?*

Not the usual sort of question he asked, but a welcome one, nonetheless.

Allie: *I'd love to.*

18

Allie

"Allie, this is so *hot!*" Savannah squeaked as we sat on her couch, wine in hand.

"I know, I can't really comprehend it," I said, taking a swig to hide my smile. I put my wine glass down and shook out my hands.

"Okay, enough about me. You're now fully up to date on all things Dax and Allie. I want to know what's going on in your world. Two weeks is a long time to be apart," I frowned at her.

"I know, but we still spoke every day," she said, taking a drink from her own glass.

"Yeah, but it's different," I said.

"It is," she agreed.

"Okay. So? Anyone caught your eye?" I asked.

Savannah just took another, very long drink from her wine.

"Oh my god! There *is* someone! I knew it! I couldn't imagine spending two weeks away from you and not have you ask me to come around once. I would like to point out I invited myself here."

"I know, *I know.* But I guess you understand what it's like. It's so *consuming,*" she tried to plead her case.

"Is it weird that I can say that I know what you're talking about?"

It certainly felt weird to say.

"No, it's not weird, it's good. I'm glad you're back on the metaphorical horse that is Wyatt Smith," she wagged her eyebrows at me.

I threw the pillow I was holding at her. She lifted her wine glass up and out of the way just in time, "Savannah!" I said, completely embarrassed.

"Oh, Allie! Come on, you're dating a *rock star,*" she said.

"It's not like that, and we're not dating we're just… hanging out," I grabbed another pillow that was in reach onto my lap. "Dax is not only *Wyatt Smith*. I don't even see him as that when we're together. He's…," I thought about it. He was so many things, and everything about the things he was, and about how I *felt* about those things, it was all intense. My mind started to spiral.

"Allie," Savannah said, snapping me out of my inner turmoil, "Don't pull away from him now that it's getting good," she said.

"I'm not," I replied, not meeting her gaze.

"Maybe not yet, but you were thinking about it just now," her single, well defined eyebrow stared me down.

"We're only just hanging out," I repeated, more to myself than to Savannah, "We haven't even slept together yet."

"So?" Savannah asked, "You don't need to sleep with someone straight away for it to mean that the relationship will work out. Sleeping, or not sleeping, with someone on the first date means diddly-squat, Al."

I frowned to myself. I knew that she and I were both thinking about Ben. I had slept with him on the first date.

"There's nothing wrong with that either though, Allie," she continued.

I looked up at her. I knew she could see and feel the fear that was pinging through my body. Every fear and insecurity that was carved into me by Ben, the need to run away and hide so that it never happened again.

Savannah reached out for my hand, "This is good, Allie. Wyatt is good, and he isn't Ben. Sometimes you have to see it for what it is. Feel the fear, and do it anyway," she said.

"Feel the fear?" I squeezed her hand back with one hand and reached for my wine glass with the other.

She nodded, "And do it anyway."

I gave Savannah a long hug before I left. It felt like for the first time in our 24 years of friendship we were setting off on endeavours of our own where we might see one another less. It felt okay, like she was there if I needed anything and vice versa, but it still felt weird that we hadn't set a date for the next time we'd see one another.

She told me again to feel the fear and not to run and hide, that if I did that then it meant that all the Ben's of the world won. I didn't like that idea at all. So, with a promise back to her to feel the fear and do it anyway, I made my way home.

The pull of comfy clothes and my latest piece of interest, *Beethoven's Sonata No. 14 in C-sharp minor, Op. 27,* was undeniable. It was an incredibly thought-provoking piece of music to play and I was enjoying the change in tone from the *Prelude in C Major.*

My phone started to buzz in my pocket.

I answered straight away, "Hello, stranger." You could tell by my voice that I was smiling.

"Long time no speak," Dax said back, I could hear the smile in his voice too, "How's Sav?"

"She's good. Lots of talking and lots of wine drank," I recounted.

"I hope you spoke about me."

"You remained in the conversation 90% of the time," I replied.

"Only 90%?" he asked, mock horror lacing his voice.

"The other 10% was filled with the act of drinking our wine, of course," I assured him.

"I supposed you'd need to breathe too, between sentences," he went on.

"I came to find that was a particularly important part of speaking. Who knew?"

"So, there's a catch to our date," he chimed in.

Our playful banter moved into a real-life type of conversation without missing a beat. That was probably one of my favourite things. When Dax had told me that speaking to me was easy when we first met, I never got it. But I got it now, talking to Dax was the easiest thing I'd ever done.

"I'm listening," I said, though I was a bit weary.

"The date will begin around 10:30PM," he explained.

"Like, at night?" I asked, baffled.

"That is usually the purpose of the 'PM'," I could hear him trying not to laugh.

I just rolled my eyes, "Okay, I'll be ready at 10PM then." That was very spontaneous, I thought.

Allie being spontaneous. Quick! Someone record the date and time.

"That's it? You're not scared about what it could be?" he asked.

"I'm feeling the fear, Dax, and I'm doing it anyway," I replied.

19

Allie

I should have had a nap. I was just wrapping on my *skeenie* and I felt my eyes starting to close.

It was 10:10PM and Dax had just messaged that he was downstairs. I had seriously considered making a coffee for myself before leaving, but it got too late and I was just too tired.

I tried to pep myself up on the way down. The excitement of my first out-in-public date with Dax, this was quite a milestone. I mean, we did go to the park, but this was a *date* date.

It was freezing as I walked out of my apartment and into the night. Dax was leaning against Aspen's black sedan like he usually was, looking far too cool and way too sexy and it was all made a thousand times better as I saw that he had two thermoses in his hands.

"Don't tell me," I said, my eyes focused on the hot beverages he held, and the hot beverages alone.

"I figured coffee might be required," he handed one to me.

I took it and launched myself at him and I kissed him with equal enthusiasm. His hand immediately found my waist and held me against him. I could feel him smiling against my lips.

"Are you ready?" he asked as he opened my car door.

"I was born ready," I said, suddenly filled with so much energy I could have sprinted a mile. Dax rolled his eyes and he closed the door on my side and jumped in his own side.

He raised his thermos to me, and I *clinked* mine against his as we sped off into the quiet city streets.

We just drove for a bit, not really leaving the city but driving to a different part of it. I was sipping my coffee when Dax reached his hand over and put it on my knee. I smiled and looked at him.

"This is new," I said.

With one hand on the wheel and one hand on my knee, he looked at me from the side as a small smile grew on his face.

"Is this okay?" he asked.

"It's perfect," I said, reaching over and combing the hair back from his face before settling my hand on the back of his neck.

We drove like that for another 15 minutes until we pulled up to a little row of shops somewhere on the other side of the city. All the shops were dark except for one. The sign read '24-hour Ice Cream Parlour.'

My throat got all tight and my nose tingled like I just downed a sparkling beverage too fast. I moved my hand away from Dax as he put the car into park.

I was wearing my signature open-mouth-trout look. Again.

I knew why we were here. I looked over at him only to find him already staring at me.

"I figured, while we were on a 24-hour operating place of work streak, that we might as well try another," he sounded so unsure, like he didn't know if my silence was good or bad.

I knew I had been kissing him a lot lately, but I didn't really care. I leaned over and pulled his face to mine by the front of his leather jacket, "This is wonderful, Dax," and planted one right on him.

"Yeah?" he asked, like he thought that there was more than one way that this date could have been interpreted.

"Yeah," I said, leaning back into my seat.

He gave me the biggest grin and jumped out to get my door. He always got my door.

He held his hand out for me and continued to hold it as we made our way across the lot to the ice cream store.

Dax was wearing a beanie but there was no mistaking, as soon as we walked into the little shop, the three on-the-clock staff knew exactly who he was.

"Holy crap," one said.

"Dude. *Dude,"* another said as he was tapping his friend trying to get their attention.

"What is— oh my god," they all stared at us, and it was my first time ever seeing Dax recognised in public. It made the fact that he was *famous* a little more real for me.

"Hey, guys," Dax said, taking off his beanie.

"Dude, you're that guy!" the shortest of all the ice cream parlour workers said.

"I might be," Dax said with a smile.

"You're Wyatt Smith!" one of the others said, "I'm seriously your biggest fan, you have no idea. Your music is all I listen to." They hurtled the words out to him like they were worried the moment would end too soon.

The last one of the three just stood there in shock. The shortest one nudged his friend, "This is Remy, he's probably your biggest fan of all of us. He even dyed his hair like yours." The short worker ripped off his friend's uniform hat.

"Dude, no way! That looks awesome!" Dax said. The boy with stage fright smiled and murmured a thanks as he ran his hand through his hair.

The one, who was his biggest fan, stepped forward, finding his confidence, "Do you think we could get a photo with you?" he looked like this was probably the best day of his life.

"Sure, if my girlfriend doesn't mind taking it for us?" he turned to me.

A lot of things happened in that moment. The first being that I became a bobble-head. Nodding my head like my neck was a spring. The second being that I lost my voice entirely, and the third being that I apparently just became Dax's girlfriend.

I took the phone from the one who was called Remy and snapped a few shots, one regular and one silly. Dax ordered us two scoops of chocolate ice cream, paid for them and led me back to the car. We sat in the parking lot on the hood of the sedan and ate our ice cream.

The silence was nice. Calming.

Dax gave me the chance to be the first to speak, content to sit in silence with me or tap away on his phone from time to time.

I could see in the corner of my eye that he kept looking at me, but it wasn't until I finished my whole ice cream that I spoke.

"Girlfriend?" I finally looked at him.

He looked back at me with such honest hope that I wanted to crawl into his lap then and there.

"Is that okay?" I saw him swallow.

"You actually make me nauseous, so I'm not really sure," I scrunched my face up at him.

Dax tipped his head back and let out a laugh that echoed through the empty parking lot around us. He set down his ice cream and tugged me to him by my *skeenie*.

"You're such a dork, Allie," he leaned in to press a kiss to my jaw, a spot I was coming to find I liked to be kissed very, very much.

"Will you be?" he asked again, so close our noses were touching.

"If I have to," I said, adding an eye roll for emphasis.

"Allie," Dax said, whining my name.

"Yes, Dax. I'll be your girlfriend," I said. Letting every lightning-storm emotion I was feeling shine through my face just for him to see, as I pulled him in for another kiss.

I asked Dax if he wanted to stay over at mine. He said yes very quickly to the point where it made me blush. I told him he could park his car under my apartment building seeing as neither Dean nor I had a car, but the apartment had a spot that came along with it.

He sent a message to Aspen letting him know he'd be out with the sedan until morning and we made our way up to my apartment.

It was like there was an elastic band between us that was getting more taut with every passing second and it was going to snap, making us collide and headbutt into one another.

I got a spare toothbrush out for Dax. Yes, I was that person who had spare toothbrushes and mini shampoos and conditioners. I mean, you never knew what the situation would call for, right?

String-bean-Dean was fast asleep in his room, so we brushed our teeth in silence before moving into my room. I quickly put on some pyjamas that were simple but appropriate for a 25-year-old and handed Dax a pair of oversized sweats that I had.

We hopped into bed, him on the right side, me on the left and we just looked at one another for a while.

Dax's hand reached out to my knee and slowly, very slowly, moved up the rest of my body, all the way up my arm until he cupped the side of my face, and then it all just exploded.

Our lips crashed in a mess of tongues and teeth faster than you could say 24-hour Ice Cream Parlour.

Just like the time on my couch, his hands roamed over every curve of my body like it was the only thing they had wanted to do in the weeks since we'd met. Lord knew mine hadn't thought about much else.

He hovered above me and I tugged at his shirt, indicating that it needed to go, toot sweet. Dax leaned back as I leaned up, helping him remove my own shirt until he leaned down, letting me feel the weight of him in a way that was incredibly satisfying and still not nearly close enough.

The kissing continued and the feel of his skin on my skin sent shivers through my entire body. His hand drifted to the elastic of my pyjama bottoms.

I certainly didn't think that *this* would be happening tonight, which made me infinitely grateful that I had taken the necessary steps to groom the day before.

Thank you, thank you, thank you.

When he moved in again it was slower and much more deliberate. He kissed me one last time before his hand, that wasn't propping him up, moved from my cheek to my neck, over the curve of my breast and down to my waist and to my hip. His mouth followed the exact same path as his hand, kissing down my whole body and earning shallow, breathy pants of approval.

I knew what he was doing and *wowzers,* I was freaking out. All I could think was, *good god, I've been blessed with a giver. Thank you. Thank you.*

I watched him as he made his descent.

Oh shit.

After I helped him shimmy off my pyjama pants, he played with the band of my underwear. His eyes flicked up in another silent request. I nodded to him as I lifted my hips slightly to help him out. I mean, it was the least I could do.

He settled further down on the bed and had a hand flat against the plane of my stomach, trailing kisses along my inner thigh that were a little too ticklish.

Christ, Allie. Don't laugh, don't laugh, don't laugh.

The first touch of his tongue was absolutely nothing to laugh about and gave me enough of an indication of where exactly the rest of this engagement was headed.

I couldn't breathe.

My responding gasp was quite clearly exactly what he was after because he didn't stop, but rather proceeded to execute manoeuvres I wouldn't be able to tell you the names of in a million years. At this point I wasn't even entirely sure what my own name was.

My eyes squeezed to the point of seeing stars and my entire body began to shake. I didn't have any self-awareness in that moment to be concerned, or embarrassed, in the slightest about the amount of times his name fell from my lips or how loud it came out.

Dax looked up at me from where he was, his eyes twinkling with satisfaction and mischief as he let me compose myself. My breathing came back down to a healthy tempo. Dax moved up to lay next to me, bringing the blanket that was folded at the end of my bed with him.

He kissed me as he settled by my side. Still on the high of what just happened, I began to let my hands roam, eager to return the favour.

"It's okay, Allie," he said. His voice was gentle, making me stop my movements.

I looked at him quizzically, "You don't want…?" I asked. I was completely aware of the situation going on beneath the elastic of *his* pyjama bottoms and to say I was zealous to return the favour was an understatement.

"Oh, we'll get to it all Allie, believe me. But just not in an apartment that you share with a guy named *string-bean-Dean."*

I laughed so hard I snorted, my hand immediately slapped over my mouth and nose, but only made us laugh more.

Dax pulled me closer, tucked the blankets around us and pulled the pillows further down the bed. The spot we had settled in was warm and neither of us were keen on moving.

We talked for a while longer in our rapid-fire-speed-dating-questions way as the early hours of the morning ticked on.

I idly traced nonsensical patterns onto the planes of his chest, and he mindlessly played with strands of my hair.

We fell asleep like that and I couldn't tell you the last time I went to sleep feeling that happy. Just utterly content with everything, especially with the body that was laying next to mine.

20

Allie's alarm went off so loudly that it felt like someone had slapped me into consciousness.

We woke up just as we had fallen asleep - her curled up to my chest without any pants on and me wrapped around her like an octopus.

It was fair to say that that was one of the best sleeps I'd had in a long time. Cliché, but still true. Allie was warm, and soft and she smelt like cherry blossom shampoo and clean laundry. With her was the only place I had wanted to be since our date in her living room.

She groaned at the sound of her alarm and moved out of my embrace to turn it off. She looked over at me and rubbed her eyes before she gave me a sleepy smile.

"Morning," she said in a raspy voice.

I smiled back before moving across the bed to pull her to me. I was leaning in for a kiss when her hands shot up, one covering her mouth and one covering mine

"No way, José," her voice was muffled from behind her hand and she was shaking her head, scuttling back.

"What? Why?" my voice was muffled too while I tried - and failed - to pull her back towards me.

"Morning breath. Or do rock stars not have that?" she asked as she reached down the side of the bed for something to put on her bottom half.

I rolled my eyes at her before giving her a poke to the ribs.

"Brat," I said.

She looked at me with mock offence and threw a sock at me.

Allie got up from the bed and grabbed her robe, "Can I request you make the coffee this morning?" she said with her sweetest smile, "I have a feeling I'm going to be late for work."

"On it," I said, giving her a salute.

She hesitated in the doorway before making a dash back for the bed and planted a quick kiss on my lips.

"Gross, Allie! Rock stars don't do morning breath, didn't you know?"

She flipped me off and then made her way to the shower, leaving me with a stupid grin and the very important task of making coffee.

Allies coffee machine was exactly what you would have thought Allie's coffee machine would be. It was small, and old and had one button that turned it on and off. It was an incredible piece of machinery, especially considering that it still worked and produced what she claimed was 'top tier brew'.

I was watching the machine drip it's liquid gold, standing in Allie's kitchen in my borrowed sweats and no shirt, waiting for her to get out of the shower.

"Woah, sorry—"

I turned at the sound of a male voice behind me. Score. I was finally getting to meet string-bean-Dean.

"Holy crap," he said, staring at me with his mouth wide open. Maybe it was something about this apartment, but both the residents had a tendency to look at me just like that.

"You must be Dean," I said, walking over with my hand stretched out, "Sorry about being half naked in your kitchen, I was just making coffee for Allie."

Dean reached out and shook my hand, "You're—I mean, aren't you?" he got very flustered, very quickly. His hand was clammy, and it took all my energy not to wipe my own hand after I moved back from our shake.

"Totally depends on what you're referring to, Dean, but in this case, I think I could be. Or, maybe I'm just a very handsome imposter," I smiled.

My phone buzzed in my pocket.

Ap: *Dax we have to head to Jane's office for a brief about the publicity stuff for the album. Are you coming back soon?*

Jane was our wonderful, incredible and just generally badass manager. She was why we were where we were in our career as a band, without a doubt.

Dax: *Coming now be back in 30 minutes.*

Ap: *Hope you used protection.*

Dax: *You can't see me but I'm giving you the finger Asshole*

Ap: *Touchy touchy. Be back soon pls.*

"Sorry, what?" I said back to Dean, pocketing my phone. He'd been speaking that whole time and I didn't hear a word.

"I was just saying that I can't believe you're hanging out with Allie," Dean repeated.

I frowned, my head cocking to the side, "Why's that?" I said. I didn't know Dean from a hole in the wall and regardless of what Allie had said, I was willing to give the guy a chance, but things were not working in his favour so far.

"Well, I just mean, Allie doesn't get out much. If I had imagined the next guy who would be standing in my kitchen was dating Allie, it sure as shorts wouldn't have been Wyatt Smith, you know? Like, how does that even happen!?" he reached up and pushed his glasses up his nose, scratching his head and laughing. Giving me a look that showed me he was 100% waiting for me to reply to that.

"I would say she gets out enough," I suddenly felt very protective of Allie, "I've actually got to go, sorry to leave so soon. It was nice to meet you though," I said with a smile, moving past him back into Allie's room. She was right, Dean was a complete string bean.

I was just pulling my shirt over my head as Allie walked into her room wearing her fuzzy robe. I handed her a mug of coffee.

She saw that I was dressed and gave a little pout, "Oh no, you're going?" she asked. I liked that she wanted me to stay.

"I am," I said, mocking her pout, "I have to go to a meeting with my manager about the dates for the press tour. It's coming up quick," I stood and pushed my hair back.

Allie nodded as she took a sip from her coffee, "Of course, that makes sense that you would have to do that."

Her response made me smile. She was so happily *Allie*. Completely unconcerned that she was an absolute weirdo and she went with it. Incredibly witty, smart, kind and very funny amongst a comprehensive list of other things, but still a massive weirdo. The thought of that made my chest feel all warm.

I walked over to her and she stretched out the mug of coffee. I took it from her and had a sip, grateful that she liked her coffee the same way I liked mine. Uncomplicated.

I then scooped her towards me, "Can I kiss you now?" I asked.

"You may," she said, smiling as my lips met hers. It was meant to be a peck, but the undeniable heat was there, simmering under the surface.

"Thank you for last night," she said, her cheeks going a bit pink.

"The pleasure was all mine," I said. Then I gave her a little smirk, "Well, maybe the pleasure was yours too, actually," I laughed as she squirmed.

"Dax!" She smacked my chest and then pulled me to her for another kiss as she took the coffee cup back from my hand. "I look forward to returning the favour," her voice was a low whisper that immediately had me thinking about puppies and the elderly to settle the stir of emotion that built up in the pit of my stomach.

The blush that rose on her cheeks was the only indication that she saw all of what had transpired just flash across my face in the brief few seconds it all went down. I would have bet you anything that she was thinking of exactly what I was thinking of.

She cleared her throat and said with a jarring amount of enthusiasm, "Okay, well, have a groovy day!"

That's a new one. My eyebrows shot up, "A groovy day?"

"Yep!" she said, popping the 'p' for emphasis. I was trying to hold in my smile. Like I said, a proper weirdo and I was definitely there for it.

"Okay, you have a groovy day too. I'll text you okay?"

"You better," she smiled.

With one last kiss, I left her place, grateful to have avoided seeing Dean again and made my way to Ap's car in the basement of her building.

Ap: *Dude?*
I will actually come over there.

Dax: *I'm leaving now*
don't get your panties in a twist.

21

Allie

I had the realisation on my way to work, at some point during the week after the 24-hour ice-cream parlour date, that it had been well over a month since I'd had the urge to buy any premixed brownie boxes. February was usually a prime brownie buying month because the hustle and bustle of the New Year died down and everyone realised no plans had been made for the second month of the year. Of course, I got the shitty end of that stick.

Had work still been shit sometimes? For sure. But I had much rather spoken to Dax about it and been pulled from that misery by his humour than make the trek to get a brownie mix in the late hours of the evening. But things were good. Things were better than good, but I wasn't about to jinx it.

Dax had continued to cook me meals most nights for the next few weeks, and I continued to rate them a 5 out of 10. We settled into a wonderful routine, alternating between his apartment and mine and it was much to my great pleasure that I got to repay him for his initial favour after our ice cream date. Repeatedly.

Savannah had asked for the details of all those encounters too many times until I called her a perv and threw a pillow at her face.

I finally got to say hello to his friends, and band mates, during one of our many FaceTime chats. I got to see Aspen a lot more than the others, and I often heard him whine to Dax about when we would all meet in person. It made me laugh. I knew that when I finally did get to meet him in person, it would feel like I'd known him forever. He had that type of personality, I was coming to find.

Aspen was also exactly how Dax had described and absolutely the sort of younger brother that would insist on calling a band *Socks and Sandals.*

I knew that Dax was going to have to leave for the press tour soon, it was hard to believe it had almost been two months since our park picnic. What I had not anticipated was that he might've had to leave earlier than planned.

We were sitting on one of the sofas in his living room, wrapped up in one another, as usual, while our food digested. Dax had made us *pho,* and yes, it was a 10 out of 10, and yes, I gave him a 5. I was starting to think that he knew that when I said 5, I really meant 10.

"How much earlier?" I hated how disappointed I sounded, how sad I felt. This was his *job.*

Way to be supportive, Allie.

Dax was playing with my fingers, turning a ring I wore around and around my finger in a mindless action.

"Not tomorrow, but the next day," he sounded equally as glum.

I decided that enough was enough. We had been down about it for about 10 minutes, but it was exciting. They were leaving earlier because they had to fit in more dates due to the success of the album so far.

"No, this will be great," I scooted up the couch from my slouched position.

"It will?" he looked at me a bit confused.

"Yes, it will. This is so exciting Dax! Your album is *killing it.* So, you're gonna have a hoot of a time promoting it and I'll be present and accounted for for all the phone calls, texts and FaceTimes," I beamed at him.

"A hoot of a time?" he sounded completely unsure.

"Like a wise owl, my friend," I combed a hand through his red hair. I had never seen it faded, come to think of it. He must be all over the dying schedule to keep it so bright. Maybe it was his hair and makeup team.

I wanted a hair and makeup team.

"It's going to be for a few months, Allie," he said it like he was trying to convince me that calling things off would be best or something. That the distance would be too big of a thing between us. What a looney.

"Oh, like… *three*?" I made sure to have it seem like that was a dreadfully long time.

He nodded.

"Bugger, well this has been great and all but maybe we should call it here," I started to move away from him, and he looked right at me, not yet catching on. "If you could move, that would be great. You're super heavy, and heavy dudes who have to travel for work are a pretty big turn off for me so…," I made a wincing face at him while shooing him away with my hands, "Not to mention you smell *awful.* What is that?" I scrunched my nose.

He finally cracked a smile and rolled his eyes, "Okay, okay. I'll perk up."

"Months, shmonths, Dax."

He was definitely about to laugh at that, which was better than seeing him broody. I kissed his temple, "It'll be fine. We'll be fine."

He grabbed my hand and planted a kiss into my open palm, tugging me back down so I was laying next to him. He nuzzled into the side of my neck and requested I stayed the night. I did, of course, and tried my best not to think about how I would soon be without the body I had come so used to having around me.

We were in bed and I was about to fall asleep when he asked quietly, "Do you really think I smell bad?"

I huffed a laugh into his chest where I was comfortably tucked.

"No," I said, taking a big deep breath in, "You smell like the—," I stopped. There was no way to say it without it being weird. I told him just that, "There's no way to explain it without it sounding weird."

"That's okay, I already know you're weird. The damage is done," His voice was muffled as he spoke with his lips pressed against my hair, "Tell me."

"You smell like lavender and mint. Like salt water. Sort of woodsy as well, I guess. And like leather, too. All of those combined," my voice was riddled with tiredness.

"That's a lot of smells for one nose to pick up."

"Mmm," was my only response and I breathed him in again, but made it very exaggerated.

Dax's laugh rumbled through his chest, it made me smile.

"You smell *clean* and *fresh*," I finished and nuzzled in closer.

"Clean is good," his voice was barely more than a whisper.

"Definitely better than whatever I was smelling on the couch earlier," I whispered back.

His laugh was a quiet interruption in the dark. It hung around us, clinging to the shadows until sleep found us both.

When Dax said that it would be like he was with me all the time, even though he would be bouncing from country to country, he wasn't wrong.

He took me on every plane trip, taking a stream of photos and sending them all to me when they landed. I sent him photos of what I was up to as well, but there was only so much excitement that could be had from doing the washing.

I didn't realise how used to having Dax around I had become until he was no longer knocking at my door at 7AM with coffee and croissants, or I wasn't waking up way too hot but perfectly content in his python-like embrace.

It was weird, but things were still… well, I hated using the word in fear of jinxing it, but things were sort of perfect.

Dax was still many things I had yet to put a name to, but some of the blanks I'd once had while explaining him to Savannah had started to fill in. Dax was thoughtful and kind. He was considerate and sexy as hell. Dax was the person I wanted to be around most, and as terrifying as that was, I was doing just what Sav had said. I was feeling the fear and doing it anyway, and so far, it was paying off.

I was walking home from work and my phone pinged.

Dax: *FaceTime?*

That was how things were, and to be completely honest, it was working a treat. His days were my nights more often than not, but we made it work. In some ways, it was like he was still just across the city in his own apartment.

Once, he had done it more than once, but I remembered this time particularly, he had woken up at 3AM his time to have dinner with me. He had gone out and bought take-out just to put in his hotel mini fridge so that come 3AM, he could wake up to an alarm and eat with me on FaceTime.

He had been shirtless and his eyes were half closed the whole time, but I laughed so hard that I inhaled a noodle and spent most of our internet date cry-laughing at the very real and completely underrated pain of having a noodle lodged in my nasal cavity.

Needless to say, that whole situation certainly woke him up and that he, too, was laughing so much he cried. The cherry on top was when Dax admitted that the food speared to the end of his fork had been the same ready-to-go bite from an hour before, and that he was pretending to eat because the food 'literally tasted like ass'. That made me snort-laugh to the point of my abdominal muscles twitching from overuse because he had been *pretending to chew* to keep up the charade. I had laughed more than I had eaten, which was saying a lot considering the size of my portions.

We broke our fortune cookies together and our date ended when I needed to go to bed and he had to have a shower and get dressed for the day.

In my mental list of dates, it had become my favourite so far.

I spent a lot of time kissing the front facing camera on my phone. It was gross, but every time I did it Dax's eyes lit up a bit so, who was I to take away his joy?

I smiled and called him on FaceTime just as I walked onto the city block my apartment building was located on. He picked up on the first ring.

"There she is," he said, smiling at me. I exhaled a bit seeing him on my phone screen.

"Shouldn't you be asleep?" I pushed the door of my apartment building open with my shoulder and then proceeded to tap the call button of the elevator repeatedly.

"We actually arrived in Amsterdam today, so it's still morning here. I am about to die of exhaustion though, so there's that," Dax had his head on a blindingly white and very soft looking hotel pillow, "Did you get my photos of the flight? Aspen fell asleep so we were balancing rice crackers into towers on his head. My tower was the highest," he gave me a tired smile.

"Of course it was," I laughed, stepping into the elevator, "I haven't gotten them yet though."

The FaceTime call moved to 'paused' for a second. Dax popped back on my screen as I stepped out of the elevator. I almost squealed with delight as he said, "They're still sending."

I nodded my head and tried to school my face into a mask of calm, but one thing I couldn't do, as everyone knew, was hide my emotions.

"What's happened?" Dax said immediately, moving his pillow up so he was propped against the headboard of his bed.

"No, nothin,." I said, "But I have to put you in my bag for a second. Can you hold tight?" I put the phone in my tote without waiting for him to answer.

"You can't woman-handle me like this, Allie!" I heard him yell from my tote.

I just rolled my eyes.

"Don't you roll your eyes at me!" I heard him yell again a moment later. I barked a laugh at his uncanny ability to know me as I lugged in the massive parcel that had been sitting outside my apartment door.

No, people didn't usually get this sort of service, however, the postman, Doug, was a solid guy. He used to deliver mail in the mornings, when I first moved into the building with Dean, as I was leaving for work. When I was still using a cane to help myself walk, we had struck up a friendship and every time I had a package, he would always leave it at my door.

I made sure to give Doug a good bonus come the holidays. As far as I was concerned, the people in our postal service didn't get paid enough.

I dropped my things in the kitchen, including my large parcel, and went back to lock the door and take off my jacket. The weather had started to warm up a bit more that I had since stopped wearing my *skeenie* out and about. It was always a sad day when the *skeenie* was put back into the cupboard until the next winter season.

"Allie?" Dax called from my bag.

"Coming!" I hurried back and took the phone out of my tote.

"Please tell me what's going on, I'm going to die from suspense as well as exhaustion," he said around a yawn.

"Okay, so this is a surprise for you and a gift for me, sort of," I said as I disappeared from the frame to get some scissors.

"I'm scared," Dax mumbled into his pillow, making me laugh.

"I bought you a dildo," I said, as I came back into frame.

"Just what I always wanted, thanks babe," he was giving me his best 'real but fake' smile.

He told me on one of our many FaceTime's since he'd been gone that that was the smile he gave to the press. He also never called me babe, so that made me cackle.

I moved the phone onto the floor and set it against one of the legs of the kitchen stools.

"Now that's what I call a big package, Allie," he said as I started to cut into it.

"Yes, well I ordered something relatively large," I replied.

"I wasn't referring to your postal delivery, and how do you even know what I'm looking at?" he asked.

I caught on very quickly to what he was referring to and spent the next few minutes coming out of my laughing fit and wiping the tears from my eyes.

Just as I was about to get back into my unboxing, Dean walked into the apartment and wasted no time coming over and inviting himself into the frame of my FaceTime call.

"Hey Wyatt!" Dean said way too enthusiastically.

"Hey man, how's it going?" Dax replied politely.

I always forgot his first name was actually Wyatt.

"Yeah, not a lot, how's the tour?" Dean went on like he was not interrupting my FaceTime with *my* boyfriend.

"Good, thanks! Hope you're well! Take it easy Dean," Dax coolly ended the conversation. Dean fumbled with his farewell before making his way into his room.

"You're so good at that," I whispered as I finished cutting all the tape holding the box together.

"It comes with the territory," Dax shrugged.

"Teach me your ways," I said. I interrupted Dax's reply as I squealed, "Okay, okay, okay!" I beamed into the camera, "Are you ready?"

"I'm ready," he said, he was smiling but definitely a little nervous.

I lifted it out of the box and onto my lap. Dax's face lost all nervousness and he was looking at me like, well, I wasn't not sure. No one had ever looked at me the way Dax was looking at me.

"You bought a guitar," he said. His voice was soft and full of emotion.

I felt myself get choked up at hearing that voice, "I bought a guitar," I replied, picking up the phone and giving my front facing camera a big kiss.

22

Allie

The days started to slowly blur into one another and whenever I tried to recount something, I found that all my memories had suddenly started to replay in my head in the form of FaceTime calls and text messages.

Savannah and I still caught up almost every Friday for dinner at our favourite Italian place, but she had been busy too. She'd applied for, and received, a promotion at work which had her travelling out of the state to the other major stadiums owned by her company. She was now in charge of something I couldn't remember the name of, but it meant she needed to do in person reviews constantly.

Whenever she was home, she always made time to see me though. It went without saying that I missed my best friend, but I was happy for her. Savannah deserved all the success that went her way.

My evenings consisted of everything I always did, but Dax was usually on FaceTime. They were in Japan now after moving all the way through Europe.

Most of the time we would be doing our own routines while enjoying one another's virtual company. I would play my piano while Dax would read or I'd be cooking (the only meal I knew which was spaghetti and meatballs, duh) while he played the guitar.

He had successfully taught me his four favourite chords and I could string them together well enough that I felt confident in verbalising the phrase 'yes, I play the guitar' and 'oh me? Yes, I can play more than one instrument, thank you so much for noticing.'

Dax had in fact enquired when I would be able to casually drop those lines into conversation. I told him he needn't worry about such trivial things. But when the time came, I would be ready. I made a point to practice them after every session I had on the piano. It didn't take too long for the calluses to form on the ends of my fingers.

My hands had always been soft. Gentle and rarely used for anything too hard or bracing. When I looked at them now, it felt silly, I guess, but I suppose that I felt like as the skin toughened on my fingertips, I had begun to toughen in other places too. Like maybe I was getting stronger as well.

Dax and I tried to have coffee together as often as possible, but as they continued moving on with their locations on their tour, the times fluctuated. I had learned the hard way that having a coffee at 1AM was not smart, so I invested in my first pack of decaf.

My midnight coffee dates with Dax had quickly become one of my favourite times and were well worth the day of yawning that followed it.

One thing was irrevocably clear though - I missed him very, very much.

23

When we left for the tour, not once did I realise that I'd never packed up any parts of my life before we set off. I didn't need to pivot, to tie up loose ends and switch mindsets. To unpack the life I lived when we weren't at home, and put away the box I delved into when we were having a break.

I didn't think about it. Not once.

I was ready for the tour to come to an end. Being away with the guys was always fun, I loved spending time on the road with them and my lack of compartmentalising on this tour was a lot easier than I had thought it was going to be.

Allie made it easy to be away though. She also made it hard. And the days that dragged because of the blinding tiredness were always well worth the nights I got to spend talking to her. So cute it was gross, right? It was still true.

The guys all gave me shit but being away had made me excited for them to all finally meet. I knew they'd love her.

It was during one of our FaceTime calls that the reality of it all hit me. Allie had mastered the G chord, and finally strung all four notes she had learned together. She was so excited, so was I.

I had taken a screenshot of her sitting there on the other end of our FaceTime, the guitar in her lap with the biggest smile on her face. It had been my wallpaper on my phone now for a while. Aspen was the first to notice and all he did was give me a big hug. I pushed him away and then ruffled up his hair, but I knew that it made him happy to see me happy. It made *me* happy to be happy.

Maybe there was something to this lack of compartmentalising thing. Or maybe it was Allie.

She had fallen asleep on our FaceTime chat after I had taken that screenshot of her holding her guitar.

She still didn't snore, and even though I told her she was a drooler, she wasn't. She was as beautiful awake as she was asleep. She just slept, soundly and peacefully. She was a very still and calm sleeper, which was probably why she never wriggled out of my hold when we did sleep together.

I watched her for a bit when, usually, I would've ended the call and flicked her a message saying something along the lines of how she had a nose whistle and that she might need to look into it, or that she had a stray booger that was fluttering in the wind of her inhales and exhales and I recorded it for later.

None of that ever happened, but she always laughed so hard, it brought out the infamous Allie snort-laugh, that I couldn't help myself.

It was that time when I watched her a little longer when I knew.

I knew without a shadow of a doubt that I was completely and undeniably in love with her.

24

Allie

People usually told you that life had a way of balancing itself out, that if you were hitting those hard days one after the other, that you would get the good times too. Well, when they issued that memo, they must've forgotten to include that it went both ways. You didn't get too many good days without a reminder of the cold hard truth; that the grass was actually much greener on the other side. That one side was far shittier than the other.

My boss was, how does one put it nicely?

Well, one doesn't. Not in this case.

My boss was the kid that never got picked for any team sport and grew up in his parent's basement until he was in his late thirties, only to be told repeatedly by said parents that no girl was ever going to be good enough for him so he took that lovely little falsity and morphed it into an excuse to grab my ass anytime he deemed the marketing corner of the office worthy of his presence.

That was the sort of behaviour that I dealt with at work, the sort of behaviour that had me always, *always*, sitting at my desk at almost every moment of the day and scuttling to the bathroom the long way so that I would have the lowest chance of running into him.

Did I still get the high and mighty tongue lashings he had to offer? Of course! All my successes were overshadowed by small and silly mistakes, but no one was ever remembered for their moments of glory, were they?

I had been in my own head while I was copying something at the printing station. I didn't hear the nauseating squeak of his too-new shoes or the chafing of his suit pants. Not until one hand was cupped on my ass. I screamed, of course, and turned so fast I saw stars, pressing myself up against the copier to get away from him.

"Good job today, Alice," he said. His breath smelt like tuna salad. "Another great campaign."

He smirked at me and walked off. He was the kind of person that walked on his toes, the heels of his shoes never touched the ground.

You'd think that was a compliment, but it wasn't. I would be met with a list of complaints tomorrow and this would have become another excuse to have touched my backside.

I felt sick, but mostly I felt angry, because no one in my office had ever bothered to stand up for me.

I walked home with my jacket off, enjoying the warmer turn of the weather and desperately hoped the light breeze would move over me and take the grime of the day with it.

I took out my phone.

Allie: *I hope your day has been much better than mine.*

I knew that they were heading to an interview, their last one, actually. So, I didn't want to interrupt anything with a call. I was surprised when he replied almost straight away.

Dax: *Oh no.*
Do I need to beat anyone up?

Allie: *Absolutely you do.*

:(

Dax: *> Photo*

I tapped on the photo and waited for it to download as I left the corner store. I had stopped in on my way home to grab some brownies. So, when the photo popped up from Dax and I saw a shot of the very same brownie box I held in my hand that he had grabbed from the internet, I let out a snort-laugh and sent him a selfie of me pouting, holding my own box.

Dax: *I'm sorry I'm not there to help you make them.*

Allie: *It's okay. This is good. You being here... well, there, but also here. This is good.*

Dax: *See you soon.*

I had typed out the words 'I love you' but quickly deleted it.

I had never wanted to send them more than I had wanted to then. I also had never wanted to hear them back so much.

I knew it the moment I realised that it wasn't the brownies I wanted. I wanted Dax.

The motions of turning on the oven were familiar. I had been preheating the oven since I was a kid. Even though the electric stove top had brought with it it's challenges, I had always been my most comfortable when turning on the oven.

I snapped the little dial to 'fan forced' and then cranked the temperature to 180 celsius.

I added the milk, butter and eggs to the premixed dry ingredients faster than you could say 'Allie can work an oven like a pro' and before I knew it, the batter was inside the oven, cooking.

While the goey-goodness cooked, I went to get changed into my comfies - a shirt that belonged to Dax that barely smelt like him anymore, and some baggy sweats. I walked out of my room and back towards the kitchen, more than ready for my brownies when my entire body went into shock. I couldn't move.

The wailing of a siren on the city street below blasted past so loud I could have been standing beside it. A window had been left open. I never opened windows, always making sure they were shut tight.

My body started to shake as the memory of my accident encompassed me like being submerged under water. A loud horn sounded in my head and bounced from ear to ear. I knew some kind of sound left my mouth, but I couldn't tell you how loud or how long ago that might have been. The lights of the truck flashed behind my eyes and my body erupted in pain. My leg and hip instantly gave out on me as I crumpled to the floor of the kitchen. I held myself tightly, my muscles refusing to unwind as I relived the moment the truck collided with my car over and over.

I didn't know how long I had been curled on the floor of my own kitchen until I was suddenly lifted and placed somewhere soft. The unfamiliar arms that had placed me there were soon replaced with strong, slim ones. A hand that had rubbed circles on my back the very same way more times than I could count, drew me from the nightmare I was reliving. The verbal commands to breathe in and out were delivered to me by a voice I probably knew better than my own.

As my body unwound, aching only now from the intensity of how tightly I had been curled in on myself, I kept my eyes closed and reached for Savannah, holding her tightly until the exhaustion took over and I fell into sleep.

25

Allie

I decided to forgive Dean for being an asshat and letting Ben into the apartment. I knew it had been a long time since it all happened and I had intended on forgiving him before now, I'd even forgotten to mention it to Savannah. But I got comfortable in my stubborn silent treatment towards him, and so caught up in Dax, that I just forgot to forgive him.

After I had woken up the next morning, still clutching Savannah so tightly my fingers ached, she told me everything that happened.

I had been on the floor of the kitchen for about 20 minutes in the end. It was almost 6PM when I had gotten home and sorted out the brownies, and by the time Dean found me, called Sav and helped me into bed, it had just passed around 6:15PM by Sav's to-the-minute retelling.

Dean had come home, found me on the floor unresponsive to anything he was saying and called Savannah straight away. Dean knew that I struggled with the lingering trauma from my accident and as far as housemates went, he had been quite accommodating, aside from leaving a window open here and slamming his door too loudly there, my triggers were never a real issue *inside* the apartment.

He'd lifted me off the floor under Savannah's careful instruction and placed me on my bed. He even tossed out my burnt brownies for me and washed the tray.

Sav had said he checked in to see if I was okay before he left for work. So, I had decided to forgive him for his prior offence. I hadn't had a chance to tell him yet, but I would as soon as I saw him next.

Sav had been home after arriving back from wherever she was for a work trip earlier in the day. I knew she had been away, and it was just stupid luck she had been at home, and even stupider luck that she had actually *picked up* Dean's phone call.

His stalkerish tendencies that overtook the first few months after they had been introduced, and his lingering creepiness after she had made it abundantly clear what she thought of his intentions, left me with no faith in her actually picking up that phone call. But she did.

Though it was a 15-minute walk to Savannah's, it was a 3-minute drive, 1.5 minutes if you put pedal to the metal. Sav knew how I felt about her driving. I thought she was too fast and too careless. I was grateful though, if it was only just for moments like this that she was such a speed demon.

She had stayed with me for most of the morning of the next day after I had called in sick to work, but I ordered her to leave eventually when she kept getting calls from her own work.

Savannah hesitated, clutching her own cup of coffee.

"I can stay, Al. Work will understand, I've been run off my feet since the promotion," she said as she perched back on the edge of my couch.

I was mindlessly trailing the rim of my mug with my thumb, "No, Sav. Honestly, I'm okay now, just tired and sore. A little foggy but I am just going to go back to sleep. I will be fine."

I gave her my best smile, but I could feel my bottom lip wavering.

Sav set down her coffee and pulled me into a tight hug.

"It's okay, Al," she said, her hand making the circle motions on my back again.

"I hate it, Savannah. I *hate* it," I pulled away and aggressively wiped my eyes.

I remembered when I wasn't like this, you know. When I could walk down the street and not have to decide whether or not I was going to brave the stroll to work without my earplugs or close my eyes as a car drove by me after dark.

When I could *drive.*

"Allie, there are things...," Savannah said, moving some hair behind my ear.

"It stopped working. You know that. I am not going to pay to see someone who won't help me," I said. I knew that wasn't all of it though, that some of the resistance had come from me. I didn't say that part, and neither did Savannah, though she knew it too.

"Okay," she said, letting it go, "will you promise me to at least think about it? There are other places. Other therapies to try too, Allie."

I had always refused the pharmaceutical side of therapy. I didn't want it.

"I promise I'll think about it," I said. And I meant it too. I would think about it. I knew there was more that I could give, but it was like nobody understood that *giving* that was almost the hardest part.

I slept for the rest of the day.

When I woke up my head felt clearer. My body still ached a bit but, I felt more like Allie.

I was just shuffling out of my room to head to the kitchen to make myself a tea when Dean walked in. We stood in the kitchen, I was fiddling with the tie of my fuzzy robe and Dean was playing with the keys in his hand.

I silently made my way over and gave him a hug.

Needless to say, string-bean-Dean and I didn't hug, "Thanks Dean."

It took him a minute, but he did eventually hug me back. He mumbled an awkward 'don't mention it' and headed into his room. At least I felt like I had successfully patched up that bridge.

The peppermint tea I was brewing called to me like a siren to the sea, and as I began to calm further I realised that amongst the chaos of everything that had happened, it really should have been a good day, the best day, really. Dax was coming home.

He'd arrive late but I had completely lost track of my phone the last 24 hours, so I had no idea if he'd even messaged or tried to call.

I immediately felt bad. We had spoken every single day for almost the last six months and then I fell off the face of the earth. I hope he didn't think I had ghosted him or something.

My mood lifted instantly. The last complete rotation of the planet on its axis brought me shit-all, but the lingering self-pity dissipated as I imagined seeing him again for the first time in three months.

I was carrying my tea to my room, set on finding wherever my phone had gone to die, when a knock sounded at my door. My heart leapt into my throat. Surely it wasn't him, it was too early. Wasn't it? Or I could have gotten the flight times wrong, or maybe he had done one of those things where he told me he was back later as a ruse, only to come and surprise me earlier. It felt like that was a very 'Dax' thing to do. Something I felt like Aspen would have also fully supported.

I turned around on slippery socks, placed my steaming tea on the kitchen island with surprising steadiness and hurtled myself towards the front door. The soreness that hung around my limbs was completely forgotten.

I threw open my front door, only to have my smile turn sour on my face.

I had forgotten that it wasn't only good things that came in threes, because it wasn't Dax at my door.

It was Ben.

26

DAX

I couldn't stop my knee from bouncing the whole flight.

I watched the light fade into dark as our plane took us home.

The tour was a huge success. The promotion of the album couldn't have gone better, and the reaction from the fans was beyond anything we could have hoped for.

I loved it all. Speaking to everyone, talking about the songs, the different parts, the writing process.

But heading home was something I had looked forward to the moment that we had left.

The guys all slept on the flight, that was the usual.

Ap woke up a few times and we played cards until he was tired enough to fall asleep again. I alternated between jotting down different lyrics into my notebook, to reading, to listening to music, to just looking out the window in silence.

As soon as the plane touched down, I pulled out my phone and turned off airplane mode. I had sent Allie a stream of messages after our last interview, mostly asking about how her brownies turned out and a request that she kept one for me, but I didn't expect a reply because I knew she would have been asleep or getting ready for bed.

After the interview, the guys and I sent her a quick photo and then I sent her a customary series of shots of the journey to the airport.

She hadn't responded to any of them. It had already been a full day for her and as we landed, it was already close to getting late.

I had been talking to Allie every day for months and months, and she had never not replied.

Something in my stomach sank.

Moving through the airport was muscle memory. Once we got our bags and headed to the cars that were meant to take us home, I pulled Ap aside.

"I'm going to Allie's," I said, running a hand through my hair.

Aspen rolled his eyes, "Dude, a few more hours won't—"

"No, something's wrong. I haven't heard from her since she finished work yesterday."

Aspen's face sobered up as his eyes scanned my own features, "Could she just be busy?" he asked.

"Maybe," I agreed hesitantly.

My brother looked at me for a while longer before he nodded his head, "Okay, let me know when you get there okay?"

I nodded back and gave him a quick hug before waving to the other guys and jogging to get a taxi.

I pulled a hat over my head and jumped into the first one that pulled up, giving him Allie's address and asking him to get there as fast as he could.

27

Allie

It was pure instinct to close the door, leaving only a sliver open. Having something between him and me.

I'd never been hit by Ben, but I had been scared by him enough to warrant the shield of a door to me.

I could smell him from where I stood in my apartment.

Ben had been drinking.

"God dammit, Allie, give me back my shit!" he yelled, even though I was less than a metre in front of him. I held in my gag from his breath.

I wasn't sensitive to the smell of alcohol. I was, however, sensitive to the smell of *that much* alcohol.

His words fell into one another like dominos.

"What are you doing here, Ben? I told you I didn't want to see you again," I said, keeping my voice calm and steady.

You're fine, Allie. You're good.

"You always thought you were so much better than me, but who's the one keeping my stuff after they were thrown out!" He flung the words at me.

"You didn't *throw* me anywhere, Ben. I'm going to ask you one more time to leave," I continued to keep my voice calm.

"You're such a *bitch,* Allie! You made me do it, you know that right? You *made* me do it all."

He stepped closer to the door. I shut it a fraction more in a mimic of his action until I was only looking out from a crack.

"Don't you fucking close the door on me Alice, give me back my fucking shit. I know you still have some of my stuff," he lifted his closed fists and smacked them so hard on the front door, it caught me off guard and I fell backwards, the door flinging wide open between us.

A look crossed Ben's face that might have been something like regret, but then it disappeared, and determination set into his features and he made to walk into my apartment.

"*Stop,*" I yelled.

That was the second time I had ever yelled in my apartment.

I really needed someone to explain to me why after 8 months of not seeing this guy, he showed up twice in the following six months.

I couldn't believe it, but he listened. He stopped.

"You take one step into this apartment Ben, and it will be the last thing you ever fucking do," I said as I kept his eye contact and brought myself up to my feet.

I was going to fall apart any minute, my legs were shaking, and my heart was in my throat.

Push through it, Allie, you're fine. You're good.

I walked up and grabbed the door, closing it again between me and Ben just as Dean rounded the corner.

"Allie? Are you okay? I heard—"

"I'm fine, Dean. Ben is drunk and was about to leave before I called the police."

Dean didn't say anything, but he didn't leave either. He stood there and it felt like he had my back.

Ben's eyes landed back on me again.

"You're gonna regret keeping my things Allie. You're going to regret it all. You don't get to just *say* that you don't want to see me again. You are not the one who *decides* that. I did *everything* for you. We were weeks into our relationship when you had your accident, *weeks.* You owe me *everything* Alice!" His voice was so loud it cracked.

"I don't *have your things* Ben! Why would I want your crap in my life?

Everything that was here I gave you in that box. Maybe, if you're so sure you've lost something, you should ask around all the other girls you were *sleeping with* while you were convincing me to pack up my life and move in with you," I spat at him, but that last part of what he had just said, that struck me hard.

I had always thought that quietly to myself, that I owed him something because he had stayed. It had *eaten me alive*. The guilt. It made it easier to believe him when he said that I had forced his hand to find someone else, multiple someones, actually, to help him feel appreciated. I could feel the bile rising in my throat.

"I never asked you to stay, Ben! No one made you stay. I thanked you, every *fucking* day of our whole relationship. It should have never been something you brought up in a fight to make me seem like the bad guy, but you *always did.* Every time! Like somehow, it was my fault for almost dying and I was… I was somehow, what, I don't know, indebted? That's not how caring about someone works Ben!"

I was yelling again. Yet another thing that had come in threes. I was not just yelling in my apartment though, because Ben was still in the hallway.

"You were indebted to me!" Ben screamed, like actually screamed into the crack of the door that I had open between me and him. I felt his spit hit my face.

I was about to yell back. I was so lost in the spiral of emotions and memories that this had brought up. That Ben, being in the hallway outside of my apartment, saying what he was saying, had dragged to the surface of my mind. I had thought I was growing stronger than that, with every callus on my fingertips I had thought I was getting tougher too. It seemed that was not the case.

"Is everything okay here?" An officer said as he stepped out of the elevator with his partner. I hadn't heard police arrive, had there been sirens I would have known. I turned to look at Dean who was walking up to me now. He lifted his phone up awkwardly as if to say, 'it was me'.

He came to stand next to me and said quietly to me first, "I asked them not to sound their sirens, cause… you know."

Dean turned to the policemen, opening the door wider, "Officers, this man is the ex-boyfriend of my roommate. He has come here twice, uninvited, and he's currently very drunk. He also pushed the door open and made her fall backwards. That's when I came out."

Ben's face encompassed a quiet fury as he set the full weight of his gaze onto Dean.

This might not be the moment, but what in the name of all that was orange was going on here. Who was this Dean, and what had he done with my Mac and Cheese smelling roommate?

"It's time you left, Ben," Dean said.

He exchanged a few more words with the police. They asked me something, but I didn't really absorb it, I just nodded. Dean's hand rested on my shoulder to move me back into the apartment.

Ben was in handcuffs. I looked at him one more time, and I hoped with literally everything I had, that I'd never see him ever again.

He turned to look back at me as the doors to the elevator opened, "I hope you enjoy being alone, Alice. No one will want to pick up all your broken pieces," he spat.

Dean placed his hand above mine on the door, I was gripping it so tightly my fingers had gone bone white, and he shut it.

I didn't move, I just stood there trying to count my breaths.

Breathe in for 10, and out for 10.

When Dean touched my shoulder, it startled me so much I jumped.

"Sorry," he mumbled.

I had held on long enough and there was nothing I could do as the tears welled and started to fall down my face. I just shook my head.

I pulled myself away from the door to head to my room.

"Allie," Dean said.

I turned to look at him.

"I'm sorry I let him into the apartment. I didn't know," Dean pushed his glasses up his nose and scratched his head. I nodded back to him.

I don't know how I did it, but I managed a few words back to him, "Thank you. I… thank you."

Dean stared back at me, sort of like what had just transpired and the person he had morphed into for the last few minutes had never even happened. He scratched the top of his head and made a sound that was kind of like hocking up a loogie to swallow back down your throat again.

I didn't wait to hear what he said after that. I curled up on my bed, a pillow hugged to my chest and let the sobs wrack through my body.

It had been a very long time since I had felt like that. Like I was the size of pea in a world full of giants.

I had forgotten what it was like, the heaviness that pressed in on my chest, the helplessness. Things had been so *good.* I had been so happy for so long and nothing bad had touched those months.

Since the baking aisle, and the couch date and the picnic and the dinners and the FaceTimes. It had all been bright, and colourful. But as I lay there, desperate to calm my own breathing and clear my mind, the greyness that had encompassed everything that I was for what had felt like a very long time, washed over the colour. It dampened the blues, the greens. The reds.

My tears had dried up, and my breathing eventually measured out.

It turned out that my phone was on my side table, probably thanks to Sav, and I just hadn't noticed it. It was on Dax's side, not mine.

Dax's side. I wonder when I had started to think of that side as his.

It was going off relentlessly. I ignored it. I had nothing to give or to say to anyone.

My eyes were looking at nothing for a while until my piano came into focus. I slid off my bed and sat in front of the ivory keys. That still felt safe to me. Ben had never touched that part of my life; he had never turned the black and white keys grey.

I closed my eyes and played every song I remembered. There were a lot of them. I played the soft ones, I played the loud and chaotic ones, I played the thought provoking and cheeky ones. It always worked, always pulled me from whatever funk I found myself in. But with every note I played now, nothing eased. Nothing washed away with the rises and falls of the music. It wasn't working like it usually did. It didn't push the weight off me. I was under water, pinned beneath a rock. That's what it felt like, like I was drowning.

I smacked the keys, the loud sound of all the notes playing at once absorbed my scream. I didn't care if Dean was asleep, or if the apartment above me had heard.

That's when I heard another knock.

My head snapped towards my bedroom door. Like I could see through it, down the hall and into the hallway. I must have been playing for a long time because my body was stiff. I had no idea what time it was, but the sound of that knock on my door immediately sent my heart into a gallop.

Thoughts of Ben explaining what happened to the police in a way that got him out of trouble swarmed through my head. I hated him, I *hated* him.

I stormed out of my room and all but ripped the front door off its hinges, the rage rolling off me was palpable, "I swear to God, Be—," I stopped abruptly.

The words I was about to catapult at him along with the anger, the hurt, all died on my tongue.

It wasn't Ben at my door.

I didn't expect the baseball cap, he was always in a beanie, but I guess with the weather warming up, March brought with it the end of the winter hat season. So, I didn't know that it was him, not right away. He took off his cap and pushed his bright red hair back. His face was a mask of worry like I'd never seen before.

My hand shot to my mouth as a strangled sob escaped me and my legs gave way. It was only a second between that moment and next, when he was before me with his arms circled around me.

His smell enveloped me. It was nothing like what I had remembered, nothing like what I thought still clung to different parts of his shirt I sometimes wore to bed.

My forehead was on his chest as my hands gripped his shirt. He might have said something to me, might have placed a gentle kiss behind my ear, but I didn't hear it, I didn't really feel it. I was just focusing on him, on how the heaviness lifted and the grey receded back. How everything became brighter when he lifted me from the floor of the doorway of my apartment, closing it behind him and settled us onto my bed. He turned the lights off, tucked the blankets around us, and hummed softly while he ran his fingers through my hair.

I suddenly knew what Dax was to me, what I had been frightened to voice to Savannah all those months ago. What made me want to run and hide. It was scary to think about, but it was also the easiest thought that had ever fluttered through my mind.

Dax was *home.*

28

I woke up in what I was pretty sure was the middle of the night, still wearing my jeans, and incredibly uncomfortable.

That wasn't why I'd exited my R.E.M though. Allie had wiggled out of my hold and was shuffling off the end of the bed.

"Allie," I rubbed my eyes, my voice was still laced with sleep and where I usually would have just rolled over and headed back to dreamland, I'd woken with the painful reminder of her face when she opened her front door.

The anger in her voice I'd never heard before and, quite honestly, couldn't really picture someone like Allie being capable of producing. And then she crumpled to the floor and held onto my shirt like it was a lifeline.

I'd never been so desperate to know what to do in a situation. *What* do you do when that happens? Why did no one ever include that in any of the advice, warranted or not, that had always been shoved down my throat?

She turned to look at me, "Oh, sorry, I tried not to wake you." Her voice was soft, but alert like she'd been up for a while.

"Everything okay?" I propped myself up on my elbows.

"Yeah, I was hoping to sneak out undetected and steal your shoes but that's okay, I'll do it next time," her voice was whispered and very serious which made me smile.

I felt a little of the weight lift, "You're a terrible robber. You're not supposed to tell the target your plans," I whispered back.

"It's part of the whole thing. Now you'll always be worried I'm going to steal your shoes," she said while standing and turning to look at me.

I tipped my head back and let out a laugh. I had missed this. The in-person stuff. I'd missed *her*.

She gestured over her shoulder with her thumb, "I was going to make tea, can't sleep," she offered me a small smile.

"Want company?" I asked.

"Yeah, but it's too late to ask anyone to come over, that would just be mean to wake someone up this early," she said, turning towards the door.

I barked another laugh quietly at her sass, grateful to see it had made a comeback and got up and followed her into the kitchen.

I sat at the kitchen island while she made two cups of tea. She turned on a few of the lamps in the living room and the light cast us in a soft glow. She sat down across from me and nursed her favourite mug in her hands. It had the question 'what the schnitzel?' on the side with a stick figure shrugging with their hands up in an 'I don't know' gesture. One of the hands held a plate with a little orange blob that I assumed was meant to be a schnitzel.

That was Allie's favourite mug and it didn't surprise me one bit.

We sat in our comfortable silence for a while. I had drunk half my tea already before she spoke.

"I'm worried about what you'll think if I tell you," her eyes remained on her mug of tea.

"Anything you say won't change what I already think about you, Allie," I replied.

"And what is it that you already think?" Her eyes met mine.

"That you're a huge weirdo with too many throw pillows." My face couldn't have been any more serious.

She cracked a smile and it pushed my worry away a little farther.

I waited for her to start. I wouldn't ask her to tell me anything she wasn't comfortable in saying, I hoped she knew that too.

She took a deep breath and started from the beginning.

She told me about her accident.

God, I swear my stomach dropped out through the floor of her apartment. She spoke through it all like it was a rehearsed speech.

It moved from the accident onto Ben's involvement in her life. My stomach suddenly reappeared and went sour.

It was like once she started to explain what her life had been like for the last few years, and what *she* had been like, she couldn't stop.

I wondered if she'd ever had the opportunity to tell someone those events from her perspective before, like she was doing with me now.

I gripped my mug tighter and tighter the more she went on. How was there *more*? Where did she keep all that stuff? Where did she keep those memories and still find the time to joke about stealing my shoes in the middle of the night?

Allie didn't look at me once while she told me about her injuries, the time in hospital and the person that Ben was, who had been to her and the way he had treated her. Why he was around just before I had gotten back and what he'd said.

By the end of it, we sat in silence again, but it just felt *so loud*. I'd been in arenas full of screaming people and *this* was too loud for me.

Nothing deserved to be that quiet, that serene and still, while I'd just learned that the person I was in love with had endured things I couldn't even comprehend.

"Why didn't you say before? Not about Ben, but the accident? Or any of it, I guess. I could have…" I didn't know how to finish that sentence.

"I guess there were moments I could have mentioned it, but I was worried." She traced the rim of her mug with her pointer.

"About?" I prompted.

"No one has ever looked at me the way you do, Dax. I didn't want that to change, how you looked at me, laughed with me—"

"*At* you," I corrected her. A smile lit up her face immediately.

"I'm sorry that your welcome-home party after something so exciting was so drab." She tucked a loose strand of hair behind her ear.

"No," I got up and walked around the island, she swivelled on her stool to look at me.

For all our banter, our back and forth and jokes and poking fun, I looked her right in her eyes, bright and clear, and urged her to believe everything I was about to say

"You don't apologise for things like that, Allie. For any of it. For your accident or for how he made you feel. None of it has ever been, or ever will be, your fault. I'm sorry if no one has ever taken the time to tell you that. I'm sorry I hadn't been here with you. *I'm* sorry that you couldn't tell me sooner. I swear, Allie, I won't ever hurt you like that," I leaned in and kissed her forehead.

I didn't know if that was good, or the right thing to say. If it was too much or too little.

Her arms looped around my waist, and that's how we stayed until I was sure our tea was cold, and the sun was going to peak up around the buildings of the city outside soon.

Allie took a big inhale, like a massive sniff.

"Are you smelling me?" I stepped back to look at her, a smile already ghosting my lips.

"Absolutely, I am. You've been gone for three months and now I realise that I've really just been smelling myself on the shirt you left here," she explained, letting her arms drop.

"You've been smelling my shirt?" I lifted an eyebrow and clamped my lips shut. Allie hopped off her stool and took our cups to the sink.

"Like my life depended on it," she replied and I cracked, a laugh bubbled out of me. I laughed, of course, but there wasn't a single part of me that wasn't elated to hear that she had been sleeping in one of my shirts.

Allie walked down the hall, flipped me off over her shoulder, grabbed her robe from her room and went to have a shower.

It was a lot later than I thought, it was almost 6:30AM and I knew the Allie would have to leave for work soon, so I decided to duck out while she was in the shower and grab some coffees and croissants. Our usual.

I picked up her keys and locked the door to her apartment on my way out, not entirely comfortable leaving it open given all the new information I had just learned. Even if Dean had stepped up, which surprised me as much as it had surprised Allie. For all his faults, he was a good guy. I'll think about buying him something orange as a thank you.

Holding the bag of pastry between my teeth, I unlocked the door to her apartment and pushed it open with my back. I turned to find Allie standing at the end of the hallway in her fuzzy robe. I lifted the takeaways and paper bag up.

"Breakfast?" I grinned at her.

"I thought you left," she said back, her voice a little too sad to be funny. Her expression looked a little too lost.

"Oh, I did," I walked by her, planted a kiss on her temple and sat the bag and cups on the counter, "I was actually running like the wind; you should have seen me," I continued as I grabbed a couple plates from the cupboard.

"Oh?" she said, her face lifted as she finally caught on. I'd be damned though, if the tightness in my chest didn't ease at seeing her light up.

"Mmm. Olympic quality," I put a croissant on each plate.

"I'm sorry I missed it," she laughed.

I walked over and grabbed her hand. I led her to a stool and pulled it out for her to sit before I took the lid off one of the coffee cups and put it in front of her.

"What made you change your mind?" she said around a mouth full of chocolate and pastry.

"I haven't had your 6 out of 10 meatballs yet," my response was spoken around a bite equally as large which earned the biggest snort-laugh I'd heard yet.

29

ALLIE

Dax walked me right to the doors of my office building. His hair was tucked away tightly into the baseball cap he had worn to mine straight off the plane and with a kiss farewell, and the assurance that Aspen was on his way to grab him, I headed into the office.

I tapped the elevator call button until the doors opened and stepped inside. I was the only one going up. It was refreshing.

I swear, Allie, I won't ever hurt you like that.

Dax's words circled around my mind like a canoe with only one paddle.

It's not like I never thought someone would say that to me, like I thought I was going to be alone forever and never share with someone the ongoings of the last three years of my life. I had thought I'd meet someone, tell them of my past and that I'd hear those exact words. What I didn't realise was that when I heard them, I'd believe them.

And I did, I believed every word that Dax had said which was… weird. And sort of freeing, like I was a little bird pushed out of the nest and I had about 4 seconds to learn how to fly for the first time or *splat.* I was kaput.

This is going to sound really stupid, but I *did* feel like I was flying, or at least moving farther away from the nearing ground rather than closer to it.

Allie: *Have a good day. Thank you*

for breakfast and smelling so great.

Dax: *I am going to sleep for forever.*
You can just transfer me for the coffee
whenever.

I huffed a laugh, taking the time to think of the perfect reply that would make him pee himself just a little, but it seemed I had taken just that little bit too long.

"Alice!" There was nowhere in the world I wouldn't have recognised that voice. Unfortunately.

For anyone who wondered or really cared, my boss's name was Bart.

Yes, exactly like the character from the Simpsons. Better yet, his full first name was Bartholomew and he used it whenever he was speaking to any other bigwigs that came in for a yarn.

I looked it up, he told everyone that it meant he was the great descendent of some important person. Anyone with two fingers and a phone could've told you that there was no version of this reality where that was true in any capacity.

I called him Bart the Fart, and I was equally excited and terrified that I would one day say it out loud to his face. I mean, could you *imagine?*

"My office," he said, pointing at the small glass square behind him. All the drapes were drawn as they always were.

I dropped my stuff at my desk before I walked in. I kept the door open as I sat down.

"Shut the door, please," he said, and I was confident he waited until I had taken my seat before he said it, just so I'd have to get back up.

That was the sort of person Bart the Fart was.

"Where were you yesterday? Take the day off when you knew you'd messed up on the campaign?" His eyebrows were raised high like he was satisfied in catching me in the act of avoiding my responsibilities.

"I wasn't feeling well. I actually spent the whole day in bed. You had mentioned on Wednesday that the campaign went well, I didn't realise there were so many faults," I replied as politely as possible, trying to keep my eyes off the sweat patches that had soaked through his blazer.

"Well, there was a shit-storm of issues yesterday with the choice of asset used for our Facebook ads, Alice." His eyebrows didn't move, like they were taped up.

"Bart, Sir, I am not in charge of the assets, that's Allegra's responsibility. I put together the plan and then monitor for opportunities of optimization through the course of the campaign," I explained.

We'd had this conversation more times than I could remember, but I was continuously impressed on how well I managed to hold myself every time. I really wanted to tell him to stick his asset up his ass.

"Alice, is your role not the *Marketing Manager*?" he said it like it was an insult.

"It is," I replied.

"Then *manage* the *fucking* marketing," his eyebrows still didn't move, but his attention did finally drift from my face.

"Absolutely," I said.

You pimple of a man.

"I'll get right on it," I stood up.

I bet you've never gotten laid.

I walked out of his office feeling a lot better with the additions to my responses I had said internally. I was a positive person. I was the sort of glass-half-full person. But even I could admit that everyone has a threshold, and I just didn't need that today.

I was thinking about all the hard days I'd hit consecutively and pumped myself up that the good days were around the corner. This world demanded balance; I could dig that. I wasn't selfish enough to believe that I was the only person alive who deserved all good days and no bad ones, but surely there was a scale or something that determined how shit one's day was and how many other shitty days they should then incur afterward.

I spent the rest of the day thinking about that. About the scale on which my days sat. I didn't just dwell on the bad ones though, I had so many 10 out of 10 days in the last 6 months that I really had nothing to complain about.

As true as that was, there was nothing that could have stopped me from picking up a box of brownie mix on my way home.

I sent a photo of them to Dax.

Dax: *I really hope I never meet your boss.*

I would accidentally sneeze in his salad.

I was laughing to myself like a mad woman as I continued down the street to my apartment, thinking about all the ways that I would one day quit and make my dramatic exit from that company. How I would really stick it to the man by throwing a stack of paper into the air and not care in the slightest who had to pick it up. Maybe photocopy my ass and print it out a hundred times and put a copy in everyone's 'in' drawers.

Once, I had walked by a little dog turd on my way to work and thought about all the different reactions that Bart would have if I placed it on his desk for him to find when he walked in.

That made me laugh even more. I hadn't entirely ruled out that particular event from ever coming to fruition. It was in the vault. Just in case.

People could judge me all they wanted, but if they had their ass grabbed by someone named Bart the Fart who perspired through his thick polyester blazer, they'd be thinking about it too.

Dax: *Want me to come round?*

Yes, a thousand times yes.

Allie: *I can feel your lack of energy from*

here. It's okay, you sleep. Message me tomorrow when your reserves are no longer depleted.

Dax: *Save one for me.*

I made the brownies.

I made them really well too.

The top glistened and the edges had a nice crust. I sliced into them and if you were imagining a nice gooey centre, you would be on the nose. They were the gooiest, and I didn't want them.

I didn't want a single one.

I waved hello to Dean as he walked in, he asked if he could have one and I wasn't defensive at all. I even told him he could have two. *Two.*

I didn't have dinner either, I thought that maybe my body thought it needed dinner before dessert, which had never been an issue before, but it had been a weird week for me to say the least so if my body's response to brownies was altered I would understand. But, the urge to gorge never came.

By the time I looked away from the brownies sitting on the plate in front of me it was midnight.

Midnight.

So that meant I had been sitting and looking at a plate of warm brownies slowly going cold for 6 hours.

I lifted my phone from where it sat face down on the counter and it unlocked immediately when it took in my face.

My phone was still open on my messages with Dax.

I sat and looked at it for a while, at the last conversation we'd had.

I grabbed the plate of brownies and threw some cling wrap over them. Pulled on my jacket and hopped into my shoes as I raced out of my apartment. I had the mind to close the door quietly as to not wake Dean, then I was full speed ahead.

I knew where Dax lived. It was a 40-minute walk from my apartment, but if I ran I could make it in half that time.

I didn't even know if he was going to be home, or awake, or whatever.

I ran, holding the plate of brownies out in front of me like I was in an egg and spoon race. My Chucks smacking the sidewalk and echoing back off the buildings around me.

I kept my eyes mostly on the ground and for every car that drove by, I turned my head away, avoiding the glare of their lights.

I managed to run for about 10 minutes.

10 minutes and I was so sure I was going to die. Oh my god.

My determination and my grip on the plate of brownies didn't falter, even though my stamina had let me down.

I walked and walked and walked.

I was standing face to face with the base of his intimidating building. My heart was thundering with the very idea that he might be up on the top floor, as well as from the mini marathon I'd just completed.

What was I doing here?

No, I knew.

I knew what I was doing here.

I pressed the call button for his floor.

Can we just… his *whole* floor.

Yeah, I'd get used to that when pigs flew.

I buzzed again, and again. The fact that it was now almost 1AM didn't stop me.

I went to buzz again but stopped myself. I had called up more times than what should have been required.

He wasn't home. That was fine, he might have been out with his brother or—

"Hello?" Dax's sleepy voice croaked through the little speaker.

I didn't even hesitate, "It's Allie."

He might have said something back, and I could have totally missed his response over the pounding of my heart, but I didn't think he said anything. There was a little wait and then the door buzzed and clanged, and I pulled it open.

My momentum had slowed down during the wait, but I still tapped the button for the elevator with a speed I wished I had been able to run here with.

It finally arrived and I hopped in, tapping the top button.

37.

It lit up without needing a card to scan and took me all the way up.

It was the longest elevator ride of my life.

My heart had calmed down by the time the doors pinged open, and showed Dax pacing back and forth in nothing but his boxers, his red hair askew in every direction.

"Jesus Christ, Allie. Are you okay? How did you get here, what—," he stopped, "are those brownies?" He had every right to look as confused as he did.

"I walked here," I said.

"You *walked* here?"

"And yes, they're brownies. They're like 10-points-to-Allie sort of brownies too," I handed him the plate and he took them, looking at the plate, to my face then back to the plate and back to my face.

"10-points-to-Allie?" He looked dumbfounded, "You give yourself points?" His face broke out into the biggest shit-eating grin.

I just seriously have no filter.

"Just blink twice if I'm right," he continued, lifting his eyebrows.

I knew my face was the colour of his hair, so I tactfully changed the subject.

"Did I wake up Aspen too?" I enquired, none the wiser, peering around him to look for his brother.

Dax pushed his hair back with one hand, letting out an exhale and clearly not as phased by my weirdness as he ought to be, "No, he went out with Rip. They don't really get affected by jet lag, or so they say." He shook his head, "You could have called me, I would have come over and gotten you and your 10-points-to-Allie brownies, or I could have come round to yours for the night or something."

I was sure he was thinking about yesterday, but that wasn't why I had walked all the way to his.

I rolled my eyes at me, "No, it's— well, I made the brownies," I nodded towards the plate in his hands, "But I didn't eat any."

"You didn't?" He looked at the plate that was clearly missing two brownies.

"That was Dean," I clarified. He rolled his eyes, earning a smile from me.

"I made them, and I didn't want them. I stared at them for 6 hours and I didn't want a single bite," I said, looking at his face.

"You spent 6 hours staring at brownies? How do you know they're worthy of 10 points if you didn't try any?" He was trying not to laugh.

"Dax!" I whined, "you're missing the point."

He sobered up but kept on his signature side smirk, "What's the point, Allie?"

"The brownies weren't going to fix it. They weren't what I wanted," my voice had dropped down, and though I was speaking low and quiet, it still felt too loud for the stillness of his apartment.

Dax's eyes darkened immediately. He took in my own features as the reason why I had walked almost an hour to his apartment in the middle of the night clicked into place.

He set the brownies down on the floor just beside me, next to the doors of the elevator. His breathing had quickened ever so slightly, and I was suddenly painfully aware that he was in his underwear, and only his underwear, right in front of me.

"Mmm?" The weight of his gaze was literally like nothing I'd ever experienced.

"Yes, well, I thought about it, and then I thought of you. And I thought of you and me, well… I mean, then *naturally* I thought of us. I guess what I'm *trying* to say is—"

"What did you want, Allie?" His voice was thick.

"You," I breathed, and I reached for him.

His hands were in my hair, they roamed down the sides of my neck and continued to move up and down my body like he didn't know what to do, where to start.

My arms were locked around his neck and my own hands had found their standard place of residence in his hair.

His hair. I tugged at it a bit, earning a throaty sound that would be my absolute undoing.

He tugged at my jacket in response, not breaking from our kiss as he pushed it from my shoulders, and it landed on the floor behind me.

He started moving us backwards and, with every step towards his room, another article of my clothing was left behind. I cast a thought to what someone might've thought if they arrived here and saw my clothes paving the way to Dax's room, but I didn't care. In fact, I sort of liked it.

I'll be damned, who was this person and what have they done with the Alice Charlotte Jamison I know.

I'd admit, taking off my slacks - the same ones I had worn to work because I hadn't changed and just spent the whole evening staring at baked goods - was a definite interruption to the kissing.

Dax unbuttoned and helped me shimmy them down. I almost *fell over* which had us both laughing. Dax stopped our retreat and bent down to remove the pants entirely considering they were a health and safety hazard. His words exactly.

That moment sort of slowed everything down. I stood back up after using his crouched frame for support as he tossed the slacks away.

He placed a soft kiss on the inner side of my knee and looked up at me. He kept my gaze the whole way up to his impressive height before his eyes roamed my features again.

"Is this okay?" he whispered as his hands moved down my shoulders to my arms.

I nodded my head, "Yes. More than okay."

He bent down to lift me up, my legs circling around his waist and he walked us the rest of the way into his room, nudging the door closed gently.

Our kisses changed then, they were no longer frantic or greedy, they were exactly the sort of kisses that said the words I struggled to find the courage to say, the words I was *afraid* to say no matter how true they might have been. The sort of kisses that made it so you didn't really need to say it out loud at all, he'd just know. He had to know.

The weight of Dax settling above me was an experience in and of itself.

He held himself up just enough, but I felt every inch of his skin against mine.

Our hands explored one another. We had done that before, I had traced the planes of his chest and felt the dips and lines of his back, and he knew my own body about as well as I knew it myself. But this was different. This felt new, this felt like *more.*

My whole body erupted into goosebumps as Dax traced the line of my jaw with his lips.

I was going to combust, Lord help me.

"You're so beautiful, Allie," Dax mumbled against my skin.

"You are," I said back, breathless.

"I know," he said, his mouth still lazily followed a path I couldn't see, but one he knew well, across the different surfaces of my body.

I snorted a laugh.

Of all the times to snort-laugh, that was not it, Allie.

Dax drew back and looked down at me with his sexy side smirk, "That was so hot, do it again."

I burst out laughing. He wagged his eyebrows at me, and I brought my hands up to cover my face.

"Oh *shit,* I'm so sorry," I couldn't stop laughing.

"I could pass some gas if that would make things even?" he enquired which made me snort-laugh again, louder.

"Dax! That's totally ruined the moment." The giggle fit finally dissipated as I met his eyes once more.

"Has it?" His face settled back into a mask of calm, of expectation and, *hot damn,* so much lust I could have caught on fire.

"No, it hasn't." I pulled him down to me and he settled his weight on me again. I sighed into him.

Dax reached over to his top drawer and grabbed something out of it. He leaned back and ripped open the little square pack with his teeth.

Fuck, I completely forgot.

20 points for Dax, cause that little detail completely evaded my mind during the almost hour stroll to get here and every moment since.

The pressure was slight to start, but the closer we became, the more intense it felt.

My eyes quite literally rolled to the back of my head and the little habit of mine that involved his name and my tongue popped back into existence after going dormant since our first encounter.

He halted as my eyes closed completely.

The only sound for a moment was our breathing and then Dax leaned down and placed a kiss on both my eyelids. Yes, it felt about as sweet as it sounded.

I opened them to see him there above me, looking at me in the way that he did.

My throat clogged with emotion.

I never wanted that to change. I'd never not want to have him look at me like that. I didn't even know someone *could* look at me like that.

"Hey," he said, beginning to move again.

"Hey," I whispered back, reaching for him.

I had never been more grateful for jet lag, or more accurately Dax's brothers lack thereof, and I was infinitely more pleased that we had the entire penthouse to ourselves.

30

Allie

Someone was yelling from Dax's living room.

The phrases *oh my god* and *she's here* were repeated over and over and then there was a knock at Dax's door.

"Go away, Aspen," Dax croaked from behind me.

We were curled up. Me, the little spoon to his big spoon. His breath tickled the back of my neck.

"I can't do that Dax. I have to come in," Aspen's voice held a bitter sweetness, like he didn't want to, but he had no other choice.

The dramatics of their family, I swear...

"What is wrong with you? We'll be out soon," Dax's voice, on the other hand, was exasperated. I had already started to shake with laughter.

"I'm giving you five more seconds to get decent, and I think you'll need them considering that our hallway is now Allie's closet."

"*Oh no*, my clothes," I breathed, embarrassed. I turned in Dax's arms, "*My clothes*!" I repeated in a whisper-shout.

He just took in my face and gave me a sleepy half smile. He kissed my nose and then without any warning, he grabbed me and rolled us over, so his back was now to the door. I made a very unladylike squeal, sort of like pig.

Not a second later Aspen walked in.

"Aspen, get out," Dax grabbed the pillow and threw it at his brother. It hit him directly in the face and then dropped to the floor. It was hilarious and I was properly cackling.

"The infamous Wallie, at last," Aspen let out a sigh of relief, and raised both arms as if in praise.

Finally, someone who is weirder than me. Win.

I poked my head up and gave him my biggest smile, "Hey, Aspen."

"Allie! Nice to finally see you actually exist and that Dax's wallpaper isn't a random photo off the internet," he winked at me, "I'm making pancakes, get up. It's already brunch time," Aspen said over his shoulder as he walked out of Dax's room.

"Brunch time?" I mouthed to Dax. He just shook his head as if to say, 'don't even get him started'.

Dax, ever the gentleman, gathered my more delicate garments and handed them to me before braving the hallway, and his brothers exuberant singing of our ship name, for the rest of my clothes.

As soon as Dax left, I reached for his phone. There I was, my guitar on my lap and smiling like an idiot. When he came back into his room, his arms full of my clothes, I turned his phone screen towards him.

"When did you do this?" My voice was the epitome of disbelief.

"When we were on tour." He climbed back onto the bed and settled next to me, placing a kiss just behind my ear.

"I think that earns you 10 points," I leaned into him.

"Oh? I get points too?" he murmured, close enough to feel the whisper of his words.

"Mmm," I kissed him. His phone was forgotten quickly, and I regretted starting to get dressed.

"Wallie! Pancakes!" Ap yelled from the kitchen.

"For the love of all that's holy," Dax dropped his forehead to my shoulder.

"I sort of hope he says that to us in public sometime," I winked at Dax, my head tipped back in laughter at the horrified expression on his face. I gave him a quick kiss on the corner of his mouth, "Mmm. We'll have to be faster next time," I leaned away from him with an exaggerated exhale and reached for my pants.

"You always know just what to say to boost my confidence, Allie."

Dax was beaming at me while he grabbed some pants of his own, but he chose to forgo the shirt. I just rolled my eyes at him and reached my hand out.

"Let's go get our Wallie-cakes," I led us out into the hallway.

Dax had quickly typed something into his phone and then chucked it on the bed on our way out. I couldn't help but wonder what that was about.

"Don't ever repeat that word, ever again," Dax pushed his hair back from his face and grimaced.

I got to meet Aspen properly then. *Properly* being defined as in person and not naked.

It was sort of noticeable when I saw him through video chat, but in person, Aspen looked so like his brother it took me a bit by surprise.

Aspen was a couple of years younger than Dax, and his face showed it. Whereas Dax's natural hair colour was black, Aspen's was a dark brown. Expressive brows of the same colouring sat above eyes that were such a bright green that you *felt* warm just looking at them. They were kind. The real difference, though, between him and Dax, was their smiles.

Dax's smile, the one I saw, the one he gave just to me, was soft and small and it was almost like it rarely ever saw the light. Aspen's smile was sun kissed and unrelenting.

Meeting Aspen was just as I thought it was going to be like. We had spoken a fair amount over the last three months, and I already felt like I knew him, so when we sat down to have pancakes, it was like we'd done it hundreds of times before.

"Those were the best pancakes I've ever had," I leaned back and patted my stomach.

"Well, we have to balance each other out," Aspen replied, setting his own fork down on his empty plate. I arched an eyebrow in question.

He pointed to himself, "Sweet," and then he pointed at Dax, "Savoury."

"Ahh. Did you know when we met, he told me that 'cooking wasn't for everyone', told me that you were the cook in the family and then proceeded to whip up a storm in the kitchen?" I said to Aspen as I narrowed my eyes at

Dax.

Aspen just sat there grinning like he had the front row seat to a show he'd always wanted to see.

"I never said I couldn't cook," Dax defended himself, still eating his pancakes.

"It was *implied,* and you know it!" I pointed an accusatory finger at him.

"Allie, you struggled to turn on your stove top," he looked at me, an eyebrow raised, daring me to keep going.

He had a point.

"Yeah, well, you've never had a box brownie as good as mine," I slumped back into my stool.

"That," Dax pointed his fork at me, "is very true. They're delicious," he leaned over and kissed me on the cheek.

Aspen wrinkled his nose at the mention of dessert that wasn't made from scratch.

I was rolling my eyes so much lately, I swear they were going to permanently remain looking towards my frontal lobes if I wasn't careful.

Dax sorted me out with the necessary things for a shower. He had one of those rain showers where the water stream just fell from the ceiling. It was incredible and I stayed in for so long that he came to knock on the door to see if I was okay.

By the time I had dried off, dressed and made my way out into the living room, the brothers were having a very quiet argument.

"What's going on?" I was standing at the top of the stairs, observing them from above.

"Aspen thinks he's going to drive you home," Dax couldn't have sounded more unimpressed.

"That would be great, Ap," I thanked him and tried to keep the gracious look on my features while I had a mental breakdown regarding my calling him by Dax's nickname.

At what point did you start to call someone by a nickname they had been given by someone else?

"I mean, Aspen. Sorry," I winced at how awkward I sounded.

Definitely deducting 5 points for that awesome little performance.

His face softened, "Ap is good, Al," he winked at me.

Only Savannah called me Al. I wonder what she would think when I told her that the nickname had now been commandeered by someone else.

"I'll take her home, Aspen," Dax interrupted my little thought bubble.

"I've met her once, Dax. I just want to talk to her," he turned to look at me. His gaze morphed from casual to mischievous between one blink and the next, "Get to know my future sister-in-law better. And plus, Allie wants to get to know me too, don't you Allie?"

I'm not sure what my face did, but whatever the visual was, Aspen's turned red from the strain of holding in his laughter and Dax looked positively mortified. My entire body erupted into goosebumps and I wanted to scream and cry at the same time.

Holy sheep shearing, grandma knitting, sweater vests.

Sister-in-law.

Get a grip Allie, hold it in.

I swallowed the swarm of butterflies that threatened to fly out of my mouth. Dax spun back towards his brother and I swear I'd never seen a man move so fast in my life .

I composed myself as quickly as I could with a promise to my internal self-hype woman to die over that little moment later in the safety of my own room.

Clearing my throat, I decided I would ghost over the entire ordeal, but not before taking a mental snap of the expression still plastered on Dax's face, the man was speechless.

I had never been a good actress, so despite my own confidence that I could pretend Ap didn't just say what he said, my voice came out in a high pitched squeak, "Then it's settled."

Any handle both Dax and Aspen had on their expressions cracked and they tipped their heads back in laughter.

Ah. Must be a Smith family thing.

I walked down the stairs, a small smile of my own on my face and gave Dax a peck on the cheek and a sassy tap on the bum before I headed towards the elevator.

"Aren't we hanging out today?" he pouted at me, shirtless and standing in his living room. He'd almost completely recovered from the whole sister-in-law ordeal.

"Tomorrow? I need to clean my apartment and do washing and gross adult things," I made a gagging sound.

"Okay, tomorrow. That works," he nodded.

I ran back over and gave him another kiss before trying for a mad dash, but he caught my arm and pulled me back. I squeaked and he laughed, it was so cute that it was gross.

"You guys are so cute, it's gross. Come on, Al," Aspen hit the call button for the elevator. He only hit it once which gave me the heebie-jeebies.

Because I couldn't help it, I stole a third kiss from Dax and tossed my most casual farewell over my shoulder, "Toodles!"

I froze where I was.

No, Allie. No, no. You literally just *slept with him. You needed to wait before the accents came out.*

"Wait, wait a second, what was that?" Dax's face was the picture of flat out shock.

I turned on my heels to look at him, completely mortified that I'd just flung out my Swedish accent impression to him with zero context given. Dax didn't know about my flare for accents.

"That was nothing," I could feel my face going beet-red.

"Don't tell me. You do impressions," he lost it, laughing without any restraint.

"I do not do impressions," I said. I lifted my chin a little higher, "I do accents and that was Swedish, I'll have you know. A very good take on it, too."

"Hold on, Allie," Dax was wiping tears from his eyes, "say it again, please, do it again." He was bending at the waist with his hands on his knees.

I rolled my eyes, stuck my tongue out and headed towards the elevator. It shut with Dax, cry-laughing while apologising and I think he was trying to assure me that it was incredibly accurate as far as Swedish accents went. I couldn't be sure, but I think he fell to his knees at the end there.

I huffed a laugh as the elevator doors closed. I thought about the next time I would see him and how I'd bring out the Scottish accent that I personally thought was my best work. He was going to wet his pants. I couldn't wait.

The silence on the way down with Aspen wasn't uncomfortable, but it wasn't like it was with Dax.

I was asking him about his day as we walked out of the elevator and into the basement parking of their building. He told me about how he was going to unpack as well and that there was a new video game out that he wanted so that he and Angus could verse one another, so he was probably going to order it online.

He was still going on when I looked from him to the entry ramp.

A car had just pulled in. It was daytime, so I wasn't being mindful or careful about the headlights of oncoming vehicles, but I should have been. I always needed to remember.

So, when the car entered the basement we were in - it was much darker than it was outside - the automatic headlights snapped on. I immediately stopped hearing things and my breathing started to quicken.

No. Please, no.

I was acutely aware of being around Aspen, and that this was not something I had told his brother when I mentioned my accident.

It all started to happen - the headlights flashed behind my eyes and I felt myself flinch away, covering my ears as the horn blared in my ears. My fingers had started to go numb, vibrating with pins and needles and I knew that I called out but what I said or how loud, I had no idea.

Like there was a door and I was being pushed farther away from it, the light to the exit getting dimmer and dimmer as I curled farther and farther into myself. It was crippling.

"Breathe."

It wasn't Savannah's voice that spoke to me then. I had all but forgotten for a moment who I was with or where I was, but I listened.

I inhaled. Not nearly enough air for what I needed but it was air all the same.

The hand that tried to soothe me was not the one I was used to. Instead of Savannah's circular motions on my back, Aspen gently dragged his hand up and down.

It was different but grounding all the same.

"Breathe," he said again.

I wasn't sure how many more times he said it, or how long I had been sitting on the floor of the garage with my hands over my ears and my knees against my chest. Aspen was sitting next to me, his hand still making a gentle trail up and down my back.

I finally lifted my head up, turning to look at him. Unshed tears of embarrassment were sitting in my eyes.

"I'm so sorry," I croaked out to him.

His face adopted a look of confusion that was so like his brother's it made me yearn to run back up to the thirty-seventh floor.

"Why would you be sorry for that, Allie? You don't ever need to apologise for having an anxiety attack. You can't pick and choose when they happen. Don't apologise," he gave me a small smile that made me want to fall apart all over again.

It's not like Sav had never told me that it wasn't my fault, that I didn't need to apologise, but for some reason when Aspen said it, when *Dax* said it, it felt different.

"I had a car accident three years ago," I explained.

"You don't have to—," Aspen started.

I shook my head, "No, no. It's fine. I have PTSD because of it. Headlights are a problem for me. It's why I don't drive," I finished.

Aspen nodded his head and was silent for a moment, "Does Dax know?" His question wasn't loaded with expectation, just with an honest enquiry. Like 'if I told him about this, would he lose his mind?' sort of thing.

I nodded, "He knows about the accident. I hadn't quite gotten to this part yet. It's a lot to absorb. I *am* going to tell him. I just don't know how," I said honestly. And it was true, I didn't know how to explain to another person that this was my every day. Not everyone got it, understood it, or even accepted it.

It was why I hadn't let my work know about it. Could you imagine Bart the Fart if he knew about it?

Aspen stood up and held his hands out to me to help me to my feet.

"Thanks for your help," I mumbled.

He waved me off as we walked the rest of the way to his beat-up sedan, "Don't mention it, Al."

"How did you—," I started.

"I had a friend in high school who struggled with anxiety. Big crowds, small spaces, that kind of thing. They taught me a lot about how to help someone in that situation," Aspen unlocked the car. It made a loud *beep* that caused me to jump, my heart rate fluttered but I kept a handle on it.

"Well, I'm grateful for your friend," I slid into the passenger seat that had become so familiar to me. It'd been months since I sat in it last, but it felt like sliding on a pair of old jeans that were just my size.

The drive back to mine was equally as silent as the elevator, but almost more comfortable.

The day was beautiful. It was warm and gave the first taste of true spring as the last of winter melted away. Despite the situation that had just occurred in the basement of Dax's building, I felt… well, I felt freaking top-dog for lack of a better phrase.

I felt like that kid at the birthday party who filled up their plastic cup with some kind of delicious beverage and then proceeded to tip it upside down then right side up super-fast without spilling the drink and everyone was like 'woah, no way!'.

That was how I felt. Like the kid who could keep their juice in their plastic cup when doing the fancy magic trick.

Not only was the sun shining, but I had just had the best sex of my *life* with the guy that I was so in love with that I was putting every rom-com I'd seen and read to shame.

I felt like a phoenix from the ashes.

Was that weird to say? Probably.

It gave me an idea.

I turned to Aspen, "Hey Ap, if I wanted to do something for Dax, like a surprise, could you help?"

Aspen's grin was blinding, "Whatever Wallie needs, Wallie gets."

31

I was in my guitar room when Aspen got home.

"Hey, Ap!" I called out.

I heard him dump his keys and then make his way up the small set of stairs.

"Hey, I have this new chord progression I was thinking would be good for the lyrics you—," I looked up to find him standing in the doorway, his hand rubbing the back of his neck and it looked like he either had some really bad gas or something bad had happened.

"What?" My heart jumped into my throat, "What?" I said again. I pulled the guitar strap over my head and set the instrument back in the stand, turning off the amp.

"Come sit for a second," Ap just turned away and headed back towards the living room. I was on his heels but didn't pester him until we sat down.

He told me everything that had happened. He told me what Allie had told him - she didn't know how to explain it to me and that though he didn't feel like it was his place, it might help to not have to tell me herself.

He mentioned the PTSD, the anxiety and the panic attack. The headlights.

It was like hearing about her accident all over again.

I knew of Aspen's friend from high school, so I knew that, by whatever grace, he was the perfect person to have been with her. I knew he would have known what to do, how to help her.

If it had been me, I'm not sure I would've known. I still felt like when she told me about the accident and Ben, that I should have said something more, done something more.

"Did she tell you about the accident?" I asked him after a beat. Once he had told me about the basement, we both just sat for a while.

"Just that she was in one," he dragged a hand down his face and slumped back into the couch with an exhale.

I nodded back.

"Did she know you were going to say something? Like, if I were to call her would this be crossing a line or something?" I pushed my hair back from my face.

"I think she assumed I would mention it. She didn't say not to, maybe she thought it would be easier this way too, for me to tell you," he replied softly.

"She's not broken, Ap." It came out sterner than I had intended.

I hated the way he was looking, like he felt sorry for her or that maybe how she looked changed in his eyes. Rationally, I knew he didn't think those things, but it was almost a reflex to think that. To defend her. To be angry at the people who treated her differently or less than, all because she had gone through something horrible and come out the other side still smiling.

"I didn't say she was, Dax," his response was equally as defensive. I knew he cared about her already, it was just the kind of guy he was. Aspen had a big heart and was all fun, all the time. A little - okay, a whole butt load - dramatic, but he could turn on his serious side faster than you could say 'Wallie-cakes.'

"It's okay to call her, Dax," his face had softened. His eyes then took on a glint that told me he had moved on from the heavy, that he had passed on what he needed to and that he was going to step back now, "If I hear any loud moaning coming from your room, I will not hesitate to post the photo of you, butt naked in a paddling pool, on the internet," he got up and headed for the stairs, no doubt to his drum room.

"For fuck's sake, Aspen. I was 5! It is perfectly normal to swim naked at that age!" I called after him, and just like that, the mood changed.

"We could totally just let the internet decide, if you're so confident!" he retorted just before closing the door.

I rolled my eyes and flipped him off. I stood up and grabbed Aspen's keys before heading straight for the basement.

She picked up on the first ring.

I was sitting outside her apartment building. My heart had been racing the whole drive over and wasn't letting up even after I had sat, staring at the window I knew looked into her living room, for the last thirty minutes.

"Hey," she sounded tired.

"Hey yourself, what's going on?" I tried my best to sound relaxed, or as normal as I usually did.

"Nothing too much. I put on some laundry and now I'm laying in bed. I was going to try and play the guitar for a bit but I'm exhausted," she yawned.

"How are your chords going?" I knew my smile was apparent in my voice.

"Yes, I am incredibly good at the four I know. I think I'm about ready for the next four," she sounded so proud.

"Wax on, wax off, grasshopper," I said in my most serious voice, I could practically *hear* her rolling her eyes.

"You know I saw you, like, two hours ago," she changed the subject.

"Yeah, I know." It was silent for a little while, but that was normal for us.

"Ap said?" she enquired. She knew that I'd know what she meant.

"Yeah, he mentioned," I replied. I jumped out of the car, letting the door close lightly and jogged across the street to her building.

"I'm sorry I didn't tell you. I *wanted* to tell you, I just thought between the accident and Ben, the third little nugget of truth would have broken the horse's back," she said quietly. I could picture her playing with the frilly edges of one of her throw pillows.

I knew why she would have felt that way. Now that I knew about Ben, I could get a grasp on her reasonings more easily. It still didn't change the fact that I wanted to be there for her.

The elevator doors opened, and I pressed the number to her floor, then I tapped the button to close the doors until they shut.

"It wouldn't have," was all I said back.

"You don't know that, Dax. It's one thing to hear it, and another to see it. It's not this romantic thing where you're a hero swooping in to save the damsel situation," I could hear her heavy breathing through the phone.

"I don't think you need saving, Allie. Maybe some cooking lessons, but that's probably about it," I stepped out of the elevator and walked the few steps to her apartment door.

I heard her huff a laugh, "Dax— Oh, one second someone just knocked on my door."

I pocketed my phone. If I could have captured the look on her face when she opened the door, I would have been the proud owner of the newest viral meme image.

She was wearing a long, bright pink pyjama shirtdress. The colour was completely not Allie, but the phrase on the front, however, was without a doubt on brand.

It had a groundhog on the front of it that had a long winded explanation about how groundhogs and woodchucks were the same animal, then proceeded to write out the corrected version of 'how much wood could a woodchuck chuck' which was, of course, 'how much ground, could a groundhog mound'.

Like I said, very Allie.

If you're imagining the writing going all the way to the bottom of the shirtdress and not just the standard slogan spacing being in the middle of the chest, then you're correct. I had to ask her at some point where she even bought her clothes.

"What the shi—what are you doing here?" she asked, a little breathless.

"I figured that you might need some help with your adult things today," I explained, running a hand through my hair.

"Dax—," she started, a little frown forming.

"I know you're capable, it's not that. I want to be there for you, Allie. I don't want to do it for you, I just want to help you do it. Make things a bit easier, lighten the load, brighten the day—," she interrupted me then.

"If I don't stop you there, I don't think you'll ever stop," she said, her frown ironing out. She was fighting a smile.

I continued anyway, "Balance the scale a bit, be the fruit to your vegetables—"

"You're just saying things now," her smile broke through.

"Be the knife to your fork—," I was very quickly running out of things to say.

"If I let you in will you stop?" she said with so much sass I could have choked, but her face was mischievous.

"Only if I get to fold your delicates," I followed her into her apartment and closed the door behind me. She barked a laugh so loudly that I jolted, making myself laugh.

It made me think of something that was completely unrelated.

"When's your birthday?" she turned to look at me as I asked.

She was familiar with our questions game, so she just went with it, "Start of December," she said, "Just before we met, actually. When's yours?"

"End of November," I walked up to her and pulled her to me. "Let me in, Allie. I can handle it all. All the parts you're worried might be hard to take, that you think are a lot. Let me decide that, okay? Let me in."

Her eyes scanned my face. She nodded, "Okay. You have to let me in too, though." Her hands rested against my chest.

"I already have," and I meant it. I knew it like I'd never known anything before. I didn't want the boxes anymore; I didn't want anything in them. Every part of my past that was locked up and sealed shut. Every part of my life I kept separate. I didn't want it.

It was exhausting, I realised.

Why had I never realised that before?

I wanted to start fresh; with Allie, the band, the guys, my life on the road and off the road, the cooking and movies and trips to the park.

I moved in and pressed my lips to hers as everything that had cluttered my mind before Allie completely disappeared.

32

Allie

"I *love* surprises, this is so exciting Allie!" Savannah jumped up and down in her living room clapping.

I couldn't help but smile back at her. This *was* exciting.

Spending Sunday with Dax was almost impossible. I had this issue, and I wasn't entirely sure if there was a scientific name for it, but if I had exciting news, or I purchased a gift for someone too early before the time it was supposed to be gifted. I *had* to tell them.

So, keeping quiet about my plan to surprise Dax and not let anything slip... I would have preferred to wax everything from the eyebrows down, to put it plainly.

But I pulled it off. He had no idea and we spent the entire day relaxing on my Facebook Marketplace couch. We started to watch all the Marvel movies from the beginning. I had seen on my Instagram feed while scrolling this photo of all the Marvel movies and the order you were supposed to watch them in. We were probably the only people who didn't realise that they all joined into one, long, comprehensive story.

We got through two and then fell asleep. Dax woke me up in the early hours of the morning and we shuffled to my room. It might've been the early morning or the way he looked half asleep but let's just say we didn't immediately hit the hay once we settled into bed.

I practically convinced myself to forget about it to make it through the week.

All the dinners at his apartment, the coffee and croissant breakfasts, the walks from my apartment to my office were everything, all those moments and the moments in between, I had spent months thinking of.

I had pictured him at my door almost every day, pictured him at my kitchen island while I made us tea. Now that I could reach out and run my hands through his hair or wrap my arms around his waist, I refused to be taken from the moment by anything, even a completely awesome and super amazing surprise like I was planning.

Now, if that wasn't the most obvious display of personal growth and self-control ever then you could slap my ass and call me Sally.

10 points for Allie. Hell, 15.

"Okay, okay, tell me the plan again but from the top," Savannah sat down on her couch and looked at me with big, excited eyes.

"So, on Friday afternoons Rip and Angus play some kind of indoor soccer scrimmage and they've organised for all the guys to participate. Don't even ask me what or how, it was just what Aspen put forward as the reason to get Dax out of the house.

That will go until about 7PM, so I will have plenty of time to get up to their apartment, make my impressive spaghetti and meatballs and set up a cute little date thing. Aspen gave me his second elevator card swiper so that we can get up with no issues. I just need you to drive me to their place and maybe help set up the little table all cute and lady-and-the-tramp like."

When Aspen had handed me his back up elevator card, he had unhooked it from his keys.

"Aspen. Don't tell me you keep your spare elevator swiper on your keys," I commented, worried.

"Of course, I do. If I put it anywhere else, I'd lose it," he said back with so much conviction I choked on my response. I wouldn't be the one to take that from him, he'd have to learn that lesson on his own one day.

"Allie, that is so cute, he is going to love it," Savannah gave me that look like she was about to start crying. Right on cue she started to fan her eyes.

"Sav! Stop it," I sat down next to her and grabbed her hand.

"This is just the best. I am so happy for you, Al. You deserve all this, all the good stuff," she lifted my hand that was clutching hers and kissed the back of it, I did the same thing back to hers.

"How's your secret guy going? You haven't said anything more about him since you told me there even *was* someone," I leaned back onto her couch.

"It's incredible, Allie. He's just, he's so *good*," she was picking at her nails, "I was thinking we could all have dinner here next week or something, and you can meet him properly too."

"Why are you so nervous? If you like him, I like him. All this secrecy has me scared though," I admitted.

"Don't be," she smiled at me, "It's all happy times, we just agreed to keep things on the downlow, and we wanted to tell you together," it was Sav's most genuine smile, so when she told me it was all good, I believed her.

I leaned over and kissed her cheek before standing and heading to the door to slide on my shoes, "Sounds perfect."

I slung my light jacket over my arm. It was warm enough outside that I would be fine in my t-shirt.

"Okay, I'll grab the ingredients on my way home from work. Will you come get me at 6?" I opened her front door.

"I will be so on time; you have no idea," she bounced where she sat and clapped her hands again.

Let him in.

I could do that, absolutely, I could do that. It might be that I already had, but now I just needed to tell him.

I wasn't sure if I was nervous for the cooking, the whole purpose of the event or for the fact that I didn't know if Dax did or did not like surprises and I couldn't imagine Aspen divulging that information anyway.

If Dax hated surprises, Ap would have loved to see it all play out and then piss himself as he recorded Dax's face. Out of love, of course.

I stopped by the corner store after work and picked up the three ingredients I required. I also got a couple of candles that apparently smelt like 'pine trees and the alpine wilderness' whatever that meant, and speed-walked back to mine.

Aspen messaged me just as I finished up at work that they were leaving for the soccer game. Dax had also messaged me saying the same thing.

I didn't even take my shoes off at the door. If that didn't accurately convey my nerves then I didn't know what could. I quickly shoved the whole shopping bag - pasta and all - into the fridge and ran to my room.

I wanted to look nice, but also like I didn't even try. I opted for a mustard pinafore with a white shirt underneath that had these cute frilly details on the neck and sleeve. I felt pretty when I wore it.

I quickly threw a few curls into my hair and barely missed burning my eyeball on the barrel as I tried to pick my phone up.

It was Savannah.

"Hey chicky, I am here! Let's get surprising!" She was 'wooing' and 'ahhing' over me while I tried to tell her I'd be right down. I seriously doubted she even heard me.

I took one last look at myself in the bathroom mirror then triple checked that I'd turned my curling iron off at the wall, cause we all knew how it felt to leave the house and think it was still on. Yep, no thanks, didn't need that today.

I grabbed the bag from the fridge and went down to Savannah. She was parked at the curb and as soon as I started walking towards her, she started to chant 'yes, yes, yes!' prompting me to put on my best catwalk display. A few more hyping phrases - 'work it and spin, spin, lunge' - were thrown my way for which I classily obliged. I landed in the passenger seat of her car with about as much grace as a hippo.

"Ready?" she asked.

"Born ready," I replied, a look of determination set into my face. These would be the best 6 out of 10, letting him all in, meatballs he'd ever have in his life.

Sav parked under the building taking the spot that Aspen's sedan usually sat in and we walked over to the elevator. I pressed the button until it arrived, and we rode all the way up.

"Holy shit balls," Savannah gasped, taking in the penthouse, "It's totally surreal to me right now that I'm in *Wyatt Smith's* penthouse. Pinch me, someone...*ouch!* Allie!" She smacked my arm.

"You literally asked me to," I shrugged in earnest before walking to the kitchen.

"Toad," Savannah mumbled as she continued to snoop around.

I set about the process of boiling the kettle for the pasta and found a pan big enough for all the meatballs. They had a gas oven and I'd seen Dax use it plenty to know how to safely turn it on to the right heat. I mean, I thought so. I guess we'd find out.

Savannah came bounding into the kitchen after the pasta water had been salted and the raw noodles added, her face the picture of complete and total happiness.

"Allie, this is so *cool* I could *die," s*he collapsed onto the island before me.

"Can you help me make this cute please? I'm worried if I take my eyes off the stove top, something will catch fire," I kept my eyes glued to the heating oil in the pan. Putting my hand just above it to see how hot it was like I'd seen Dax do, too.

Savannah took her job in lady-and-the-trampifying the kitchen island with so much gusto I struggled to keep my composure. Her tongue was poking out her mouth in concentration the whole time.

Sav had brought a tartan tablecloth and a little basket with breadsticks for the middle. I had no idea she was going to do any of that so my whole body was about to split and leak gooey love everywhere, but again, my attention had to remain on the meatballs that were now happily sizzling away.

By the time I turned around, the island had been transformed into a table for two at what could have been the cutest, hole-in-the-wall, family owned Italian restaurant you'd ever seen.

"Sav," I exhaled, my eyes went a bit glassy, "that's so top tier, you have no idea."

"Yeah?" She double checked.

"Absolutely perfect," I reached out my hand for her to come over and gave her a big squeeze.

"Okay, I've gotta run. I'm having dinner with *my* guy tonight as well. He will be at the restaurant soon so I'm gonna jet. Call me if you need anything, I won't be too far away, and good luck!" She kissed my cheek and waved at me from the elevator.

I turned back to my meatballs. They were now completely cooked through and appropriately seasoned with salt and pepper. I dumped them into the strained pasta that was sitting in the pot and added in the jar of sauce.

I mean, it looked the same as always. I was smiling to myself as I grabbed a couple bowls out of the cupboard, mentally going through what I wanted to say.

I was toying between 'hey Dax, things have kind of levelled up lately, you know, with you learning all my deep dark secrets and the awesome sex, I guess what I wanted to say was that I love you'. I didn't think it was half bad, there was also 'these meatballs might be a 6 out of 10, but yours are a 10 out of 10'. It wasn't an immediate winner, but I was keeping it in the bank, just in case.

Aspen had messaged letting me know they were on their way back so I started to dish out the pasta portions.

I even found some cheese in their fridge to sprinkle on top just as the elevator pinged, indicating someone had arrived.

Oh, what? They're not supposed to be here yet, shit, shit, shit.

"Dax! Aspen!" A voice called. A *lady* voice, and not one I knew.

What the...?

"Boys?!" They called again.

She hadn't seen me. She had walked straight through to the living room and stood at the base of the stairs that moved into the hallway.

She turned around and spotted me. As soon as she did, she let out a yelp and her hand flew to her heart.

"Oh, holy pine nuts, you scared me so bad!" Her hand moved from her chest to fan her face.

My mouth opened and closed but nothing came out. I clutched the serving spoon, still piled with spaghetti and meatballs.

"Wait, *wait, wait, wait.* This is crazy. *Stop it!"* She covered her mouth and sort of pranced over to me, her heels clicking loudly on the marbled floor. I, all of a sudden, felt very short wearing my Chucks.

"You're Allie, right?! This is *so cool.* It is the best to meet you! I'm Jenna!" She said enthusiastically, pulling me into a hug. Her perfume stung my nose and made my tummy roll a bit.

"I—," I started, but she cut me off straight away.

"Oh. My. Gosh. This is *so cute.* Well, I know this absolutely cannot be Daxy, I think we both know he needs to learn a thing or two about romance, am I right?!" She knocked me with her elbow.

"What?" My heart was picking up pace. Who even was this person?

"I mean, he has no issues with the physical stuff - but you don't need me to tell you that!" She laughed and then tapped my arm, like *I* was supposed to know that *she* was supposed to know that too?

How did she know that? Why was she talking about it like she knew about it recently?

Please, no. Please, please, please, not Dax.

"I'm sorry, but how did you get up here? You need a card." Was that rude? It felt rude.

I couldn't help it though, I thought I was going into shock. My heart was racing, my palms were sweaty, and my hands were starting to shake a bit. Dread coiled in my stomach, my mind was racing with every possibility, but there was only one that made sense.

Please, please, please, no, no, no.

She held up a swipe card with a look of confused astonishment.

I should have known. Every time he was on his phone, every time, he was talking to someone else. Stupid Allie, you're so stupid. He never let me see, he always said it was nothing.

"I have a key, silly! Like you, I would imagine, or else how did you get up here! Did Dax give you his main one? I thought I had his only spare," she looked at me. Her eyes bright and unblinking, the picture of satisfaction oozing from her features and all while I felt my brain have a power outage and my heart suffered an earthquake.

I dropped the spoon I was clutching with a white knuckled grip back into the pot and dashed for the elevator. I'd never clicked a call button so fast in my life. I could feel the tears welling and spilling over one by one. The click of her heels echoed from behind me and I think she might have been calling my name, but everything was so muffled. The smell of her perfume clung to my shirt. I was going to throw up.

My chest hurt. *Everything* hurt.

I threw myself into the elevator, prompted the doors to close as fast as they could and pulled my phone out of my pocket with shaking hands. Savannah picked up on the second ring.

"Allie? Are you okay?" She sounded worried, like she knew, like she might have had a feeling.

I choked a sob, "I'm so stupid Savannah, so, so stupid. I should have known. I should have just *asked* who he was speaking to every time. He was always talking to someone. God, how could I believe him? Everything he ever said, how could I have *believed him?*"

"Allie, calm down I can't understand you. I'm coming. I will be there in 5 minutes, don't walk anywhere, okay?"

"He's just like Ben, Sav, just like Ben. How am I so stupid? How could he—," I broke off into a strangled sob. The sort where you can feel yourself about to be sick. The ones that make you want to curl into a ball and never move.

"I'm coming, Allie. Okay? 3 minutes."

"Don't hang up," I managed to say, though I couldn't for the life of me see how she understood a word out of my mouth.

"I won't hang up. I'm right here okay? 2 minutes, Al."

I could barely see in front of me, my eyes just pouring with tears. I didn't really care if someone saw me, heard me, whatever.

I had clicked the button to the basement without even thinking of it.

"I'm in the basement," I sounded calmer. I didn't feel calmer.

How could this be happening? How?

"1 minute, Allie," Savannah said.

I let the phone slide from my face as I walked into the basement and slumped against the wall next to the elevator. The waves of painful realisation continued to crash over me, everything I had worked so hard to move past was coming up to meet with vengeance. With a questioning cruelty like 'how dare you move on from those feelings? That place?'.

When slender hands reached out to grip my forearms, it scared me so much, I screamed.

I properly screamed.

"Allie, it's okay, let's go. Come on."

"Savannah, how could he? *How could he?"*

She never replied, she just helped me into the back seat and took off, getting us as far away from Dax's place as possible.

33

Aspen and I were almost home when Jenna's name popped up on my caller ID and I remembered she needed something for Phoebe.

"Hey Jenna, sorry I know you need the stage—"

"Wyatt, I'm so sorry," she interrupted, sounding frantic, "So, so sorry. I had no idea what I said, what she might— I was just trying to be nice." She sounded like she was about to cry. I was completely lost.

"Woah, slow down. What are you talking about?" My knee started to bounce. Aspen gave me a nervous look.

"I didn't know she was going to be here, Wyatt. I swear. I was just trying to be nice, find common ground. I wanted to be her friend," Jenna pushed all the words out all at once, like saying them faster would make things better.

"You didn't know who was going to be where, Jenna? Where are you?" Aspen's eyes widened as he sped up, mumbling curses under his breath.

I shot him a look of confusion.

"Allie. I didn't know Allie was going to be here or I wouldn't have come. You're always home on Friday nights, always," she explained.

My heart stopped. I felt it stop.

"What did you say to her, Jenna?" I didn't recognise my voice.

"I... well... I was just...," she was fumbling with her words.

"What the fuck did you say to her Jenna, what did you do? *What did you do?*" I didn't even wait to hear what she said before I hung up the phone.

"What's going on Aspen?" I was breathing so fast my lungs were burning.

"She wanted to surprise you, Dax," Aspen started as he picked up even more speed, "She wanted to cook you something, something about meatballs. I don't even know. She wanted to make it like a dinner date at a restaurant but at ours because you can't really go out. She wanted to surprise you."

Aspen flew into the basement parking of our building and I was out of the car before it had stopped. The elevator had never taken so long to come down to us, or so long to take us to the top.

I stopped in my tracks. The whole set up. The island, the food.

She made her spaghetti and meatballs, and her bag was still sitting on one of the chairs of the island like she'd had only one goal when she left and that was to leave as fast as possible.

I didn't even notice Jenna walk up to me, "Wyatt, please, I am so sorry, I didn't think."

"You don't ever *think,* Jenna! Ever." With that I turned on my heels. Grabbing the keys from Aspen and heading back down to the car.

Pick up, pick up, pick up.

Allie's number went to voicemail every time.

"Dammit!" I smacked the steering wheel, a zap of pain went up my arm.

I drove straight to her apartment, threw the car into neutral and ran to her building. I didn't even bother with the elevator, taking the stairs two at a time to her floor.

I wanted to bang on the door, I wanted to break it down. But I didn't.

I took some deep breaths. Calmed myself down, swallowing the emotion lodged in my throat.

I knocked on Allie's door lightly.

"Allie?" I called, "Allie, please. It's not what you think. Let me in, let me explain."

No one answered. I didn't even hear any shuffling behind the door.

I went to knock again when the door cracked. It was Savannah.

She looked behind her and then slid out into the hallway. She just looked at me and the warning from the first time we met crept back into my mind.

"Savannah, I swear it's not what she thinks," I pleaded.

"I know," she nodded.

"I mean it, Sav— what?" I was trying to process what she'd said.

"I know it's not what it looks like. Angus told me. He's inside with Allie now," she inclined her head towards the door, "He explained it to her, too."

What a relief.

"Can I see her then?" I went to move towards the door, but Savannah stepped in my path.

"No," she crossed her arms. Savannah was slight, she was shorter than Allie and slimmer too, but for all of that, the look on her face made me step back.

"What?" I knew I looked as confused as I felt.

"You didn't tell her about Jenna, Wyatt. You *work* with Jenna, she's the person who freaking touches up your *hair!"* She whisper-yelled the last part.

"That doesn't mean anything to—," I started.

"To who, Wyatt? To you? Or to Allie? She told you *everything.* Do you know how hard that was? She even plays her piano for you, Wyatt. She doesn't even do that for *me. Me!* For all that you know of Allie, how could you not know that while she was opening every single part of herself up to you, because you *asked,* the fact that you weren't doing the same, that it wasn't even a consideration, malicious or not, how do you think that would make her feel? After everything you know. Ben? Her mum? The accident? The trauma?" Her face told me she could keep going, but she was choosing not to.

Savannah took a deep breath like reliving all those parts of Allie's life were hard for her too.

"She's not damaged, or incapable, or… or meek because of any of it," she went on.

"I know that. I've never thought that." For all that I was falling apart on the inside, those words held strong. I'd never thought anything different. How could I? Allie was probably the strongest person I knew.

"But she is not invincible, Wyatt," her voice had dropped down to where I could barely hear her.

"If I could just *tell* her, explain why I hadn't said—," the words were hollow as they waited to be spoken.

Why didn't I tell her? Why didn't I just unpack all the boxes, all the things I placed neatly together. It was because Allie was more than all of it, she was better than all of it. It didn't make sense to bring it up, to show her all those things.

"She needs time," Savannah reached for the door, she gave me one last look and then closed it gently, leaving me in the hallway. In a spot I had stood more times than I could count.

I could walk to the exact place before her door with my eyes closed, but I had never felt more desperately lost in my life.

34

I had nothing to say.

Nothing to say that would make anything revert to the way it was last week.

That was the first time in my entire life I didn't feel like I had anything to put to paper. Nothing to type into my phone or scribble into my notebook.

I sat and stared at my phone all weekend. If I wasn't watching my phone waiting for it to ding, I was staring at my guitar, wishing for something to shove me towards it. Something that I could do, or write, or play that would help.

I didn't know what to do.

The elevator pinged to our floor late Saturday afternoon. I didn't know who it was, but I knew who it wasn't and that was enough to not really care who it was at all.

Angus sat down in the chair across from me and placed the little elevator swipe card on the coffee table between us.

I looked over at him, I could feel the pleading expression on my face. My skin tightened and I suddenly felt like I couldn't get enough air into my lungs.

"Wyatt—," The tone of his voice said it all.

Neither he nor Savannah had said anything about why he ended up with her and Allie in her apartment. I had guessed he'd found someone, was seeing someone, now I knew it was Savannah. I was happy for him. I was. More than that, I was glad he had been there to explain, as selfish as that might have seemed.

I leaned forward and rested my elbows on my knees. I let my head hang for a second before I met his eyes again and pushed my hair back with both hands.

"She's not coming," I said what I knew he was dreading having to relay, "I didn't keep it from her because it meant something to me, because I didn't want her to know," I said to him, even though he already knew.

"I know," Angus said. The look in his eyes was the look they all gave me every time I ended up alone again. Like they wanted to help, to fix whatever it was that always made me end up back at square one.

"I'd tell her anything she wanted to know, anything," I said to him again.

"I know," he repeated.

"This wasn't how it was supposed to happen," I said softly. I think I was probably talking more to myself than to Angus, and not to Aspen who I knew loitered in the hallway behind me, forever unable to restrain himself from eavesdropping.

"Is she okay?" I asked.

Angus gave a small shake of his head and I swear my whole body pulsed in a shudder of pain.

I did that. That was me.

"Sav is with her now, still. She won't speak but I told her Wyatt, I explained everything to her. Just give her time to digest it. To process it," Angus walked over and placed a hand on my shoulder.

Time.

He bid Ap farewell on his way out, but I couldn't move my gaze away from the key card he had left on the coffee table. Aspen's spare indicated by the little 'A' he had written into one of the corners with a sharpie.

I knew that it was meant for his name, but I couldn't stop thinking that it should have been for Allie.

I lasted until Monday midday before I messaged her.

Dax: *Hey*

She never wrote back.

She didn't write back in the afternoon or the evening, not even through the night. I stared at my phone all night just waiting for the screen to illuminate, but it never did.

I lasted until Wednesday morning before I called her.

*Heyo, this is Allie, I'm probably busy learning a second language or maybe just on the toilet but leave a message and I'll get back to you toot-sweet. *Beep**

I hit her message bank every time. I called her three times, three times in a *row* and every time I got the same voice recording.

I knew she wasn't going to pick up, and though I had hoped, I knew I wouldn't hear from her at all on Thursday.

Friday morning came and went, so did midday and then the little digital clock on my phone ticked from 4:59PM to 5PM and I couldn't wait anymore.

The time she needed, I couldn't give her anymore. I needed to see her, hear her voice, hear her say something. *Anything.*

Aspen was out with the sedan, so I grabbed the keys to the Jeep that we had and made my way to the basement.

When we had a lot of time off, we liked to go camping. Hiking and trails and the outdoors. The quiet. That's what the Jeep was for, but it would do for a cross city sprint.

I parked in the regular spot outside her building. It was 5:20PM and I knew she would have probably just gotten home from work.

I wanted to know if she was making brownies. If she had made them at all during the week.

Did she get takeout and give some to Dean? What were the leftovers she had felt she needed to pay him back for?

Did she start to learn a new song on her piano?

Was she still playing her guitar?

I felt like I knew the answer to that last one already.

I walked across the street to her building and walked in. Grateful, for the first time ever, for her terrible security that didn't prevent anyone from walking in the front door or calling the elevator.

I stood before her door. I didn't want to knock. I wanted to just open it and walk in like I had before, when she knew I was coming and left it unlocked. I knew that if I tried the handle it wouldn't turn open like it did then.

I knocked on the door softly.

There was shuffling and then the door opened to show Dean standing there in something that wasn't orange for a change. A pair of sweatpants and a shirt, they were both grey.

"Dude! How are you?" He stuck his hand out in a shake.

I reached out my own hand, "Hey Dean, how are you?" I asked him, giving him one of my most special 'press smiles'.

"Yeah, I'm actually pretty good. Heading out of town this weekend," he nodded his head as he spoke, "Bro, I'm sorry, but Allie said, if you showed up, not to let you in."

My chest ached at that, "I just need to speak to her for a second, Dean."

Dean must have learned from Angus how to pass on the pity look fast, because his eyes cast the same saddened stare at me.

"Wyatt—," he started.

"Sorry Dean, but I'm coming in," I pushed by him causing him to bump back into the door. He called after me and I threw an apology at him over my shoulder and rushed down the hall. He didn't bother following me as I saw him dawdle into the living room.

I stood outside her door. That was the closest I had been to her in over a week and I had a sinking feeling it might be as close as I'd ever get again.

I had to explain though, I had to try and let her know *why*.

I lifted my hand, freaking the fuck out the entire time. I was terrified.

I knocked.

"Allie," I said, "God, Allie, please. Please let me explain," I whispered through her door.

I couldn't hear anything on the other side, nothing.

But then there was some rustling, like the covers were being thrown back and I stepped back from the door, backing up the hallway a bit the way I'd come in.

Allie opened the door to her room gently, peaking at me through the crack in her door before she opened it wide.

I already felt how this was going to go.

Please, no.

She stepped out into the hallway, wearing the oversized sweatpants I had once borrowed from her and an oversized shirt. My shirt.

One of the many band T's that cluttered my closet, the only thing I ever really wore, when wearing a shirt was required. The one Allie had on said *The Smiths* across the front.

I couldn't move my eyes away from the shirt, I couldn't stop looking at *her* in my shirt. I tried to swallow and found the emotion that had clogged in my throat made it near impossible.

Allie moved her eyes from my face down to the shirt that she wore, she was gripping the bottom of it tightly.

I moved my gaze back up to hers. Her seafoam green eyes were made impossibly bright by the heartbreaking redness that surrounded them. I knew she had been crying. I knew she had probably been crying while I waited for her texts and her calls.

I swallowed again, "Allie, I swear there is nothing going on. Jenna and I dated *three years* ago. I haven't even had another girlfriend since her. Until you." I was impressed at how steady my voice sounded.

"But you didn't tell me, Dax. You didn't tell me anything. And you were always…," she trailed off, like she remembered something and got caught up in the memory of it.

"Always what, Allie?" I took a small step towards her.

She just shook her head.

"I'm trying, Allie. I'm—," my voice cracked; no steadiness left, "I'm not good at this. I've never done more than one thing before. It was either one or the other for me. I could never *mix*. Something always suffered. I was never *good* at this," I motioned between her and I, hoping that she knew what I meant, "I'm trying, Allie," I said again.

Tears slid down her face as she looked at me, as she took in my face. Her eyes scanned my features like they had done on our very first date, when I knew she was looking for a reason to say no, but she didn't find one. I could tell as I watched her, watching me, that she had found a reason this time.

My chest was pierced with the most aggressive sort of dread I'd ever felt.

No.

She nodded at me, a small, sad smile ghosting her trembling lips. I lifted my hand, I wanted to hold her. To wipe her tears, to do anything. But I didn't, I let it drop back to my side.

"You're rock. Rock and roll. Electric guitars and drums and, and hard notes and rough edges…," she sniffed, wiping her checks of their tears, "I am classical. Sweeping, and gentle. Strong but soft." She looked back at me again, "They are too different. They don't mix, Wyatt."

I flinched. I actually *flinched*. I don't think I'd ever flinched in my life. I took a step back away from her.

Wyatt. Not Dax.

She wasn't finished, "This isn't fair for you or me, I can't do this silence. This in between. I think… I think we need to figure some things out."

I'd never nodded my head so fast, "Allie, I'll—," I started but the look on her face silenced me.

"Apart," she whispered, fresh tears falling down her face.

"What?" I said.

No.

"Apart," she repeated.

I couldn't move.

"I can't— I can't *believe* you anymore. Everything you've said, every word I want to believe but it sits in my stomach like lead weights and I can't—"

"Allie, I told you already, there's nothing—"

"I know what you said, Dax. I heard it from you, from Savannah, from Angus. I can't believe it though. I told you *everything*, you know *everything*. I thought I knew everything too, but you kept that to yourself. All the parts of me that I can't face, you saw them all. I never saw any of those parts from you. I thought you just didn't have any, not that you were *keeping* them from me. I think maybe you need to face those parts yourself. Like I need to face mine," her voice was so calm.

I didn't know how her voice was so calm, even as she couldn't stop crying, yet my entire world was being shaken.

"I thought I could do that with you," she said.

I looked up to her eyes again.

"I don't think I can do that anymore," her bottom lip started to tremble again, "Please, Dax. You need to go." It wasn't more than breathy words, but they rang clear as day as they moved right through me.

I wanted to scream.

I wanted to grab her and make her see, tell her I knew, *I knew* that I fucked up. That I didn't mean to, that I didn't even know. That I thought I didn't have to compartmentalise things to function, to do good. To *be* good. That I thought I could have it all, that for a second it felt like I *did* have it all.

But none of it came out, I didn't say any of it as I turned around and walked away.

35

Allie

As soon as he turned to walk away, I wanted to pull him back.

Every word I had said to him, that I had spent days and days planning to say, I wanted them all to disappear like smoke in the wind. I wanted to take back every broken look that crossed his face, every hesitation that he had. I wanted to take it all back.

But he turned to leave, and I didn't move. I didn't call after him.

Even if I did grab him back, I knew the words he'd said would still sit heavy like they did when I heard them just before. I knew that anything he'd ever say would sit just the same. I knew I'd never be able to look at him with such a clear knowledge that he was right there with me.

I didn't know if he had ever been right there with me, I felt like I didn't know him at all.

I just watched him leave, saw him round the corner and disappear from my sight.

I scrunch my eyes up and prepared for the loud bang of the front door that would come as he left. I stood there as tense as ever for longer than I realised, because the *bang* never came.

He had closed the door so quietly, I hadn't realised he'd left at all.

36

Every step away from her was harder than the one before.

I took the stairs because the thought of waiting for the elevator… I wouldn't have been able to do it.

I could feel myself losing grip, losing whatever leash on my composure I had. So, I did the only thing I knew how to do.

Everything that was Allie, that was scattered around my mind like a well-loved home, I gathered it all up. All the bits of her, the brightness, the everything, I gathered it all with every step I took and placed it all into a box I didn't realise existed. A box I never wanted to exist. The one that was clearly labelled 'Allie'.

I packed every single piece of her up, the throw pillows, the shoes by the door, the coat on the hook, and sealed it in that box in my mind. Then, carefully, I moved it to a place I would rarely ever go looking for it, to the back corner where there was hardly any light. I placed Allie's box gently there as I got in my car and sped too quickly, as far away from her as I could get.

It had been dark for so long by the time I got home, I was honestly surprised that the sun wasn't up yet.

I had driven out of town, going nowhere at all, only knowing that I was *moving*, and that was good. That if I stopped moving, I would fall apart.

Then the storm that had raged in me settled, and I had packed every part of Allie left in my mind up too well, too tight, that things looked normal. They didn't look *right*, but they looked like they did before I met her. And so, I drove home.

Aspen was asleep on the living room couch when I walked out of the elevator. Well, he had been asleep, but the ping of the elevator had caused him to stir.

"Dax?" His voice was laced with sleep.

"Hey Ap," I went to walk by him and head straight to my room. I dumped the keys for the Jeep on the hook where I had grabbed them from.

"So?" He sat up a bit.

"So what?"

"Wyatt." He stood up.

"It's done. She asked me to leave, so I left," I kept walking to the steps that lead up into the hallway.

"So, go back?" He said it like it was the simplest thing in the world, and maybe it would have been.

"No," I stopped at the base of the steps, "it's over, Aspen. Leave it alone."

"No, you need to go back. Tell her again, explain it to her again," he walked towards me. He raised his voice, determination and worry rolled into his words.

"No!" I turned and screamed at him, "No, Aspen. It's over. Did you not *hear* me? It's fucking *finished*. So, drop it."

"Dax—," he started again, and I knew what he was going to do, he was going to keep pushing.

"Jenna was right, Aspen. I'm closed off. I can't *do* more than one thing at a time. I can't be good for Allie and for the band and for me all at once. I can't let people in. I couldn't even let Allie in, she had free rein while everything else was packed up tight," I pointed to my temple.

"You can go back, Dax. Go back and fix it," he said again, so resolved like he thought I was an idiot for not having that idea first.

"Aspen, stop," I continued up the stairs, praying he would let it go.

"Dax," he said my name louder. I turned around to face him, standing outside my bedroom door, the words left my mouth before I could stop them.

"Aspen. Just stop, you never fucking *stop*. It's done. It's finished," I pushed my hair back from my face, "God, you're just so… just focus on your own fucking life for once, leave mine alone. Dammit, Aspen." My voice hurt from the strain of the volume I spat the words out at.

I didn't wait for him to say anything else, couldn't bear to see the look on his face, so I walked straight into my room and I put that in a box too.

37

DAX

Aspen didn't speak to me for a whole week after I had yelled at him. We'd even rolled into April and, every month without fail, he came up and gave me a 'pinch and a punch for the first day of the month'. This was the first time I could remember that he didn't do that.

I didn't speak to anyone that week at all.

I had woken up well before the sun. Sleep, as usual, had refused to find me again and all I could do was think about what I had said to Aspen.

I had shoved that encounter in a box labelled 'do not open' but it rattled around and made so much noise I couldn't ignore it anymore.

I had decided that enough was enough, I needed my brother back and I needed to apologise in a way that I knew he would accept without a doubt.

So, naturally, I decided to bake him something.

I made him cinnamon rolls, with extra icing. They were his favourite and there was literally nothing he wouldn't do for one.

Usually he made them himself, with sweets being his specialty and savoury being mine, but I knew that if I concentrated, I could whip up a batch that he would hoard in his room.

It took me two hours.

Two whole hours and I couldn't even let the dough, that I'd already rolled out into perfect little swirls, rise a second time. I knew the second rise was important because Aspen always said 'second's the best' as his baking motto.

In a pinch, to accelerate the whole rising process, you could put your baked goods somewhere very warm, or so I heard, and so I turned the oven on high and set them right in front of it. I wasn't really in a position to be taking those kinds of risks considering the weight of apology these buns would hold, but beggars couldn't be choosers. I had to put all my eggs in one cinnamon dusted basket and hope for the best.

By the time Aspen wandered out of his bedroom, yawning and unstable, just emerging from sleep, they were ready, glazed and placed in the middle of the kitchen island.

He stopped in front of them and then looked up at me.

"I was wondering how sorry you'd be," he said, swiping a finger across the top of them and tasted the frosting. He lifted his eyebrows and irked his head to the side slowly before picking up one of the rolls and taking a mammoth bite.

He was chewing for about 15 seconds before a grin broke over his face and he said around a mouth full of food, "You're forgiven."

I looked at him and I seriously had never wanted to cry so much as I had in the last week. This was shit, everything was just so, *so* shit, but things were always less shit when Aspen was on my side.

"Yeah?" I asked.

"Yeah," he took another bite, "You're a massive wiener, but yes." His smile grew even wider.

"I'm sorry," I couldn't quite smile back.

Aspen finished the cinnamon bun he had shoved so gracefully into his mouth before he wiped the icing on his cheek away with the back of his hand.

"I focus on your life because I love you. When you're happy, I'm happy. When you're good, I'm good. That's why. I will always try and do what is best for you, even if that makes you angry," he picked up the tray and held it gently, like it was the most precious thing in the world.

"I know," I matched his stare. He held my gaze until he was satisfied, nodding his head slightly before turning to leave.

"Good, now let's stop talking about this stuff before I barf," he flopped down the couch and turned on the TV.

I smiled and followed him, feeling a little lighter than I did before, and desperately wishing I had taken a bun out of the tray for myself, because there was no way he was sharing.

All the shows sold out for our tour.

They all sold out within an hour of the tickets going live.

I was so proud, so unbelievably proud of my friends and what we had achieved. We were living our dream and it was incredible.

In the month that led up to the start of our tour, we planned and then replanned the set list.

The new album had gone nuts, but our others had crowd favourites that we needed to incorporate into our performance as well.

Aspen had really let his freak flag fly when planning out what we would wear on stage. He had bombarded Phoebe with phone call after phone call as well as individual links to different Pinterest vision boards that he had created for everyone.

We practised for hours. Every day. Hours and hours and hours until the calluses on the ends of my fingers and on my hands had started to form their own calluses.

We landed in London for our first stop. It was one of our biggest shows and the crowds were insane. The way they welcomed us onto the stage - there was no feeling like it. It was amazing. Luke walked right up to the edge of the stage and screamed right back. Then we all followed suit. That's how we started our tour, it was euphoric. It was humbling.

Our shows were set out to be three per city and they were spaced with a day in between. Our previous tours hadn't always been like that, but considering the size of this one, it was planned with more time and made longer.

The shows, I mean, we nailed them, one after the other. And only once so far had Rip spun around, smacked into me and caused me to fall on stage.

I finished the song on the ground, and we didn't miss a beat. After that particular show, none of us could stop laughing.

We still yelled and screamed before and after every performance, of course, and getting to spend time with my closest friends was everything I could have wanted.

I repeated it to myself every day.

This is all I could have ever wanted. The guys, the road and my music. The fans, the stadiums. I didn't need anything more than this.

You eventually missed the quiet and the down time, but those memories we made on tour, everywhere we got to go together; it made the fast pace and long days worth it.

A couple months of hopping from city to city, saw us making our way through Europe slowly and surely on what was the first leg of our tour, and I was perfectly fine.

I was perfectly fine not thinking about anything other than what I needed to do.

The routine was simple.

Get up, get dressed, either do something or don't, sound check, get ready, concert, do something or don't, the next day would come and be filled with either doing something or not doing something and then we did it all again.

The box that was unpacked in my mind was the one that was clearly labelled 'tour'. It always sat just within reach and it was never taped shut but only ever closed very lightly.

Everything in that box had a place and I knew where to put it. I kept it in the light where I could always see it, even if the things were packed away temporarily.

I didn't look to the corners of my mind that were dimmer, dustier.

There was nothing for me there anymore.

"Dax?" Aspen waved his hand in front of my face.

"Mmm?" I looked to him quickly before picking up my forgotten fork and diving into our takeaway food. The consensus had been Chinese food, but I had requested something else. Anything else.

I was eating Greek food. It wasn't so bad.

We were in the hotel room that Rip and Luke were sharing, a movie was playing, and we were all eating.

"Did you hear anything that I said?" Aspen took another bite of his food, but his expression darkened.

"Sorry, I was thinking about something," I mumbled around a bit of food. I wasn't hungry, to be honest.

"You're not dealing with it, Dax," he said.

"Dealing with what?" I asked.

I knew what he was talking about.

Don't say it, don't say it.

"Allie." Once her name left his mouth, everyone stopped talking and all eyes were on me.

"I'm dealing with it fine, Aspen," I pushed my plate away. I was sitting on the ground in front of the couch and moved back to lean against it.

"It's been over two months and you've been on autopilot," he set his own fork down.

"I'm fine. The tour is going great, the shows are awesome. What more is there?" I looked at him. I shouldn't have made the non-verbal dare for him to say it because if there was anyone who would take it on, it was Aspen.

"I didn't say anything about the shows, Dax. That is one part of everything. You've done it again. Picked one box and only opened that one, everything else is suffering," Aspen was still looking at me. Before I could even reply he spoke again.

But that wasn't true. Things suffered when I *didn't* do that.

"You haven't written a song since the press tour, and that was three months ago, over three months even," his eyes flicked to Rip.

"You were doing better before, bud. You seemed happier. Brighter, even. We're just—" I cut Rip off this time.

"I was happier, Rip," I looked right at him. Not angry or mad, just showing them exactly what they were fishing for. "I had absolutely everything I had ever wanted and now, I don't have it anymore. So, now that it's been said out loud, let's move on, okay? I'll be fine," I looked at Aspen and tried to convey to him that I heard what he said, but I just didn't *want* to hear it. Not right now. Maybe not for a while longer.

In his defence, he'd said nothing to me about any of it until now. About me or about her.

He nodded his head a bit before he looked at Angus briefly.

Alright, that's enough for today.

It was hard to be around them when someone mentioned her name. Angus had struck a friendship with Savannah so it happened a lot more than you would think. He said 'friendship' but I knew they'd been seeing each other since before we'd gone on the press tour. I also knew that everyone knew except for me, that he'd told everyone but me.

Well, I knew, of course. I wasn't blind. But I also knew that he hadn't said it to me out loud yet because he thought it would bring Allie back up in conversation and it would suck for me.

It did suck.

It was the fucking worst, but I wasn't going to tell him that.

I got up and said goodbye to everyone before I headed back to my own hotel room.

Me, Angus and Aspen all had our own, where Rip and Luke shared a suite. We all took turns sharing verses getting our own space. Whoever had the foresight and patience to organise that schedule deserved a medal.

The walk down the hall was long, but it was nice and quiet.

I always had a thing for hotel hallways. The carpeted floors and the silence that sort of pressed in on you from either side. It was reminiscent of a recording booth at a studio, the way it felt. I liked how everyone whispered when they were walking from their room to the elevator even though they never had to. It was like being in a little pocket of the world in between different moments. It was calming.

There was one good thing that came from all this, if you were one of those people who really dug deep until you could pull anything together that resembled a silver lining - Jenna had stopped speaking to me.

That sounded mean, I knew that. But I was relieved.

She smiled and I smiled, and we were civil when we had to be. She did her job and fixed me up to be stage ready and that was it. She didn't tell me that I was emotionally closed off anymore. That I needed to be fixed and that my behaviour wasn't normal.

Phoebe tried to talk to me a few times while she was getting my outfits ready. About how sorry Jenna was, how she had read the situation wrong, how she had read *me* wrong.

I obviously told her it was fine, I was over it and no hard feelings.

I knew that Jenna was sorry. Her apology was there and so I took it and got on with my day, but it didn't change anything. It didn't bring Allie back or remove the fucked up situation I found myself in.

I took a very long and very hot shower.

I had just finished trying to dry my hair and cringing at the red colouring that stained the white towel when someone knocked at my door.

I opened it to find Angus on the other side, "Hey man, come in," I left the door open and walked back to throw the towel into the bathroom, "I'll be surprised if they don't charge us for all the towels I have ruined with this freaking hair colour," I laughed as I walked over to him and threw myself onto the bed.

"You're the one that thought red hair would be cool," he snickered.

"It *is* cool," I countered.

He waved me away, his face returned to a more neutral expression.

"What's up?" I tucked a hand behind my head.

"I wanted to talk to you about something," he rubbed the back of his neck with his hand. It was a habit we all had, I wasn't really sure who started it, but we all picked it up.

Ah, he was finally going to spill the beans.

"Shoot," I smiled at him.

"Alright," he took a deep breath, "Sav and I, well, we've been seeing each other for a while. Since before the press tour, actually," his eyes got a little wider like he was watching a scared animal that had been cornered against their will.

"I know," I said.

"What?" He looked dumbfounded.

"I know. Of course, I know, Angus. I think it's awesome," I chucked one of the pillows that was next to me at him. He caught it.

"You do?" He clutched the pillow to his chest.

I suddenly felt like the worst friend ever, that I had been so in my own head about my own situation that I had made my friend feel *bad* or scared to tell me something this exciting.

"Of course, I am. My situation has nothing to do with you. Savannah is awesome, Angus. I'm genuinely happy for you. I'm also glad you finally told me," I laughed.

"Okay," he smiled a bit, then cleared his throat, "How would you feel about her coming to visit for a few weeks. Maybe a month," he spoke slowly, like he was worried I was going to crack and go insane.

I wasn't going to lie. It could have still happened.

"You don't need to ask me that, Angus," I felt my own smile slip away.

"I do," he nodded.

"You don't. I'm not any more important or in charge than you are."

"No, you're not. But that's not why I'm asking," he gave me a knowing look.

I took a deep breath, "I know why you're asking," I looked down at my hand and started to pick at my nails, "And it's okay. Thank you, but it's really okay. I'm fine, Angus. Invite Sav, it will be a relief to have someone else besides you four around," I looked back at him and beamed a smile.

A smile of his own had begun to spread across his lips, "Okay. Alright, I'll ask her. You're sure that you're sure?" he asked one more time.

"Yes, I'm sure that I'm sure," I huffed, "you don't need to worry about me, I'm all good," I said as he chucked the pillow I had thrown at him back to me.

He got up and reached out his hand for one of our traditional slap-shakes, grunted and walked back towards the door to leave my room.

He hesitated like he was going to say something, then he shook his head to himself.

He opened the door and threw a wave back to me and just when I thought he was really going to leave he turned around and looked at me, like he had to really build himself up to that moment.

"We all worry about you, Dax. All the time," he said quietly before he left, the door clicked shut softly behind him.

Well, I didn't expect that.

From Aspen? Always. And Rip was the only other one that was ever vocal about anything to do with what the guys thought about me and my... I don't know, my life, my business. Angus though, he had never said a thing to me.

His words ran through my head.

We all worry.

What was I doing?

I think maybe you need to face those parts of yourself. Like I need to face mine.

That's what she had said to me.

I wasn't facing anything, I had gone over and over every box in my mind, every compartment and made sure that things were tucked away tightly where they needed to be, there was no overlap, none at all.

I couldn't bear it. Because suddenly, Allie had touched every part of my life, and I refused to face any of them because of that, everything I had worked toward would cease to exist.

I had always done this. And when the band took off, there was nothing I wasn't prepared to do to get it where it needed to go. The rest of the guys were just the same. But everyone, slowly, had started to let life in as the years moved on. Aspen was like me, focused and unrelenting, but the more I looked, *really* looked, the more I saw what he did outside of the band.

There had been no event that happened where I let someone in and I lost everything because I spread my attention too thin, because I had too many fingers in too many pies. I had never let anyone in. I had never wanted to and then, all of sudden, I never could.

It worked in my favour, eventually, because I learned all too quickly that when fame came into play, people often wanted to skip the queue from acquaintance to blood relative in a matter of moments. That everyone looked at you for something that you could give them, that no one ever really wanted to return the favour because they didn't care.

But then there was Allie, and she hadn't wanted anything except to show me where the baking powder was. She hadn't wanted anything other than me. And still, *still*, I couldn't let her in.

But wasn't that why I was where I was anyway? Because I couldn't, because I *refused* to face anything, everything.

I looked at my guitar case that sat against the wall next to my bed. I took a deep breath and on the exhale, I launched for it. I grabbed it and put it on the bed quickly. I unlatched the buckles on the side and lifted the lid.

I looked at it.

I stared.

I took another deep breath and lifted the instrument out of the case and onto my lap. I took out my phone and set it in front of me. My hands were shaking a bit but I kept going, kept breathing.

I opened the notes app and selected the one I hadn't opened in a long time. I hadn't touched or thought of in over three months.

I opened it then and slowly scrolled through the notes. It was full.

I read every single line, every word and phrase. I read them all over and over again and with another deep breath, I fit my hands onto the frets of my guitar, an action that was as familiar as saying my own name, and I began to write her song. Finally.

38

Allie

It had been almost three months.

June stared back at me from the little calendar that sat on my desk at work. And not even the start of June with its start-of-the-month, endless-opportunity-for-growth vibe. We were glaring frighteningly close to the end of the month and I felt like I'd been sleepwalking through life.

Or maybe like I'd tripped on a hill and just gave up on stopping myself and rolled down to the bottom. That was probably more accurate.

You also didn't need to tell me how ridiculous it was that I seemed to be considering the starting point of all time as the last time I saw Dax.

I was completely aware of how the entire situation looked.

Have you ever said something when you were mad, and wished that you'd just counted to 10 like all the 'control your anger outburst' articles online told you to do? Yeah, well, I felt like that was where I was at.

The classic Allie-over-thinker scenarios had resurfaced and I'd gone through every single moment from meeting Jenna - still wanting to replace her sugar with salt - all the way to what Angus had said, to what Savannah had said, right up to the moment where Dax flinched from my words.

I knew I was in the right to say what I said, I knew that I still had every right to hate that I was kept in the dark. That I was the last to know about everything. That I was spilling my literal organs out while he kept all his dirty laundry tucked away.

But you don't just stop loving someone, no matter how much they might have sucked in a certain moment.

I wanted to hate him, but I didn't. I was glad I didn't.

So, it had been almost three months since I wished I could have had the courage to explain to him why I did what I did. Why I said what I said.

Why I felt the fear in probably the scariest moment I'd experienced with him and decided to turn around and run away instead of face it. Because that's what I did at the end of it all, wasn't it?

I ran away.

I might have hated myself a little bit for that, but mostly I hated Ben. Beyond that though, I hated that I let him win all over again.

I had been standing strong for months. My arms stretched above me and holding the metaphorical world above my head.

It took two seconds to feel it come down around me. To climb out of the rubble was exhausting. It had taken weeks and even then, it was only because I had used up the entirety of my three years of sick leave staying home.

The clock on my phone finally ticked to 5PM. Letting out the world's largest sigh, I packed up my stuff and headed out of the office, straight to Sav's.

Summer was in full swing and as much as I loved the cold, it was refreshing to leave the office while the sun was still up. Even as boots remained a staple, though they were about ready for a replacement, I swapped my work slacks and sweaters for skirts, brightly coloured tops and the occasional cardigan that offered no warmth but emphasised modesty.

I lingered outside Savannah's building while I waited for her to get home. When she arrived, she pulled me in for a bone crushing hug.

"Wine?" She pulled back from our hug with a knowing look.

"Isn't that what Friday afternoons are for?" I wagged my eyebrows at her.

Sav dialled a number into a keypad and then scanned us through another door before we made it up to her floor. The security at her building never ceased to amaze me but she had assured me on multiple occasions that it was normal, and my building was the odd one out.

It was within mere minutes that I found myself on her couch, a throw pillow in my lap, and taking a huge gulp from my glass of wine.

"Sweet petunia, *yum,"* I grabbed the bottle off the coffee table to get a look at the label. "This is new?" The enthusiasm in my voice should have been shameful, but it wasn't.

"Someone at work recommended it and of course nothing can be labelled unbeatable until it has the Sav and Allie stamp of approval," she said.

"Very true," I took another sip, "How was your day?" I set my glass down, thinking I needed to moderate myself or else I'd have to crawl home.

"My day was… well, it was good but stressful," she said, looking at me.

"Stressful how?" I enquired. Savannah's job involved a lot of travel and I knew it wasn't always easy for her.

"Stressful about the day coming to an end, not really about the work," she clarified.

"Oh?" *Oh no*. Something was coming.

She set her wine down and did the hand-rub-clap thing that indicated her internal hype session had concluded and she was ready to talk.

"Shit," I mumbled, grabbing my glass of wine and throwing caution to the wind. I'd roll home if I had to at this point.

"No, no, this is fine. It's fine, it'll take two seconds to say," she straightened her posture and turned to face me.

I groaned and took another big swig of my drink.

"Angus and I are dating," she pushed the words out quickly.

I started to choke on my wine and a little came out my nose. It wasn't a pretty sight.

Sav jumped off the couch to grab me a tissue before she settled back slowly into her original spot.

"Are you kidding me, that's what you had to tell me?" I was still dabbing my nose with the tissue, "Freakin' flapjacks, Savannah, I already knew that! Don't scare me like that, I thought you were going to tell me you were getting a cat or something," I sneered at her.

"What do you mean you know? How could you know, we've not told anyone!" she countered, looking completely shocked.

"Wait, are you saying that you didn't know that I knew?" My eyebrows hit my hairline.

"Allie, come on this is important," Sav looked as exasperated as she sounded.

"You're darn tootin' this is important. I outsmarted the people reader of all people readers. What's the date and time? Quickly let's take a photo," I twisted and held my phone out in front of me; Savannah looked positively distressed and I looked a little crazy.

"Perfect," I smiled at her and put my phone away, "You can continue now," I took a sip.

"Thank you," Savannah rolled her eyes, "How did you know?" she asked, her face getting a guarded look like she thought I might have accidentally walked in on something.

"Good grief, whatever you're thinking, stop it. I figured you two were together when he came with you to get me from Dax's," I said. It started off strong but by the end you could hear my voice drain of any type of enthusiasm.

"Allie," she reached out for my hand. I just waved her away.

"Was that the big news?" I asked.

"No, well, not entirely," she took a deep breath, "I'm leaving to go visit him on tour."

"You're what?!" I squeaked.

"Tomorrow," she added on quickly.

"What?! Savannah! How could you only tell me now?" It was an ode to me that my eyes didn't fully pop out of my head.

It would have usually earned me 5 points, but I didn't really think about that rating system anymore. Not since I had added an extra column to the scoreboard.

"I know," she cringed, "I was worried how you'd react."

I felt my face soften, "Savannah, you know I'm always happy for you. If you're happy, I'm happy."

"I know, I just—," she hesitated, "you seem better. I didn't want to ruin that." She gave me her standard Savannah pity eyes.

I was about to tell her to knock it off when she really hit me with a stinker.

"I think you should come," she sounded so resolved.

I just stared at her while I composed myself.

I swallowed, "I'm not going with you, Savannah."

"Allie—," she started.

"No, Sav," I cut her off, "I won't go. It's not even a possibility. Plus, I am almost entirely sure that I am the last person that he wants to see." I picked some invisible fluff off the pillow in my lap.

"He would, Al. Of course, he would. You don't know that," she replied softly.

"I do know. You weren't there, you didn't see his face. I was so mad. So, so mad at him, at everyone. I felt like a joke. I was hurt, and at the time it felt worse than Ben, so, so much worse," I still didn't meet her eyes, but she sat and listened anyway, "It doesn't really matter now, anyway. He left. He heard everything I said, he knew everything, and he left." I said.

"You told him to leave, Allie," Savannah said.

"I know. I thought he would have maybe fought a little more though," I took another sip.

"You would have hated that," she leaned over the coffee table, grabbing the wine bottle and topped up both our glasses.

"I know," I nursed my now full glass.

"You have to tell him, Allie." Savannah settled back into her spot.

"No, I don't. But you go, have fun. I am so happy for you Sav, honestly," I looked up at her finally, "You deserve all the happiness. So, go. I'll be right here when you get back."

"Okay," she said but sounded unsure and her voice was thick.

I put my glass down and shuffled towards her, "Don't do that, Sav."

"I don't want to leave you," her eyes glazed over.

Sav had always looked after me. I never tried to make things difficult, but I knew that she had always worried, especially the last few months.

"You're going to have the best time," I replied.

"I know."

"Didn't you once tell me to feel the fear?" I lifted an eyebrow.

She rolled her eyes, "That was different," she retorted.

"Maybe, but it still applies. I'll be fine. I have string-bean-Dean and Wendy from the Chinese place."

"Allie!" She pushed me away from pulling me into a hug.

"I'm so happy for you, Sav," I hugged her back tightly.

"Thank you," she whispered.

That's how we stayed for a long while.

"This is good. Let's hug for a long time so we get sick of each other and you spend the night at the airport," I patted her back

Savannah laughed and pulled away, "You sure you won't come?" she asked one more time.

"He won't want to see me, Sav," I picked up my glass of wine.

I don't think I could have conveyed accurately just how much I wanted to get on that plane with her.

39

DAX

Savannah arrived with no less sass and flare than she had the last time I saw her.

Maybe not the last time, seeing as that was when she stopped me from seeing Allie. I didn't blame her though. If I was her, I probably would have stopped me too.

Angus' laugh was deep and rumbling and I hadn't heard it as much as I had since Sav had joined him.

It was no surprise that we saw him for only the hours that he was required to have an instrument in his hands for the first three days after her arrival, but once they got *that* out of their system, they had come to join us for our usual evening hangouts.

We'd landed in Spain and Aspen and I were sharing a room during this particular stop.

The crowds hadn't let up once this whole tour. Every show and every signing that followed was bigger than the last. We had thought that the first show of this entire tour was the biggest we'd get. We were wrong.

I hadn't been nervous about seeing Savannah, at least I didn't think I would be, but my heart jackhammered while we waited for their arrival and as soon as they walked into Luke's hotel room, where we had all taken residence for the night, she walked right up to me and gave me a hug.

"Hey, Wyatt," she said, stepping back.

I rubbed the back of my neck with my hand, "Hey, Sav. It's nice to have you here," I smiled at her. It was no word of a lie.

"Good to be here," she smiled back.

And that was it, no more and no less.

We sat down and chatted for a bit. We all took turns versing each other at Mario Kart and when I finally won a race, I stood up.

"Where are you going?" Angus frowned at me.

"Early night for me. Today's show wrecked me," I patted him on the shoulder, "I'll see you guys tomorrow though. Have a good night," I turned to Sav, "Night, Sav," I passed on to her separately.

"Night, Wyatt," she smiled back at me.

I welcomed the hot shower and took the time to wash my hair. Tomorrow we had a day off and I had to go get the red touched up before our next show, it had faded to a weird orange colour. I never usually let it get that bad.

After ruining another white towel, I pulled on some sweats, forgoing a shirt, and pulled out my guitar.

It was liberating. Like a flood gate had been wrenched open. Anytime I could, I reached for the guitar.

I had started five different songs, but there was one that had stuck out to me, one that I worked on the most.

I had just begun reworking the bridge when someone knocked at my door. I thought it was just Aspen. He almost always forgot his key card to get in which surprised absolutely no one.

It wasn't Ap, though.

"Savannah, hey. Everything okay?" I moved back from the door and grabbed a shirt to quickly pull over my head. She walked in and shut the door behind her.

"Yeah everything's okay, I just thought I'd come and chat," she said, moving to sit on the bed that didn't have the guitar on it.

"Are the guys okay?" I sat opposite her on my own bed.

"Yeah, they're still playing Mario Kart," she smirked.

We sat in silence for a bit, it was incredibly awkward if I was being honest.

I rubbed my hands up and down my thighs and just as I went to speak, so did she.

It broke the tension at least.

I cleared my throat and decided I would approach the conversation like ripping off a band aid, “How is she?”

I couldn’t even meet her gaze as I leaned my elbows onto my knees and let my hair fall in front of my face a bit.

“She’s okay,” Savannah replied quietly. I looked up and found her staring right at me.

I tried to read her face, but I knew that Savannah had a good hold on people, meaning she probably also had a good hold on herself. I doubted I would be able to pull anything from her expression even if I tried.

“Is she happy?” I asked, just as quietly as she had spoken. Like if I spoke any louder, the very building around us would crack and fall to pieces.

Sav’s eyes searched my face a moment before she spoke again. I wasn’t entirely sure what was there anymore.

“I would say that she’s trying in that department too,” she replied evenly, she really had a lock on her expression.

We sat there looking at one another for a while, trying to pull something out of the other that neither was willing to give up. Of course, Savannah knew what I was doing.

“I won’t tell you anything that she’s said about you, Wyatt. There’s a friend code with that type of stuff, and anyway, it would be breaking her trust.”

“No, I know.” And I did.

I kept my eyes on Sav, because it became very clear that she had just let slip something slip, and knowing Savannah, she didn’t do it by accident.

Allie had spoken about me.

She’s spoken about me.

My heart was pounding so frantically, if I looked at my shirt close enough, I could see it beating. If I thought about that for too long it gave me the heebie-jeebies.

I knew that I was done living my life out of boxes. I had known it even when I wasn’t doing anything to try and change it.

I wanted 24-hour ice cream stores and early breakfasts and facetime calls.

I wanted shoes off at the front door and 6 out of 10 spaghetti and meatballs.

Mostly, I wanted to tell it all to Allie, I *needed* to tell her. Even if she heard it all, saw all the dusty boxes and taped up memories, and asked me to leave anyway. At least I would have told her everything I should have right from the beginning.

I wanted the constant stream of messages, the rapid-fire questions. I wanted to know if her day was good or bad or in-between. If she needed brownies or if she needed me, like she had once said she did.

Like I needed her.

A small smirk started to appear on Savannah's face as her eyes tracked every thought that passed over my face. Everything I wanted to say I knew she read clear as day.

"I need your help," I said and I knew she knew exactly what I meant.

"Perfect, I already have an idea," she beamed.

40

Allie

Savannah had been gone for an entire month and I'd never been so happy to see the end of July in my life.

Not only had the romantic notion of leaving my place of work with the sun still up melted away in the relentless heat, but I was hot, and sweaty, and blubbering like a baby while I waited at the gate that Savannah's plane had just arrived at.

I couldn't pick her up and bring her back, but Savannah had actually driven herself to the airport when she left, so I caught the train, then the bus, and made the short walk into the terminal I knew she would be at. The plan was to see her after she had gotten back, but patience wasn't really a strong quality of mine.

I spent most of the day reorganising my wardrobe, as most 25-year-old city dwellers did on a Saturday in the summer, and then I got to the airport two hours early.

She walked out of the double doors that were held open and as soon as she saw me, her face scrunched up in an ugly cry, just like mine did.

I ran up to her and pulled her into a hug so tight I even struggled to breathe, but she didn't shake me off for air, she just hugged me back.

Savannah told me all about it. She arrived in Spain and then travelled through with the band to all the major cities they were playing in that country and flew out the same time they did to head to their next stop.

I focused on nothing else except for her experiences and she was so happy. She'd even gotten a tan.

Of course, we had spoken while she was away, but this was different, hearing it in her words as opposed to text messages and photos.

It was amazing, every single part. And Angus was amazing too, for him to have caught Savannah's eye, of course he was.

"What about you?" she turned to me from the driver's seat. We had collected her bags, found the car quickly and were already on our way back to hers.

"I joined a gym," I said to her, looking straight.

"A gym?" she asked.

"I've already run an entire kilometre without stopping. It took me almost two weeks of going every day, but I did it. The first time I tried to run, I almost wet myself," I snorted, turning to her.

Savannah kept looking from the road back to me.

"I also bought a CD. It has a range of different siren noises on it," I kept looking straight ahead.

"What?" Savannah's head whipped to me so fast, I was surprised the car didn't swerve.

"I have listened to it on the lowest volume, with my earplugs, three times," I said.

"And?" She looked dishevelled.

I maybe should have waited to tell her about this until she'd parked the car.

"Dean had to come in the first time and turn it off. The second time I managed to listen to it for 12 seconds before I had to get up and turn it off, but no attack. The third time I managed 30 seconds and I could breathe clearly through it. Sort of." I was staring at my hands.

"Allie," Savannah's voice broke, causing me to look at her. Her eyes were brimmed with tears and she gripped the steering wheel tightly.

"I figured I could try it myself, the whole exposure thing, little by little. I read about it online," I mumbled.

Savannah just nodded her head and wiped her tears away.

"I'm so proud of you, Al," she tried to say, but her voice came out as a strained whisper. I reached over and she grabbed my hand.

"Next is moving on from the brownies," I said with a smile and Sav choked a laugh, letting go of my hand to wipe her cheeks again.

"Step by step, let's not get carried away," she retorted.

Step by step was right. This was good, I felt good, like I was moving back into a version of myself I might have known once upon a time.

I huffed a laugh, "Maybe you're right, maybe not the brownies yet." I went back to picking my nails, and absolutely refused to think about the fact that the brand of brownie mix I bought had changed rather suddenly 7 months ago.

And maybe it wasn't the brownies that I wasn't quite ready to let go of.

41

Allie

If the month of August was a real person, I'd kiss its feet - not considering the Roman Emperor for which the month was renamed by and in representation of, of course.

The tail end of summer was finally upon us and the cooler nights were dropping their fractions of degrees with every day that passed.

I had managed to rope Savannah into coming to the gym with me from time to time, and the day she also ran a whole kilometre without stopping, we celebrated by getting totally shitfaced in her apartment while watching *The Office*.

We'd both called into work 'sick' the next day, as I'm sure you could imagine.

A lot of things had started to change, actually.

Change wasn't really something I yearned for. I was a planner and I liked to know what was happening. I was the sort of person that had to Google suspenseful parts of movies so I could know what happened *before* it happened.

So even the *notion* of change was completely out of my comfort zone.

I had finally run an entire 3 kilometres on the treadmill. I did celebrate with a family sized pizza for one, but all in moderation, you know.

It might have been the adrenaline of that accomplishment, but the next day, when I walked into work with my head held high and Bart the Fart decided to cop a feel as a way of praising my last campaign launch, I turned around and grabbed his chubby little wrist.

There were two different ways that the whole situation could have gone, but I decided to run with it.

I looked him in his beady eyes and said with the most steadiness I'd ever had, "Bart, if you touch my ass one more time, it will be the last thing your sweaty little sausage fingers ever do," I maintained my attention on his face. "If you like the work I do, you can thank me in an email. Have I made myself perfectly clear?" My heart sped up and pressure started to form behind my eyes at what I'd done.

It took him a minute to come to, but he nodded his head so aggressively that his whole face wobbled before he tried to pull his wrist out of my grip.

I let go, turned around and carried on making copies at the printer. I had absolutely no idea how I managed to keep my composure for the rest of the day.

I went straight to Savannah's and broke down on her couch, but she couldn't outline a bad thing about what had transpired.

"If you lose your job, then fuck them, Allie. It's time you moved on anyway. God, you're just— I am so proud of you. Who are you and what have you done with the Allie I know? I'd like to send a postcard wishing her well on her new endeavours, but this new, confident version is amazing." She grabbed both sides of my face and planted a big kiss on my lips.

I shoved her a way, "Savannah!" I wiped away her slobber, she just laughed and tried to come in for another one.

But it was true, everything she said.

I liked this version of me better too, and also, Bart the Fart could shove it where the sun don't shine.

Sav: *Are you sure we have to go to the gym today?*

Allie: *Yes. No backsies-outsies.*

Sav: *What if I'm sick?*

Allie: *I saw you yesterday...*

Sav: *It came on suddenly, and it feels contagious.*

Allie: *I'll see you at 5:30PM!*

Sav: *I've changed my mind, I want my postcard to request the old Allie to come back. The one who thought running was a waste of bodily fluids.*

Allie: *That's the spirit!*

The gym was closer to Savannah's house than it was to mine, but it was close to work which made it a good fit for both of us.

I walked in to find her already there, geared up and ready to go.

"This is an incredibly drastic change of tune," I walked by her and headed to the change rooms.

"I decided today was going to be my 3 kilometre day," she yelled after me.

Savannah did in fact run 3 entire kilometres without stopping once.

I had done 3.5 and we decided that the best thing to do in that circumstance was have wine and pasta.

String-bean-Dean was MIA for the entire rest of the week. He was on some tech conference retreat thing that ran until Sunday, so I was halfway through my Dean-free week and though we got on, I was *loving* it.

"You can have a shower first. I'll order the food," I said to her as I unlocked the door to my apartment, kicking off my shoes.

Savannah mumbled her agreement and kicked off her shoes too. I chucked my keys in the hallway bowl and dumped my gym bag on the chair next to it. I started to make my way to the kitchen, and it took me a second to realise that someone had been in my apartment.

My walking slowed down, and I reached out to grab Savannah's arm.

"What?" She looked at me confused.

I put a finger to my lips to tell her to be quiet and then pointed towards the kitchen island, "Someone put that there, and it wasn't me," I whispered.

"What? The card?" she asked, her voice was just as quiet but she was humouring me, like I was completely overreacting.

"Yes, the card!" I whisper-shouted.

She just shrugged at me, pulled her arm from my grasp and headed down the hallway to the bathroom.

My heart was pounding like crazy as I walked right up to the card and picked it up.

It was white and completely blank on the front. I couldn't help but note that it was incredibly good paper stock.

Not the time, Allie.

I flipped it over.

I held on to the edge of the island for balance. My heart was galloping, and my nose started to sting from the sudden dump of emotion that crashed through me.

On the back of the card was a messy scrawl in black sharpie. It read:

"My favourite type of music is Classic Rock. – D"

Oh my god.

A shuffle from the hallway caught my attention. My eyes were blurry from the tears that made their descent from my rapid blinking. My brain was frantically, desperately, trying to figure out what was happening.

"What?" I looked at Savannah. She leaned casually against the wall of the hallway, "What's this?" I didn't even recognise my own voice. It broke my own heart a bit, I could tell that it might have broken Savannah's too.

The devastating hope that tumbled out was everything I had made the decision to move past. To better myself; take those feelings in my stride, and get on with my life.

It was only then that I realised the door to my apartment had been left open, and in the threshold stood the same boots with too many buckles. The jeans that were tight and black and moved into a worn and faded band T - this one had *AAR* on the front of it.

There was no jacket, but there was the same face that had no right being in the 24-hour corner store that was a 1-minute walk from my apartment in the late hours of a freezing December night. And the bright red hair.

But most of all, I had no idea how he came to be standing in the doorway of my apartment, looking at me like I was absolutely everything he needed. Looking at me in the way that only *he* had ever looked at me. In the way I never wanted to be without.

I, on the other hand, was looking at *him* like an opened mouthed trout. Wonderful.

"What—," I started to say, looking back at Savannah for help. For *anything.*

She just walked over to me and grabbed my hand, placing a soft kiss on my cheek.

"Feel the fear, Allie. And do it anyway," she looked right into my eyes, and she kept on looking until I nodded.

She picked up her shoes and patted Dax's chest on her way out.

I was left standing in the middle of the kitchen, watching as he moved into my apartment and closed the door behind him.

He sat down and took off his boots, like he was in no hurry at all, before he walked toward the kitchen. He came to a stop just that little bit too far away. If I reached out to him, I might have been able to graze his shirt with my fingertips.

I looked up at him, still blinking through the tears that spilled, still trying to piece together what was going on. I'd forgotten how much taller he was than me, even without the boots.

"How are you here? Shouldn't you be in Europe, or, somewhere not here?" The words came out in a strangled whisper.

"Yes. Technically," he pushed the hair back from his face, "We had a week break, so I flew back for a few days," his voice was equally as soft as mine. He tucked his hands into the front pockets of his jeans.

"I don't understand," I tried to clear my throat, but it wasn't really helping, there was no way to hide the absolute shock I was in.

Dax walked right up to me then, like it was a split second decision, and it took every ounce of willpower to not move a muscle. To not grab onto him and bury my face in his shirt, not to run my hands through his bright red hair.

He stopped so close to me that if I took a big enough breath, my chest would touch his. I had the feeling that we'd been right in this moment before.

He reached up slowly and moved the back of his finger down my cheek, wiping away the onslaught of tears that wouldn't stop falling.

I felt like I was always crying lately.

"Allie," his voice was a whisper, heavy with the same emotion that was wrapped around my own vocal cords, "I was stupid," he frowned as he spoke, looking at me but sort of *through* me. He grabbed a piece of my hair and moved it behind my ear. I wouldn't have been able to move, even if I tried. My eyes were glued on his face.

How is he here right now?

"And scared, I think," he went on, "I only knew that everything I'd ever wanted was right in front of me, in everything you said and did. The things we did together. I wanted *that* to be my whole life, I wanted to forget everything else. I mean, I've had girlfriends, Allie. And I will tell you anything you want to know." He looked so serious but as per Allie, a bubble of laughter erupted out of me followed by the biggest eye roll I'd delivered in, what felt like, a very long time.

Dax's face broke out into one of his signature side smirks. It would take some getting used to again, I thought, as my stomach did a flip.

"I don't care about your girlfriends, Dax," I gave him a small smile as I sniffed, but it fizzled quickly, "I was so mad, and hurt and just wanted to disappear. I had always been the last one to know about everything and when the going got tough, really tough, I ran away." I wished that I was wearing something other than gym gear, wished I could have the hem of a shirt to grab onto for support.

"You didn't run away, Allie. I did," his face held such openness, it made me wonder why I ever thought I'd never be able to believe anything he said again. How that, in a million years, could have ever been true.

"I asked you to leave, Dax," I retorted quietly.

"I shouldn't have though. I put every single thing that we did, every memory of us, I put it in a box, and I sealed it up. I refused to look at it. That's what I do with everything and everyone in my life," his voice was shaking, drawing my eyes up to his face, "But I had never wanted to do that with you. With us."

"You were always on your phone," I blurted out.

"What?" His eyebrows lifted a bit.

"Every time we were together, you were always on your phone. You never let me see it, and every time I asked you said it was nothing. On our first date, at the ice cream shop, even the day after we, you know, *got it on* for the first time. That one really rocked my boat, let me tell you," I gave him a look that said 'you couldn't even imagine my inner turmoil because I held it together like you wouldn't believe' look, "I thought that it was Jenna, or someone, who you were speaking to. I wasn't prepared to go back to that reality Dax, I'd—"

"Allie," he cut in gently, silencing my babble of an explanation. I didn't really know where it was going to go, just that there was so much I needed to say to him. Three months of stuff.

"I was writing you a song," he said simply.

"You were what?" It was my turn to look a little lost by his words.

"Whenever I was on my phone, I was writing you a song," he just stared at me.

I stared back. I traced the lines of his face like my life depended on it. I never thought he would be standing in my kitchen again.

"I'm—," my apology was cut off by his own.

"I'm sorry, Allie. There's nothing in my life that I don't want you to know about. There's nothing in yours that will ever be hard to face. I honestly don't think I could go another day without trying your 6 out of 10 meatballs, or hearing you snort-laugh right as we're about to *get it on,* as you say," he wagged his eyebrows and I couldn't stop the laughter that poured out of me along with the tears. They weren't sad though, they were happy.

I was a big, snotty, hiccuping, laughing mess. *This* was what happy looked like.

Dax reached his hand up to the side of my face and I wasted no time leaning into his touch.

"Is this okay?" he asked, slowly leaning down to me.

"I mean, I thought I would be able to move past the nausea, but you really just have this *odour…*," I offered him a small shrug and my best 'don't look at me, I don't make the rules' expression.

Dax tipped his head back in laughter. A sound that hadn't filled my apartment for months, but was quite clearly the exact thing that was missing, the thing that made it a *home* for me.

Before his hand slipped from my face, I grabbed it and tugged it back. Dax looked down at me, his face drunk on happiness and I wasted no time pulling him down to me.

"This is perfect," I said and I pressed my lips to his.

42

Allie

Just because I had used up my sick leave didn't mean I didn't have any annual leave saved up. I hadn't taken a holiday in the entire time I'd worked for the pet store, so when Dax asked if I would go back with him on tour - I had never sent my request for leave to HR so fast, the action wasn't even visible to the naked eye.

We packed up an entire suitcase filled with things that Dax was certain I'd need, or come to want. If there was anyone who I would be taking packing advice from, it was a guy who travelled the world most of the year.

It was clearly no surprise that I was flying back with Dax. Everyone had been waiting at the concert venue that we had to go straight to from the airport and I received hug after hug after hug. Aspen refused to let go and it took Dax, Rip and Luke all chipping in to peel him off me.

I saw Jenna, who rushed over and apologised to me repeatedly, she spoke so quickly it sounded like pig Latin.

I had forgiven Jenna a long time ago, so I passed that knowledge onto her. I mean, I wasn't about to invite her over for a sleepover but, I didn't hold her accountable for the downfall that happened.

I gave Dax a kiss on the cheek and reached into my bag for my earplugs.

"Okay, I'll see you after the show!" I waved over my shoulder at the guys as I left.

"What? Where are you going?" Dax tried to look at me as he was having his hair styled.

I honestly didn't really know why they bothered. They got so sweaty, and Dax ran his hand through his hair so much, that anything that was done to it prior to getting on stage in terms of style was a lost cause.

"I'm heading to my spot at the front of the stage," I answered, holding up my earplugs to him, "I am, after all, your biggest fan." I threw a wink over my shoulder and made my way to the mosh pit.

43

Allie had been on tour with the band for two months, she stayed with us through the end of our Europe leg and all through our South American one.

Two things had never worked so well together. Allie and the guys got on like they'd been friends their whole lives.

Autumn had set in completely and the weather was cooling down everywhere we went. I smiled to myself often about the fact that Allie would be whipping out her *skeenie* when we got home, something she was quite verbal about in terms of her excitement.

Every show we played; she was in the front row.

Every city in every crowd was different, but she was always there. The constant that would always be.

She sang every word to every song.

"Alright guys, how are we all doing tonight?!" I asked the stadium on one of our final shows. Their response was so loud that, of course, Luke had to yell right back at them.

"We want to thank you all for coming out here tonight, you guys have been awesome!" They yelled back at that too, and Aspen threw in a little beat on his drums as emphasis of what I said.

"There's one more song we'd like to play for you tonight. It's brand new, so you've never heard it but—" They screamed and screamed.

My eyes found Allie's and hers were already on mine, along with the biggest grin ever, as she threw in her 'woos' and 'yeahs' with everyone else.

"This one is called 6 out of 10. I hope you like it," I said as I looked right at her and God, I wish I would have taken a photo of the look on her face.

Every song I ever wrote had become about Allie. It sounded cliché, but it was true. Everything could now be tied to her, and it made every show we played that much better.

But this song. This song was really *about* her, and I finally got to play it for her. Telling her everything, from every moment since the baking aisle, how there had never been any doubt that she was everything I'd ever been looking for. The person who could finally help me unpack all my boxes.

Epilogue

"Did it go in?" Allie yelled as she twirled around.

The penny sat to the left of the fountain after what was now her fifth attempt at tossing it over her shoulder into the water.

"Oh, crap," she huffed as she went to pick it up again.

Two years.

Two whole years, and another two albums later, and Allie had been there for all of it.

She fought me on it first, but eventually she agreed to move into the marketing team for the band and ditch her job at the pet store with Bart the Fart.

It was two years of songs written about Allie. Of her at her piano and me with my guitar.

We were currently in Italy and she insisted that every fountain within a 5-kilometre radius of our hotel had to be visited and she had to make a wish in all of them.

I wasn't one for questioning her motives, so I went along with it.

I had ditched the red hair the year before, reverting to my natural black. Allie had been devastated when I told her, she said she'd paced all day waiting for me to come home.

As soon as the elevator doors pinged open and I walked out… let's just say that Allie wasn't disappointed in the slightest and I was hard pressed for time on moving us both to our bedroom before she got the upper hand.

"There's something wrong with these pennies," Allie pouted as she returned to her position to try and toss it in again.

"There's nothing wrong with the pennies, Allie. You just have terrible aim," I smirked at her from where I stood to the side.

She turned to me and stuck her tongue out.

Getting her composure, she closed her eyes and murmured something too low for me to hear and flung the coin behind her. She turned instantly and was already jumping up and down when the little *plop* indicated that her wish had been accepted.

"Alright, where to next?" She beamed as she walked over to me, grabbing the map I held of the area of the city we were in.

"Are you sure that we need to go to every fountain?" I asked, trying not to sound like a drag but this was our fifteenth fountain. *Our fifteenth fountain.*

She even found all the little ones that weren't huge tourist attractions and insisted they were probably the most important ones to go to.

"Uhm, do turtles have shells?" She gave me a look that said 'I think you've lost half your brain. Of course, we have to go'.

I barked a laugh and followed as she grabbed my hand and headed, with absolute certainty, to our next destination.

We had doubled the amount of fountains, bringing the grand total to 30, when Allie flicked her last coin in.

I watched her every time, and every time I couldn't help but love her more.

She turned to me, opening her eyes with a smile already on her face. She walked over, completely content with what she had achieved for the day.

"What?" she asked, trying to read my expressions.

I knew what my expression looked like; her cheeks had started to redden as she dropped my gaze.

"You know," I started, and she looked back up to me. Her eyes widened a bit at whatever she saw on my face, "I have travelled the world more times than I can count," I said.

"Hello, Mr. Humble," Allie countered and poked at my side.

I grabbed her hand and pulled her towards me, earning a yelp of surprise from her.

"I meant that I've been here, to this exact city more times than you've probably been to the public toilet in your nearest shopping centre," Allie scrunched up her nose at my analogy making me laugh, but I kept going, "and this is the first time I've done this. This is the first time that I've walked around the city on my day off, or seen literally any of the fountains we went to today."

I kept my eyes on her and her face softened a bit as she listened to what I said.

"You opened my eyes, Allie," I tucked one of my arms around her waist and pulled her even closer. I just couldn't stop looking at her.

Her face was getting redder and redder, "Dax, if you keep looking at me like that, I might actually combust," she groaned, hiding her face in my jacket.

I smiled into her hair, planted a kiss on the top of her head and waited for her to look back up at me.

She did look up, eventually, and there had never been a more perfect time.

"Marry me, Allie," I asked her.

She didn't hesitate, didn't even wait a second to reply.

"Yes," she breathed and pressed her lips to mine.

Aspen & Poppy

CELINE L.A. SIMPSON

All The Best Notes

(MTME Book 2)

For my brothers, Clarke and Kirk.
I wouldn't be me if I didn't have you.

If you've ever been scared to reach out with both hands for the things that you want, if you've ever been scared to jump for those things that are just out of reach, this is for you.

1

January 5th

I'd never been to this bar.

Actually, frequenting any kind of bar was so far down on my list of things to do it wasn't even on the page. I was only out due to equal parts support of my best friend, celebrating her random and unexpected though not at all unwelcome visit, and out of fear for the safety of my goldfish, Natalie, who'd been threatened with waterly harm if I didn't agree to join her on this expedition (an incredibly below-the-belt maneuver in my opinion).

"Aren't you having *so* much fun?!" Leah projected her voice with startling hardiness. It not only made her dance partner jump, but an older gentleman who I'm pretty sure was dozing with his fingers *in* his beer jolted awake and sloshed his beverage on his wife? Sister? Cousin? *Mother?*

"Uh-huh!" I lifted up both thumbs in front of me while bopping from foot to foot. My shoes were sticking to the ground. *Sticking*. If my feet weren't heavily laced into them I was positive I'd have already lost one.

I just really wanted to go home to the caramel popcorn recipe I'd been hyping myself up to make and my half typed out post for Natalie's instagram account, *@queen.nat.the.first*.

That wasn't something I shared with too many people, but Nat was a star. With over two hundred and fifty thousand followers online, it was probably more respectful to call her what she really was: an icon.

"I think it's getting late!" I called back, my voice at a much more suitable level.

"It's only 10:30!" Leah's voice was filled with what I could only assume was happiness due to the fact that she thought, with great amounts of delusion, that it was still early in the evening.

"I have work tomorrow?" I tried again.

"Tomorrow's Saturday." Leah stopped dancing. With hands on hips she stared at me like she was hoping that I could feel the mental wedgie I knew she was delivering.

Her complete lack of movement made me realize I was still bopping from foot to foot with my hands *still* raised in front of me…*still* giving her the thumbs up. I dropped them to my sides immediately, rubbing my palms down the front of my jeans.

"Stock take?" I wasn't even sure what that would entail in a job like mine. The way my voice heightened in pitch did nothing for my case.

"Poppy, I leave tomorrow, and plus, you *promised.*"

"No– *no,* I never actually–"

She was giving me her puppy dog face. It looked more like she was trying to get spinach out of her back molars while attempting to scratch her nose without using her hands.

"Uh, fine. *Fine.* But I'm going to the bathroom."

"Perfect! Yes, good." She was smiling in a way that was so severe I felt my own face begin to morph into a less-than-ideal picture of concern, "Nothing like emptying your bladder to increase your comfort levels. You'll be lighter. Better for dancing!"

Leah turned away from me in a flourish of leggy movements that didn't entirely make sense to me and I had to remind myself repeatedly that I was in fact, very fond of her and that my friendship with her was totally worth being pushed – no, sorry, *catapulted* – out of my comfort zone. Threats to Natalie's life and all.

In a twist of unusual luck, the ladies room was blissfully empty. Not a tinkle to be heard or a thorough lipstick application to be seen. I didn't need to pee, but I *had* needed some peace and quiet. My bag remained where it was when we'd left my apartment; slung across my body, tattered and fraying at the edges.

I looked away from it and back to my face, swallowing the lump in my throat and studying the haunted way I now looked.

Sometimes I looked at myself and had no idea who was looking back.

'Breathe, Pen.'

I could hear my brother's voice in my head as clear as if he were sitting next to me. I let my eyes close against the pressure that bloomed behind them. Pressure, but never tears. Not for as long as I could remember.

'Big deep breaths like you're about to blow out all the candles on your cake, but don't release it so fast. Breathe out like it's your breath moving through the trees outside. Slow and steady.'

As a kid I'd always been easily overwhelmed and just like everything else, Casimir had always known what to do. As I got older, he'd obviously stopped talking to me like I was eight, but no matter what those were always the memories that surfaced first.

I had makeup on my face but it seemed like an inconsequential thing to be concerned about over needing to feel the cold water on the heated skin of my cheeks.

When I opened my eyes again they were clearer. The light amber color seemed brighter and their identical nature to that of my brothers didn't create a yawning chasm in the pit of my stomach, but rather made it feel like he was looking right back at me. The pink tint to my cheeks made me look pretty, like I was happy to be at this very shitty bar.

Running my fingers through my long chestnut waves, I took a final deep breath, popping all the overwhelming thoughts and feelings back behind the door in my mind they'd managed to creep out of. A practiced mental maneuver so familiar to me it had become second nature over the last decade.

Only then did I head for the door, sure that I might be able to get at least another hour out of the evening.

Maybe.

Thirty minutes for sure.

My eyes were glued to the toes of my own boots and it became evident that, when a much larger pair of boots I didn't know entered my line of sight, I'd just encountered my first roadblock of the evening.

"Excuse me," I said. The perfect picture of politeness.

"I was dancing beside you on the dance floor just before." The voice held the gruff timbre you might expect from a man who smoked too many cigarettes. Like someone with a sort of hacking cough that walked around smelling like a suffocating blend of ashtray and Axe body spray.

"Excuse me," I said again, finally lifting my gaze to look at his face. I think he could have been handsome, maybe he even had been once upon a time. He wasn't anymore.

"I wanna buy you a drink." He delivered the words with a slur and an outrageous amount of confidence. I sort of wanted to ask him if he had any tips on how I might lift my own.

"Oh," I gave a small nod. "No, thank you."

"That's no way to thank a gentleman." He lifted his arms up and placed them on either side of me against the walls. A trifecta attack of displaying the pit stains of his flannel, providing me with a fiercely unwanted odor, and blocking me in even more than he had been before.

"I'm here with someone," my voice sounded as impressed as I was, which was not. At all.

"I think she's just fine in the company of her dance partner."

"I wasn't talking about her." That was a big fat lie. I was quietly impressed with the way it rolled off my tongue.

"Who, then?"

"He's over there," I gestured in the vague direction of the bar with my heart hammering in my chest.

Just as I'd hoped, the oaf turned to get a look at who I was (not really) gesturing to.

I didn't waste the opportunity to duck under his arm, getting a real heady whiff of the stale smell that I was certain would impact the results of my next eye test on account of the burning that ensued.

"Hey!" he called from behind me.

The tone change of his voice made my heart pick up. I tried my best not to run and held in the scream that wanted to purge itself from my soul at the feel of phantom hands grabbing for me.

I was panicked. I was actively *panicking.*

The part of the bar that was closest to the bathroom was occupied by someone who I hadn't noticed at first, but judging by the way his head hung low and how he nursed his beer I'd wager he'd been there for a while and wanted nothing more than to be left alone.

Dark brown hair that looked almost black peeked out from under a baseball cap that didn't really look like it fit with the rest of him. He wore a leather jacket that spanned the broad expanse of his back, leading down to black jeans and black boots.

My only regret was having to ruin his evening. "Excuse me?" My voice sounded more sure than I felt about actioning this plan.

He didn't move other than a slight tensing to his shoulders.

I took that like I hoped it was intended – a better sign than being told to fuck off – and let the rest of the words practically fall out of my mouth, "You don't know me but my name is Penelope, or Penny or Poppy, most people just call me Poppy and I really need your help. Would you mind, uhm, quickly kissing me?"

Well, that got his attention.

"I–what?" His face angled a little more towards me but he still didn't look at me.

"Please? I–" My heart was going so fast I could feel myself immediately starting to sweat, and not in a cute way. "There's someone..." Words had escaped me entirely and it seemed I'd also begun to forget all the words in the English language. "He smells terrifying. *Please* kiss me?" There was a desperation in my voice that I was sure he heard as clearly as I did.

"Hey, you!" The rumbling baritone of the guy sounded behind me.

"Oh, crap." Nope. That was a bad plan. A very, very bad plan. I decided to tell him that and make a run for it. "This was a very bad plan. I'm really sor–"

Baseball cap dude only hesitated for a second. He moved so quickly I didn't get a chance to see his face and then his lips were on mine.

I wasn't sure who was more shocked, him or me.

In the same moment my entire body melted against his. His hand, rough and calloused, reached up to cup my face. His thumb pressed against my jaw with just enough pressure to angle my head in a way that gave him better access to my mouth and I was suddenly made entirely of fireworks. I was an actual open flame.

His tongue swiped at my bottom lip sending a zap straight down my spine.

Woah. Woahwoahwoah.

A small sound escaped me, half surprised shock and half surprised whimper, wholly enough to snap him out of whatever was happening.

He pulled back with a jolt and dropped back onto his stool. He gave off a shocked, surprised and concerned vibe that made me feel like I'd approached him without pants on. The way he pulled his hands from me abruptly left me in a freefall straight onto the stool next to his.

My lips tingled from the fresh memory of where he had just been. Oh my *God,* I just kissed a stranger.

"I just kissed a stranger," I mumbled against my own fingers, frowning to myself. The path-blocking-oaf no longer a thought in my head. "I just–"

"Actually," I could hear the smile in his voice even though he still hadn't looked at me. "*I* kissed *you*."

I gripped the lip of the bar and turned myself around, resting my elbows on the sticky surface that was arguably worse than the dance floor, "But I asked you."

"I've never heard someone say an individual 'smelled terrifying' but oddly enough, I knew exactly what you meant. Plus, you asked me *twice*," he clarified.

"Thank you for that." I dropped my head into my hands.

"Which part?"

"That guy was…" I trailed off, equally as grossed out of his existence as I was with the surface beneath me.

"Yeah, I figured." He took a sip of his beer.

I took in his profile while he pulled his cap lower over his eyes.

"Can I buy you a drink? To thank you properly?"

"Not necessary." His decline wasn't rude, but more unexpected. It was obvious to anyone with eyes he wanted to be left alone, but I clearly had zero social reading cue skills.

"You kiss a lot of distressed women, then?"

Wow, smooth Poppy.

"Only those who ask me twice."

"Ah." I nodded. I felt my face relax into something that resembled a calm, natural sort of comfortability. Was I flirting? Was it *working?!* "So, that's your angle, then?"

"Good cop, bad cop. You're familiar I'm sure."

"Oh yes, you make a great good cop."

"Oh?"

I saw just the hint of a tug at the corner of his mouth.

"Very soft lips," I whispered at him conspiratorially.

The tentative tug at the corner of his mouth got more pronounced and it felt like I had a wild horse galloping in my chest.

"Do you make a habit of not ever looking at the people you rescue?"

"Oh, not really," he said the words on the back of a sigh. Not so much weary as it was knowing. "I was enjoying this conversation though."

"And if you look at me, it will become…unenjoyable?" I frowned. Maybe it wasn't working. The flirting, I mean. I instinctively leaned closer. Baseball cap dude had piqued my interest.

"No, it will be different though." He sounded reserved, maybe even a little disappointed. That was the moment he angled his body towards mine and looked directly at me.

2

January 5th

I was certain I was going into shock. My fingertips started to tingle and I wasn't entirely sure I could feel my nose on my face anymore.

"Oh my–" my voice cracked on the second word.

"Please don't scream," he implored, genuine worry on his face. His tone was calm and gentle like he'd done this before; soothed women on the edge of a mental breakdown.

"*Oh my God*," I whispered this time. "You're–"

"Yes," he nodded, looking at me like he still wasn't sure I wasn't going to scream.

"Do you have any idea who you are?" I couldn't stop whispering. Did my voice box even work anymore?

"That feels like a loaded question, Poppy."

"Mother of pearl," I felt my eyes widen. "You know my name." For some reason that startled me, and my hand flew to my chest.

"Yes, you told it to me when you asked me to kiss you."

Right.

"Twice."

...Right.

"Great balls of *fire,* I just attacked Asp–"

"*Please,* don't say it," he whispered with a small amount of distress. Eyes pleading. Whole *face* pleading.

"Say what?" It was very hot in here. "Are you hot?"

"My name, and like, thermally?"

"Please don't arrest me. I didn't know you were...you. Is it a crime? To have come up to you like this? Oh my God, I'm a felon. Do I need to address you with a title?"

"Give me a second, I'm trying to unpack everything you just said." His brow was still furrowed in concentration, like he was trying to take everything I said seriously, but also trying very hard not to laugh.

"I don't think my legs are working. Am I walking?" I couldn't tear my eyes from his face.

He leaned back to get a better look at the stool I was sitting on and, by default, my legs that were still clearly dangling.

"I don't think so, but I've been wrong before."

"I'm so sorry, I really didn't know you were...*you.*"

"It's okay, no one's ever told me I have soft lips before so, I'd say this was a win-win."

That had to be a lie.

"I think I'm melting." I was still whispering.

"You're not melting." He grinned at me and my heart did a big, massive belly flop into my chest.

"I can't look away from your face," I admitted in a hushed tone.

"That's okay. If it helps I can also look at yours until you're able to?" he whispered back.

"That's–actually, that would be great."

So, there we sat. Staring at each other like this wasn't one of the most peculiar moments of either of our lives.

"...This is actually really cool for me," I broke the silence, unable to stop the way that very feeling took over my whole face so much my eyes crinkled, despite the context of the entire situation.

His lips tilted up in almost a bashful smile.

"Am I coming across cool?"

"Super cool." His face turned implicitly serious.

"You're sure?"

"Absolutely." His lips twitched once before settling back into his serious expression. "You know, you don't have to whisper anymore," he said, picking up his beer to take another sip, not breaking our eye contact for a single second.

"Oh, this is my voice forever now," I said.

"Well then, here's to hoping you never need to call out for someone across a long distance."

"I figured there would be people surrounding you."

"Like members of the public?" He quirked a brow.

"Or security," I countered.

"Ah." He nodded, "Usually, yes. His name is Jason, but I snuck out."

"Woah." My eyebrows lifted in surprise, "That's very bad cop."

"You assumed I was a good cop in the first place."

"Touché." My eyes relented their need to mentally grip onto his face and I finally blinked. It occurred to me then that I'd just had a conversation with a man for what must have been a good couple of minutes without blinking.

Wonderful.

Right, if I'd ever had a cue to leave, that was it.

"Okay, well," I cleared my throat and started to reach into my bag for my phone. "I am *very* sorry, again, for asking you to kiss me. Had I ever thought about this actually happening," I gestured between him and me, trying not to let my stomach flutter at the quick glance I gave his mouth. To lips that had just been pressed to my own. "I assure you, with great sincerity, that was not how I would have gone about it."

"That's okay, Poppy. It was fun, I've never rescued someone from such terrible peril before." His smile was so genuine it was hard to resist the urge to inscribe 'national treasure' onto his person. "Did you need a lift or anything?" He finished the last of his beer and stood up.

"Oh, no." I didn't think I'd ever been so flustered in my life. "That's alright. I'll just find my friend and—"

Leah McDonaugh:
Alright you social butterfly!! I am looking right at you with some fella at the bar.

Leah McDonaugh:
I refuse to salt your game, so I'm going home with Hank.

Leah McDonaugh:
Henry?

Leah McDonaugh:
Harold?

Leah McDonaugh:
Harry! It's Harry

Leah McDonaugh:
It might be Hunter actually

Leah McDonaugh:
Don't wait up sissy, love you! (super proud of you!!!!)

Leah had sent those messages ten minutes ago and if her lack of presence in this crappy bar was anything to go by, she'd ditched me.

"Great." I shoved my phone into my back pocket, hopping off the stool and mentally calculating the odds of me getting home safely on my own. Between Mr. Ashtray-Axe and the general vibe of the perimeter of this bar, I'd say they were fairly low.

"You sure you're good?" I hadn't realized he'd moved to stand beside me. His hat pulled down low once again, hiding every part of his face.

"Yeah, I'm–"

"Come on, I'll give you a ride." He nodded his head towards an emergency exit door to my left.

I was already shaking my head, "I can't ask you to do that."

"You didn't. What's a ride between two people who've kissed?" He looked up enough to shoot me a wink that caused every part of my body that had skin on it to flush.

"I don't know you, though." I was grasping at straws for reasons unbeknownst to myself.

He was trying his best to take my words seriously, but it was clear he was getting a kick out of this. "If I had a pension for never dropping women home after offering a ride, I would have picked a drastically different career path."

Well, he had me there.

I hesitated, knowing I'd already infiltrated what I was sure was meant to be a quiet evening just for him but torn with the reality that Leah had left me here all on my own.

"Really?"

"Really. Fame and crime aren't super complimentary as far as I know." He'd already started walking, reaching the door and pushing it open before I finally convinced my feet to move.

Alright, this was happening. It was really happening.

Aspen Smith, the drummer of the biggest rock band in the world, *Lady Luck,* was driving me home.

3

January 5th

I trailed behind Aspen walking down the dark alley next to the bar and finally taking him in. He was tall and broad and looked like he smelt *very* nice. But I already knew all that.

It was weird that I knew this man more than strangers should know each other. I knew that his eyes were green and his hair was a dark brown. I knew he'd played the drums since he was in single digits and that he liked to bake sweet things. I knew he and his brother started a band that was now that band was the most popular rock band in the world and that even though he could sing, he never did and always declined with the most dazzling smile I'd ever seen.

My eyes lingered on the broad expanse of his shoulders and they didn't stop until they had landed right on his–

"I can feel your eyes either burning a hole into my back or really enjoying the shape of my ass," he called out over his shoulder. "I can't quite be sure of the placement." There was just a hint of a smirk flashing from under the brim of his hat. He walked with his head down and his hands in the pockets of his jacket. It was the walk of someone familiar with remaining inconspicuous when needed.

I pulled my coat around me tighter, blushing like it was what I did for a living and jogged up the extra couple of steps so that I was walking next to him. "Sorry, this is kind of nuts though, you're...*you*."

"That's true," he said. Not in a conceited egotistical way, but rather just acknowledging that what I said was just factual.

"And you were just *here*, or I guess *there*." I nodded my head back towards the bar and watched him from my peripheral vision.

"That's also true."

"And the bar we just walked out of was...well, it was pretty dingy."

"True again."

"Goodness, I don't think I've ever been so right in my life." I turned to face him fully and couldn't stop the grin on my face, or how it widened impossibly when he chuckled quietly. I felt the sound seep into my skin, making me shiver. My body immediately wanted to draw closer to it. To hear it again.

We reached the end of the alley and I stopped, looking for the sort of car that I figured would belong to a rockstar. What I hadn't anticipated was the car that he walked up to.

I rocked back on my heels as if I'd been punched right in the sternum.

My heart lodged in my throat when he stuck the key into the door and thumped his fist just above the handle twice while rattling the key and for a second I was fifteen again, watching my brother do the exact same thing.

"I don't know why we can't get a new car, Cas," I'd said, sliding into the passenger seat when he finally got his door to open.

He got into the car not a second after me, the frame creaking and groaning as it adjusted to bear his weight. Casimir reached across the center console to flick my forehead before tsking. He shoved the key into the ignition, turned on the car and put it into gear. "Just because it doesn't work perfectly doesn't mean it doesn't work well," he replied and peeled out of the parking spot.

The memory was over as fast as it arrived.

My face must have said it all because Aspen looked up and immediately frowned, tentatively walking back towards me. "Are you alright? You look..." He didn't finish the sentence, he didn't have to. I already knew how I looked.

"This is your car?" It sounded like my throat was closing up, like I was struggling to breathe. I think I might have been. I started to count my breaths, trying to calm my frantic heart.

He looked back over his shoulder with a little smile on his face, "Isn't she a beauty?" He asked the question but voiced it as a statement. It was clear that this particular mode of transport meant a great deal to Aspen and the idea of that made something in my chest tighten. He blew the car a kiss before turning back to face me.

"When did you–" The words got stuck in my throat. I swallowed and tried again, unable to tear my gaze from the car. "When did you get it?"

He didn't reply for a little while, long enough that I forced myself to drag my eyes back to his face. His head was tilted to the side. The expression he wore was curious, as if trying to figure me out was suddenly at the very top of his priority list.

"It was Wyatt's first." The way he spoke was unsure, like the words he was speaking were private things he didn't ever share, but for some reason he'd decided to trust me with them. "He got it when he was eighteen and when he headed off to college a year later he gave it to me. Having the car helped with not having him. Been in the family ever since."

Aspen frowned immediately after the words left his mouth, dropping his gaze to his boots. Any other time I might have struggled to keep my eyeballs in their sockets at the casual reminder that Aspen's older brother was Wyatt Maddox Smith, the frontman of *Lady Luck* but out of everything he'd just said, it seemed like the least important part to me.

I nodded my head, trying to get my shit together so that this person I'd literally just met didn't think I was deranged, or for some undisclosed reason repelled by 2000 model Ford Tauruses.

But I *knew* that car.

Not just in the way that you know metal cases that moved around on wheels. No, I knew *that* car like the back of my hand. Or, at least, I'd known one like it.

"Do you…have a thing against geriatric sedans?" He quirked an eyebrow and tucked his hands back into his leather jacket. It was cold, but I'd forgotten about the bite of the air around us.

"No, I—" My voice sounded far away, like you could tell it was traveling from whatever distant memory I'd been captivated by just to spill out of my mouth. I lifted a hand to point in the general direction of the vehicle in question. "My brother used to have a car just like that."

"Oh," he nodded, glancing at the car again. "A man of good taste, then." Aspen's grin was so bright, it was hard not to feel its warmth even when the chill around us had started to make my eyes water. "Come on, it's fucking freezing and I like all my parts attached."

I snorted, "I'm sure you're not the only one."

I started to walk towards Aspen and couldn't help but think how weird this was for me. I thought of my brother every single day, sometimes they were happy thoughts, sometimes the memories were so debilitating it knocked the breath right out of me and I couldn't speak through them. Something like seeing a car that was the same color, make and model of the one he had loved so much would have sent me into a spiral that could have lasted days, but Aspen's cracking laugh reached across the distance between us, wrapping around me like a lasso. It yanked the first step from me, coercing every other that followed until I was standing in front of the passenger door.

I pretended not to notice the little tremble in my hand when I reached for the handle. The part of my brain that couldn't help but highlight it for once didn't put up a fight as I deluded myself into rationalizing the shaking as a mere repercussion of being out in the cold and my total lack of gloves.

"Shit!" Aspen yelled. The sound unrestrained and propelled from his vocal chords with the entirety of his lung capacity.

I screamed like a banshee and turned to take in my surroundings so quickly my head swam. "What?!" I panicked further when I couldn't immediately identify the threat he so clearly had.

"What?!" I said again, giving up on looking around me to settle my panicked gaze on him. But he wasn't across from me where he should've been, getting into his side of the car.

"Penelope," Aspen's voice came from directly beside me and I screamed. Like, unrestrained with the entirety of *my* lung capacity.

"What," *heave,* "in God's name," *heave,* "is *wrong* with you?!" I smacked his chest in outrage before I took in his face and he was, well, he was outright beaming at me.

Shocker.

I smacked him again but this time he held my hand in place against his chest and I felt the rumble of laughter that shook his body.

"Sorry, *sorry.* I realized I didn't open your door for you. My mom would have had me by the balls. Actually, maybe not my mother, but I'm sure someone's mother would have."

"Sounds like you're incredibly comfortable with a lot of mothers," I mumbled, still

scowling at him.

"Oh, very. I share bathwater with them all on rotation." He reached in front of me for the handle of my door, still smiling like he was having the time of his life. I tracked his movements with my eyes until he was back in his original position. "Your chariot awaits, milady," he bowed, flourishing his hand a little.

I tried to hold back my eye roll and failed, "You're not what I expected, at all."

"And what did you expect?" He sounded genuinely curious and so I thought about it for a second before answering. It was important to me, for whatever reason, that I was as honest as I could be with him.

"Well, aside from never expecting to actually meet you, ever, I thought you might have a little more ego. Definitely a more environmentally damaging car. Definitely some sort of security team that you couldn't give the slip. Some ink. A deviated septum, maybe."

"Ink?" He was very clearly trying not to laugh.

"Yeah, you know, like maybe some dice on your bicep, or a spider web on your elbow."

"Like the fuzzy ones that hang from your rear view mirror?"

"I was thinking more like your band logo."

"That would make more sense, yes," he laughed.

I tried to keep my face as relaxed as possible even though my blood pressure was spiking to no doubt incredibly unhealthy levels at the feeling of another rumbling laugh beneath my palm.

"Well, no deviated septum here." He jumped to another of my previous assumptions. "Though it's oddly flattering that you've thought about my nasal cavity," he replied without missing a beat, and then he frowned. "Do you think lots of people have thought about my nasal cavity?"

Aspen looked so genuinely concerned about that reality that I couldn't stop the laugh from bubbling up and out of me.

Definitely not what I'd expected.

"Come on," he said, eyes twinkling and looking at me like he'd won something precious just by making me laugh. "Get in and I'll take you home."

"I can't," I said, my turn to set my gaze on him.

"Why?" A crease appeared between his dark brows, making me notice just how green his eyes were for the first time, even in the dim light from the street lamp nearby.

"You haven't let go of my hand," I said, dropping my gaze from his face to his mouth briefly before settling on the hand he still held beneath his, pressing it to his chest.

"Oh," he sounded as surprised as he looked, which made me smile, *again.* He released his hold on me and stepped back a little, opening the door wider.

Buckling my seat belt while he walked around to his side, I did everything in my power not to observe the interior of his car. Not to look for things I knew wouldn't be there, like the rip in the roof at the back, or feel for the bubble stickers I had placed under the glove compartment as a kid.

Aspen knew the way to my house without even needing to put my address into maps on his phone.

"That's kind of impressive," I said, looking at him with raised brows.

"It's been known to happen once or twice," he winked at me before turning his attention back to the road. He held the steering wheel in one hand and let the other rest on the gear shift.

There was only one word for how he looked right now and it was fucking *delicious.*

I'd been doing a stellar job not thinking about how he'd kissed me for the whole drive. I hadn't thought about the warmth of his lips on mine, or how they felt, or how his thumb had dragged along the edge of my jaw and–

"Penny?" I didn't need to look at Aspen to see the amusement that would no doubt cover his features. I could hear it plain as day in his voice. I knew immediately he'd said my name more than once. It also occurred to me that it was the third version of my name he said, like he was trying them all out for size.

"Mm?" I was glad for the darkened car so that he couldn't see the blush that encompassed my entire body for the second time that evening.

"We're here," he said. His eyes flicked to the little town house right across from us. The porch light turned on, just how I left it. The windows were dark so I knew Leah wasn't home yet.

"Oh," I wasn't surprised by the disappointment in my voice, I was surprised by the real, honest to God knowledge that I'd just said it that way out loud.

Out. Loud.

"Oh!" I said again. Entirely overcompensating and noticing, with no small amount of horror, Aspen physically jumped from the exclamation.

"Thank you, for the lift and the rescue. This has all been incredibly bizarre." I meant it only in the best of ways.

"I've enjoyed our time together equally as much, sweet Poppy." He turned the car off then turned to face me. The total absence of the engine rumbling made the silence seem much heavier.

"Sweet, huh?" I asked, my voice entirely too loud in the confines of his car.

"So far," he replied, his eyes twinkling with laughter.

I watched Aspen in the same way he watched me, with curiosity and bewilderment and a touch of confusion. It made me wonder what he saw, because I was always careful to keep myself in check. To keep all the heaviest and most desperately broken parts that had never healed no matter how many years passed in a safe place, away from direct sunlight. Where the things that I felt too strongly waited with years of learned patience for me to let them out. To give them space to breathe when I didn't need to worry about being seen or heard or noticed.

I'd tried a few times at the start, to feel them in front of Leah, but it hurt her to witness that in me. I knew it did and I was so blindingly terrifying that I'd scare her away that I just...stopped.

My mind had learned when it was best to keep that part of myself quiet, to only let that side of myself show when it was safe to do so, which was when I was alone. When it was dark and the entire world around me was quiet.

It was probably the car, with its all too familiar interior that somehow convinced me to speak. To let a trickle of the words that circled around my mind relentlessly out in the presence of someone I didn't really know at all.

"It was nice getting to ride in a car like this again," I admitted. I'd been thinking that the entire car trip. Ignoring the pressure in my eyes every time it surfaced, knowing it would never amount to anything.

It was just that the seat beneath me felt so familiar. The smell of this car, though different, somehow seemed to still have the undercurrent of pine and vanilla, Casimir's favorite blend of air freshener that he religiously kept stock of in the boot. I felt convinced at that moment that if I got out and checked, there would be a box tucked in the back right filled to the brim with them.

"Your brother doesn't have his anymore?" His question was so innocent, and I never wanted to answer it because right there, in that question, my brother was still alive. He was still breathing, and blinking and *living* inside of Aspen's mind and it made my chest cave because it had been almost thirteen years since he'd been any of those things in mine.

"Casimir died when I was sixteen." I was struck stupid by the oddity of feeling brave enough to say the words when I was looking at Aspen. This person I didn't know, this stranger I'd met in a bar. Like I could say the words and not hear the sound of the gun going off as acutely as I usually did. Not feel the way the same bullet that ended the life of the only person who'd ever been just *mine* also embedded itself into me. Not feel the slight pinch in my shoulder every time I moved my arm that existed because of the bullet that had never been removed.

"Poppy." I could hear the sadness in his voice for me and it was clear then that was the name he had settled on.

Even though I'd just met Aspen Smith, I knew that making him sad was the very last thing I ever wanted to do, so I smiled.

"It's okay," I whispered, just like we had in the bar. I pretended not to feel the phantom weight of the tears that never surfaced well up in my eyes.

He didn't tell me he was sorry for my loss, or that he knew how I must have felt. He just looked at me and it was enough.

"This has been incredibly bizarre," I said again, still whispering. My chest felt a little lighter at the slight lift of the corner of his mouth.

"Certainly was a first for me," he whispered back.

"Bye, Aspen." I reached for the door.

"Ap," he said, his voice not a whisper but still soft enough not to pierce the night around us. "All my friends call me Ap."

I turned to look at him, keeping my face serious. "Friends, huh?" I asked.

"For now." His lips lifted in a shy sort of lilt and I wanted to commission paintings in its honor.

"You say that to all the girls under duress you rescue with a kiss." I opened the car door and stepped out, taking one last moment to lean down and look in at him, knowing full well it would be the last I'd ever see him like this.

"Only the ones that ask me twice."

4

January 6th

Aspen

"You alright, Ap?" My brother's voice sounded in my headphones from behind the glass of the recording booth.

"What?"

The metronome counting the beats for the song we were recording stopped at the sound of his voice. I realized at that moment that I had absolutely no idea what song I was supposed to be drumming to.

"You're distracted," Dax frowned.

To everyone all over the world, he was Wyatt Maddox Smith. Lead singer and rhythm guitarist for *Lady Luck.* But to everyone who really knew him, who really loved *him,* he'd always been Dax. I knew my brother, and he was about to say that I'd been working too much and I needed to take a break.

"You're working too much," he heaved a heavy sigh, like he should have noticed that already. "Let's take a break."

Told you.

"I'm good. Sorry, just lots on my mind." I let the drum sticks roll between my fingers.

"Oh, I bet," Rip, the lead guitarist in *Lady Luck,* said from his spot next to Dax. "I take it that's code for 'yes Rip, the date you set up was incredibly successful'."

I gave my friend the middle finger before signaling to run the track again.

We were in the middle of recording our next album. It was past midnight and our producer and longtime friend, Adrian Douglas, had long since headed home.

We met Adrian when we were just starting off as a band. A bunch of kids who knew nothing about anything except how to play the instruments in our hands.

Adrian had just welcomed his second baby into the world and was running on less sleep than any human ever should. We sent him home early when he went to the bathroom and found him half an hour later asleep on the toilet with his pants around his ankles.

The plan had been to record the drums for at least half the songs we'd already established the rhythm guitar and vocals for. That meant eight songs needed to be done before we could wrap things up.

We were done with five.

I'd long since rid myself of my shirt and sweat was dripping off the end of my nose. I took off my baseball cap to push my soaked hair back before readjusting it backwards and starting the song again.

It was a real honest to God effort to push Penelope-Penny-but-everyone-calls-me-Poppy from my mind. To quiet the chatter of every thought that raced through my head like they were on a loop pedal. It was an effort, but as soon as I pushed all the noise away and let myself lower into that place I always descended to when I was drumming, where I was in control and integral and my purpose was crystal clear, the next two hours flew by.

Dax walked into the booth with a towel and handed it to me. His face was the picture of pure elation. Stepping back, he leaned against the door frame and ran a hand through his jet black hair. "That was good, Ap. Really fucking good."

"Yeah?" My own smile matched his.

Nothing had ever felt quite as *right* as making music with my brother. As feeding off the excitement we both shared when things were going the exact way we had imagined. When a song came to life that had been only four notes strung together or pre-recorded in the voice memo app on Dax's phone. Or a drum pattern I'd been tapping out over breakfast while absentmindedly scrolling on my phone that Luke, our second rhythm guitarist, had recorded without me knowing.

There was nothing I loved more than playing in a stadium of thousands and thousands of people and meeting my brother's eyes, knowing that we did it. We fucking *did it.*

"This album's going to be next level," I said, unscrewing the top of the water bottle he tossed to me and drinking down the entire thing.

"Fucking wild," he laughed, shaking his head before heading back out to Rip.

I followed behind him, running the towel over my hair and flicking off the lights.

"So," Rip said from his spot on the couch, "How was the date?"

"You waited that whole time just to ask me that?" I threw the damp towel right at his face.

"Dude, what the fuck?" Rip threw the towel off him so fast it was a testament to his fight or flight instinct. "Just trying to help you get laid. Sue me."

"Maybe you shouldn't think about my dick so much, it's weird." I dropped down beside him, closing my eyes.

"I only think about it because I care about you." He said the words with a genuineness that told me he was being a hundred percent serious.

"I want you to try and listen to the words that exit your mouth," Dax said, eyes alight with delighted entertainment as he swung from side to side in the desk chair across from us.

Rip just flipped him off before turning back to me. "Come on, Ap. Give me something. She seemed really into you."

I peeled open one eye and shot a quizzical look at my friend, "That so?"

"Yeah, I mean," he frowned, "Why? Was it really that bad?"

"Well," I hesitated for only a second, flicking my eyes to my brother who was looking at me with the same level of excited curiosity before I looked back at Rip, "It certainly wasn't *good.*"

"Was she wearing lime green?" he asked with complete seriousness because I had once, *once,* mentioned that the color had made my head hurt when I looked at it for too long.

"Hated the drums?" Dax chimed in.

"Thought Narwhals were mythical creatures?" Rip asked, making both Dax and I give him a double take.

"What? No, she–" God, I really didn't want to say it. My eyes flicked to my brother again and I saw the moment it clicked for him.

"No," he said, face darkening with the sort of sad anger it always did because unfortunately, this had happened before. A lot.

"I believe her exact words were, 'So, when you say *married,* you mean he's totally not seeing anyone else?'" My impression of her voice was probably off, but I'm sure they got the gist.

Rip's eyes widened comically and Dax just rubbed a hand down his face.

"But she literally said specifically that 'If Mr. Smith is open to a date, I'd love to meet him!' That's what she said."

"And it didn't occur to you to double check which Smith she was referring to?" Dax asked incredulously.

"You're *married!"* Rip exclaimed like no one in their right mind would assume she meant Dax, and that was because our friend was about as descent of a guy as you could get.

"Hey, it's okay, honestly." I closed my eyes again, wishing I could just fall asleep there. "I ended up sneaking away for a beer at that bar *Cherry's,* and—"

Poppy's name was on the tip of my tongue. Her hand beneath mine, against my chest, and the way I knew she didn't think I'd be able to see her blush in the dim light of my car. The feeling of her body melting against mine, molding to me so perfectly that I'd never felt more wanted in my life.

I got up abruptly. "I'm gonna head home." I walked back into the sound booth and grabbed my shirt, tugging it back on along with my hat.

"And what?" Dax asked, confused eyes assessing me.

"And it was nice to have a quiet beer for once." I gave him a little shrug before grabbing my keys where I'd dropped them on the table next to the couch. I didn't want to tell them about Poppy. I felt protective of the memory of her in my head even though I'd only met her once.

She'd been my peaceful moment. My rare blissful quiet at the end of what had been a very loud day and for once I wanted to be selfish. I wanted to keep this one, incredibly *good* thing for myself.

"Message when you're home, boys," I said over my shoulder. "Hi to Allie from me too, please," I tacked on, not waiting for either reply.

Dax and I used to live together before he moved out of our penthouse and into a place with his wife, Allie. I'd lived in the penthouse alone for a full six months before I realized how much I hated it. At first, I thought it was just because I'd lived there with my brother, and then I didn't, and that was why it felt so…*off*. So, I moved into a new penthouse in a different building. Smaller, with less rooms but bigger windows.

I pulled into the mostly empty second basement of my building that only I had access to and punched the code into the elevator that would take me all the way to the top floor.

When the doors opened into my apartment, I was greeted by a dense sort of darkness only broken apart by the glittering lights of the city that trickled in from the windows. I didn't even bother turning on any lights and headed straight for my bedroom, not bothering with the lights there either, instead going straight for the shower.

Every time my brother, or Allie, or Rip, or any of the guys in the band asked me about the new place I told them it was perfect. Bachelor life was much better now that I lived somewhere that was just mine.

That was a year ago and I think they all still asked me from time to time because they knew it was a lie every time I delivered the same practiced reply. They knew in some way that it covered a blistering truth that reared its ugly head every single time I came back to this empty apartment. That it didn't matter if I was here in the penthouse, in a house of my own or even in a studio apartment. It didn't matter if the furniture was new or secondhand or if the entire place smelled like a home cooked meal, because I was still the only one there. It was still *silent*.

I didn't like silence, and the longer I was in it the harder it was to tolerate.

It made room for unruly and unwanted thoughts to circulate and accumulate and get louder and louder and *louder.* I hated the quiet almost as much as I hated sleeping.

To be fair, I hadn't always hated sleeping, but over the last couple of years it had gotten worse and now I only did it when I physically couldn't keep my eyes open any longer, like tonight.

I'd been up and drumming well before the sun rose and met the guys at the studio barely after first light.

I let sleep take me simply because I had no choice. No choice but to be consumed by the silence. No matter how much the frantic, racing beat of my heart protested against the very idea of it.

I'd woken three hours later heading straight for my soundproofed drumming room with twitching fingers. Beats and patterns already built up in my head to an unbearable point to compensate for the absence of noise that surrounded me in every corner of every room.

The moment my drum sticks were in my hands my body started to relax. Only feeling completely at ease when my body was dripping with sweat and my muscles were screaming with the victory that there was no longer space for silence to exist around me.

5

January 11th

Poppy

"And you wonder why I didn't tell you in person." I rolled my eyes, picking all the best parts of the stir fry out of the container.

Leah was doing the same from where she sat in the form of FaceTime in front of me.

Alright, she *had* been doing the same thing. *Now…*she sat with her mouth wide open and half chewed Chow mein on full display.

"Leah, your mouth. Close your mouth," I said around my own chews. "Also, I thought you got all your wisdom teeth removed?" I squinted close to my phone to get a good look.

"I can't," she said, eyes wide with disbelief, "You've blindsided me. And only the top two."

"I haven't blindsided you."

"Is nothing sacred anymore? What happened to the best friend code, sissy?" Her eyebrows were now almost one with her hairline.

Dropping my chopsticks back into my stir fry, I set the container to the floor beside me and heaved a breath, giving my phone my full attention. "Okay, I'm *sorry.* But I don't know what you expected me to do even if I did tell you. You got home at like 3:00 AM and fell asleep on the couch with your jeans halfway down your legs. I'm not entirely sure they were up when you walked through the door." I gave her a pointed look which earned a sly smirk.

"I can't confirm or deny that theory but you're right, I was in a sex haze."

"Precisely."

"I could have seen him before I left." That little smirk disappeared immediately, replaced once again with a scowl.

"How would you have managed that?"

"You could have called him!" She sounded truly incredulous now and it wasn't like I didn't know why. Leah, like me, and honestly like most young girls and women...actually literally *anyone* of any age, loved *Lady Luck.* Leah had a poster of Wyatt at the back of her closet that I'm certain she's kissed on more than one occasion.

"And how would I have done that?" I crossed my arms over my chest, ready for what was coming.

"Have you suddenly forgotten how to use a phone?"

"I actually didn't get his number."

Leah didn't reply. She didn't even *blink*.

I leaned in closer to my phone to see if she had actually frozen. "Leah? Are you there?"

"YOU DIDN'T GET HIS NUMBER?" she screamed into the line.

I'd gotten so close all you could see was my forehead. I was sixty percent sure I'd peed a little. "No, I —"

"You're saying, you bumped into *Aspen Fucking Smith* outside that dilapidated bar and you *didn't get his number?"*

"No. It seemed redundant." I was putting on a confident exterior but I'd thought the same thing over and over and *over* since Friday night. I'd never had any intention of asking for his number, it didn't mean I hadn't wanted it though.

"Penelope." Her tone had changed completely.

She said my name in the same way she'd said it when we were eight and I told her that Tommy Green said he didn't like me back. Or like when we were eleven and we'd found out she had made the volleyball team and

I hadn't. Or like when I moved in with her and her family after I'd lost Casimir and on the six month anniversary of his death I admitted to her in the quiet dark of her butterfly decorated bedroom that I didn't really want to be here anymore.

"It was nice though," I cleared my throat. "You know? Like one of those passing moments between two strangers. Like the universe knew what you needed even when you didn't and then you part ways, forever changed by that single encounter."

Leah's face softened more with every word I spoke. "Forever changed?" There was no one in the world who had known me better than my brother, but Leah had always come in at a very close second. "You like him." She was beaming at me so big it was like she had marshmallows stuffed into her cheek. Or maybe a buttload of Chow mein.

I rolled my eyes, "Everyone likes him."

"Mmhm, but you like *him.*" She wagged her eyebrows, funneling another dumpling into her mouth.

"We interacted for like, an hour."

"Stranger things have happened," she countered.

Preaching to the choir, sister.

"I can't believe you met the drummer from *Lady Luck,*" she said again in a quiet reverence that I'd once shared with her.

But when I thought of Aspen Smith now, I didn't think of him like that. The man I'd collided with, who I'd asked to kiss me twice. Whose laughter had reverberated beneath the pads of my fingers and wrapped around my nerve endings, setting every part of my body alight. He was so set apart from the version of him I'd thought I'd known and all I wanted to do was learn all the other things I didn't know about him now too.

They were all just big, crazy 'wants' though. Things I wanted for myself but knew I'd never have.

"I miss you already," I said, wishing she was right beside me again so I could wrap my arms around her.

"Me too, sissy," she said, blowing me a kiss. "Not long now until your birthday, will you come home? We missed you over Christmas and you know that Mom and Dad would love to see you."

"I'm not sure yet, but I'll let you know as soon as I do."

"Alright, sounds good." She smiled at me the same as she did every year, knowing those words were just a cover for the answer I eventually gave, which was no.

I would always be grateful for the way Leah's parents took me in. The way they had made space for me in their lives when they hadn't needed to. When my own father hadn't wanted to.

But no, I wouldn't go back.

We said our goodbyes and I cleaned up my apartment on autopilot.

I had picked up a new wisteria plant for Nat's fish tank and quickly posted about it, typing out the caption that sat below her cute little face: *I am officially a crazy plant fishy #mymombuysmyplants #isthatweird?*

It was only once I was in bed did I let myself think about the one word that always rattled around in my head. It felt like a song I had heard once and loved, but now struggled to remember the way it began.

Home.

People threw that word around too much without really knowing what it meant to them; it was their hotel room on holiday or the city they were born in and moved from at age one. The first apartment they rented for three months on their own with a terrible upstairs neighbor and the bathroom with no door.

I didn't think any of those definitions were true.

To me, home was a feeling. It was so consuming and overwhelming and the very act of leaving it shook the foundations of your whole entire world. It *hurt* to leave it.

It was the hardest goodbye that ever existed and the happiest hello every single time.

I didn't have a home now, but I knew that feeling because I had it once before. I knew what it was like to have it with every cell of my body, which was why I knew what it was like to live without one.

It was the driving force behind my need to move so frequently.

I managed to wake up and move through life every day because of the rules I had put in place for myself. I called them 'Poppy's Life Rules'.

The first of many was keeping myself firmly split in two. It didn't sound healthy, but it simply just *was* and had been since I was sixteen. One half was for me, the other for the world. I had as much interest in sharing that part of myself as I was certain people wanted to witness it.

People were uncomfortable with pain. There was never the right thing to say, or do, or way to act, and soon enough it became too hard for everyone and people did the only thing they thought they *could* do, which was step away.

And away, and away. Then they were gone and that was it.

The second was that I always, *always*, made sure to call Leah, or at the very least message, no less than three times a week.

The third, and most important, was never to stay in one place for more than a year.

As soon as I'd set off on my own, I had needed something to hold on to. That 'thing' became a fierce determination to find that feeling again. There was only one way I figured how to do that, and that was to chase it. To cover as much ground as possible as fast as I could.

It made sense to just move on every year on the date I moved first.

April fifth.

It was three months away and it was coming too fast and too slow all at the same time. I didn't know where I was going next, only that I was going.

I had to go. It wasn't a want, but a need. I *needed* to find that feeling again.

Home.

The very idea of being without it for the rest of my life terrified me right back into my sixteen year old self, admitting my darkest secret into the quietness of the world.

So, that's why I moved. Because everyone deserved that feeling, even me.

I hoped by the time I found it, I'd believe that.

6

January 12th

I saw him coming out of the corner of my eye and I knew exactly the sort of expression my face was making and I couldn't do a thing to change it.

"Woah, there she is!" Todd said and I immediately wanted to throat chop him. "Popsicle, give me some." Todd held out his knuckles to me and like every time he did that, I stared at his hand with immense confusion.

"Heavens," I mumbled, pressing my thumb against the pressure point that existed between my eyebrows to alleviate the immediate headache that surfaced.

I knew what a fist bump was, I'd given and received many in my life. I would even go as far as saying that I was a *fan* of the fist bump. I just refused to A: acknowledge that's what he was asking from me and B: respond to the nickname 'Popsicle'. Ever.

"C'mon, Popcorn, I explained it to you yesterday." His eyes narrowed a little but his classic smile that showed too many teeth stayed firmly in place.

I wondered then if the casual use of a term of endearment usually reserved for one's father sat as uncomfortably between us for him as it did for me. My guess was not.

"You did, Todd." I didn't deny his claim, he'd explained it to me everytime I didn't fist bump, which was always.

I drummed my fingers on the counter, doing my best to ignore his hulking figure next to me while I waited for the microwave to finish heating my food. I usually timed my trips to the staff kitchen perfectly, missing Todd at least three out of the five days in the working week. Todd reminded me of the sort of guys in high school that were cool because they were mean and then grew up but didn't grow *out* of any of their habits.

"So, when can I get that date?" He stepped a little closer to me and the same marginally uncomfortable feeling that washed over me as always arrived right on cue. I wasn't totally sure what it was about Todd, but from the moment I met him a little light flashed in my head with a voice attached screaming '*Alert! Alert!*'.

The most aggravating part of it all was Todd didn't even work near this kitchen. He had his own kitchen, all the way over on his side of the office which meant he purposely walked over here when he knew I was having lunch.

Gross.

I had immediately become a conquest for Todd from my first day here, and if I knew him (I didn't really, but from our contained interactions I sort of had an inclination) then I knew that Todd didn't particularly like the word 'no'. So, on the days that our schedules unfortunately collided, he cornered me in this kitchen and asked me out.

"Sorry, Todd. My answer hasn't changed and I still have a boyfriend."

There was no reason why he should have, but Aspen Smith immediately popped into my head. He just appeared right in my occipital lobes out of a puff of smoke. *Bam!* There he was.

He'd done that pretty much every single day so far this week. Like always, I delivered an appropriately placed mental flick to my own forehead at the swell of unruly emotions that surged at the very idea of putting 'Aspen Smith' and 'boyfriend' into the same sentence and relating them to me. It wasn't healthy for my lady bits.

It was also delusion. Those words *couldn't* exist like that.

One moment delivered by the universe, I reminded myself.

Never to be repeated again. I chanted over and over...*because you were the idiot that didn't ask for his number....even if you'd never use it.*

I gave Todd a quick tight lipped sort of grimace, clocking thirty seconds left on the microwave.

Fuck it, cold Thai was better than Todd and his overbearing cologne.

I grabbed my food, a fork from the drawer and made for the exit. The *only* exit.

Todd stepped in front of me, crossing his arms. "You know," he said like I wasn't trying to escape his presence, "you've said that every time I've asked you and I've never seen him. You don't even call him on your lunch break and I've never heard you talk about him to anyone."

Todd was a big guy. He filled up the entire door frame with his head almost touching the top. I had to crane my neck to the point of pain to see him and I knew nothing about the image I posed was intimidating.

I pushed every thought of Aspen from my mind and squared my shoulders, looking up, up, *up* at Todd, "The fact that you know whether or not I call my boyfriend on my lunch break is incredibly alarming."

"You know what I mean," he smirked, casually leaning his shoulder on the door like he wasn't actively demonstrating all the traits of a creep. "Go out with me, come on."

"Nope."

"Penelope–"

"I'd like to get by, please." I pretended not to notice the way his toothy smile stopped looking like a smile entirely and more like he was baring his teeth at me like a rabid dog.

Coming back to reality, I sat down at my desk and ate my leftover Thai in peace, deciding to work while I forked cold Cashew Nut Chicken into my mouth. I actually really liked my job and the thought of leaving it when I inevitably moved on sent a small surge of regret through me.

I was a transcriber. People submitted things like voice recordings, interviews, presentations, and I listened to them. Turning all their spoken words into written ones as I went. The only qualification I'd needed was an above average word-per-minute typing speed and the ability to sign an NDA.

It was a desk job just like any other, but there was also always something new to learn, too. For example, today I learned that Jupiter had a moon called Io and, unlike Earth's moon, that one actually had multiple hundreds of volcanoes. Volcanoes that *erupted,* making it the most active moon in the solar system.

Fucking, *woah*. That was something I'd definitely fist bump over.

"Hey, P," Jessica, who worked three cubicles down from me said. Just her eyes framed in thick, black rimmed glasses visible over the top of my cubicle wall.

Jess was an incredibly kind, single mother of two that had always been welcoming without being overbearing. She was the perfect sort of work friend and the total opposite of Todd.

"Hey, Jess." My smile was genuine and even though I couldn't see her face from the nose down, I knew she was smiling back.

She walked around to stand in the entry of my cubicle, her turtleneck a bright yellow under her long, crocheted overalls.

Yes. *Crocheted.*

"Oh, new sweater?"

"You like it?" She beamed at me before reaching up to fiddle with the collar.

"Very much," I beamed back. There was no need to let her know the bright, highlighter-like nature of most of her clothing had me fearing for the health of my eyesight. Jess loved in-your-face colors and if they made her happy I was convinced that was all that mattered.

"Get through much today?" I asked, noticing for the first time it was 5:30 PM and I was officially off the clock.

"I had a court case." She wagged her eyebrows at me.

"Ooo!" I gasped, looking at her with real, genuine excitement.

"We're talking about a granny running through not one, not two, not *three,*" her voice rose steadily with every number, "but *seven* red lights. All within twenty minutes of one another."

I whistled. "Holy smokes."

"And the best part," she went on, whole body almost vibrating while she bobbed on the balls of her feet.

"I'm not sure I'm ready." I closed my eyes and pressed my lips together.

"Her first name was Ina–"

I cracked an eye to see Jess's face was going red with her effort not to laugh.

"—and her last name," the laughter broke through and she crossed her legs like she was trying really hard not to pee her pants, "was *Minit.*"

I gripped the armrests of my desk chair and released my own belly laugh. Half from her story and half from the contagious effects of her own bubbling laughter.

That was precisely the state both Jess and I were in when our boss, Winston, a young man who was roughly six years my junior strolled over like he was already in on the joke.

"Ladies," Winston said, leaning on the top of my cubicle wall and smiling at us in a way that made his top lip completely disappear beneath his mustache. "This seems like the place to be."

"Oh," Jess struggled valiantly to collect herself. "Hey, Winny. Just telling P about the flatulent properties of cauliflower." She delivered that line with a wink that closed both of her eyes.

Winston, bless his heart, nodded before giving Jess a double take. "Oh," he immediately became flustered, "are you…are you alright?"

"Oh, yeah," she said, waving him off. Her cheeks reddened slightly and she dropped her eyes to the floor. "Just bloated."

Winston, *Winny*, nodded sympathetically and Jess looked mortified. It was well known in the office that he took the responsibility of the constitution of staff members rather seriously. A weird thing for any workplace superior to hone in on and make their niche, but Winny was a weird guy so it sort of made sense.

Rumor had it that one time, Rahoul from accounting was having some serious bowel issues and Winny passed him a diluted gentle laxative under the lavatory door.

"Well, I just wanted to see if Poppy was coming to the staff Say No To The January Blues party, but actually, Jess you haven't RSVP'd either."

"Undecided," Jess said in a perfect blend of kind yet confident.

"Same," I jumped on the back of her self-assured train, "but I'll let you know soon."

Jess waited for me while I packed up my stuff so we could leave together. She asked me about my week, I asked her about hers, and it was perfect because she didn't push when I offered her the surface level pleasantries that only an acquaintance required.

Todd called out for us to hold the elevator from across the office and Jess responded by hitting the 'close door' button with vigor.

We parted ways in front of the building, her going one way and me going another. Forty minutes later I was sliding my key into my front door, shooting off a quick message to Leah in response to her last text at lunch time on whether or not it would be possible for Aquaman to *actually* exist.

Me:

Yes, I'd like to think somewhere out there, Aquaman really does exist.

Leah McDonaugh:

Superman?

Me:

Of course.

Leah McDonaugh:

Ant-Man?

Me:

God, I hope so.

While that conversation was happening via text, I also hopped into Instagram to send her a couple of memes I'd saved about never growing out of our emo phase and how, weirdly enough, the crossover that was happening between country songs and punk rock music was totally our vibe.

"Hey, Nat." I leaned down to plant a smooch to the glass of my goldfish's tank. Natalie was fourteen years old and, besides Leah, the closest thing to family I had now. She had been a gift from my brother on my fourteenth birthday.

I sat in my apartment eating one of the pre-made meals I'd spent last Sunday prepping for the week (a new thing for me, I'm not entirely sure it's going to stick), laughing intermittently at the meme's Leah was sending through, and then proceeding to share that humor with Natalie.

I'd just gotten into bed when my phone rang.

"Hey sissy," Leah said around a yawn with her face far too close to the camera, her hair twisted around a pair of tights in what was her fourth attempt at getting those heatless curls that she'd yet to have any success with.

"Hey sissy," I said back, peppering my phone camera with kisses.

She gave me the run down on her day first, telling me about how she was determined to learn calligraphy before the new year but couldn't figure out how to use a quill.

Leah was a photographer. She had stayed in our hometown and exercised her personable, approachable and people-loving qualities to build a thriving business that specialized in newborn photo shoots. In her spare time, she was on a never ending search for the perfect hobby. Calligraphy, it would have it, was next on the list.

"I feel like if you attacked these things alphabetically, it would create some order to your chaos."

"You make a valid point," she conceded, but made no further comment, letting the conversation end right in the middle of its existence. My friend danced to the beat of her own drum, and for a long time she had taken me by the hand, keeping my feet moving along with her own when all I'd wanted to do was stop.

Aside from those couple of times in the first year I'd officially become a part of her family, I hadn't said a thing to Leah about any of what reeled in my head. The whole new version of myself that coexisted with the person I used to be, that just constantly screamed behind that door in my mind. But Leah had done her best, and it had been enough for me.

Sometimes I would be bursting at the seams with it. With all these emotions and feelings and anger. Things that made me mad and hateful and painfully sad. I was always unwilling to unleash it upon her, unable to fathom the concept of hurting someone else I loved in any capacity in any way, ever again.

The thought I might do that still filled me with obscene amounts of guilt at random points in my day, but I was selfish with Leah. Utterly unable and unwilling to let her go.

"And your day?" Her eyes had already started to droop. "Quickly, tell me about your day." Leah reached up and pinched her eyes open, reminding me of that scene in the Mr. Bean movie where he used toothpicks to keep his eyelids from closing.

"I have a good one for you," I said around a bubble of laughter, diving into the tale of Ina Minit, Todd, Winny and the January Blues party I didn't think I would go to.

"How's Rahoul?" she asked.

"I think he goes to the bathroom on a different floor now."

Leah nodded her head like that made perfect sense to her.

I almost told her about my thoughts of Aspen. *Almost.* But I didn't.

When we hung up after a very dragged out series of air kisses, I ended up just laying there, wide awake and thinking solely about Aspen Smith.

'It was hard to be gentle with myself when my stomach was in knots and the very idea that I'd somehow mistaken this universal gift as a once off when it was intended to be something more than that. It made my hands clammy.

Something more. What did that even mean? It meant everything and nothing all at the same time.

It was helpful when I reminded myself that while I didn't ask him for his number, or fax number or what direction of the city I should be directing my smoke signals, he also didn't ask for any of those from me.

And then I felt stupid and naive all in the same breath because he was a man that actively had thousands of pairs of underwear thrown in his general vicinity more times than I really wanted to think about on a yearly basis...and I was me.

My lungs filled only to expel a heavy sigh and the sheets that clung to my legs were now too stifling.

Of the things that I'd learned about Aspen in the hour that I'd met him, *really* met him, it was that he was a decent human. That, for some reason, he'd needed to sneak away from his own security guy to have a quiet beer in a crappy bar and had been too nice to tell me to get lost. And he kissed me to save me from a man who had smelled terrifying and had somehow known exactly what I meant.

There was also the asking twice thing.

I could still feel the swipe of his tongue along my bottom lip. I hadn't been able to *not* think about him without my stomach tightening and the severe and sudden urge to squeeze my thighs together. It became abundantly clear that a single kiss from Aspen Smith had been more satisfying than some of the actual sex I'd had.

By some, I meant all of it. All twenty minutes of every combined encounter.

All four times it happened.

You know what, make that three and a half. I still couldn't fully comprehend the five seconds and single thrust delivered by Henry Lexington in the backseat of his beaten up truck the day after my seventeenth birthday constituted as actual sex. Leah still couldn't contain her laughter even now, doing what I'd never actually admit was an impressive impersonation of his high pitched, *'oh, yeah!'* that spanned the duration of both the start and the end of my very first time.

It made me think about the way my body had buzzed to life with Aspen and how, for that moment, it was as if I'd never known what it was like to be awake before. That another person could make me feel like that. That if having the bare minimum of Aspen did that to me, what would it feel like to have him do *everything* to me?

I'd known him for a heartbeat and already he'd pulled more from the dark, quiet part of my mind than anyone ever had.

That terrified me for two reasons: the first was that I wasn't sure I would survive reliving the things Aspen seemed inclined to pull from me, knowing or not. The second was that I knew, without a shadow of a doubt, that the only thing sharing those things with him would achieve would be to hurt him, just like they'd done to Leah.

My thoughts were a broken record that had played on repeat in my head for the last six days because the only way I'd ever see him again was from the nosebleeds with him on stage.

And, you know, maybe in that moment it might feel like he looked my way, squinting into the farthest part of the stadium. For a second he might remember the girl he drove home in a car she secretly loved more than he did.

That's enough, I thought to myself. Rolling over onto my side and closing my eyes. *That's enough because it has to be.*

7

January 13th

Aspen

I knocked my boots against the side of Dax and Allie's house. The snow fell from my shoes in clumps and the sign I had gifted my brother and his wife for Christmas last year rattled from the impact.

The hand carved – arguably priceless – artifact read *Wallie's Place*, where it had been lovingly nailed off center and on a bit of a slant right next to their front door.

"It's off center, Ap," Allie had said, trying to line her body up with the part of the house it should have been positioned in.

"And it's...I think it's crooked," Dax said, chewing on his bottom lip while he tilted his head to the side.

"So, perfect?" I asked, standing next to them in their front yard while it snowed.

They both walked over and wrapped their arms around me, sandwiching me between them.

"Perfect," Allie said, looking across me to give Dax a watery smile.

"Perfect," he said, looking at her in the same way.

The memory settled against my heart as something warm and familiar as I stepped inside and let the door close behind me.

"Heyo!" I called down the hallway, the gentle sounds of classical music and laughing trickling down to me.

"I called it!" Savannah, the girlfriend of Angus, *Lady Luck's* bassist, and Allie's best friend shouted with tremendous passion.

"You're two minutes late, that means Luke wins," Allie said, the image of her poking her tongue out crystal clear in my mind.

"I won?" Luke sounded delirious, "I never win!"

"You didn't win," Savannah deadpanned. "*I* won."

"I guessed your arrival time, Ap! *I won!*" Luke flew around the corner, charging at me with such intensity that all I could do was move my hands to cover my balls and brace for his weight when he jumped onto me.

"You didn't!" Savannah yelled after him a moment before I saw the bright blonde of her hair charging at me. I released an *oof* at her making what had to have been a running jump onto me as well.

"*Hey*!" Sav's voice was incredulous and I couldn't help my smile, "I'm light as a feather."

"Yes, ma'am," my voice was muffled by Luke's arm in front of my face.

I spotted my brother from the end of the hallway, his black hair still damp from a shower and his eyes glinting with mischief.

"Wyatt, no," I pleaded, moments before he launched down the hallway, calling for his wife and adding himself to the pile.

"Fuck me," I grunted. "I'm going down."

"Not without me!" Allie called, and the top of her brown hair was the last thing I saw before my knees buckled beneath me.

"I got that one!" Angus called from the direction of the living room, the pride at finally managing to capture a photo of the 'Aspen Pile', as it had been so lovingly dubbed.

"Did she make it?" Savannah called from somewhere in the pile of people above me.

There was silence while we waited for the result.

"She made it!" Angus yelled, throwing in a few '*woop*'s and '*fuck yeah*'s.

He was, of course, referring to the amount of people I managed to hold up before we all fell. Last time, I crumbled like a shortcrust moments before Allie had managed to add her weight to the pile. This time, I'd held out.

"Why do we do this again?" Luke asked, offering me his hand to help me up.

"I—" Allie started but stopped immediately and looked back at me from halfway down the hallway. "I actually have no idea."

"Neither," Savannah said, grinning at Allie while she fixed her brown waves, stopping her from looking like she'd just been electrocuted. we

"It just makes sense," Rip called from the living room. "Now hurry up, this game won't play itself."

It was Friday night, which was games night and the one night a week, when we weren't touring, we made sure we all got together as a family. It was something we had sort of tried to do a couple years ago, but Luke's ex-girlfriend had never really cared for them. They always ended up being a boys hangout which wasn't any different from what we always did anyway.

When Angus and Savannah moved in together, Luke moved in with Rip and suddenly family games nights became everyone's favorite part of the week.

Our game of choice had always been charades. It continued to baffle mostly everyone present because none of us could actually act that well. Allie, on the other hand, had held tight to what she continued to describe as 'her truth' that she was exponentially gifted at this game. Any time anyone even attempted to allude to her that she was just as bad as the rest of us like, for example, pointing out to her that penguins didn't *skip,* Dax either threatened or followed through on grievous bodily harm.

Teams were decided based on couples and households, but Luke and Rip just sort of adopted me into their duo. I knew the question was coming, I saw it in four sets of jittery stares that made the spot right next to me appear a thousand times more vacant than it actually was.

"So," Luke started, completely ignoring the elbow to the ribs delivered not so subtly by my brother, "where's your girlfriend?" He wagged his eyebrows at me.

I felt the same pressure on my chest that made itself known every single time I was placed into a situation where I didn't think I could follow through in the way people expected. I didn't want to answer the question, wasn't really sure *how* to answer it. How to do it and not picture his face falling. So, I did what I always did. I gave him my biggest smile. The one with the dimples.

"Oh, I'm sure she's somewhere out there," I huffed a laugh and settled back into the couch, tucking my hands into the front pocket of my hoodie.

The moment the words left my mouth, 'somewhere out there' came to me vividly in the form of the back alley street outside of *Cherry's*. I felt the moment my mouth went dry, filled with the remains of every word I had wanted to say to Poppy but held back for fear of *what,* I wasn't exactly sure.

Fear of everything, probably.

I thought about her and it felt like I was falling, like the ground was racing up to meet me over and over again but I never made contact.

Poppy. *Poppy.* I liked the way her name sounded in my head almost as much as I liked saying it out loud. She'd given me three different names to choose from, like she'd wanted to let me make up my own mind of who she could be to me.

She hadn't known me at all when she'd stumbled to my side and asked me to kiss her.

The look that took over my face was utterly involuntary at the memory. That she had taken the time to introduce herself with three different names in the midst of what I could have only assumed was a great and terrible panic. I'd thought about the way it felt to have her pressed against me more than I'd thought about anything in a long time.

"What's that look?" Allie had come to sit next to me without me even realizing it. She spoke quietly, considerate of the incredibly attuned listeners around us.

"What look?"

"*That* one." She pointed right at the middle of my face.

"Just thinking." I let my head drop back to the couch. "Not something you witness frequently, I'm sure. Living with he-who-must-not-be-named."

"It does always look painful when he does it," she frowned, nodding her head in agreement. "Like a cross between trying to focus his eyes on something too close to his face and remembering how he called the moment wrong when our neighbor Mike was trying to hand him something but Dax thought he was going in for a hug."

My head rolled to the side with laughter, able to imagine that exact moment perfectly. "What a dingus."

"The biggest dingus." Allie's smile was bright and clear as she stared at my brother across the living room with nothing but pure, unfiltered love on her face. "So," she continued, "that look?"

It had been a long time since I was caught between not wanting to let someone down and wanting to keep something for myself. I didn't want to lie to her, but I *did* want to be selfish with the thoughts in my head.

Selfish.

The very idea of it pushed me to say something.

"I met a girl," I whispered the words to Allie in the same way that Poppy had whispered to me, and I cursed myself for the thousandth time that I hadn't asked for her number.

You assumed she wanted to give it.

I did, for a second. And that had been all for me, I thought. So, I didn't ask.

"Oh?" Allie whispered back. "Just once?"

"Mm," I hummed, focusing on something in the bookshelf across from me. "Just the once."

"No number?" She quirked a brow, remembering that when she and Dax had met, they faced a similar issue.

"Must run in the family," I winked at her and she rolled her eyes. The truth was, I'd almost driven to the bar three different times on my way here but I reminded myself that even if I went back there, she wasn't going to be there.

That wasn't the first time I'd managed to have a beer at *Cherry's* on my own without anyone seeing me or following me there.

There were paparazzi almost permanently camped outside of my apartment building and even though they tended to leave us all alone, at least when we were home, only snapping a photo of us coming or going and no real pursuits of any kind. One of the biggest selling points for my new apartment was that there were two exits: one went out onto the public street, the other was a little bit of a maze to get through with a fence that spanned back almost a whole block and three different gated entrances depending on where you were going. That's the way I usually went when I really didn't want to fuck with them.

Namely when I was heading to *Cherry's.*

Even if they did catch on and happened to be at one of the other gates, I usually had enough time and skill to lose them without much effort. The Taurus had never let me down.

"She's not going to be there, if I go back," I mumbled, my eyes darted to my sister-in-law who had really become more of a best friend to me in the last three years.

"Might not be," she nodded, "but she might be, too."

I thought about not at least *trying* to see her and the idea made my chest ache. It made my body hurt all the way to my fingernails.

"Yeah, she might be."

If she wasn't there, I'd let it go. I'd give it one shot and then I'd force myself to stop letting her consume every single thought I had.

"Thanks, Al." I gave her a quick kiss on the top of the head before I headed for the door.

"Hey, where are you going?" my brother called from behind me.

"Out!" I called back, the word not even fully out of my mouth before the door closed shut.

Not even ten seconds later my phone was buzzing in my pocket. I reached for it on instinct, to pick it up, to be there for whoever it was that was calling, whoever it was that might need me. I knew, rationally, that it was probably Dax, and that he was inside his own house with all of our friends.

Safe.

I knew he was safe, but the panic that started to claw at my throat at the reality that I was seriously considering not picking up was making me feel sick.

I had just gotten into my car when the buzzing stopped. All I wanted to do was turn the car on and put it in drive.

Poppy. Poppy. Poppy.

Her name was echoing in my pulse. I could feel it in my fingertips.

I couldn't do it.

"Fuck," I grunted between clenched teeth, digging my phone out of my pocket and pressing redial immediately on my brothers name.

"Ap?"

"Hey!" I shoved every ounce of cheerfulness into that word. "You all good?" I kept the smile on my face because it made it easier to keep the smile in my voice. To keep it from cracking and letting the panic that was clouding my vision seep through.

"Yeah, I just…you sure you're okay?" He sounded worried, and suddenly I had gained a bit of clarity. That I hadn't thought about how he'd feel, any of them really, if I just walked up and strode out. No explanation, no nothing.

My gut twisted.

"Sorry," I said, rubbing my eyes. "Sorry, Dax. Yeah I'm good, I just—" I started to explain but it was Allie who cut me off, pulling the phone from my brother.

"I can't believe you called him." I could hear her frown as she attempted, and failed, to keep their voices from traveling through the phone. "He's a grown man, Wyatt. He doesn't have to always explain to you where he's going."

"He just stormed out without even —" Dax's voice cut out completely.

"Aspen?" Allie asked, calm as ever. "We're all good here, I promise no one will call unless it's an emergency. And we'll text first."

"You sure?" No one had ever come quite as close to seeing through me as Allie did. I think it's because, in some ways, we were the same.

"I'll use the emergency word."

"Schnauzer?"

"Schnauzer," she repeated in confirmation. It had been her idea to implement an emergency word. If I was ever unable to pick up her call, if the call was followed by the emergency word then I'd know it was important. If it wasn't, I didn't have to call her back. She suggested it one time, ever so casually, first saying she wanted to do it for herself.

She said she panicked if she couldn't answer the phone for whatever reason.

That was a lie.

Allie had suffered a car accident so bad I couldn't even recount to you all the injuries she'd sustained. The experience had left her with PTSD which had, more often than not, sent her into these debilitating panic attacks.

It had been almost six months and she hadn't had a single one. After years of working hard on her own and then, eventually, going to see someone again.

So, panic from the sound of sirens and headlights? Sure. Unanswered phone calls? No. That was all me and she knew that I knew, but we'd never spoken of it aloud.

"Schnauzer," I repeated, double checking.

"That's the one. Have fun and good luck." She hung up the phone and I waited another five minutes to see if any other calls would come through.

I heaved a heavy breath before turning on the car, remembering my single minded focus from before.

Poppy. Poppy. Poppy.

I'd built it up in the twenty minutes it took to drive there. Built it up some more in the five it took to park the car, then I waited for the feeling of panic to go away. To do this one thing for myself. To go in and see if she was there.

She could be. She *might* be. But that meant in some roundabout way I was assuming I deserved this. Deserved to get to know her, or to take her out to dinner. To put her number in my phone under one of the three names she'd given me to choose from.

I wanted to. I really fucking wanted to. But I couldn't get out of the car.

I sat there for twenty three minutes before I finally made myself turn the car back on to head home.

The head lights shot out in front of me, immediately illuminating a small frame with heaving shoulders.

She stood there like she'd come running from wherever she'd been. Like she was equally as shocked to find herself standing in front of my car as I was to see her there.

"Poppy." Her name just fell out of my mouth, like the word wanted to run straight for her and bring her back to me. Seeing her standing there sent every single thought flying from my head, draining every drop of panic that had been poisoning my body from the moment I walked out of my brother's house.

It was just her. All of a sudden exactly what I wanted became very clear, and it didn't seem so selfish to reach out and take it.

I opened the car door, the frame creaking as I stepped onto the road. I didn't stop until I was standing right in front of her. Amber eyes, wide and unsure, looked back at me. Her hair in a plait down one side.

"Poppy," I whispered into the space between us.

"Hey, Ap," she whispered back.

"I want to have dinner with you," I said, not entirely sure on the logistics of how that would work, but she nodded anyway.

"Okay," she still whispered, her breath making a cloud between us.

"And I'd like your number," I added quickly, "please." My eyes darted between hers and the lips I was doing my very best not to think about, especially when they started to curve into a small smirk.

"That delivery felt weird," I said, reaching up to push my hair back from my forehead. "Let me try again." I turned around and walked back a few steps before facing her once more and reapproaching.

Her lips clamped into a tight line in an attempt to take this as seriously as I was.

"Don't laugh," I said, turning around and going back to try it for a third time.

"No laughing," she replied, shaking her head with a small frown.

I walked up to her again, stopping only when we were toe to toe. "Poppy," I started, "can I please have your number?"

Her eyes didn't dart around my features but instead they glided, like she wasn't in a rush. Like she wanted to remember what she was looking at.

"You can," she said, "but only because you asked me twice."

8

January 19th

I didn't know that he was going to be there. I actively convinced myself that he wouldn't be, and if he was, it wouldn't have had anything to do with me.

Every time I reached for the door to walk into *Cherry's* I turned around and walked away. I ran into three patrons on three different occasions who I was sure thought I was in the process of losing my mind. It took twenty minutes of hardcore talking myself in, then out, then back into the idea again before I walked in.

It had been this blinding sort of panic when my eyes went straight to the stool he'd been at and it sat empty. The very first thought that entered into my head was *'no'.* Powered by genuine disbelief that he *couldn't* be there. That was when I'd run. Moving through the bodies of Friday night clientele and sparing only a single thought as to how, in all the world, Leah had found *this* bar and decided it was the place to visit. This place I'd never heard of in a part of this city I'd never even thought of going to.

A universe moment.

The thought seeped through no matter how many times I knocked it away, only disappearing completely when I found myself standing in front of Aspen's geriatric sedan, right where I knew it would be. I didn't need more light than the same faint glow of the nearby street lamp that had made his eyes glitter like stars to know the body behind the wheel was his.

My heart had been galloping so fast. Thumping like the beat of a drum I was sure he'd hear, and then he turned on the car.

I'd been able to admit to myself in that breath you take between big moments that it seemed this was the first time in a very long time that I'd run *towards* something instead of away. It was terrifying and exhilarating and made my heart ache with a mixture of joy and betrayal when I watched him step out of his car and realized that I was precisely where I needed to be.

Aspen's number was now saved into my phone as 'Ap'. He'd handed me his phone right

there and watched as I entered it. I then watched as he changed the name from Penelope to Poppy. When I added him into my phone as Aspen, he'd plucked it immediately from my grasp and changed it to Ap.

With every conversation we had it became more apparent that I actually didn't know anything about Aspen. That knowledge thrilled me. He continued to be unpredictable, never doing or saying or replying with anything I remotely anticipated which meant I was constantly grinning at my phone like a fool.

At the start of the week I hadn't been able to focus on a single thing. So, in a compromise to myself, I put my phone face down next to me on my desk. It did nothing for my productivity because my eyes darted to it multiple times a minute waiting for the telling buzz that indicated a message.

The first time it had been Leah, just as it had been the second time. That was when I decided to put myself out of my own misery and text him first.

Me:

I've tried to write the word 'bio' three times and each time somehow managed to write 'nip'

He replied immediately and it sent my heart careening right into my esophagus.

Ap:
Extraterrestrial communication? Are you wearing your foil hat?

Me:
I thought I was wearing it when I left the house, but now I can't remember…

Ap:
They're onto us

Ap:
Hide in the men's bathroom immediately

Ap:
The last stall (very important)

Ap:
I'll be there with provisions and you'll know it's me because I'll knock three times in quick succession

I'd snorted so loudly that Jess thought I was choking on my food and ran over in terror, immediately delivering the Heimlich without first confirming my ailment.

"Breathe!" she yelled with alarming vigor. *"Breathe, god dammit!"*

Jess had arrived with a small bell the next day and sat it on my desk. "Just so that never happens again," she muttered, "this is the choking bell."

I could only nod and watch her leave, but not before she stopped in front of my cubicle and with only her eyes to be seen murmuring a reassuring, "I have one too," and headed back to her desk.

Leah demanded a choking bell for Christmas that evening.

I was sitting on my couch last night when my phone went off again, my heart role playing a prison break the same way it did every other time Aspen messaged me in the last week.

Ap:

Roughing it without support of, or access to, amenities humankind has developed to make life a breeze?

In full fledged fool mode, I grinned at my phone. Aspen had taken to sending me definitions through the day of different things. I assumed it was a way of him just letting me know what he was up to when the first few had been the definitions of 'studio', 'drums' and 'burrito', but now I severely doubted it.

Me:

Camping?

Ap:

You've been practicing, Poppy

I read my name like I was hearing him say it and my body erupted in goosebumps. I could practically feel the way he'd whispered it against my skin, like a question and an answer all rolled into two syllables.

Ap:

Liquid substances falling from great heights?

Me:

Oh no :[

Ap:

I believe in you

Me:
I'm perplexed

Ap:
Your vocabulary is so hot

At least no one was around to deliver the Heimlich on account of my howling laughter that time.

Me:
I believe you're flirting with me

Ap:
It's become my favorite thing to do

Holy balls.

Me:
Either rain, or maybe a waterfall?

Ap:
You're very good at this game

Me:
So you're saying I won?

Ap:

A really close second :D

It was the first time in a while where falling asleep had been difficult on account of something positive. I wanted to meet every single one of his messages with a reply of my own that went off just as fast as his came in, but I always seemed to fall asleep first. It was like the man didn't rest.

My favorite conversations were the ones where he called, and he did that a lot. Aspen was an incredibly entertaining text-volley partner, but it was easy to pretend he wasn't making me feel the things I was starting to feel when they were words on a screen.

Hearing his voice come through the phone was like being struck by lightning. It woke me up.

"Picture this," he said, voice clear and unburdened by sleep like I thought it would be so early in the morning. Yet again, not what I'd expect from a rock star though I'm fully able to admit I was leaning into a stereotype there.

In my defense, I'd never met a rock star before.

I had just stepped off the train and was making my way up and out of the station, a smile already on my face. "Occipital lobes at the ready," I replied immediately.

"You're so smart Poppy…" he paused for only a second followed by a sound that resembled severe devastation. "Oh my *lanta*."

"What's wrong?" My chest swelled with panic.

"I don't know your last name. We've been talking all week and I never asked your last

name. This is so much worse than forgetting your car door," he grumbled.

All that did was make me smile wider.

"I won't tell the mom's you have on rotation if you don't want me to."

"You really *do* like me."

"Hart," I laughed, replying to his dramatics. "That's my last name."

"Your name is Poppy Hart?" He sounded in awe and my eye role was unstoppable. "That's a beautiful name." His voice was full of a quiet sincerity that I was coming to understand as his default setting. Aspen Smith, I realized, was a labrador.

"Thanks, Ap." It had always been my name, but all of a sudden I liked it a whole lot more.

"Do you have a middle name?" It sounded like this was equivalent to Christmas for him.

I couldn't not laugh, "Yes. It's Elizabeth."

"You have *got* to be joking. I think I'm dying."

"What's yours?" I giggled. *I giggled.* I was giggling? I think I needed to add a new rule to Poppy's Life Rules but I was, all at once, finding any of them difficult to recall.

"You don't know it?"

"I'd like you to tell me," I slowed my steps, knowing my office building was coming up but not wanting the conversation to end.

"Okay Poppy Elizabeth Hart," his delight was an audible, tangible thing through the phone, "my name is Aspen Killian Smith."

"Well," I said, doing my absolute best to remember everything about this moment and the man I was talking to. To remember that no matter what, I had felt like *this*, "That's a beautiful name."

Aspen had texted me the entire day meaning I had gotten zero work done. As soon as I was off the clock and out the doors of the building, waving to Jess as she headed off in the other direction, my phone rang with an incoming call.

He spoke, continuing our text conversation, as soon as I picked up.

"Hiking to a waterfall," he said, sounding like he was playing a video game in the background, "that's what I think we should do."

Now all I could do was imagine Aspen playing a video game, maybe just in sweats? Maybe he might not have a shirt on.

I cleared my throat, “I thought the answer was camping?”

“It was. However, upon further pondering,” he paused to swear softly, “sorry, zombies. Anyway, I figured being out in the middle of nowhere in the dead of winter was probably not ideal for your toe tips.”

“You might be the first boy who’s ever thought about my toes tips.”

“Boy?”

“Sorry, man.”

“*Man*?” His voice rose a full octave on that single word.

“Guide me, please,” I laughed, stepping onto the train.

“No,” he sighed, “man feels right. I might just need to do some pull ups against the window in the nude to earn the title.”

“What an interesting definition.”

“It’s either that or lather myself in baby lotion and pose for a charitable calendar.”

“Option B please.” I was joking, of course. In saying that, I was also grateful that he couldn’t see the way my face had flushed raspberry pink at the thought of him covered in oil.

We’d spoken about absolutely nothing, but we did talk.

I’d realized I didn’t really find myself caring that nothing more had been said about his proposed dinner date or that his sidetracked comment on hiking to a waterfall was equally exciting as it was unanticipated. Talking to Aspen had been consuming all of my thoughts. I couldn’t even recall everything I’d transcribed in the last five days when normally I’d have learned at least a handful of new things by now.

It really was all I’d been thinking about with every single part of my brain so when I sat down and stared at my laptop with the web browser open to potential rentals available in three different cities, my heart sank.

Because I was leaving.

It didn’t fully register in my own brain what I was doing until my phone was pressed to my ear and Aspen was picking up on the second ring. The words just poured from my mouth.

“I’ve seen you in person twice.”

"That's true." Aspen seemed to have a knack of picking up on whatever I was feeling, his tone was soft but serious.

"Maybe I don't know you that well," I said, staring at the listings of apartments I already knew I'd hate on the screen.

"Oh, I know what this is about. You missed the column about my favorite color combinations in *Rolling Stone*."

"I must have," I said, the grip I had on my panic slipping just a little.

"The one about my taste in music in *Mojo*?" he went on, his voice full of feigned outrage.

"No, I caught that one."

"Perfect!" It sounded like he slapped his hand on his leg. "You're half up to date."

My quiet laughter fluttered between us and I could picture him so clearly, somewhere, anywhere, sitting down and smiling into his phone.

"Ap," I whispered.

"Poppy," he whispered back.

"Are you busy?"

"I am not."

"Would you like to come over?"

"More than anything, yes."

I had no idea where Aspen lived, but thirty minutes later there were three knocks in quick succession at my front door and there he was, right in the doorway to my house.

"Hey," I sounded breathless. I *felt* breathless.

"Hey." His responding grin was something that I wanted to see everyday. It was like looking right into the sun and I wanted nothing more than to always be able to see the imprint of it when I closed my eyes.

He brushed so close to me when he walked in and I'd never been so aware of someone else's body, clad all in black as he was and smelling faintly like pine and violets. Aspen was tall but it didn't hurt my neck to peer up at him in the same way it did to look at Todd. He moved like someone who used their body, who was comfortable in it. Someone who didn't really like to sit still.

I didn't like where I lived. In fact, I hated pretty much every place I'd ever rented but looking at Aspen Killian Smith standing in my living room, it was like the walls of my little town house sagged in relief in the same way I did.

Right in that moment, of all the places I'd lived since I was sixteen, this one had just become my favorite.

9

January 19th

It occurred to me moments before I knocked on Poppy's front door that I'd gotten myself out of the house so fast that I forgot to put on both underwear and deodorant. But I wanted to see her.

Actually, I wanted to see her again the moment I dropped her off at home last Friday. From the literal second she closed her front door with a little wave and an uncertain tilt of her head, but I didn't want to be *that guy*.

Too forward and pushy.

So, I waited. I waited for her to say outloud what days suited her for dinner, or if hiking to a waterfall was what we were going to do on the weekend. If she had asked me to sit on her couch and hold her yarn while she crocheted, I would've done it.

Being in Poppy's orbit was where I'd wanted to be all week, and I'd never wanted to be anywhere else when I was behind my drum kit. With drum sticks in my hands and a beat in my head.

We'd been in the recording studio every day. Long days that were tiring but the songs were coming together in a way that surpassed even our last record, and that experience had been borderline religious. There was only one thing that was stumping us so far, and all five of us agreed that we'd yet to find what was going to be our first single for the album.

The first song we were going to release. We had a bit of time, it wasn't planned to be released until the start of April and we were only halfway through January. Dax just thought we needed some perspective and so the call was made that we would take the week off. We'd worked right through Christmas and New Years and he'd declared that what was missing was our ability to 'chill'. That's where hiking with Poppy was meant to come in.

Poppy was still staring at me, her back pressed to the front door, her hands ringing nervously in front of her.

"Shoes?" I asked, pointing down at my boots.

"No, they're fine," she smiled at me, but it was timid. I'd seen Poppy look shy before, but never worried, not like that.

"I wanted to see you." I couldn't help the single step I took back towards her.

"You did?" Her eyes widened a fraction and I'd bet if she could've, she would have stepped back.

"Yep." I sunk my hands into the front pockets of my jeans and rocked back on my heels. "Pretty much since I dropped you off at home last week." I let my eyes wander, trying to figure out what it was about being near Poppy that made it impossible to not say the things that were in my head. To not *do* the things I wanted to do.

Both habits I had rid myself of a very long time ago.

She just watched me, unmoving, and so I took the lead feeling weirdly confident about every step I took further into her house. It was small and...bare.

It was not the sort of home I had imagined for Poppy. I'd thought of colors, of patterns that didn't match and paintings either too small or too big for the walls she'd put them on. I had imagined carpets so fluffy they swallowed your feet and plants that crept along walls and window sills.

Instead there was a serious absence of color, like she'd intended for it to be plain and unwelcoming.

That's when I noticed the boxes.

There were some in the living room, some to the side of the kitchen, some at the base of the stairs.

I felt her eyes taking in every movement I made while I took in everything around me. I pointed to the boxes, "Going somewhere?" I flicked my eyes to hers and found her already looking at me. Our eyes clashed for a second and it seemed to be enough to break whatever trance she'd fallen into.

"Oh. No." She pulled the sleeves of her sweatshirt over her hands, crossing her arms over her chest. There was more to that answer than that but it felt like a violation of her privacy to ask, even though every part of my brain screamed for me to find out.

Why the unpacked boxes? Don't tell me you're leaving when I've only just found you.

No, I wasn't going to do that. Instead, I did what anyone else would do in my position. I focused on the fish.

"That," I pointed at the tank and walked over to sit on a stool at the breakfast bar of her kitchen, "is a lovely fish."

Watching Poppy right then was like seeing the moment the sun had finally burnt away the remaining clouds after a storm, showering everything in light again. She beamed at me with pure, undiluted joy and it was like I'd been punched right in the chest with a flaming fist. I would have everything I'd ever need if I could have this girl look at me just like that for the rest of my life.

Poppy was beautiful. Like she was the very image of a spring day with her bright amber eyes and chestnut hair.

"Aspen," she said, walking over to sit on the stool next to me, both of us just there looking at her fish. "Meet Natalie." She looked at me like I should be extending my hand towards the tank.

I did the next best thing I could manage in a pinch and bowed my head in reverence. "Natalie, the pleasure is mine."

"Nat," Poppy leaned towards the tank, "this is Aspen Killian Smith. We like him."

"We do?" Her words had taken me off guard and now I wanted more of them. I wanted *all* of them.

"Oh, she likes you," Poppy said, conveniently hurdling right over my question.

"How can you tell?" I leaned in as close as she was, peering at the little floating orange sparkling blob.

"She's fluttering her fins extra fast," she murmured, her nose almost pressed to the side of the tank.

"Is it some kind of mating call?" I mused,

"That's definitely one possibility," Poppy nodded.

"Should I be doing it back?"

"Not on the first date, Aspen!" She looked at me in mock horror before a small laugh escaped her.

The noise triggered something in my mind, notes forming into the beginnings of the sort of song Poppy would be. The longer she looked at me, the more somber she got, like that brief moment of sunshine was only a sliver between thick, rain heavy clouds.

"There was a reason I thought you should come over," her voice was unsteady and I wanted to reach out to touch her.

"You *do* want to ravish me." The corner of my mouth tipped up at the way a light pink flush made its way up her neck. I wanted to follow its accent with the tip of my tongue.

"No? Okay," I tried again, leaning my elbow on the counter beside me. "You've heard about my baking ability?"

"Well, it *was* in *The Stones*."

"You did read it!" It had worked for a second, her eyes brightened and the crease between her eyes smoothed out, but only for a second.

"Aspen," she said my name the way you'd read the start of the last sentence of a book. It had this note of finality to it that made my hands feel heavy and my teeth ache. It felt very much like this was going to end before it ever really started and suddenly I couldn't breathe.

I was under water and she was above the surface, just out of my reach.

"I'm leaving," she pushed the words at me unceremoniously, like they frightened her almost as much as they frightened me. And they did, those two previously insignificant words strung side by side had become terrifying.

I felt my smile falter. I'd never been so taken off guard that I'd let it slip before and the moment her eyes flicked to my mouth I saw her own expression fall too.

"It's a rule that I have. For myself, not for, like, the general public." She was ringing her hands in front of her again. "I don't stay anywhere more than a year," she explained, and I was trying really hard to hear the words.

I swallowed, bringing my attention back to my own expression, keeping the right one in place. I didn't know what else to do, everything felt too loud.

"Okay," I whispered.

Silence so heavy and claustrophobic settled around us like a blanket. It was the first time I hadn't ever wanted it to end. I didn't want the words to fill it that I knew were coming. I wanted to sit in it, before things changed and the possibility of Poppy becoming mine was still a reality.

In the absence of noise, Poppy frantically started to fill it. "I've moved every year since I was eighteen," she said with rushed words like they explained everything.

"Why?" The word was out before I could stop it.

"I'm —" she cut herself off and I knew she'd pulled some invisible leash on herself. "It's complicated."

I nodded even though nothing had ever made less sense to me. "How long have you been here?"

She knew as well as I did that what I'd really asked was how long until she wouldn't be anymore.

"A little under three months," she whispered. "Until I go."

"Where are you going?" Another mental check that my expression was still relaxed. Calm.

"I don't know," her voice shook and her chin quivered and I couldn't take it. All I wanted to do was *fix* it. Poppy's eyes fluttered before she dropped my gaze and I knew, before the words even left her mouth, that they were a lie. "It's complicated."

"Okay," I whispered.

"You make me," she started to talk, her wide amber eyes flittering around my face with uncertainty until a look of determination set her brows in a small furrow. "You make me feel *a lot*. More than I have in a long time and I wanted to tell you right away because I, well, I'm sort of a one woman band."

"You're using a band related metaphor?" I smiled at her. I couldn't help it, even though every word she spoke was equivalent to a paper cut between my fingers.

"What do you think?" She grinned too, and I knew it was despite herself.

"Impeccable decision making. Please, continue."

"I'm…I'm a…"

"…One woman band?"

"Yes. *Yes*. And you're sort of…*challenging* all of that which I think…I *know* will end up with you getting hurt and the thought of that makes me sick, Aspen. So I needed to tell you now." Poppy stopped only to take a big breath and kept talking. "I don't date, like, at all. It's never really been something that's made sense with my lifestyle. I've just never been anywhere long enough for it to matter, and it hasn't mattered really, until recently. I just don't date. See people. Have relationships. Except for Leah…and Nat." Her hand flew up and gestured helplessly at her fish.

"Okay," I said again. I was trying to take in everything she'd said and I was trying to do it calmly because I was confused and worried and not really okay at all and Poppy was very clearly nervous.

"*Okay*?" She didn't whisper back that time, the word came out in full force. Whatever she'd expected from me after her one-woman-band explanation, that hadn't been it.

My ribs groaned at the effort of keeping my lungs from exploding. It felt like I'd inhaled a big breath and couldn't let it go.

I picked my next words for Poppy, not for me. "That's okay."

She just nodded, clearly determined to be pleased with this conversation regardless of the small crease still lingering between her brows. Just like when we were standing in front of my car, the consequences of my own wants didn't seem to cross my mind.

"Can I still see you, until then?"

"You…are you sure?" Relief and shock colored her words in equal parts.

"We're friends, Poppy. Plus, it's surprisingly hard to find a fellow Taurus enthusiast around these parts." I reached my hand out, palm up between us because I couldn't stop myself anymore. My entire body seemed to thaw against the chill that had unknowingly settled in when she didn't even seem to think about it and placed her hand in mine. It stung, the warmth of her hand against the coolness of mine. Her skin was soft, fingers unhurried as they traveled over the calluses on my hand over and over.

"I can believe that," she nodded.

"You're a dime a dozen," I still whispered because anything else felt too hard.

"Now you're just trying to ravish me." She lifted her eyes from our hands. It felt like I was getting another peek of sunshine and all I wanted to do was bask in it.

I had thought about Poppy in every way a man could think about a woman. I wanted to walk down a busy street with her tucked into my side. Arrive home and find the lights already on and Poppy curled into the corner of the couch. I wanted her hair fanned out across my pillow, her hands fisting my sheets and my lips on every single part of her body.

That was when my control slipped and I finally, *finally*, just let my eyes roam over her. Thick socks revealed the expanse of her golden legs. Her shorts looked soft and well loved and disappeared under the oversized sweatshirt that devoured her whole.

"So," I swallowed, needing to change the direction of my thoughts before I did something incredibly inappropriate in front of her fish. "About dinner. I don't think it's such a good idea."

She nodded even as her face fell. It happened so fast I don't even think she realized it. Seeing it happen was equivalent to the ground slipping out from under me. "Unless you're partial to a camera in your face along with your entree."

"Oh." Her eyes flicked back to mine. She'd forgotten that was a reality for me, because even though she had known who I was when we'd met, she didn't look at me in the same way she had when the realization hit her. Poppy looked at me like she could see behind the curtain that separated the

Aspen the public knew and the other parts of myself that not even my family saw. Like she could see every part of me, even the parts made completely of glass and prone to shattering and wanted to keep me anyway.

"Mm," my voice was rough, my head filled with images of Poppy beneath me. Above me. Of all of her *everywhere.* "So, how about hiking?" It was a small grace that I was sitting down.

"Does a waterfall exist somewhere in there?"

"You *are* very good at that game and here I thought you were just Googling the answers."

"I like to hike," she said, her attention focused on where her hand still rested in mine.

I had her for three months.

It made it easier to think of what I wanted knowing that I was never going to be able to keep her.

"Hiking it is, sweet Poppy."

She looked up at me resembling the loveliest version of the Cheshire Cat, "Sweet, huh?"

I wanted to run the pad of my thumb over her bottom lip, to trace the shape of her face and never forget that if nothing else, someone had looked at me like Poppy was looking at me right now. Like she'd follow me anywhere if I only asked her to.

"For now," I said, squeezing her hand and letting the smile on my face turn into something real, something hers.

10

January 20th

The request for Aspen to stay with me had been on the tip of my tongue. It seemed absurd that he didn't feel the way even my house wanted to keep him, his warmth and sunshine and goodness. But, that would have been cruel.

I had asked him to come to tell him I wasn't staying. To do the right thing, and be upfront about my situation.

Well, as upfront as I could have been.

Aspen was the sort of person you wanted to trust fall into. He was solid and present and if I let myself want him like that, it would only end up hurting him. I was already breaking so many of my own rules by entertaining the idea of a friendship with him.

I could admit that even though I had Leah, I was lonely. I was always achingly aware of that fact but I forced myself to endure it.

It was what I deserved, what was for the best. It was what worked *best.*

So, when my eyelids had started to droop shut and he tucked the blanket up further around me that we'd been sharing while watching a movie, he stood up to leave.

Ask me.

That's what his face had said when he tucked a strand of hair behind my ear. When his fingertips blazed a trail with the lightest touch down the column of my throat.

Ask me to stay.

But I didn't, and I knew he wouldn't ask to stay either.

That seemed hard for him, asking. That second time outside of *Cherry's* when he'd asked for my number I thought at first it was nerves that made his eyes uncertain, maybe even a little afraid. I was sure now that wasn't it at all. Ever since then he hadn't asked for a single thing more, not like he'd asked me for that one thing.

Aspen leaned forward, pressing a kiss to my cheek, lingering for only a breath too long before his long legs led him away from me.

I gripped the blanket he'd tucked around me so tightly my hands began to ache, just so I wouldn't chase him down. I was about to fold, to give in and demand he come back, even if it was just to sit with me, just to *be* there, when my phone went off with a new message.

Ap:

I'll see you bright and early, we're going
to hike the shit out of that waterfall trail.

Ap:

Goodnight, Poppy.

And then not a moment later,

Ap:

Goodnight, Nat.

I cursed my alarm to the deepest, darkest pits of hell when it blared *'I'm walking on sunshine'* directly into my right ear at the butt crack of dawn. For some reason I felt optimistic about the act of waking up if the thing to *wake* me up was a bright, happy diddle I felt fondly about.

I now hated that song with the ferocity of a hard done by hedgehog.

My eyes were still pretty much closed when I locked the door to my house and followed the sound of the rumbling engine that idled out front. That's why it had taken me a full three seconds to realize that was *not* the sound of Aspen's car.

The passenger side window was already down and he was grinning at me so wide his eyes were almost closed.

"Aspen," I said, my voice full of the sleep I had been very much still in only fifteen minutes ago.

"Poppy, have I ever told you that you look the *most* beautiful in the mornings?" He sounded genuine and I wanted to flick his nose.

"Aspen," I tried again, "this isn't your car."

"This is my *hiking* car," he corrected. "Actually, It's my brothers but he keeps it parked in my garage.

I was silent while I just took in the hefty piece of machinery that was his Jeep Wrangler, but then he added on, "and that was absolutely not a euphemism."

As hard as I tried, the smile I'd been holding back tugged at the corner of my mouth while I just stared at it.

His car, I mean. It was huge, I wasn't even sure I'd be able to get in without looking like I was trying to mount a horse. "Guess I was right about one assumption," I said, rubbing my eyes. "You do own a less environmentally friendly car."

Aspen leaned over just as I clicked my seat belt in, leaving a chaste kiss on my cheek like it was something he'd done a thousand times before and I felt the contact of his mouth on my skin all the way to the ends of my eyelashes.

"This," he put the car into drive and peeled out of his park, looking no less delicious than he had in the Taurus, "is not my car. So technically you're still wrong. But if it makes you feel better, this is a hybrid." He shot me a quick wink before focusing his attention back onto the road.

Aspen was dressed precisely how you would expect for someone going hiking in winter and not at all what you might expect someone who favored jeans as tight as the ones he wore. Aspen was decked out (still all in black) with hiking boots that looked well worn, black, form fitting cargo pants and a sweatshirt under his winter coat. His dark hair curled around his ears under his beanie that had a big *Lady Luck* logo on the front of it.

"So, Poppy Elizabeth," he said after a minute, the barely noticeable tug at the corner of his mouth let me know he had been very aware of my perusal. "What is it that you do?"

Aspen didn't manage to run out of any questions for the entire hour and a half drive it took to get us out to what he had only divulged as 'his spot'. Insisting it was like a family recipe, only passed down when you became of age.

He'd said that right as we passed by the sign that said 'Frosted Lakes Hiking Trail'. By the time we were there he knew almost everything about what I did Monday to Friday, including the story of Miss Ina Minit and Jupiter's Moon, but minus Todd.

With my hand held firmly in his grip, Ap led us through overgrown terrain to get to the hiking trail he insisted was a much easier walk. I could tell he was excited, mainly because he was narrating almost everything we did.

"We're just going up this hill now, you okay?" He checked over his shoulder, giving me a little grin before tugging me along. He followed it up only moments later with, "We're going down this hill now. Oh, hey look, that's one of my favorite trees! See the roots? They're so twisty that if you look at it from right over…*here*," he held me in front of him so close my entire back was pressed to his chest, his arm wrapped around me and resting on my collarbones, "it spells 'Ap'."

I turned my head to peer up at him, catching another of his big, bright smiles that I knew were real, knew were all Aspen. I had never been that great at reading people, but it was right then that I had the sort of realization that took your breath away. It was knowing that he was choosing to share something he loved with *me,* of anyone, anywhere, ever. It made me think that maybe one day – if we'd had the time – I'd have known this big, hiking, drummer with glittery eyes and rough hands better than I knew myself.

"That's pretty cool," I said, my voice suddenly thick and I didn't think too much about what it meant when my own hands came up to grip the arm he had wrapped around me.

We made it to the path, known not only by the well worn dirt that spanned either side of us and the snow that dotted the edges left from a fall a few days ago, but also by Aspen's announcement.

"We've made it to the path!" He held both arms out to either side of him, as if this wasn't a public trial but a place that was all his, that he was proud of.

The path was wide enough in most parts that we could walk side by side, only going single file in the tricky bits. Ap made sure he was in front of me when it was a steep decline, or that he held my hand and led the way on any rough uphill parts.

It made my body want to turn to jelly.

I had to make it a rule for myself that any time I felt like removing any article of his clothes I would chant *'just friends'* six times in my head.

It had, thus far, not worked in the slightest in deterring any such mental behavior on my part.

"So," I said, a little out of breath. A little from him and a little from a particularly tricky bit. "You know what I do, now you have to tell me what you do."

"I thought you read my articles?"

"Mostly everything I know about you I knew before I met you. That's weird, Aspen," I said.

"Alright, what's something you know that's weird you didn't find out yourself?" He held a hand out to me and helped me over a log.

"I know one time when you were really drunk, you went to pee but missed the toilet and ended up going all over Angus."

"Ha!" He barked a laugh so loud birds flew out of trees around us. "I totally forgot about that. Okay, yes those are the sorts of war stories that regular people might not know about one another, but that has nothing to really do with *me*."

"Alright, I know you love to bake."

"That phrase lives on half the shirts I own. Try again."

"That you thought swapping places with your sibling didn't only apply to twins and you tried to get Wyatt to take your math test in the second grade."

"I've forgotten all about these! Poppy, keep going, this is wonderful."

"You're not seeing my point at all," I scowled at him.

"Please?" He jutted out his bottom lip and I immediately wondered what it would be like to take it between my teeth.

"I know your preferred brand *and* style of boxers." I didn't meet his eyes on that one, because I knew for a fact, knowing that about a stranger was definitely not normal.

"Oh?" I could hear the mischief in his voice.

"See," I said, "the only way I should know that is if I'd seen them myself."

"Are you picturing me in my underwear, Poppy?"

"I--*No*."

Boy was I ever.

There were so many other things I could have said, but I went for the option that sat closest to his genitals.

"It's okay," he leaned in to whisper in my ear and the heat of his words made me shiver. "I've pictured you too." He pulled back just enough to shoot a wink right at my shocked face.

Aspen took my hand in his after that, doing me the favor of not making a note on how I was flushed from head to toe, and proceeded to tell me as much about himself as he could.

Aspen hated running, he *loathed* it and he was terrified of publicity events because he was constantly nervous he'd say something that would upset someone without meaning to. He'd always liked avocados from his earliest memories, his parents were nice people, but they weren't a close family and he and Wyatt didn't ever really go home. He'd been a theater kid at school which was why it was common knowledge that he could sing very well, though he'd decided that when it became his brother's thing, he just wouldn't do it anymore.

"Do you sing in the shower?"

"Loudly," he slung an arm over my shoulder and smirked down at me.

"That's something I didn't know." My arm wrapped around his waist on instinct. "Can I hear you sing?" I asked the question not thinking it would be a big deal, but I felt him stiffen at the question and the very moment I was about to take it back he spoke.

"I mean, sure, maybe if it's just the two of us I could —"

"Why did you do that?" I asked, more curious than anything. His face completely transformed with the weight of his frown.

"Do what?"

"Say yes when you didn't want to? It's okay that you don't want to, Aspen."

We'd stopped walking, locked in this stare off where he was trying to find an answer to whatever questions he had running through his head in the same way I was trying to find the answer to mine.

Then my stomach growled. This big, grumbling, echoing sound.

Just like that, his very real, very Aspen grin was back in place and that conversation was going to have to be left for another time.

"You're in luck, Poppy Elizabeth Hart." He swung his backpack around to his front and pulled out two ziplock bags containing sandwiches with the crusts cut off.

"You cooked lunch!" I was absolutely as excited about that reality as I sounded.

"No cooking involved, sweet Poppy."

"I can't believe you packed lunch."

"I figured you ate food."

"First you think of my toe tips, now my stomach? Is this how friends are supposed to act?"

"Where we're concerned, absolutely."

My cheeks hurt from the way my smile took over every muscle in my face. "You cut off the crusts."

"I didn't know your preference, so better safe than sorry." Aspen suddenly looked incredibly shy.

"Well, you were right. I don't like them," I said, taking the one he handed to me.

"Like I always say," he said, sitting down on a rock off to the side and patting one next to him for me to join, "trust your sixth sense."

"When do you say that?"

"That would be the first time."

We ate in companionable silence until three quarters of my sandwich was gone and Aspen had moved onto his third granola bar. We tried to be oblivious, but it was hard not to be conscious of the day getting away from us.

I handed him my empty ziplock back, intending on finishing the last few bites of my PB and J on the hike.

Silence with Aspen was like knowing you'd locked the deadbolt of your house without second guessing it when you were on the cusp of sleep. It was certain and safe and the sort of silence that I imagined people thought of when they were looking for a quiet moment to ground themselves, to regroup. The only downside was the racing thoughts in my head.

A tug of war of joy and dread that I wasn't doing the right thing by being there, but in the end the side of my brain that insisted I lived in the moment won. Mostly because I knew that there would come a time I would recall moments like the one we were in and I'd be glad I kept it close until I could see the imprint of it on the palms of my hands, even long after I'd let him go.

"Are you waterfall ready?" Ap reached his hand down, pulling me up effortlessly.

"I've never been more —" The words got stuck in my throat and then a scream ripped from me with such jarring brutality I was sure I saw the trees tremble around us.

My scream didn't stop. As if it was being pulled right out of my fucking *soul,* it just got louder and louder. The sandwich went flying out of my hand in what direction, I had no idea. Aspen made some maneuver with his hands that looked like he was all at once trying to punch the air and grab some invisible perpetrator.

"*SNAKE*!" The word finally burst out of my mouth in a frequency that could be heard by human ears. "*SNAKE*!" I repeated, like it was suddenly the only word I knew.

I didn't think another second on my decision to launch myself directly at Aspen.

To his credit, he didn't even seem remotely phased by what was happening.

My hands grabbed at his backpack, at his jacket, at his arms and shoulders and chest. Things that I would have really liked to have taken my time in touching for the very first time, but this was life or death and I was in pure flight mode. I didn't stop my ascent up his body until one of my legs draped over his shoulder and my hands were holding onto his head while he turned in a circle trying to get his bearings without being able to see.

"You know," he reached up and parted my fingers so he could see out between them, "in a weird turn of events, I feel like I've been training for this exact moment."

"It's winter, there shouldn't be snakes in winter, Aspen!" My voice was nothing more than a pathetic rasp.

While I did my best to keep the next lot of screams secured in my chest, he explained a number of things to me. The first being that it was, and he stressed this as being really important, the size of his forearm.

"You have massive forearms," I squeaked, keeping my eyes locked on the beast.

"I'll be honest, that's a brand new compliment for me, Poppy, and I would like to take the appropriate amount of time to unpack that later." His voice was still muffled by the part of my hand that covered his mouth. "The sun's out, love, it was probably just trying to catch some UV." Aspen delivered that fact like it was cute.

Cute.

I didn't take a single breath while I watched it start to move, slithering away like it hadn't just shaken the foundations of my sanity. It was at that point that I realized that it was very, *very* silent and I was very, *very* wrapped around Aspen's still form.

He moved slowly like he didn't want to startle me, reaching up and around for me in the same way he had done for his backpack, pulling me around to his front. The light green of his eyes had all but disappeared on account of how large his pupils had become.

His eyes were half lidded and his mouth parted while he kept me pressed to him in a hold that was both too strong and not strong enough.

My heart started to pound for an entirely different reason than it had before. Images of the sort of underwear I knew he was wearing filtered into my mind, of how solid he felt beneath my hands, how he still smelled like violets and pine trees even after we'd been hiking for hours.

Aspen started to let me down. He did it so slowly I'd become hopeful that it would never end. On my way down I felt every single part of his body with every single part of mine. I wanted to climb back up just so he could do it again.

And again. I wanted the fast pass and to only ever do this for the rest of my life.

The way he was looking at me didn't lighten up, the heat in his eyes or the way his gaze dropped to my mouth didn't change.

"I feel like you handled that with incredible grace," he murmured. Even though his words were supposed to be light, there wasn't any humor in his voice. It was strained with whatever he was battling against in his own head.

"I appreciate that," my voice was so gravelly that it hurt to speak but I was glad for the cover up, otherwise it would have been very clear exactly what I was thinking.

"Poppy," Aspen whispered, his hands still holding my waist, the tips of his fingers digging into the side of my ribs like he was desperate to hold me there, to keep me close and all to himself.

"Yes?" There was no mistaking the shake in my voice that time.

"I think I'm going to kiss you now." He was already leaning in.

"This is breaking so many of my rules." I was impressed with myself that I'd managed to say that much. At least I couldn't say I didn't try.

"Which ones?"

"Pretty much all of them," I swallowed.

"I think I'm still going to kiss you," he said again.

I'd spent so long telling myself no. Reprimanding myself over and over for *wanting* more than I had, even as I'd continuously tried running towards that very thing without any hope of ever finding it.

"Okay," I said, knowing it was wrong, knowing that I shouldn't. "Yes," I said again. "Okay." Just as his lips met mine.

I had tried my very best to remember what it felt like to be kissed by Aspen.

Tried to remember the way his lips fit against mine and how it felt different to exist in my own skin when his hand came up to hold my face. I had been so far off pinpointing the remnants of how it felt now that I was comparing the memory to the real thing.

I wasn't ready for it like I thought I'd be. The feeling of his rough, calloused hands moving to both sides of my face.

The first kiss was gentle.

He pulled back to look at my face. Eyes darting to the points where his hands touched me before moving back to my eyes and then down to my mouth. It looked like he was trying to convince himself it was really happening. I knew that because I was doing the same.

"Friends don't kiss like this, right?" I whispered, because I knew that they didn't and I wanted him to help me break my rules. I moved my hands up to hold onto his wrists, to keep him in place.

"It's different in every part of the country but I'm pretty sure it's standard here," he said, lips breaking apart into a little smile that made his eyes shine a brighter green than before.

"Okay," I said, falling into the lie and lifting up on my tip toes, "that's good."

This time when Aspen kissed me, he did it like he was trying to tell me a secret.

His lips were *so soft* and every swipe of his tongue against the seam of my mouth made my body jolt with little zaps of pleasure, going off behind my eyelids and traveling down the length of my spine to settle low in my belly. Every touch of his lips on mine overwhelmed me. I was completely made of helium right then with no hope of ever being a regular woman ever again.

Aspen's hands shifted, one sinking into the roots of my hair, gripping hard, and the other to the middle of my back, pressing me further into him.

I couldn't help the sound that escaped me. I tried to hold it in but I was becoming a person I didn't recognize with every second that his hands were on me.

I stiffened, completely embarrassed that that had just happened. This was not something I had experience in, feeling like I was being unwrapped in the best way (cue all three and a half of my sexual experiences, please).

I tried to pull away but Ap's grip on me tightened, "No," he said, his lips hovering over mine. "Don't go."

"I—" I wanted to explain to him that the noise was an accident. That I hadn't meant to, but I didn't get a chance before his lips were back on mine and I was suddenly no longer standing on the ground.

Aspen moved us around like someone who knew the trail we were on like the back of his hand, leaning me against a tree with my legs around his waist and I could feel *everything*. His hands were slow but seeking as they made their way under my coat. The expanse of his broad palms against ribs, the very tips of his fingers skimming the underside of my breasts.

It was involuntary the way my hips started to circle. Moving and seeking the friction he had made me absolutely desperate for and, *sweet slipping sanity*, this man was well endowed.

"Poppy," he said my name like a curse word and all it did was serve to short circuit whatever parts of my brain still worked the way they should've been.

"Yes?" That didn't sound like my voice, it didn't feel like my hands that were hungry to touch the warm skin I knew lay just under his sweatshirt.

"I have to stop touching you, but I can't," he admitted, like it was a truth he hadn't ever wanted to share. "But if I don't," he continued, his mouth tracing a line along my jaw before it settled against my ear, "especially with you doing *this*," he dropped his hands to my hips and delivered one, mind altering grind of his own, "I'm probably…I'm *definitely* going to do some very bad things to you."

"Bad?" The word was an incoherent gasp. What I actually meant to say was, 'yes fucking please'.

"Yeah." Aspen was breathing hard and my eyes were completely focused on the way his throat worked as he swallowed. His eyes were looking down to where he was *still* grinding against me. "I can think of at least four different laws I'd like to break right now that include both you and this tree, but I'm not sure you'd like that."

"Is that what friends do here too?" My whole body was shaking. Could he feel it?

"Oh, I'm pretty confident it is, yeah," he said, voice strained, "but not on public hiking trails and not before dinner."

This man had the willpower of a saint.

"I'm not that hungry and I've always liked nature," I said, still breathless and gulping and wriggling against him.

He nuzzled his head into the side of my neck, releasing his laughter in warm bursts against my flushed skin that made me dizzy. He started to pull away slowly and it injected this bizarre fear right into my blood that this would be the last time I'd be held like this, looked at like this, by him.

"Ap." What was I supposed to even say? I wasn't sure, but whatever it was I wanted to say it all.

He rested his forehead against mine before lowering his mouth to me again. Testing and tasting and exploring, pulling more of those noises from me that I was coming to realize he liked. Aspen pulled me from the tree and slid me down his body once again like he'd heard every wish I had thought.

"You're actually killing me," he said.

I was shocked because they had been the words on the tip of my tongue. In the end, I just stood there looking like...well probably like I'd respectfully been ravished by the drummer of the biggest rock band in the whole fucking world.

Aspen turned away, his hand already reaching into the front of his pants to sort out what had to be the biggest penis I'd ever almost come into contact with.

I took the opportunity to drop my hands down onto my knees, bending at the waist. I was wheezing, I could hear it.

It was an involuntary reaction at the reality of what had just happened.

I didn't manage to collect myself in time to play off that entire experience as anything but religious. I righted myself after he'd already turned back towards me, a sly lift to his lips lingering, probably because I no doubt resembled a range of blush colored produce and that was perfectly acceptable to him.

"What if we see another snake?" I said, lips still tingling and head still swimming while I tried to take steady steps on wobbly legs to slide my hand into the one he held out for me.

"Then we'll resume our previous positions." Aspen started dragging me along behind him before stopping abruptly. In the same movement he turned around in, he reached for me, taking my face with his hands once more and kissing me in a completely different way than he had just moments ago.

This one was desperate and wanting and achingly familiar to all the knotted, messy emotions that were currently learning the choreography to *Footloose* inside my stomach.

"Friends?" he asked in a whispered tone after letting go, his tall frame bent over with his forehead resting on my shoulder.

"Definitely," I said back, unable to stop the smile from creeping into my voice.

11

January 24th

Poppy

"You know it's not common practice to take your goldfish to the movies, right?" Leah asked around a mouth full of popcorn.

"Of course." A small frown formed between my eyebrows at her need to state the obvious. Natalie was tucked under my arm hidden gently beneath the confines of my jacket in her travel tank while I walked with practiced ease that meant her water didn't slosh at all. "I'm not sure what that has to do with anything, though."

"No, all good, just checking." Leah was chewing so loudly it wasn't like she was just in my ears but actually living inside my brain.

"I'm walking in so I'm going to have to hang up in a second." I headed to the back of the theater and claimed a seat in the back left corner and set Nat up on her own chair.

"God, I am *SO* excited for this movie, Miles Teller can come to mommy."

"Leah, you can't keep referring to yourself as 'mommy'." I scrunched my nose up. "We've talked about this."

"It will scare the children. Yes, yes. I know." I could practically hear her eyes rolling.

"Okay the trailers are starting, call you after."

"Love you, sissy," Leah whispered as they started on her end too.

"Love you more."

I quickly snapped a photo of Nat in her theater chair and posted it to her instagram: *'Just a fish, ready for a little Miles Teller. #cometomommy'*

I snorted to myself and decided to let Leah find that one all on her own. Most of the captions I wrote were in some way inspired by my best friend.

We tried to do this once every couple of months. Leah and I would find a movie we both wanted to watch and search high and low for theaters in our own cities that were playing them at the exact same time. She would go on her end, and I'd go on my end and it would be sort of like we were doing it together.

I started bringing Nat about four years ago when I was overwhelmed with unyielding guilt at leaving her out of all the fun. That's when I discovered travel containers. I always just moved her from house to house in a big bucket that sat in the passenger footwell of whatever moving truck I'd rented, the whole travel container thing totally changed the game for us.

I wasn't as big of a fan of bringing her out nowadays given she was going to be fifteen in April (sort of, that was when Casimir had gifted her to me. I wasn't even sure Natalie was a girl, it was just the vibe I got), but every so often I made an exception.

Leah had been pleading her case, leaning really heavily into the 'pros' of her 'pros and cons' list on why *Top Gun Maverick* needed to be our next movie. Most of her points revolved around the actors Miles Teller and some other guy named Glen.

I admittedly was enraptured with the movie and, after it was done, proceeded to talk animatedly to Leah about it all the way to the station, on the train and right to the front door of my house.

"This is going in my top five," Leah said, her own keys jingling on the other end.

"Like, life moments?"

"Bless, sissy, but no," she sighed and I could tell just by the disjointed sounds on the other end of the phone that I plopped down on my couch almost the exact same time that she plopped down on hers.

"Fair enough. I suppose you do have a more exciting life than me."

"I actually reject that statement. Right now, at this moment, you have the number of a famous drummer right in your phone."

My immediate reaction was to exclaim some sort of profanity and tell her she was losing her marbles, but then I remembered that actually, that was true. It wasn't the reason why I'd struggled to stay focused at work for the last few days, though.

No, that was more along the lines of still coming to terms that I had left his body pressed against every part of mine and just the thought of that made every part of me, mind body and spirit, erupt into tingles. That I was all but a stiff wind away from collapsing into a heap of goo if I really let myself remember the way it felt to have him speak words that had no business being as sexy as they were against my skin. That my stomach had learned all on it's own how to do the Can-Can when I remembered his laugh, his hands, his warmth, his *hands*–

"Poppy?" Leah called through the phone like she was projecting her voice through a megaphone.

"And now I'm deaf." I scowled even though she couldn't see me.

"You didn't answer my question," she whined while I reached for my laptop and lifted the lid.

Every warm and tingly sensation went cold at the web browser pulled up for apartments in Banks City. It was about a six hour drive away from where I was now in the city of Blazewood and the destination I'd decided on.

"I didn't hear your question, but I need you to help me look for apartments. Nothing I've looked at is decent," I grumbled, refreshing the page and looking through the same listings I'd looked at last night.

Leah was quiet on the other end for so long I pulled the phone from my ear just to see if we were still connected.

"Sissy? You still there?" I clicking over to page two. "I can send you the link."

"Poppy," she started, speaking slowly and with just the right amount of hesitation that I knew immediately what conversation she was going to broach. It was one we'd had many times before. "You just settled into the place you're at now. Actually, that's a lie, most of your stuff is still in boxes and you have one glass unpacked. We had to take turns drinking water when I was there."

"Leah, you know I don't like to stay put for longer than a year." The words were rehearsed. They were the same ones I said every time we had this conversation because this need to keep moving was connected to the part of myself that lived behind that huge, metal, impenetrable door in my mind. The one I only unlocked and opened when it was just me and I didn't have to worry about what came out or who would see it.

My voice sounded calm but also like I'd just sat bolt straight. Muscles locked to brace for an impending attack, but even I could tell I was exhausted.

"Yeah," she started, and I could picture her chewing on her fingernails. "I know but I just thought that eventually, you'd..." She didn't finish that sentence, but I knew what she wanted to say. That eventually I'd settle down, that I'd find somewhere that stuck. Eventually I'd stop searching, or looking, or seeking, or running.

"He wouldn't want you to be living like this, Penelope."

"Leah." Her name was a warning not to keep going. Not to push. Her simple mention of my brother made that door in my mind rattle.

"No, I have to say it because I'm it." *Push.* "I'm who you have and if Casimir was here he'd kick my ass for not saying the words out loud. He'd hate this for you, Poppy." *Push* "All of it. Always moving, never settling down, never just *stopping*. And I think you hate when I bring it up so much because you know I'm right."

My eyes stung with the tears that weren't there and my chest was heaving with so many things; with anger, and hurt and sadness and guilt. Aching with the need to release words I didn't mean and things I'd never in a million years would ever want to say to my friend.

I bit my lip hard enough to draw blood, until I was sure I could speak without my words being overpowered by one of the hundreds of choking hollow sobs I'd swallowed down in front of her.

This was why I'd split myself into two. I knew she wouldn't recognise me if she saw the person I became when all of the darkest things I felt and carried came out, and I knew she wouldn't want to stay.

"But he's not here, Leah. So, I guess it doesn't really matter what he'd say." I ended the call and did my best to forget the words so full of truth she had spoken, and the words so full of lies I had spoken back.

It would matter.

There were so many things I needed to tell him. To hear him say back. But that was impossible.

I spent the rest of the night staring at listings for apartments I already knew I hated before even stepping foot into them, still surrounded by boxes I hadn't unpacked for so long that I really didn't remember what was even in them.

I walked into the staff kitchen the next day at work on autopilot feeling like everything was wrong after my conversation with Leah the night before.

We hardly ever fought. It was almost impossible for there to be anything said that we couldn't fix right in the moment with either a sarcastic quip or a dose of reality in the form of calling the other person out on their shit. I know that's what she did last night and even though there was a big part of me that knew what she said had some truth in it, it wasn't the same. She didn't know the whole story and I knew that was my doing.

I knew that she hurt when I hurt. That was just one of the things that her heart was made of. Leah was an empath of the highest level, another reason why I'd made the decision to deal with all the very hardest things that had ever happened to me in the way I had. I'd always had Leah, before I'd been stupid and selfish and impulsive and the sole reason my brother had lost his life. For a long time I think I felt like if I didn't have Leah, if she hadn't been there for me the way she'd been, I'd have disappeared completely.

So, that's pretty much the way things were going so far today. Sad, lonely, guilty. All those wonderful things were what made up the Poppy of the present, which explained entirely why I had to sit on the floor of the train and fix my shoes after putting them on the wrong feet before I left the house.

My phone started to buzz in my hand. My heart immediately started its departure from the vicinity of my body when it was Aspen's name staring back at me.

"Hello, Poppy," his voice rang through crisp and clear.

"Hello, Aspen." My smile spread across my face like perfectly, ooey-gooey melty butter on warm bread because I couldn't help myself. This, *this,* was the Aspen-Effect.

I put my leftover spaghetti that I found right at the back of my fridge from so long ago I actually couldn't remember when I'd cooked it, into the microwave and punched in two minutes for it to heat up.

"I'm calling about our second date." He delivered the words so casually it took me a second to realize what he'd said.

I completely missed the bench I intended to lean on again.

"*Fuck me,*" I mumbled, catching myself before becoming intimate with the floor.

Aspen gasped dramatically, "But you're at work?" The sounds of cymbals and movement came through the phone. "I haven't ever had an office job. Do they let you do that sort of thing now?" He was laughing without laughing, I could just tell. "Is it too forward of me to say that your assertiveness is a real turn on? I think I'm turned on."

"You think? Like you're not sure?" I could feel the heat taking over my face, so conflicting at the laughter trapped in my chest and the guilt from my conversation with Leah that lingered at the back of my throat, sour and upsetting.

"No, I'm sure," he said. "Very, very turned on." His voice was full of the things he was feeling. The perfect sound to the look that I knew would be on his face.

That one so like the sun.

"Aspen," I sighed, "We're just friends, remember? Friends don't date."

"That's not true," he countered.

"It's not?" I knew it was. I also knew friends didn't kiss pressed up against trees or know all the places one another might be soft or very, very, *very* hard.

I'd learned that as well as hiking and a penchant for creating peculiar definitions for common words, Ap enjoyed toeing what had fast become a very murky line, one we'd both been walking since last weekend. The problem was, I really, *really* liked how murky it had become. Especially when I let myself forget all the reasons I drew it in the first place.

"Why do you think brunch became such a big thing?" Aspen delivered that line like it was a truth as old as time.

"That's not at all true."

"I wholeheartedly disagree. Friends have been dating since the 30's," he said around what now sounded like a mouth full of food.

"The 30's?" I wondered when I would stop being surprised by this man. Probably never.

"Now," he continued on, undeterred, "our second date."

"Popsicle, my girl!"

My stomach dropped immediately at Todd's arrival. I feel it pertinent to mention once again that his desk was so far on the other side of the office that you couldn't even *see* this kitchen. Actually, I knew for a fact that you had to first walk by the kitchen on *that* side of the office to get to *this* one.

"Lord, no," I mumbled into my phone, turning the screen protectively in case he tried to see who I was speaking to for some unhinged reason, not that I expected him to know who 'Ap' was.

"*Whose* girl?" Aspen sounded curious, but there was something in his voice that sounded like raised hackles.

I could see it now, how he'd save me from this incredibly unwanted and recurring life-mare. The scene played out in my head immediately; Aspen would appear out of nowhere, stepping into this office kitchen that always smelt faintly of corn, and in a strange but not completely unwelcome chain of events, he'd fling a drumstick like a throwing star. It would embed itself perfectly in the wall between Todd and I like an impassable barrier. I'd be speechless, maybe taken aback, but still impressed and Todd would fall through the floor.

I was losing my mind.

I cleared my throat, "Hi, Todd." I wonder if he could tell how uninvited this conversation was.

"Who ya speaking to, Poompaloompa?"

"Did he just call you *Poompaloompa?*" Aspen asked, sounding absolutely affronted for me, I did my best to ignore him in favor of getting rid of Todd.

"I'm on the phone Todd, do you mind?" If I sounded like I'd just sat on a thumb tack, it's because that's how Todd made me feel most days.

"Is it that elusive boyfriend of yours?" He said the words in that sort of exaggerated way that you used when mimicking what your siblings said in an effort to piss them off. I really hoped Aspen still spoke to me after this.

"Yep." I felt like I shouted the word. Delivered it in the sort of way that made me feel like I should have accompanied it with a fist pump or a high kick.

"Oh my god," Aspen whispered, sounding like he was bouncing up and down with excitement.

"Yes, that's exactly who I'm speaking to." I tried to keep a pleasant look on my face but it really felt more like a cringe and suddenly I really needed to pee.

"Oh, Poompaloompa. This is a real gift, what you're giving me right now. Maybe even the best thing I've ever witnessed." Aspen's delighted laughter trickled through my phone and now I wanted to steal a single sock from each of his pairs and hide them from him forever for being entertained by my misery.

Todd's face did a lot of things in that moment and the few seconds that followed, none of them good and all of them made my palms sweaty.

"I don't believe you. Come on, let me see your phone." He actually went to grab for it.

"What? *Hey—*" I took a step to the side just as the microwave beeped with the now heated pasta I no longer wanted.

"Is this dude serious?" Aspen's voice was harder now. No trace of the light hearted joking from before.

"Ap, I'll call you back." My feet had gotten so hot they started to slip around in my socks and all I really wanted to do was run to Winny and report that Todd has intestinal issues of his own and personally requested his assistance.

"Penelope, don't—"

"I finish at 5:30," I whispered quickly. "I'll call you then." I ended the call before I could hear his reply, ducking around Todd to grab my food so quickly he didn't have time to block my path with his bulky frame.

The entire ordeal had turned my stomach so bad, every bite of my pasta tasted sour. In an effort to prove how much Todd *didn't* get to me, I ate every last bite.

Take that, Todd.

Like when most things set me on edge, I poured every ounce of brain space I had into doing my job right until the clock on my desk showed 5:30 PM on the dot.

The seconds waiting for the elevator to arrive left my mind wandering to the conversation I had with Leah again. The reminder of how things had ended made me feel sick to my stomach. I couldn't remember the last time we'd fought like that. That was the exact moment Todd called out to hold the elevator and I once again pretended not to hear him.

I tapped the call button again frantically, breathing through the swirl of nausea that refused to dissipate by clinging to the idea of calling Ap back to talk about our friend-date as soon as I was out the doors of the building. It was completely inappropriate (Poppy, meet line-drawn-in-sand-you-drew-yourself-with-purpose-and-good-reason) but the thought improved my mood drastically. I was so improved that I didn't notice the black sedan parked just outside my building, or the tall, dark figure that hopped out wearing sunglasses and a baseball cap and a thick winter coat that was way too heavy for the mild day we were having. Not until he was standing right in front of me.

"Hello, Poppy," he said, grinning down at me in a way that made my knees wobble and my heart stop.

12

January 25th

Poppy

"Oh my god, Aspen!" My hands fluttered haphazardly on either side of his face like somehow that would help disguise his identity to the outside world. I really couldn't say why, but it felt helpful. "*You're outside my building!*"

Those were the actual words that came out of my mouth. Not '*seeing your whole person with my own eyes is the biggest relief I've ever known*' or '*is it weird that I've thought of you so thoroughly I accidentally signed off an email with your name instead of mine today?*'.

"I told you where I worked once, and only sort of, how, *how,* did you even remember that?"

"It may surprise you to know that I listen to the words that come out of your mouth. Also, typing into Google 'transcribing company on Eastborne Avenue in Blazewood' produced exactly one result so, here I am." He paused for a second, a small frown growing bigger by the millisecond between his brows, "That's creepy, isn't it?"

"In a very flattering way, yes." My reply seemed to be good enough for him because he looked utterly delighted at that. The look on his face did its job in distracting me from my panic, but only for a second.

"Aspen," I whispered to him frantically, "you're still *here,* at my *work*."

"Yes, I thought we already covered that in a creepy but flattering way," he leaned in closer to me, whispering back.

"But what about the—" It was at that moment I noticed them from the corner of my eye. The paparazzi.

"Shit." He'd noticed what had captured my attention and pulled his hat down lower over his head, like that would all of a sudden convince the men in the distance with the very big camera lenses that Aspen was not in fact who he really was. "Sorry, Poppy. I thought I lost them."

It was at that exact moment that Todd exited the building. He looked up from his phone and came to a standstill right in front of us.

"Pop tart," he said, adding yet another name to the ever growing list of things that made me want to scream into a trash can in an effort to curb my desire to kick him in the balls. "Who's this?"

I'll admit, I froze.

In my freezing, I considered for one, teeny weeny moment saying that Aspen was my boyfriend, because then Todd might actually leave me alone. Here was a real life man who knew my name. First, middle *and* last. What more proof did Todd need than that?

My stomach lurched with a serve and soul shuddering wave of nausea so intense I reached out to grip Aspen's jacket sleeve on reflex. But then I thought of the men with the cameras, and the fact that Todd was probably a whole four seconds away from realizing who was standing in front of him. I forced myself to swallow the feeling down as best I could.

The real issue here was that Aspen was clearly thinking of a plan of his own.

I knew that he'd probably put two and two together, realizing that this was in fact that hemorrhoid of a human he'd overheard on the phone.

It should have surprised exactly zero people that at the exact same time that Aspen said, "I'm her boyfriend", I decided to deliver a cool and collected, "He's my cousin."

...*Super.*

The only way to describe how I was feeling was sort of like how someone *might* feel when they knew they were about to be electrocuted. My grip on his sleeve tightened so fiercely I was worried I'd never be able to unfurl my fingers. We'd have to cut off his jacket sleeve and I'd forever be forced to walk around with the reminder of this exact moment clenched between my phalanges.

I turned to look up just as Aspen looked down at me. Just in time to see his green eyes, so bright they looked luminescent, widen to a comedic size and his lips thin in what was a very valiant effort of keeping a neutral expression. He was *enjoying this.*

I could tell my own expression had turned incredulous because he had to close his eyes, shaking his head minutely as if fighting every urge he had *not* to burst out into tear-filled, joyful laughter.

"Woah," Todd sounded like he'd just been tasered. "You're…you're *dating* your cousin?"

I was really going to throw up. "Hold on. That's actually not —"

"Holy shit, Poppy? You're dating your cousin?" Todd cut me off with the same exact question I'd been trying to answer which seemed on all accounts unproductive to me.

On instinct I moved a little closer to Aspen, the gentle woodsy pine scent with his signature hint of violets made me feel a little less like I was about to barf my brains out. It was getting so bad I could feel the sweat starting to pebble on my hairline.

I'd been anxious before, but never like this.

"Your friend looks a little green, Pop tart," Aspen's voice strained with the obvious effort of trying not to laugh. Meanwhile, I was panicking because his casual use of the color 'green' sent a jolt through my whole body and my hand immediately clamped over my mouth.

Satan's blazing balls, I was *really* going to throw up. Really, really, *really.*

Just when I thought all hell was going to break loose and my soul was screaming for someone, *anyone* – I might've even settled for Todd at this point – to help me, the barnacle in question finally looked right at Aspen.

Ah. We were so close. *So, so close.*

There had been a minute there where we'd have been able to get out of this without Todd looking at Aspen and realizing that the drummer of *Lady Luck* was standing two feet in front of him, and as far as Todd was concerned in that moment, dating his own cousin.

There was no way he wouldn't have noticed.

Todd was a firm believer in casual Fridays at work, and I could remember maybe one time where he hadn't worn a shirt that had something to do with *Lady Luck* on it.

Todd's mouth went slack at the same time as his nostrils flared. The exact moment he realized who Aspen was.

"Ap," I whispered, knowing he could hear the stress in my voice with a hint of relief, the latter from the miracle that it was words that came out of my mouth, not regurgitated spaghetti.

"Yep," he replied, letting me know that he too saw how this was all about to backfire a lot faster than perhaps originally thought. With his arm still around my shoulder, he backed us up towards the Taurus.

From then, it happened very quickly.

The passenger door opened, firm but gentle hands pushed me in, Aspen's mouth close to my ear whispering a rushed "*Go, go, go!*" And then he was running. Sliding across the bonnet of his car like he was James Dean reincarnated, with a grin so big I took another mental snap. Another moment for me to hold, hopefully tight enough that even when I closed my eyes years from now I'd see it as clearly as I did right then.

"You have absolutely no idea how much I've wanted to do that my whole life," Aspen panted, out of breath and sparkly eyed.

Todd had his phone pulled out just as we were pulling away from the sidewalk.

My face was frozen in place as I tried very hard to think through exactly what happened, but my spiral was interrupted by a loud, unrestrained laugh from the man beside me.

"Did you see his face?" Aspen wheezed with both hands gripping the steering wheel.

I also wanted to laugh. Sort of. I was dizzy, so I also wanted to lie down.

Mostly, I wanted to empty the contents of my stomach but the very chaotic way things had just descended out of control momentarily pushed that unfortunate desire from my mind.

"Aspen, he thinks I'm your cousin." I was unable to do more than whisper.

Ap did a double take at the look on my face. I was certain he was confusing my need to hurl with fear of the hole that we'd both just happily plopped ourselves into.

"Well, on the upside, maybe if he thinks your sexual desires are a little under the burrow he might leave you be? From what I heard over the phone–Poppy? Woah, *hey...*are you okay?" He reached over to tuck a loose bit of hair behind my ear and if I hadn't been in absolute peril I might have lost my *ever loving mind*. Maybe, I would've had time to bear witness to the opposing parts of myself partaking in some serious hand to hand combat. Fighting over being wooed and reminding myself this was absolutely not what friends did.

"He thinks I'm having sex with my cousin," I said the words out loud and couldn't stop the immediate onslaught of full body tingles that pushed me over the edge into hysterical laughter. That's when it really hit me. It hit me in a very big way. "Aspen, I'm going to throw up." My hand clamped over my mouth.

His face fell instantaneously. "Wait, really?" He looked at me with serious concern and even though he was double checking, he'd already pulled the car over to the side of the road. "Poppy, it's not that big of a deal, I swear–"

I didn't get to hear the rest of the words that came out of Aspen's mouth, because every single bite I ate for lunch was suddenly staring back at me from the road in front of me.

"I'm going to puke in your bed." The words were a pathetic grumble that I pushed out of my mouth for the third time. The room was spinning faster than I was sure anything had ever spun in the history of time and space. All

I really wanted to do was keep my head tucked firmly beneath Aspen's jaw while he carried me through the elevator doors and into his penthouse.

It was silly, maybe, but I'd imagined walking into this very place so many times. Thought about how it would look and feel and smell. Wondered how Aspen would decorate his home and if I'd be surprised or proven right in any of my predictions.

Let's just say being carried bridal style while fretting that there were chunks of spaghetti on my shirt was absolutely not how I had envisioned it coming together.

At all.

"That's okay," he said, dropping a gentle kiss onto my forehead and heading straight for what I assumed was somewhere I could wrap myself around a toilet and never leave.

"I smell like puke."

"A little."

I tried to whack his stomach but I'm certain my hand didn't move at all. "You're not supposed to agree with me." I wanted to cry.

"We're about to rectify the situation." He quickly opened a door that led to a clean, but clearly very masculine bathroom from what I could make out in the small crack between my eyelids. The second he did it, it was like my body knew it was safe to let loose again.

"Oh no." They were the only words that made it out of my mouth before Aspen set me right in front of the toilet and I tried not to think about the fact that I sounded like a pterodactyl screaming into his porcelain throne.

"Your toilet is very clean," I said between heaves.

"Thank you," he said, sounding close and far away at the same time. His voice too soft and too loud. I could feel his hands combing back my hair and wondered if it possible to be smitten and so embarrassed you could die all in the some moment? Because that was me.

"I think my soul is trying to leave my body." My voice echoed around the toilet bowl.

"The door is closed so it can't get out, we'll put it back later." Somehow, that was incredibly reassuring and all I could do was nod before I was hit with another round of wretches.

"Aspen." His name was a barely audible rasp. "You need to leave," I said when I could get in a breath.

"Not gonna happen." But then he turned around and went straight out the door we'd entered in.

Once he left, I was confused for a while before deciding I'd clearly hallucinated the last few minutes of conversation and had obviously reached the end of my tether. It was clear to me now that I was going to die from this.

I didn't hear him come back on account of the banshee that seemed to be squatting in Aspen's plumbing so I jumped with an undignified squeak when a cool, damp washcloth was pressed to my forehead. I didn't even have it in me to tell him to leave again, in either reality or via hallucination, because the small relief from what he was doing pulled a moan so guttural from my body it was possible to confuse me for a bison in heat.

He stayed there with me until my body was cramping with nothing left to expel and I was so exhausted I was pretty sure I fell asleep with my head in the toilet.

"Poppy," Ap's voice was gentle and soft and I wanted to wrap it around me forever.

I peeled open my aching eyelids to see a very concerned version of Aspen's face peering down at me.

"I think we need to get you cleaned up."

"What's happening to me?" I croaked out, letting my body flop to the tiled floor. "I'm dying."

"You're not dying." His hand was rubbing circles on my back, voice still gentle.

"This is karma."

"Oh? What did you do that was so bad?"

I knew he was joking, but if he knew what I'd done, he'd never look at me the same again. There was nothing that I could say, even if I wanted to, the words just wouldn't come out because more than anything, I was a coward.

I don't think Aspen thought I was a coward at that moment though, I think he just thought I fell asleep with my head next to his toilet for a second time because he whispered my name again, his hand still gentle on my back.

"Mm?" It was all I could muster to say.

"I think you have food poisoning. What did you eat today?"

Just the thought of it had my body heaving again, but nothing came out. "Oh no." I tried to drag in gulps of air. "It was the spaghet—" Another heave.

"Spaghetti?" He said the cursed word for me.

"It was at the back of my fridge," I said, refusing to look up at him. "It tasted sour."

"You *knowingly* ate sour spaghetti?" He sounded incredulous but also incredibly entertained.

"I was sticking it to Todd."

"Oh, Poompaloompa," Aspen sighed, like he knew this had 'Poppy' written all over it.

"And now I am covered in barf and you're calling me by Todd's nicknames."

I cried. I really, truly cried. It had been the first time in over a decade and this was what got me.

His thumb swiped under my eye, catching a runaway tear. "How you haven't jumped his bones is beyond me."

Aspen graced me with a beautiful grin when I dared to finally stare up at him. "Do you think you can stand?"

I gave a small nod and accepted his help to get to my feet. The dizziness hit me immediately and I reached out unceremoniously for anything to hold onto.

"I've got you, Pop." And he did, his hold on me was firm and strong.

"Dizzy," I mumbled, keeping my eyes closed tight. "Just set me on the shower floor and turn the water on, I'll be okay."

"I can't stress enough how much I'm not going to be doing that."

"Aspen, you can't help me shower." It took all my energy to look at him with as much passion as I felt about that situation.

"Yes, I can."

"But you'll see me naked." Even as I said the words there wasn't any real worry to be felt. The idea of Aspen seeing me naked didn't scare me, it almost seemed inevitable. It was entirely possible that was the bacteria talking.

"Poppy, you need help because you're not well. I promise my eyes won't wander but if you really don't want my help I can call Allie." He sounded so genuine I didn't even consider the fact that he was only saying it to appease me.

"You're never going to be able to look at me again. All my sex appeal just, *poof*. Gone. You'll think of me and only ever be able to think of the words 'pterodactyl mating call' and 'toilet'." I blame the delirium from two week old spaghetti bolognese for every word coming out of my mouth.

Aspen didn't say anything as he reached for the hem of my shirt, a silent request for me to lift up my arms. I didn't fight him because I knew I didn't want anyone else here with me but him.

My shirt dropped to the floor next to us and I could see through my half lidded eyes the way his eyes flicked to the scar on my shoulder. Aside from that moment, his eyes never left my face and he didn't say anything about it.

"Poppy," his voice was quiet but firm, "believe me when I say that I think you might just be the sexiest woman I've ever met in my entire life. That I've thought of you in ways a friend really never should, even in this part of the country, and that nothing about you being unwell because you decided to eat month-old pasta will change that for me. Except that I'm actually pretty impressed you downed an entire portion of something that no doubt tasted like actual feet."

"Two weeks," I mumbled half-heartedly. "And much worse than feet."

"I promise," he said again, "I won't look until you want me to. Okay?" He didn't move, not a single muscle until I nodded my head and then he reached for the button of my pants. Stripped completely down and not fully comprehending that it was the firm, rough, calloused grip of Aspen's hands around my waist keeping me up right, I was led to the shower.

I was certain that Aspen kept his word because his hands didn't leave my waist from where he stood at my back. Actually, I was pretty sure he still had all his clothes on as he murmured where to grab the soap and where to reach for the tooth brush prepped with a little strip of peppermint toothpaste, which he'd also promised was new.

The next thing I remembered was a big, fluffy towel that smelt exactly like Aspen being wrapped around me moments before a shirt that smelt just the same was pulled over my head.

My favorite part was the body, warm and solid that held me like I was this incredibly precious thing and I wondered then, because it had been so long since I'd known it and I couldn't be certain, if maybe this was what finally coming home felt like.

13

January 25th

ASPEN

Poppy was asleep by the time I tucked her into my bed.

It was a weird realization that, as an adult, I'd never required the use of a bucket up until that moment. I opted for the next best thing and put my least used pot next to the bed along with a glass of water.

Poppy was restless. Soft little mewing noises coming from her every so often as she kept herself tucked into a tight ball in the middle of my bed.

I watched her feeling helpless and infinitely stupid. Because it *had* been a stupid idea to show up at her work. Stupid and selfish because she didn't realize it yet, but there would be paparazzi camping outside from here on out thanks to my reckless, impulsive decision. It was like my brain malfunctioned at the very idea of being close to her and every rule I lived by just went out the window.

I had spent a long time doing right by everyone around me, regardless of what it cost me. Thinking of everyone before myself because the mere thought of *not* sent me into such an intense panic I was certain my heart would give out on me. The beats thumping through my body like a vibration so intense there was no way I could cope with it.

I didn't realize my hands were tugging so hard at the roots of my hair until another of Poppy's mewling cries broke the spell. There was a reason I was the way I was and this was the perfect example of why things were better when I thought of everyone else before myself.

I ran a hand down my face swallowing back a groan at the thought of how I was going to explain this to her when she suddenly sat up, eyes wide and terrified with a hand over her mouth. I sprang for the pot so fast I literally tripped on the edge of the rumpled rug that had never sat right beneath my bed, landing with a loud and painful thump on the floor. Scrambling to my knees I had the pot in her lap and her hair pulled back while she gripped it like a lifeline.

Poppy was a lot smaller than me, but it became that much more noticeable with her frame swallowed up by my shirt. It made me want to protect her at all costs. To make sure that she always felt safe and cared for and happy.

The thoughts came at me so abruptly my body actively jolted backwards. I had known Poppy for barely three weeks and already it was becoming increasingly hard to remember any time before where I *hadn't* known her. To imagine any time in the future where I would have to refer to her in the past tense as someone I'd known once. It sent an ache through my whole body so visceral I almost needed to use the pot she clung to.

Her body trembled through the contracting waves of her stomach trying to dispel something that was no longer there for a while until slowly, she started to relax.

"I'm okay," she croaked, handing me back the pot and looking so defeated it made me feel helpless all over again. I reached for the glass of water and handed it to her.

"Just take a really little sip." I didn't let go of the glass as she did just that, a small thrill zinging through me at her trusting me to help her. "That's my girl."

The words slipped out. I was almost positive Poppy didn't really register them, not when she mumbled a small "Thanks," and started to settle back down into the covers.

In reality, Poppy was not mine.

Even covered in my shirt, in my bed. The very idea that she wasn't mine all of a sudden made my hands go numb. For fear of reaching out to hold onto her without any intention of ever letting go, I started to move back to my spot against the wall where I'd dragged a chair from the dining table just to keep an eye on her.

Her hand reached out to grip mine, holding on with about as much strength as a squirrel.

"Aspen," she whispered from her spot facing away from me.

"I'm here." I was ready to do just about anything to make her feel better.

"Do friends cuddle in this part of the country?" Her voice was raspy and weak but I could imagine the hint of humor she'd probably intended to ask the question with.

No. *Nope*. No, they didn't.

Not by any definition even I had of the word, but because there wasn't that much more damage I could do tonight, I lifted back the covers and climbed in behind her.

Poppy was warm and soft and smelt like my body wash as she nestled back into me. I did everything I could to think about absolutely anything except the way her ass was now pressed firmly against my crotch. Her perfect, round, mouth watering–

"Is this okay?" she asked, still wiggling her hips. The movement made me hiss and I reached out to grip her waist in a very desperate attempt to keep her still.

"Poppy, if you do that again I think you might actually kill me this time," I said around the strain of keeping my own shit together.

In an effort to diffuse what was about to become a much less friend-like situation than we were already in, I grappled for anything to help. Somehow I settled on that one time Dax and I nailed an empty fruit crate to the top of my skateboard from the bottom and didn't think much about it when he stepped on it and immediately impaled his foot on a nail. There was blood everywhere. My little seven year old self had never seen so much blood all at once before. Dax was so worried we'd get in trouble that he used the hand he'd held over the hole in his foot to cover my mouth, thus transferring all his foot-blood right onto my face.

My body relaxed as any fear of Poppy feeling my painfully hard cock against her ass was completely and totally averted.

"Oh," she sounded a little more awake now. "Sorry."

"It's okay," I grinned, giving in to temptation and nuzzling into the side of her neck.

This was the sweetest sort of torture. Poppy was *right here* and still completely out of my reach. Her hands wrapped around my forearm that I'd wound gently around her, mindful of her stomach.

She was so quiet for so long I thought she'd finally fallen asleep, but then she spoke softly into the darkened room around us. "I'm sorry I ruined our second friend-date."

"This was actually far better than what I had planned."

"Oh, good." It was incredibly satisfying that I knew without looking that she would have delivered that with an epic eye roll if she'd been well enough.

"I have a photo of you sleeping with your head in the toilet. I think I want to blow it up and hang it on my wall."

"That's really sweet of you, Aspen."

"I know." My voice was muffled from where it was still pressed to the skin of her neck.

Poppy's body relaxed further into me.

By the time I spoke again there was no space between us at all. "You didn't ruin anything," I told her and meant every word. "I'm sorry I showed up at your work unannounced and that your best friend Todd now thinks you're sleeping with your cousin."

Poppy's body shook with laughter until she groaned and curled in on herself a little more. "No," she gasped. "No laughing, please."

"Got it," I said, pulling her back into me like I'd held her exactly like this before. Because that's how it felt, like my body knew hers, like her being in my bed was exactly how things had always been.

"I can't believe you saw me naked and covered in puke," she groaned. Her hands left their place on my arm to cover her face.

"I promise that I kept my eyes directly on your shoulder blades." I dropped a soft kiss on the slope of her neck. "I feel compelled to let you know; you have sublime shoulder blades."

"Aspen," she started, her reprimand sounding only half serious.

"I'm glad I was with you," I said seriously. "The idea of you dealing with this on your own makes me feel insane." I let the truth of that statement hang between us, wondering if she was able to read between the words I had spoken to the ones that I hadn't.

"Aspen, what are we doing?" she whispered, "I told you, I'm leaving."

"Because you only stay for a year and then you move on because you're looking for something you can't explain because it's complicated," I finished the explanation for her, as if the words hadn't been burned into my mind when she'd said them the first time.

"Yes."

"Why?" The single worded question left my tongue like a slingshot. I was breaking so many of my own rules tonight. I hadn't really expected her to answer, so when she did I held my breath for fear she'd stop.

"Because I'm scared. Because —"

"Because?"

Just when I didn't think she'd reply, her whispered words pierced the quiet between us. "I'm not always good, Aspen. There are things that I've done that I can't forget."

I wanted to say so many things to her then. To break apart every word she said and have her explain to me *why*. To explain to me *how* she, this person that when I was around her I might as well be standing right in the warmest part of the sun, had ever been allowed to feel like that.

"Things are better this way," she said before I'd even had a chance to organize my mind. "And, you know, I get to see all these different cities, and meet all these different people and no one gets hurt. It's just better this way."

It sounded like a line she'd rehearsed in the mirror. The inflections of her voice so unlike the person I'd come to know.

"Poppy," I said, swallowing thickly at my own nerve, "I don't believe you."

"I know." Her whisper was gentle as it seeped into my skin and splintered right into my chest. In what was the most honesty I think I'd ever had from her she added, "Me either."

I wanted to push her, to tell her that it sounded to me like she was doing a whole lot of running in the wrong direction. That of everything she'd just said, there was only one part that was true, but I think she knew that. I could feel the beat of her heart as I held her, felt it speed up at the same time that she moved her hands back down to my arm and gripped it tightly, like she wanted to use me to anchor herself here. To this bed, to this apartment, to this city.

The grip she had on me said it all, that this was something that she had carried with her for so long that she probably couldn't separate herself from it. Suddenly, the very idea of her being in pain was completely unacceptable to me. Unbearable.

"You know," I whispered against the back of her neck, "this might be poor timing but you look really hot in my shirt."

Poppy snorted so aggressively I couldn't breathe through the laughs that rocked through me, unable to control it in the slightest even as she pleaded with me to stop, that when she laughed she couldn't promise it would be spaghetti free.

"The depth of tone you got on that sound was incredible," I wiped the tears from my eyes on the back of her shirt and moved up on an elbow to try and see her face.

"If my puke covered nudity didn't send you running, that'll do the trick."

"Actually, I think you just uncovered a new kink for me."

"You're saying all the right things to make me forget you're doing this completely out of pity."

"You think I'm *pity*-flirting with you?"

"Of course," she sighed and finally rolled onto her back. It was just her eyes that seemed to reflect the small amount of light getting into the room. Only the barest outline of her features were visible but I didn't need even that to know how beautiful this woman was and that it didn't have a single thing to do with how she looked on the outside.

"Penelope, I'm so confident that, given the opportunity, I'd seduce the shit out of you."

"You will find no arguments here, Aspen Killian."

That surprised me, "Is that right, Poppy Elizabeth?"

Her face morphed into the picture of cocky confidence that sent a zap of electricity right down my spine, "Aspen, I'm confident that you could seduce a wet paper towel if given half the chance."

"I'm oddly flattered by that sentiment."

"You can put it right in your 'flattery basket' next to all my thoughts about your nasal cavity." Poppy rolled her eyes and a small, breathy laugh left her igniting those same notes that rushed through my mind the first time I heard it.

We didn't speak after that. It wasn't unbearable or suffocating or seemingly louder than any stadium I'd ever played in, not like it usually felt when I'd laid in this exact bed without her.

I pulled her tighter to me and she seemed to hold me just as hard.

"Thank you for looking after me," her voice was so small and anything I wanted to say back got stuck in my throat because it felt like it had been a very long time since anyone had looked after Poppy.

I kissed the bare, warm skin of her shoulder and tried desperately for the right thing to say back.

Poppy fell asleep in my arms as the words continued to evade me, leaving me wide awake for the rest of the night, thinking instead about all the ways I would keep looking after her if she ever decided to let me try.

14

January 26th

Poppy

The first thing I realized as I slowly woke up, was that it felt as if I had been hit by a relatively large vehicle. The second thing that struck me was that for one, weirdly terrifying moment I thought I was back in my childhood bedroom. The one with glow in the dark stickers on the ceiling and posters of all my favorite bands covering the walls top to bottom.

But I was in Aspen's room.

It was *his* glow in the dark stars on the ceiling but he was nowhere to be found. The room around me was so incredibly dark it seemed like it was the middle of the night. It was then that a minor wave of nausea pulsed through me. A gentle and completely unwelcome reminder of everything that had happened yesterday.

Me throwing up out the door of Aspen's car.

Me hugging his toilet bowl making enough noise to raise the dead.

Me needing to be showered with the support of the very man in question.

"Oh, for the love of Pete," I moaned, sinking deeper into his bed. This was just freaking *dandy*. I mean really, just great.

He told me I had sublime shoulder blades. *Sublime. Shoulder blades.*

The only saving grace of the moment was that he wasn't here to witness me coming to terms with my reality. All I knew was that there was no way I was heading into work in my current state. If it wasn't from the residue of the sour spaghetti, then it would be on account of wanting to avoid Todd at all costs.

Swinging my legs off the side of the bed, my foot landed right in the cold metal pot that had been placed there. Was it weird that that made me melt a little? That's when I heard a loud and very unmistakable bang come from the kitchen followed by and equally loud, *"Fuck."*

Standing slowly just to test the capabilities of my still tender body, I was glad to find myself without any dizziness or the need to throw up and set out to find Aspen.

And find him I did.

His penthouse was filled with incredibly comfortable looking furniture in creams and dark greens with big windows that let in copious amounts of light. I counted at least five sets of drum sticks on my way to wherever I was going and that made me smile too.

This was the way I had imagined getting to see his space. It made so much sense to me, somehow, that there was a set of drumsticks balancing precariously on top of a picture frame in the hallway.

Aspen's penthouse made it feel like we were right up in the clouds. Like we were in a bubble away from the world and that helped ease some of the tension in my shoulders.

He was in the kitchen, like I assumed he would be, wearing an apron tied at the back in a big red bow. Like, the waist straps of his apron were actually made of ribbon and tied in a huge, kind of poofy looking red bow. His hips were swaying from side to side and I knew in my soul it would be a real shame for me to make myself known and bring whatever was happening in front of me to an end.

Scratch that, it would be worse than a shame. A crime. It would be a crime.

That was the moment my stomach cramped, catching me off guard and causing me to squeak and Ap to turn on his heels. As soon as he saw me — I don't even really know how to explain it, but the way he looked at me felt like taking a deep breath when you really needed it.

"Hey," he said, waving a gloved hand my way and I finally got to see the front of his apron. It had a massive picture of his brother and sister-in-law on the front with a speech bubble from both of them that said *'Wallie loves this baker'*.

"Hey," I grinned back.

"How do you feel?"

"Well, I haven't thrown up yet."

"An immediate win, then." He gave me a little wink before turning back to whatever he was doing. "Take a seat." He looked back over his shoulder and gestured towards the kitchen island which was...covered in baked goods.

"You have stars on your ceiling," I said, sliding onto the first stool I walked towards.

"Big fan?"

"The biggest. Hey, Aspen?"

"Mm?"

"What are you doing?" And I really was curious because there were enough baked goods in front of me to open a small establishment.

"Well, Wyatt called an emergency session because he had a dream about a song he thinks could be our single but I had to bail. I've learned that everyone's usually a lot more forgiving when I show up with The Goods." He was gesturing to all the things he'd baked; cupcakes, cinnamon buns, croissants, little tart thingies. I assumed they were 'The Goods'.

"Bailed on recording? Like your album?"

"That's the one."

"But why?"

"I couldn't just leave you here on your own."

"But I have to go to work?" I was asking a lot of questions, and as much as I didn't want to see anyone, I knew I still had to at least attempt to go. That's when Aspen turned around, putting whatever he'd been fiddling with in a bowl and covering it with a dish towel.

"Poppy," he started the sentence like he was worried I'd accidentally thrown up my brain last night. "What time do you think it is?"

"Seven?"

"Okay, look," he started, reaching behind him to untie his apron, "it's clear this is going to be a real shock to you…but it's half past one."

"In the morning?" I squeaked, completely choosing to ignore the very clear, bright blue sky outside of the windows. "Oh my god, I'm going to lose my job. I can't show up *and* be sleeping with my cousin in the same twenty four hour cycle, Aspen!" I was panicking, clearly, but I had to hand it to him, he was oddly ready for this.

"Please don't be mad at anything I'm about to say."

"Well, that's a promising way to begin a sentence!" My voice was rising and my stomach was cramping and I really felt like I was about to shit myself.

"So your phone wouldn't stop ringing, and I tried to wake you up, but you were out cold. Like, *cold* Poppy. I stopped breathing while I watched to make sure you hadn't."

"Good grief." My hand unintentionally flew to clutch my non-existent pearls.

"I know," he waved me off, "it was terrifying. So, I picked it up. Your phone…"

"Dear god." I covered my face with my hands.

"Winny's great, and aside from asking me if I was your cousin, he seemed very understanding of how unwell you are. I explained everything to him in graphic detail. He seemed super concerned with your fiber intake, though, even when I told him all was well on…*that* end of things." Aspen frowned like he was still trying to make sense of that. I didn't have the heart to tell him he never really would, it was simply something that just *was.*

"Anyway," he went on, "I clarified I wasn't, in fact, your cousin and that you'd need to take today off because of the whole sour spaghetti thing. I also promised to sign his favorite pair of socks."

"Oh." I dropped my hands. "Well, that's not so bad."

"I'm hoping that if I arrive in the morning they'll still be relatively fresh."

"That's a good plan." I nodded my agreement.

"And then Leah called. Well, actually she FaceTimed."

I covered my mouth at the very real way Leah would have absolutely died.

"Needless to say she was *not* expecting me." Aspen's face said everything about how he was still recovering from whatever transpired.

"Did she pass out?" I was absolutely giddy.

"She excused herself out of frame to scream. It made me jump."

"You're an excellent spot, Aspen Killian," I beamed at him, feeling at least fifty percent better than when I'd walked out here.

"Thank you, Poppy Elizabeth." He bowed slightly and my heart did a flip flop. "I was a little scared for most of that conversation to be honest so I don't really remember much of it except that I nodded a lot and I promised to tell you that she said you guys were not fighting anymore and she misses you. Then I ducked out quickly to feed Nat, came home and started baking."

He breezed right over that last little bit so quickly I had to rewind in my own head to confirm it was really what he said.

"You—" I swallowed, "you left to feed Natalie?"

"Yeah, and before you say anything I know that's super weird but your keys were in your bag and after you fell asleep last night you kept saying 'dinner time, Natalie Jean. Dinner time!'." He cleared his throat and reached up to rub the back of his neck. "So, I just thought–"

I propelled myself off the stool and right at him before he could finish that sentence. There was no hesitation on his side in wrapping his arms around me and holding me close.

"Thank you," my voice sounded thick with the emotion that was making my eyes mist over. I don't think anyone really knew how much Natalie meant to me, including Aspen, but even without knowing, he *knew*.

It didn't feel so scary then to share a little more with him, to crack that door to the parts of myself I kept tucked away open and let this one story out. It didn't scare me to do it at all and I didn't think Aspen would mind hearing it. It took a few tries, but eventually the words came. Tumbling out like they had that first night I met him.

"On my fourteenth birthday I came home from school and Casimir had her tank set up on the tiny kitchen counter in our apartment," I whispered, the words to this story familiar but unused, like they were covered in a thick layer of dust. I gripped Aspen harder, ready for the shakes that would start to overtake my body like anytime I relived a memory that had to do with my brother but even as I gripped him, I didn't tremble.

I stayed right there with him, in the present.

"I'd asked him for a dog for months. I even wrote him a letter explaining in detail all the things I'd do to look after one." A watery laugh escaped me and I didn't realize until that moment that I was crying and subsequently soaking Aspen's shirt. I pulled back confused to see these phantom things that had never actually fallen real and wet on my face. "Oh crap, sorry." I reached out to wipe at his shirt but he just grabbed my wrists and pulled me back to him, wrapping his arms around me and kissing the top of my head.

"'*Goldfish are the dogs of the sea, Pen.*' That's what he'd said, and I didn't even care that factually everything about his statement was false." Aspen laughed at that. My eyes closed involuntarily at the rumble I felt reverberate through his chest. "I was so excited, regardless. She reminds me of him now, like I still have some of him with me."

We stayed like that for a while, for so long that I wasn't even sure how to break the hug, so I just said the first thing that came to mind.

"I'm really glad you're not my cousin." I looked up in time to see Ap tilt his head back in a laugh. I made sure to soak up every rumble and sound, determined to add it to the growing list of things I never, ever wanted to forget.

"I don't have the words to say how glad I am you're not my blood relation, Poppy." He kissed the top of my head for the second time that morning and it had immediately become one of my favorite things he did. "Speaking of, if you're feeling better tomorrow, I have our next friend-date planned."

"Should I be scared?"

"Wasn't our last one wonderful?"

"I almost died via snake, but sure."

"That's right, you complimented my forearms."

"We remember that story in dramatically different ways," I grumbled, finally pulling away from him.

"Alright, time to get you fed, sweet Poppy." Aspen turned back around towards the stove. The mention of food, and namely the thought of consuming something sweet, made my stomach roll.

"Ap, this all looks amazing, but I'm not sure —"

"Oh, no pastries for you, Poompaloompa." He walked towards the stove and lifted off the lid of a pot containing a simmering, and incredible smelling soup. "You're getting homemade chicken noodle soup. Good for the soul."

It was very clear to me then that Aspen was the human version of chicken noodle soup.

I had no idea what I was going to do because I'd drawn this line between us but somehow in the last nineteen and a half hours it had been criss-crossed over so many times that I was barely able to make it out. I'd told him right in the living room of my own house that I could only be his friend, namely because I didn't want to *just be* his friend, but I couldn't stomach the thought of hurting him in any way and I panicked.

I knew that no matter how many times I double checked, this wasn't something that happened to people on accident. That you just *found* someone who soothed your rough edges the way Aspen did for me. People didn't simply just *fit* together the way we did. Without force. With such little effort.

His hands on my waist, his teeth dragging along my neck, his declaration of imminent law-breaking activity. Not fast and aching like that, or even slow and patient like the strong band of an arm around my waist or his tender kiss on my bare shoulder.

I'd never wanted to be a fugitive so badly in my whole life as I had with him on that trail. I'd never wanted to stay *still* so desperately.

That Aspen would only ever be my friend seemed completely and totally ridiculous.

"Thank you for looking after me." It was all I could think to say, and I hoped he could see between the words I had spoken to the ones that I hadn't.

You're soup, Aspen. You're good for my soul.

"Thank you for letting me," was all he said, reading those unspoken words loud and clear.

15

January 28th

Poppy

"Are you sure?" Aspen asked for probably the twentieth time just as he put the Taurus into park at the curb outside my house.

The porch light was on, just like I'd left it before heading to work Thursday morning. But now it was Sunday night and it was a little hard to believe how much had changed in such a short amount of time.

"It really can only go up from here." I looked over at him, at the crease that seemed to live on his brow permanently over the last forty-eight hours.

"You could relapse?"

"Highly improbable." I rolled my eyes. This wasn't the first time he'd mentioned relapsing as a possibility.

"Okay, but *if* —"

"If I feel unwell again I will let you know, yes." I couldn't stop the way my features softened.

"And about the paparazzi..." He let the sentence hang between us, reaching up to rub the back of his neck. He took his hat off, pushed his hair back and put it back on in its usual backwards state before he looked at me.

I knew he felt awful about it. I was positive that he'd been dangerously close to popping a blood vessel in his eye considering how constipated he looked watching me eat soup Saturday morning before I all but demanded he spill whatever beans he was coveting.

He first told me about the fact that now that they'd followed him to my work and seen us together, they would probably have an interest in me. *Then* he followed it up by saying there may be an interest because there were actually already photos circulating of the two of us.

I was completely and totally ill equipped at being able to manage media attention. I didn't even want my own phone camera in my face taking photos, let alone one that could capture the amount of detail the lenses I saw on Thursday afternoon outside my office could.

I was scared, nervous and irrationally worried that none of my keys would properly lock any of my doors or windows and I'd walk into my kitchen to find it littered with men armed with big cameras. But I'd meant what I said when I told him it was okay, and we'd figure out how to work through it.

"Ap." I waited until he looked at me, his eyes still pleading and full of guilt, "It's all going to be okay. The only issue is that I'm going to have to think a lot harder about whether or not I have panty lines in my work pants when I leave the house."

"Poppy." His head tilted to the side in a way that said *'be serious'.*

"Aspen." My head tilted to the side in a way that said *'I* am *being serious'.*

"Now," I unclicked my seat belt and turned to face him fully, "thank you again for looking after me in what was arguably one of the more embarrassing moments of my life. Good luck tomorrow, please tell your friends I'm sorry I kept you from recording and," I held up my hand to stop him from speaking just as he took an inhale, "yes, if anything happens with the men with cameras, work or Todd, I will call you."

"I've already sent Jane a message on everything, including what we can do to make sure they leave you alone for the most part but…"

"I know, you can't promise anything but Jane is the best and will do everything she can." I recounted the words he'd said repeatedly over the weekend. Jane was the manager of *Lady Luck* and apparently 'the best and most sparkliest human', according to Aspen.

"Okay," he'd said on the tail end of a huge exhale.

"Okay," I said back, giving him my best reassuring smile.

Aspen had a knack for taking care of people. It had been weird and awkward to be on the receiving end of that at the start, like hugging a stranger and being unsure of where to put your hands.

Letting someone take care of me when I could do it myself was something I avoided completely, but from the moment his smile reached all the way to his eyes upon the unveiling of his chicken soup, I'd been a goner.

I knew that he knew I was finding it…weird. To say the least. Not because it wasn't appreciated. Especially considering how lacking in energy I had been for most of our time spent together, dozing in and out of consciousness and completely unable to take care of any of my basic needs. It was just *foreign*. Even when I had stayed with Leah's family for my last two years of high school, I'd never let them take care of me like that, and they never pushed the issue hard enough for me to try and let them.

There was a part of me that revolted at the idea that I'd sipped on ginger ale and snacked on saltines that Aspen had left on his coffee table because he'd looked up the best things to eat to help a sensitive stomach. At waking up to find myself covered in a blanket that smelt like him. To wake up again halfway through a movie and feel the warm press of his body right next to me before his gently whispered question of, "You okay?"

Waking and not feeling him close but knowing he was near based on the sounds of him in the kitchen. Coming to again and trying my best to pretend I was still asleep so he wouldn't stop the way he was running his fingers through my hair.

Revolted because I was *relieved*.

Relieved to fall asleep and know when I woke up he'd still be there. To know his presence even when I wasn't truly aware of it.

To be around Aspen was to feel safe and cared for. Wanted. *Needed*.

I didn't deserve any of it. Still, I wanted to hold on to him with both hands in the same way I was doing to all the memories I'd been collecting. To feel its burning imprint on the very bones of me. Wishing for it to leave its mark because even though I didn't deserve any of it, I wanted it. I wanted *him*.

Before I knew what I was doing, I was leaning across the console. In my head, I was totally thinking about giving him a hug, but halfway across it changed to a *friendly* kiss on the cheek.

Once again, Aspen had plans of his own and somehow, some way, our faces ended up on the same flight path and then there I was, pressing my lips against his.

Yep, that's right.

I had my lips pressed right to his with my eyes wide open, staring right at his face so hard that he'd become a cyclops. There was a moment, probably more than one, where I could have – *should* have – removed my lips from his face and ran from my front door like my ass was on fire.

None of those things happened.

Aspen's hand moved slowly, like he was trying to be careful not to startle me. The tips of his fingers dragged up the column of my throat making my entire body erupt in goosebumps before settling on the side of my face, cupping my jaw with a grip that was both gentle and firm. I was so totally and completely lost to him then.

His lips moved against mine, coaxing them open and I could do nothing, *nothing*, except relinquish every bit of my control and just do as he bid.

Kissing Aspen again was nothing like it had been the first time or the second, and even then I'd been so helpless against him. So overwhelmed but the way it felt to be touched by him, even for the short time it had lasted. Shocked at how much more I wanted even knowing all the rules that I would break.

He wasn't in a rush now, not like he had been at the bar with my quiet frantic requests or the hike with the threat of being found at any moment. No, actually, he was taking his sweet time if the languid, exploratory strokes of his tongue had anything to say about it.

Every single movement set my entire nervous system into overdrive, until I felt every swipe and nip and flick of his tongue against mine in every part of my body. Until I was too hot and too cold.

I reached up to grip the wrists of both hands that now cradled my head, angling me in whatever way he wanted to kiss me deeper. To kiss me harder. To taste me in every way he wanted and I didn't do a thing to stop it. I don't think I could have even if I wanted to, and I'd never wanted to do anything less in my whole life.

It was like he was trying to figure out a way to imprint this moment in his mind, like he'd thought about that first time and second time almost as much as I had.

He kissed the corners of my mouth delicately, leaving feather light pecks and open mouthed kisses along my jaw.

He pulled back a couple times, his eyes moving across my face. That little crease between his brows was nowhere to be seen but instead replaced with a slight lift to his equally swollen and reddening lips before he pulled my face back to his.

I couldn't tell you how long he kissed me on the quiet, darkened street out front of my house. Couldn't really put into words the way my entire body ached at the sounds that rumbled in his chest. That climbed out of his throat and danced across my own tongue. Each reverberation sent a pulse through every bone in my body, imbedding himself there. Right in the very core of me so that I'd have no choice but to remember him for the rest of my life. Have no choice but to admit that two people had never fit better together as we did right then.

It could have been minutes. I hoped it was hours.

There was a tipping point, maybe a mutual understanding of how temporary this moment was and how much neither of us wanted to lose it when our hands became more frantic and I wanted more. I couldn't stop the way I reached for the hem of his shirt to tug over his head, which he obliged without any complaints. The material and his hat discarded somewhere in the backseat.

He pulled the lever beneath his seat sending it careening back as far as it would go, which was way more arousing than it had a right to be, and in a display of what could only be described as admirable upper body strength, he hauled me up and over to straddle him.

"Oh," I hiccuped. It was definitely a hiccup because I was entirely incapable of speaking any real words. In all honesty, I was having a hard time thinking about pretty much anything with the feel of Aspen, rock hard beneath me.

"You okay?" His chest was rising and falling as fast as my own.

"Super okay," was my well thought out reply and then my hands were in his hair and his were up the back of my shirt – *his* shirt – because I had been wearing his clothes all weekend even though mine had been washed and dried. It was like a frenzy. I had no idea how I could stop and I really didn't ever want to. Aspen was warm. He was this inviting, safe, solid person and it was as terrifying as it was a fucking respite to realize that I wanted to stay right where I was, in his orbit.

I've never felt like this in my entire life, I wanted to tell him. Willed the words from my brain to jump into his. *I've been running since I was sixteen and you make me want to stand still.*

"Poppy," his voice was a whisper against my lips, bringing me back to the moment where I realized my fingers were aching for how hard they were gripping his shoulders.

"Yes?" My whole body was vibrating as if the tectonic plates of my soul were shifting.

"I—," he started then stopped. "Penelope I want…I want *everything.* I want to kiss you and touch you and *feel* every single inch of you…but not as friends." I saw his throat work on a swallow and mimicked the action.

All I kept thinking was *'how am I supposed to let him go?'*

"This is not what friends do, Poppy. And I know you made it really clear and I get it, at least I'm trying to but–"

"I don't want to be your friend, Aspen." The words were up and out of my mouth before I had time to think through the consequences of what speaking them to life would mean for me. For *him.* "I've never wanted to be just your friend but—" I interrupted him to say it all, or at least as much as I could.

That 'but' hung between us like a live wire. Its existence unwanted but absolutely necessary. That 'but' was every single part of me that lived behind that hulking, impenetrable door in my mind that I kept so much of myself behind. But some parts had snuck out, hadn't they? One I'd even willingly gone to retrieve. To share with him and somehow I hadn't fallen apart, and he hadn't run away. Not yet.

"Okay," he said, both knowing and not knowing everything that hadn't been said at the end of my unfinished sentence and still picking me anyway.

Aspen didn't even get to finish the word before his lips were on mine again. His hands were on my hips, encouraging me in a very valiant way to keep moving them the way I had been. It was a heady feeling, to know it was my body that his hands were trailing over. My shirt he was pushing up. *My* mouth that was capturing every sound that was coming out of his.

"Poppy." I felt my name more than I heard it. I wanted to feel him speak it everywhere, I realized. On every single part of my body.

"More," I gasped, *"please."* I trailed my nails down his chest, obsessing over the warmth of his body. Aspen was lean and defined and fit. The body of someone who spent a very long time playing the drums day after day, year after year.

"Fuck," he groaned into the crook of my neck. I had never been so turned on in my entire life. "Poppy, wait–" The words sounded painful as he gritted them out and my hands stilled on the button of his jeans.

"You don't want to?" I was so out of breath it should have been embarrassing.

"Oh, I want to." The grin he flashed me soothed the sting of his rejection just a little. "Believe me. But not here."

It sucked because every word that came out of his mouth just made me want to rid him of his pants even more, but he was right. I deflated immediately, my body leaning away and landing right on the steering wheel, eliciting a jarring and all too familiar blaring horn.

Casimir had what he would always refer to as 'gentle road rage'. He insisted on confusing people who made him angry by blaring his horn and then smiling and waving as he drove by them. The sound of that car horn was imprinted in my mind as much as the chipping pale green paint of our kitchen cabinets were and the mind numbing screech that the windows in our living room had made every time you tried to open them up even a little.

It was like a bucket of cold water had been thrown over me and I suddenly felt stupid for wanting things I knew I couldn't.

I climbed off Aspen and sat back in the passenger seat, embarrassed and ashamed of everything I had been so willing to do, the pain I had been so ready to cause. "I'm so sorry, I–"

"No," his voice wasn't harsh but it was direct, enough for me to whip my head around to face him. "You won't apologize for any of that, and neither will I." His eyes were *so* green, sort of like our old kitchen cabinets.

"I'm not usually like this," he said after a second, looking back at the dark street in front of us. "It's like my mind stops doing the things I've forced it to learn to do. To make the decision I've always forced it to make. With you I just keep doing the things I want even though I shouldn't."

He was so quiet, not saying a thing as he fixed his seat, grabbing his shirt and hat from the back and a hoodie that he must've kept back there, a very much needed addition now that the car had been off for a while and the cold was seeping in.

"So, before I do all the very wrong and dirty things I would like to do with you, we're going to sort out that 'but'."

"You heard the 'but'?" Of course he'd heard it.

"Oh, yeah. Don't you worry though, I have a plan." His smirk was devilish.

Ever the gentleman that he was, Aspen walked me right to my door.

"Do I get a hint?" My stomach was in knots. It was fear and excitement all balled into one because I wasn't entirely sure what I'd agreed to when I spoke out in what had been a very thick haze of lust.

"Trust, Poppy. It's all about trust." He nodded like that one word held all the answers of the universe. His face betrayed nothing while I, on the other hand, was gearing up to scream into a vacuum.

"Goodnight, Poppy." Aspen left a lingering kiss on my cheek that gave me something akin to an adrenaline rush, no matter how much more tame it had been than what we were just doing in his car.

"Night, Ap." I practically slurred the words, my mind and body working against one another.

I stared at my phone all night waiting for a message to come through from him. Typing out my own and then deleting it entirely. Staring at my ceiling and hating that it wasn't home to glow in the dark stars. All I could think about was the sticky note that he'd taped to the side of Natalie's tank of a stick figure waving and the other sticky note on the counter right next to her explaining that he was worried she would get lonely and thought his drawing would keep her company until I came home.

I could think about very little else other than his declaration of never doing the things he wanted until me and how I hadn't thought much of it at the time but I needed to know what he meant.

The events of the last seventy two hours ran through my head as I got ready for work the next morning and made the journey on complete and total autopilot into the city, wondering what he was going to do. Feeling giddy and happy and excited.

I was all of those things, but they all held the bitterness of guilt and dread and fear and pain and it only subsided when I settled on the unwavering decision that I knew I couldn't just be his friend. And so, I would let myself have him in whatever way I could get him and then I'd let him go like I'd always planned on doing come April fifth.

April fifth. When I would leave. The day I hated and loathed and wished never existed.

It wasn't perfect as far as plans went, and I was certain now that I would hurt him but not so bad that he wouldn't recover.

That's when I heard someone yell my name from across the street a moment before their huge, massive, has-to-be-compensating-for-something camera lens came into view.

"Oh, crap," I muttered and ran like a bat out of hell into my office building.

16

January 29th

ASPEN

"The prodigal drummer returns," were the words that my brother hurled at me moments before a pillow was thrown directly at my face. It was then followed by a notepad and someone's shoe.

"*Ow*," I moaned, huddling into the door frame I'd entered through and covering my face. "That could have resulted in a paper cut for crying out loud!" My voice was muffled by my hands, but I was definitely yelling, so I knew they heard.

"Guys, give him a break." Angus strolled over to hold out his hand to help me up.

"What do you mean, 'give him a break'?" Luke mimicked the words back in his best Angus impression which, actually, wasn't that bad. "You're the one who threw your shoe at his head."

And he was right. My hand was still hovering between us as I let my eyes fall on Angus's feet. One shoe clad and one completely bare.

"Dude." I felt my face scrunch up. "Who doesn't wear socks with their boots?"

"I was in a rush," he shrugged, sliding his hands into his pockets like he hadn't just basically admitted he was a psychopath.

"I'm incredibly alarmed that I didn't know this about you and we've been friends for, like, twelve years." I helped myself up and delivered a much deserved whack to his balls for the aforementioned shoe throwing.

Angus doubled over. "I don't do it often," he wheezed before falling right to the floor.

"You've never bailed on a recording session, ever," Rip announced from his usual place on the couch and I swallowed down the bile in my throat. Making the decision not to come to the studio when my brother called and asked had made me so sick I threw up. Twice.

"It's true, I thought you were joking at first," Luke chimed in, "but no cigar. Rip believed it so much he bet on it."

"Woah, big money exchanged hands then?" I said, settling in the tiny sliver of free couch space that Rip had left free and trying to emulate the picture of ease just as he gave Luke the finger.

"So," Dax said, swiveling to face me from where he sat in the captain's chair of the studio, "before Adrian gets here, and because you literally refused to answer any of my calls or texts –"

"You didn't use the emergency word," I rebutted immediately, trying to ignore the black hole of guilt that seemed to live in the middle of my stomach since the very moment I said I couldn't make it. Poppy had been sick in my bed and it had been between her and Wyatt. Between her and Luke and Rip and Angus.

These guys were my family and I'd be there in a heart beat for them. Drop everything and show up and fill in, and I had done that. In a lot of cases to my own detriment, because the very idea of *not* doing it sent me into such a panic I couldn't breathe. That if they needed me and I didn't go, something would happen. Someone would get hurt and I wouldn't have been there to stop it.

I'd done that since I was seventeen. But...*Poppy had been sick in my bed.*

So, I let my phone ring out every time. It was only when Allie texted that I replied.

1/2 of Wallie:

Not using the emergency word just triple checking you're okay?

Me
I'm okay. Poppy's sick...

1/2 of Wallie
Does she need anything? We can be there in however long it takes to get from our house to hers? Yours? The hospital?

Me
I got it, Al. Thanks x

1/2 of Wallie
xxxxoooo

"Or anyone else besides Allie," he finished with a scowl.

"Can't not reply to Allie," I said with a shrug, the justification backed by a choir of mumbled agreement.

"So, want to tell us why you bailed?" Dax leaned forward, his elbows on his knees. This was not like him, at all. It was *so* not like him, actually, that I...

I groaned, "You guys are such assholes, you know?" I gave my brother a flat look.

"I don't know what –"

"Oh, cram your cramhole." I pulled my hat from where it sat in its usual backwards position on my head, a must have to keep the messy waves out of my face when I was drumming, and pulled it down over my eyes.

"God, that's a good movie," Angus piped up from his position still on the floor.

"Totally. Dude, maybe our next game night can be a movie night!" Luke's eyes lit up like the fourth of freaking July. "I vote we watch *Dodgeball*!"

"We're getting heavily off topic here," Rip chimed in, which told me one important thing.

"Alright, so the bet was between you two then, huh?" I gestured between Rip and Dax, my hat still pulled down over my eyes. They didn't even try to deny it.

"So?" Rip nudged my knee with the tip of his sneaker.

"You're not going to let this go, are you?" I peeked from under my hat.

"Forty bucks says not a chance, buddy boy." Rip's grin was huge and I wanted to hit him in the balls too, but I knew he'd evade the attack and then get me back twice as bad for daring to try.

I heaved a deep sigh, my fingers starting to twitch with the want to play drums after so many days without it. I couldn't remember the last time I'd gone a single day without doing *something*.

"I was looking after my friend," I relented. "She had food poisoning."

"Your *friend*? Did you say 'she'?" Angus asked, sitting up but still cupping his balls, eyebrows scrunched together in deep confusion.

"But…all your friends are here?" Luke added, looking equally confused.

"That's not true," I said, moving my hat off my eyes.

"The girls are a given," Dax chimed in, equally as puzzled.

"I have…*other* friends." It was hard to not look at any of the four different pairs of eyes that were currently on my face.

"No, you don't," Dax said, leaning back into his chair and crossing his arms.

"Oh my god." Rip bolted into a sitting position and pointed a solitary finger right at me, "Aspen's got a girlfriend."

"No," I swallowed, trying very hard not to think about last night. The feeling of Poppy settled around me was a solace like I'd never known, and then me and my fucking big mouth told her to stop. "I have a *friend*…who is also a *girl*. There is a substantial difference."

"*That*," Luke said wiggling his finger in my direction, "is a substantial *lie*."

"You bailed because of your new girlfriend? He spent the weekend with his *girlfriend*!" Rip had a stupidly huge grin on his face. He didn't sound pissed in the slightest, he sounded fucking *elated*.

"She had food poisoning, and she went home Sunday night when she was feeling well enough so whatever's in your mind, cast those thoughts very far."

"I wasn't thinking about anything." The look on his face said otherwise.

"You were thinking about me having sex. It's written all over your face." My hand fluttered between us.

"How do you know what my face looks like when I'm thinking about sex?"

"Because you think about sex all the time, you pervert," Angus called out.

"Then it's settled," Dax said with a look on his face that gave me no confidence of assured good behavior before swinging his chair around to face the mixing console. "Aspen will bring his new *friend* to our next Fun Friday Family Fiesta night."

"I won't be doing that," I said to deaf ears.

"When the girls aren't around, I'm not sure it's entirely necessary for us to use their name for it." Rip had grabbed his guitar and started messing around with a tune I'm assuming had something to do with the emergency recording session on Saturday and just like that, the conversation was over.

I had a few rebuttals, but was it a little twisted that now I had a reason to push the topic of her attendance? At least, eventually? I knew Poppy kept to herself, that beyond anything she might outwardly defend, she *made* herself take a step back from people and places that might threaten her plans to leave. She'd already drawn a line with me even though it had been well and truly crossed now, by both of us. Maybe introducing her to the rest of the people I cared about would do more than I could in changing her mind.

The sound of a song I hadn't heard before trickled into the room around us. Dax and Adrian, who arrived around the time the word 'pervert' left Angus's mouth, were huddled together while everyone listened to what they had created over the weekend.

"Holy shit." It was really the only thing I *could* say.

"Dude," Dax said, beaming at me over his shoulder, "I told you!"

"For the drums we were thinking–" Angus started, but I cut him off almost immediately.

Already taking off my shirt and replacing my cap where it sat on my head, "No, no. Wait, I got something." Stalking straight for the drum kit, I gave the signal to my brother to start the track again, and then I just let loose.

Again and again the track ran. Listening and reworking different guitar riffs and solos, and even changing some of the vocal melodies as Adrian worked his magic, transforming the song from a general idea into probably one of my favorite songs we'd ever created.

We were in there all day, the outside world zoned out completely the way it always did when we worked together. When we played music together, we settled into this place where we were all in sync, knowing what one another was thinking and feeling.

"Hey, Ap," Dax's voice cut in through my headphones, "that was insane. Can you run that part just after the bridge again, but like *'dum, dahdahdahdah budum dum'* and then that thing you just did with the hi-hat but more intense and a little longer right until the quick stop for a beat before coming in strong for the last chorus? Does that make sense?"

"Yep, I think so. Like this..."

As soon as the song ended, I locked eyes with my brother through the glass and the grin on his face said everything I was feeling.

"That's our single, Dax." I knew my expression matched his own in every way.

"That's our fucking single!" he yelled, standing up with his arms stretched wide and head tipped back in howling laughter.

Luke and Angus had jumped on Rip where he sat on the couch and I took out my phone and snapped a photo of them all from my spot in the booth behind my drum kit. I quickly posted it to my Instagram profile, something I didn't do often but tried to do enough to keep engaged with our fans. Immediately, comments started coming in.

I just slipped my phone back into my pocket when Dax's phone started to ring through the open channel from his mic.

He picked it up which meant it could only be one person and then his laughter was bouncing off of every wall, louder than before.

Everyone was looking right at him when I'd finished pulling my shirt over my head and dropping onto my spot on the couch.

Everyone's eyes might have been on my brother, but his were on me.

He looked diabolically *jovial* as he spoke into his phone. "No, sweetheart," his mouth quirked up at the side, “I had no idea that Aspen was sleeping with our cousin.”

17

January 29th

I'd rushed into the building with the sort of panic that you possess when you're out having dinner at a restaurant wearing that pair of white jeans you bought three years ago and hadn't been brave enough to don until that very day, and then realized half way through your tuna tartare that your period had arrived two days early.

That sort of blinding panic covered me head to toe in the form of a fine mist of perspiration. My heart rate had only started to calm down on my trip from the ground floor up the eighteen levels to the office. It was incredibly off base of me to think that everything would have been just as it was the last time I was here.

My heart rate skyrocketed all over again when I stepped out of the elevator and there wasn't a single set of eyes not watching me. I did this weird crab-style-grape-vine walk to my desk, thinking it would be more inconspicuous than just walking there normally.

I'd been also very off base with that assumption too.

Huddled down beneath the protective walls of my cubicle I pulled out my phone to…do what? I could call Leah, but I genuinely thought she'd be more of the 'trust fall into this new adventure' mentality than providing me with anything remotely helpful, and there was no way I was going to call Aspen. Not for something as inconsequential as creepy camera people outside my office and the skin-itching sensation of twenty different eyes staring at you unblinkingly all at once.

For one, twenty people would have been nothing to him. This man who had once agreed to sign the bottom of someone's foot. For two, I knew he hadn't done a bunch of things he really should have done over the weekend for his new album and *Lady Luck's* next tour in order to stay with me. There was no way I was disturbing him now that he was actively doing those things. And third...well, we'd already spoken about this. About the cameras and the attention as a likely reality to whatever it was we were doing.

Our...*friendship*.

It would probably solve all my problems to tell him right then and there that it was too much and he needed to stay far from me because of some far-fetched excuse, like my gentle constitution couldn't handle the attention.

I knew that if I said words that sounded something like that they would seem stupid to us both but he'd believe me. Whatever the case may be, I was not going to be doing any of that, so I bundled up all the things I probably *should* do and shoved them behind that door in my mind to dwell on later. There was so much behind there now I half wondered how there was any room left. That's when my choking bell caught my eye from where it sat on my desk, right where Jess had left it.

I was teetering on the edge of an impending panic attack when I grabbed the bell and rang it like an enthusiastic town crier.

There was a loud thump, a surprised yelp that was more than likely Jess falling off her office chair and a handful of seconds before she flung herself into my cubicle.

"I'm here!" she panted, pushing her glasses up her nose. "I'm—" Jess didn't finish her sentence before I grabbed her hand and pulled her beneath my desk with me.

I started to explain everything to her before her ass even hit the carpet about what happened. A dam opened up and more words than I'd spoken to anyone that wasn't Leah in a short space of time since I was ten years old and explaining to my brother that I was certain unicorns were real and just in hiding from the world.

I told Jess everything because it felt like I owed it to her as my single in-office friend to reassure her that she hadn't put her constant attempts at companionship to waste on a real weirdo. I told her about Aspen, and Todd and how I was absolutely not engaging in coitus with my cousin. That there were people with cameras outside and they were calling *my* name.

"First of all, I'm trying super hard not to fangirl right now because I love *Lady Luck* so much I walked down the aisle to an acoustic version of *Feel the Fear* by them and even though that marriage was about as successful as trying to form a diamond by squeezing coal super tight in between your hands, I am confident the song is what enabled it to last long enough to give me my boys." Jess was talking very fast and I felt like I'd learned more about her in the last ten seconds than I had over the last nine months. "Second, I know he's not your cousin," she whispered, the corner of her mouth pulling up ever so slightly. "They stopped me when I was on my way in and asked me if I knew who you were and why Aspen Smith was seen here on Thursday afternoon ushering a young woman into his car. And that they'd spoken to a man named Todd who told them your name was Poppy." Like she couldn't physically contain it, her face split into this look of wicked delight that reminded me of Leah, "I told them that Todd had been caught multiple times in compromising positions with a toilet brush and often asked people around the office to neigh at him in greeting, so anything he said was likely unhinged garble."

"I am so impressed with you right now," I couldn't stop my own super look of impish satisfaction or the growing feeling of needing to laugh regardless of the current situation.

"But, that's not all, I have to tell you," she paused, her smile falling from her face, "I told Winny already in case he could help but he already knew. I —"

"There you are," Winny said, his head peeking down under the desk like Jess's mere mention summoned him, making us both jump. "Poppy, I think it's best you quickly come with me."

"Hummus?" Winny offered from the other side of his desk, a look of serious concern in his eyes.

"I'm okay, thanks." I gave him my best *'I swear, I'm regular!'* smile.

Winny had a minifridge in his office full of a range of high fiber snacks, including some homemade chocolate peanut butter balls. "They're a family recipe," he'd said the first time he ever offered them around the office after I'd started. "My grandma used to make them for me."

It made a lot of sense that his fixation on healthy bowel movements was hereditary.

The cat was out of the bag, especially knowing that Winny had actually spoken directly *to* Aspen on account of my trying to exorcise the spaghetti demons from my body. Between him and Jess, I had quite the support system at work considering that Todd had, as assumed, flapped his massive pie-hole telling everyone that I was sleeping with my cousin.

"I sat down with him and explained," Winny said as soon as he ushered me into his office. "He was quite convinced that everything I was saying was false and threatened to sue the company."

"On what grounds?" I'm sure my face looked as unimpressed as my voice sounded.

"When I asked him that, he said *'These grounds!'* and then just walked away. So I'm not sure." Winny was frowning like he was still trying to navigate what Todd could have meant.

I let my head fall into my hands and followed it with a groan of defeat, "So, everyone here thinks I'm sleeping with a relative."

"What's important is that we know the truth." Winny just nodded to himself, swiping a carrot stick into the hummus he held close and crunched on it thoughtfully. It felt obvious to me that that was actually *not* the most important part of everything that had transpired.

"So, what does this mean?" I looked up at my boss and prepared myself for the fatal blow of being let go. Instead, he lifted up a finger for me to hold on and hopped up to yell for Jess out his office door.

"Hey P," she murmured, sitting down next to me looking equally as confused.

"Oh god," I looked from her to Winny then back to her. "What is it?"

"Well," Winny looked at Jess then back at me, "Jess, well–"

"You can't fire her!" I stood up without my own permission. An accusatory finger flung dangerously close to the hummus Winny had once again picked up and clutched to his chest. "This has nothing to do with her. Just because we're friends doesn't mean anything. If that's the issue then we're not friends. I don't even know her!" I sounded deranged and a chance look at Jess told me she was grateful for what I was trying to do, if not marginally afraid.

"Fiddle-faddle, Poppy!" Winny's eyes looked like they were about to fall out of his head. "Please sit down, neither of you are losing your jobs! Heavens."

"Oh." I dropped back into my seat unceremoniously and Jess reached over to grab my hand.

"Thanks anyway, P." She squeezed my hand and I squeezed hers back.

"I've called you both in for a couple reasons. Firstly, Poppy, I asked Jess to come in as I thought you might find comfort in having a friend nearby."

"Oh," I said for the second time in as many minutes and quietly wanted to die.

"There are a few things you should know about Todd's behavior on account of his false beliefs around your private life."

My head dropped into my hands again and I wanted to melt off my chair but Winny, undeterred as usual, pressed on. "He said that he was going to expose you both as the 'trichophobes you are'."

Jess's expression was one that almost had me peeing my pants. Especially when she added with the perfect amount of hesitancy, "I'm positive he doesn't know what that means?"

I nodded vigorously, positive of that too, and then I was struck with a thought that twisted my stomach worse than the spaghetti: what if he'd gone out to the news outlets? I hadn't seen anything, but I hadn't really been looking at the news either.

"So," Winny went on, oblivious to the way I was slowly losing my mind, "as you can imagine he's caused some unrest in the office and that's brought me to my second reason for having you both here. I've decided to postpone the Say No To The January Blues party until February. I let the rest of the staff know in this morning's meeting but you two were the only ones not there so I wanted to let you know discreetly now."

Ah, yes. We'd been under my desk.

All I could think, besides the fact that this could already be circulating in global news, was that Winston had absolutely no idea how to appropriately read the room. I could hear that internal voice inside my head rising to a dangerously high pitch that spoke to mental breakdowns and spontaneously changing one's legal name to something rebelliously otherworldly like Gwendelyn or Fantasia.

The faces of Aspen and his brother and their bandmates flashed through my mind and I was certain I was on the precipice of losing it completely.

'It', more than likely, being my dignity.

Winny gave Jess and I the rest of the day off on account of emotional distress caused by another member of staff and that was how we found ourselves down the street in the back table of a little cafe that Jess came to for lunch sometimes.

"I know the circumstances are less than ideal," Jess said, taking a sip from a coffee that was placed in front of her in something better resembling a small bowl rather than a mug, "but I'm glad to finally get to do this with you."

There was no maliciousness in her tone. Honestly, there was nothing but pure, unbridled delight and it just made me feel even more like an asshole. Jess and I had always gotten on like a house on fire since my first day at work. She'd sat with me for our entire lunch break that first day in the office kitchen and even valiantly defended me against Todd who'd had his sights set on bringing me as close to the brink of constant food regurgitation as possible from day dot.

In the office? You would actually look at the pair of us and think we probably had our own two person book club and drank wine together on

Thursday nights but in actuality, we waved farewell at the front of our office building at 5:30 PM and left whatever budding friendship we might've had right at work.

I knew it was me. I was the reason and it was because the thought of putting down roots anywhere terrified me beyond any reasonable comprehension to anyone outside my own mind.

"Jess…" I started, determined on putting together some sort of explanation but she stopped me there.

"No, please." She put her bowl-mug down and gave me one of her genuine smiles I was familiar with. "You don't owe me a single thing. You're a private person, there's nothing wrong with that."

"I am," I nodded, grateful for the out she was providing me.

I wasn't quite sure if it was the realization I had with Aspen the night before or knowing that she defended me to the paparazzi outfront of our building. Maybe it was the realization that I had been ready to defend her to Winny at any cost, even without fully realizing that it was something I would do before the moment arrived, but I found myself not wanting the out she was giving me.

"I, uh, move a lot."

"Oh, that's fun!" She grinned, leaning back in her seat.

"You know, not really." I realized the words were truer than I thought. "It's actually exhausting. But it makes it hard for me to make friends." That was *sort of* the truth.

Jess's eyes softened with the kind of understanding that I wasn't sure she actually grasped, but it was comforting to know that she was trying for my benefit.

You know what? I have no idea if she did or didn't grasp what I was saying because I didn't know Jess at all, and that made me infinitely sadder than I'd been when we started our conversation.

"That makes sense. My boys travel back and forth between me and my ex, then sometimes with their grandparents, then back to me. It's been a really unpredictable routine, actually, for the last year or so. We can't seem to nail down the best way to raise them together." She found something on the table in front of us worth picking at and kept her eyes lasered in on it as she kept speaking, "Anyway, that's not the point. Well, actually, it kind of is. There's a group of five or six kids on my street and they're the best group of kids. Just really...*nice*. You know? But the twins–"

"Twins?!" I pretty much yell the word right at her. I had fallen right into the clutches of Jess's story. I knew she had two boys, but I didn't realize they were twins.

She laughed and it was this beautiful, proud, joyful sound. "Aiden and Leo." She was glowing as she said their names. "They're seven. I can't believe I never told you they were twins!"

"Identical?" I was in awe.

She nodded, "It has been my biggest struggle and also my greatest source of endless entertainment. They're *very* identical."

"Jess, holy *jeepers*. You're my hero."

She blushed bright pink and it made me want to introduce her to Leah right on the spot. "Thank you, but I really just meant to say, I sort of understand what you mean. The boys have never wanted to make friends with the kids on our street because they're too upset about the idea of missing out on things that they would just prefer to be set apart all together. One of the little girls had a party and invited them but they were with their dad that weekend and couldn't make it. It only happened once, but I think they could see what the pattern would look like, and decided to stop hanging out with them."

"That's heartbreaking," I said, meaning it. I could feel how much my face had fallen. "Surely that doesn't matter, they would all still be able to hang out when they're with you?"

"That's what I said, but they don't see it that way," she shrugged, like this was something she had tried to broach with them and had yet to get through. "Anyway, sorry that was a very long walk for a very short drink."

"I feel like I know you, like, thirty percent more in the last five minutes than I have learned the whole time I've known you."

"Me too!" This time, she shouted the words at me and we both dissolved into a fit of unrestrained laughter when the entire cafe went pin-drop silent at the outburst.

It was another thirty minutes before we got up to go, our coffees had long been drunk and Jess now followed both Leah and Natalie on Instagram. We'd parted ways with an actual hug and tentative plans for wine at my house soon as our next after work activity and a promise to see one another tomorrow.

A free day wasn't something I'd had in a long while.

Days off during the week were not at all like free days on the weekend when you tried to cram all your resting into a measly forty eight hours and half of that time was dedicated to cleaning out fish tanks and wiping down the outside of the fridge.

So, I took the opportunity to wander the city. I bought myself a coffee from four different places I'd never been to before and decided not to dress myself down on how I only had a quarter of each. I made a point to enjoy my own company and refused to let any thoughts in from the part of myself that usually creeped out when I was alone. The part that reminded me of *why* I was so alone. Alive and alone when I shouldn't have been, when I had been the person to put someone I loved in a situation they shouldn't have ever been in yet in some cruel twist of fate I was the one who had walked away.

It might have been selfish but I didn't want to think about any of it. For once I wanted to remain in this lighter side of myself, the one reserved for company. I spent the entire day marveling at the realization that I might have just solidified the first adult friendship that I'd ever made with another woman that wasn't Leah and I was feeling a little…nutty about it. *Proud.* Like I was finally grasping the concept of what it meant to be 'high on life'. I even went so far as to berate myself a little at all the times I'd taken the side of a cynical heart whenever I'd seen a bumper sticker or a shirt on a stranger sharing that exact sentiment.

I hadn't realized that I'd essentially spent the whole day walking around with four cold coffees that it was already dark by the time I headed to the closest train station and straight onto a waiting train.

The look on my face was a goofy version of happiness as I began planning all the ways I would tell Leah about Jess. How she'd probably want to fly in ASAP to meet the person behind the choking bell. How I would tell Aspen and how his face would light up because even without knowing, he'd *know* the importance of this moment for me.

It had been nice while it lasted, but I should have known better than to think it *would* last because It was at that moment that I looked up to see the man across from me reading a magazine. The exact magazine happened to be *Rolling Stone* with *Lady Luck* right on front.

My eyes zoned in on the man just to the right of Wyatt, who had his hat on backwards and a cheeky smirk on his face. His green eyes danced with the sort of mischief I'd had the pleasure of seeing up close.

The fear and panic that had only just begun to descend into my stomach when I'd been sitting in Winny's office sparked back to life with vengeance. Todd and his super massive big flapping mouth hadn't been shy about sharing factually incorrect news with our entire floor and I'd been silly enough to leave him unmonitored in an easy-to-approach location by the nosy men with big cameras during our sidewalk confrontation. People who would have asked him questions he would have had absolutely no problems answering.

The echo of my fear ping ponged around every nerve ending in my body in the least enjoyable way possible, reverberating with every step I took during the walk from the station to my house.

I wasn't sure, but I might have also been muttering to myself which would have sent anyone with any modicum of sense running in any direction away from me. That's why I released a blood curdling scream when I walked right up to my house and came face to face with a broad, yet not immediately familiar, man sitting on the steps leading up to my house.

"Poompaloompa, *ow*." Aspen clutched the sides of his head in a very dramatic way and I just stared at him for a whole three seconds. Half because my eyes had been tethered to the toes of my boots while I walked and now they struggled to adjust to the outline of him loitering on my lightless porch, and also because I was relieved and shocked all over again that this man was, in a very real way, *mine* in some capacity. At least right now.

"I come bearing the gift of food?" He said it like a question, like he was unsure if he should be sitting on the steps of my house.

I was overwhelmed. The door I had sealed shut was rattling, determined to break free of all its locks. Jess's face and the way she had hugged me goodbye. The way I missed Leah and wanted her there at coffee with us and then there was him. Solid, safe and *good.* This man who's career I was certain was going to come to a crashing end because of me but also wanting to be told it would be okay by no one else but the very man who's career I might be responsible for ending.

That was the driving force that made me launch myself right at him. His solid form had suddenly become the only *right* thing I'd ever wrapped my arms around and when his arms held me back it was like I'd never taken a deep breath before and if I had, it had never been this easy.

18

January 29th

"He offered you *hummus?*" Aspen's face was this mix of confusion and, what I would classify as, misplaced awe.

"You're focusing entirely on the wrong part of the story." I pinched the bridge of my nose while I paced. I had been pacing since we walked into my living room and Ap sat on the couch with his take out food on his lap.

"You're right, just…can we circle back?"

"Yes, we can. But this is important, Aspen." I stopped in front of him but I found myself completely unable to meet his gaze.

It was then that he seemed to realize that there was in fact far more to this explanation than Winston's hummus.

"Poppy." He reached out, but I stepped back away from him because the truth was, this situation could be really bad and there was no doubt that it was my fault.

I wasn't looking at Aspen so I didn't see the flicker of concerned hurt that I knew would have flashed across his face. It didn't matter though, I felt what it did to him in the shift of the air around us.

"The thing is," I started again, keeping my eyes on my hands which were twisting in front of me. "I should have known that he was going to tell people about the whole cousin thing. We left him right there on the sidewalk. He even had his phone out when we left. I wasn't thinking straight but *now*..." I took a deep breath, knowing it was taking far too long to tell him what had happened in my day. Mainly because it might be the thing that removed him from my life. Something that in all honesty should have already happened.

"Poppy, you're kind of making my chest hurt with the suspense." Aspen's tone was joking but I knew that he was on edge because of my poor delivery.

I sat down next to him, still not meeting his eyes. My voice was small and my heart was galloping, "Todd told the whole office about the cousin thing. And the paparazzi stopped my friend Jess outside of the office to ask her questions about me and so I think that he probably would have spoken to them too."

The feeling swimming around in my stomach was dread because as I said it outloud it was becoming more real that this was the sort of thing that would snowball, not just for Aspen, but his whole band. One member getting bad press would turn into an opportunity for things to be written about the other members too.

"Aspen, I'm so sorry. I think–"

"He did," Aspen cut me off and I finally looked up at him. His face was this calm mask of understanding but his eyes were...they were *twinkling*. Like, they actually had a sheen that I would have probably placed as the result of tears of laughter. He was clearly trying not to laugh and I was obviously trying not to cry and one of us was missing something very important.

"Dax had a great time announcing to everyone that if I was sleeping with our cousin, it was news to him. The biggest flaw in the story was that we don't actually have any cousins."

"You what?" I had reverted into a toddler, unable to have one single thought and follow it to completion.

"Todd did speak to the paparazzi, but because I'd told Jane straight away she was on high alert for news of the impending stories so when they popped up today to be printed tomorrow she was all over it. God, I love that woman."

He paused for a second, like thinking of the right path in his mental fork in the road to go down before he kept talking. "Plus, our entire family tree is all over the internet and…no cousins. No one would believe the articles regardless. If stories do get out, which I'm sure there will be, it won't mean anything and they'll die as fast as they were written." Aspen fell back into my couch, the once large-looking piece of furniture now looked entirely too small for any respectable living room. "Anyway, Jane called Allie, 'cause none of us were answering our phones, and Allie called Dax and you know everyone always answers for Allie. She was all 'Did you know Aspen was sleeping with your cousin?!'." He rolled his eyes as if to say, *she knows we have no freaking cousins.*

"I've been thinking about how I can get her back. I was thinking maybe brownies with salt, not sugar–"

He stopped talking the moment he saw my face which was, as you could imagine, a weird mixture of '*what the fuck?*' and '*what the* actual *fuck is going on?!*'.

"*Aspen,* how are you so *calm?*" I was trying, and failing, to keep my cool.

"Because, *Penelope,* this sort of thing happens all the time and that's why we have people in place to make sure stuff doesn't get too far where it could cause any real damage. But this isn't that sort of *stuff.* The world will not end if someone thinks you're my cousin, which they won't. The next article they'd read would probably be about how eerie it is that Dax and I don't have a bigger family and how that somehow is a direct juxtaposition on the state of our careers. People write the *darndest–*"

"You're not taking this seriously, Aspen. This isn't some small thing, this could ruin–"

"I *am* taking it seriously." His face changed a little, showing the side of him that didn't freely give beautiful smiles.

"No you're *not.* This—"

"I know, Poppy. I get it. Todd scared you and that's made you scared for me. I'm not going to get sappy here because I know this is a serious discussion but you being scared means you care and…well, I'm pretty fucking stoked about that." The side of his mouth tugged up and he shrugged like he couldn't help himself. "But that's beside the point. I know what it's like to be scared about the press and scandals. I have seen how stories get spun out of control, I *know* how vicious the media can be. That is not going to happen here. It's one guy who apparently neighs at everyone in your office building. They're going to think he's insane."

His face softened a little as he looked at me, and then he said a little more quietly, "I'm okay, Poppy."

"They wrote about that? The neighing?" I asked, momentarily taken off guard.

"Yeah, just this morning, and something about a toilet brush," he said, trying not to laugh.

I opened my mouth to reply but thought better of it. I shook my head and got the conversation back on track because it was and *wasn't* the point, "Don't you think that it's a sign that this," I waved between us, "is not a good idea?"

"This?" he waved between us, "is an *awesome* idea. But *you,*" he pointed a finger gun right at me, "are determined to believe otherwise."

"I'm still leaving." It was a last ditch effort. I wasn't determined to believe otherwise. I wholeheartedly believed…*wise.*

I saw the way Aspen's throat worked on a swallow and how his mouth quirked at the side. It looked forced now that I knew what a real smile looked like and the way even the smallest of them transformed his entire face.

"I know."

"This is an omen," I tried again, going so far as to get up off the couch and take two big steps away from him. When I turned back to face him, he'd stood as well and set down the bag of food.

"Omens can be good." He took a step towards me, his face now completely serious.

"I'll hurt you, Aspen. This can't end well," I whispered between us, desperate for him to leave as much as I was for him to stay and knowing full well that was the very last of the strength I had reserved to push him away.

"Then hurt me." He took that last step towards me until there was no space between us at all.

I was done for. So absolutely *done* for.

Would it matter, I wondered, if even knowing this was likely the very thing that would send me to hell had my previous transgressions not done the trick, that I tried? If I was at the big, flaming gates of hell and said to Lucifer himself, *'Hey, big Lu! Well, I tried!'*. Would he believe me and turn me away? Or would he say the very words I repeated to myself day in and day out…*'Maybe. But not hard enough'*.

Aspen's hands were rough and warm when he touched me. One reaching around to hold the back of my neck and the other settling on my lower back. I was putty in his hands. I was someone who'd never been awake before this very moment. I was clothed and very much wished to be completely naked, to say to him *'You can look everywhere, not just my shoulder blades. You can touch me everywhere'*.

His lips had barely touched mine, both my hands in tight fists at the front of his sweatshirt already so lost at the mere *thought* of him that I didn't care what noises were coming out of my mouth. Didn't care that I could feel the flush that I was sure covered my whole body spread up from where my stomach was in knots, making my neck redden and my cheeks tingle. How I could feel it moving down, settling between my legs with a pulsing ache I was sixty percent sure could absolutely kill me if left unattended.

Aspen's kiss turned harder. More desperate. Using the hand he had pressed on my lower back to press me flush with him, he'd just slipped his tongue into my mouth when my phone started to go off.

And I mean it was *going. Off.*

I'd put it on the loudest volume thinking that if Ap called about something with Todd I didn't want to miss it. That entire thought process backfired on me so severely that I shoved him from me in shock. He didn't move an inch but I managed to propel myself back from him with such ferocity that I was going to have to think about what I would do with the dent that now resided in the drywall behind me thanks to my elbow.

"That's my phone," I croaked, like it was some revelation that he hadn't been totally aware of.

"Are you okay?" He made a point of leaning around me to stare directly at my elbow-hole in the wall and pressed his lips into a tight line.

"I should answer my phone." I was losing all my brain cells and for the second time today, I wanted to perish immediately.

"While you do that, I'll put us some dinner." He plucked the bag of food off the coffee table and pressed a kiss to my temple. He didn't say a single thing but I felt his smile nonetheless and it made every part of my body turn a little more into jello.

My phone rang out for another second before I dove for it. Really, I shouldn't have answered the device under any circumstance. I had a flaming hot Cheeto of a rock star divvying up take out between my single plate and single bowl in my half unpacked kitchen and I was answering FaceTime from…I hadn't even checked it before answering but I really, *really* should have.

Leah had filled her lungs with enough air to sustain a deep sea free dive and was thus able to get right to the reason for her phone call.

"Before you say a single thing I just want you to know that I get why you don't date, and even though I'm confident your isolation is the reason you have so many fewer wrinkles than I do, I have held out hope that something was going to happen to remind you that you're a real life woman who deserves to have great sex with hot men. I am *confident* that Aspen is said 'hot men'. Or man. He's your hot man."

"I…" Oh my *fucking God.* "I have lots of great sex." All the noise from the kitchen went completely silent.

"Oh?" Her eyebrows hit her hairline. "Pray tell, Penelope, when was the last time you had an orgasm because of a real life penis?"

"Definitely in the recent past. Leah, *please–*" I whisper-shouted at my best friend but it was no use. Not only did she know it was a lie, but my house echoed worse than the Grinch's cave lair and to make it even better, my phone was still on full volume and wouldn't go down no matter how violently I pressed the button.

"Errrrrr," she screamed the noise into the microphone of her phone, pressing her mouth to it so closely that all I could see was one perfectly groomed eyebrow. "You've had sex with like two people and your dry spell

has lasted five years."

"Four people," I mumbled on reflex and hated myself immediately for participating the tiniest bit in this conversation that I was completely aware was being overheard right now.

"Three and a half," she tutted in mock seriousness. "We agreed that Henry Lexington didn't count as a full point."

I wanted to scream into a pillow. I wanted to be swallowed by a black hole. I wanted to change my name to something obscure like Nebraska and live as a recluse in the Swiss Alps.

"And also," she said on the back of another deep breath.

"Leah, *wait*–"

"No, this is important and I knew you'd try and stop me."

"You can say anything you want later, but right *now*–" I was getting hot and cold flashes.

"No, I won't be silenced, Poppy. Do you know how many photos are going around of you guys out front of your office? You guys look *incredible* together. Like, I am talking a perfect fucking *match*."

"Thank you, but you need to stop talking, like right now." I was trying to tap the call end button, but my fingers were so sweaty that the grip on my phone was less than ideal and no matter how many times I tapped the big red circle with the 'x' in it, her big pretty face was still on my phone screen.

It was too late though, Aspen was standing in the doorway from the kitchen to the living room with the biggest – and I mean it was *absolutely behemoth* – shit eating grin on his face holding one bowl and one plate, both piled monstrously high with food.

He kept his eyes on me the whole time, taking measured steps until he was sitting right beside me and then he did the unthinkable. He leaned into the camera frame and without dropping his smile even the smallest bit delivered a cool, calm and collected, "Hey, Leah."

Well, that shut her up real fast.

What neither of us were prepared for was the scream that followed her 'caught with her pants down' expression.

My phone went flying from my sweaty grip and the food Aspen had been carrying dropped the last inch to the coffee table with a clatter.

Everyone was silent. The only noise coming from Nat's water pump in the kitchen.

"Poppy?" Leah's muffled voice came from somewhere behind the couch but I was too mortified to move, even when she started chanting my full name to the tune of Three Blind Mice.

Aspen was the one to make the first move. Reaching down the back of the couch, he retrieved my phone and faced Leah front on even though I knew he was a little nervous given her last two responses to seeing his face.

"Please don't scream again. If we're going to be friends you should know that it scares me every time you do."

"I've done it twice," she countered and I could visualize the single raised eyebrow she favored as her visual examination point.

"And it was equally as frightening the second time." Ap placed my phone against a rogue pile of books so that Leah was facing the pair of us before he picked up the bowl of food and placed it in my lap.

"Poppy," he said before shoveling the first mouthful of food into his mouth, "was just starting to tell me about Winston and his hummus."

"Fuck the hummus," Leah said, her own bowl of food materializing out of thin air, "have you heard about the choking bell?"

"I have not!" Aspen's genuine enthusiasm sent a pang through my heart and my hand on reflex reached up to grip my shirt right about the traitorous organ.

My eyes volleyed back and forth between the two of them and I was momentarily floored with the notion that these were my people. At least for right now, they were both completely mine and a splinter of the weight I carried around with me shifted, making breathing a little easier.

"Poppy!" Leah shouted like she'd said my name more than once. "Is she there?"

"Mm," Aspen said, looking right at me with something that looked a whole lot like what I was feeling and leaned in to kiss my jaw, the spot erupting in goosebumps. "She's here."

"Poppy, tell Aspen about the choking bell. Aspen, this is what we're getting for Christmas so when you get yours you still have to act surprised. That's a must do with Poppy and presents, even if you know what they are."

"Roger that." Ap saluted the phone before giving me a wink.

Leah was done waiting for me to start and launched into the story of the choking bell herself. I watched Aspen nod along like it was the most incredible story in the whole world.

I did something dangerous, then: I let myself see – really *see* – how he fit into my world. Even when I was certain he couldn't, that I couldn't fit into his. That I might even be the person who *ruined* his world, I could see it.

The thing that terrified me the most was that it almost felt like this was the feeling I'd been running towards, that all my searching had been for this exact moment whether I felt like I deserved it or not. And because I'd already done one dangerous thing this evening I decided to do another.

I let myself imagine what it would be like to unpack all the boxes I had still taped shut. To revel in the relief of how it would feel to stop running, of the blinding joy I felt at the possibility of staying still.

19

February 3rd

"I can't do it!" Poppy yelled from the top of the rock climbing wall.

"Yes, you can," I told her for the fifth time from my position on the ground acting as her belayer.

"No, I can't. This was an awful idea!" she bellowed, smooshing herself closer to the wall.

"You just finished climbing the whole way up verbalizing an essay on how this was the best date you'd ever been on." I knew she could hear the smile in my voice. I was in a particularly good mood because when I'd picked her up and told her this was a date right from the get go she didn't fight me on it. Poppy merely looked at me with her big, amber eyes and released a sigh with a small smile before nodding her head and whispering, "Okay."

"I lied. I'm a big fat liar. I'm going to be stuck up here forever."

"No, you won't–"

"Tell Leah I love her," she yelled again.

"Poppy–"

"And look after Natalie, the password to her instagram is her name backwards, four exclamation points and the numbers zero, two, one, four." By the time she finished speaking her voice had trailed off into a little whimper.

If this place had been packed, I'm sure we would have drawn a crowd, but I'd called ahead and booked the place out for the afternoon so it was just Poppy, me and my security guy Jason who was hanging by the front door trying not to laugh. I came here often enough that the owner knew who I was and trusted us both to climb safely, so he was tucked up and away in his office on the second floor. I made a note to send him a couple tickets for the first show of our tour as a thank you. I'd called last minute and it was only because he was a real, honest to Zeppelin legend that we'd been able to book the place out on a Saturday afternoon.

Jason released what had to be the start of a chuckle and I shot him a glare that had him promptly leaving the center to stand out front.

"Poppy," I started again, "I need you to take three big, deep breaths. Can you do that?"

"I don't know," she squeaked.

"One," I took a deep breath and watched as she did the same.

"Two."

She did it again and I saw a small amount of tension leave her body.

"And three…I thought you were having fun?" I asked in all seriousness because I was sure I hadn't picked this wrong.

"I was." She sounded at least thirty percent calmer.

"And now?"

"I didn't realize how high I'd come." Her voice was muffled on account of her mouth being pressed almost directly to the wall. "It's way too high and everything's moving and if I open my eyes I'll pass out."

"Okay, but you know this rope I'm holding onto?"

Poppy nodded her head jerkily without actually looking at me.

"Well, that means that I control whether you fall or not. You don't have to climb down, you can let go and I'll drop you slowly."

"I'm heavy," she cried.

"Sure you are, and I'm also a star fish that lives under a large boulder." The tone of my voice said it all and my heart tripped over itself at the small giggle she released.

"I love Patrick," she said, still talking directly to the wall. "He's my favorite."

"Another thing we have in common." I grinned even though she couldn't see. "Remember when I said it was all about trust?"

Poppy was silent for a bit before her muffled reply came, "Yeah?"

"Well that's what we're doing, we're getting right of that pesky little 'but' because you're going to learn to trust me."

"I didn't think you were being *literal.*" She was yelling again.

"Literal is the best approach. Now, do you trust me?"

"In *theory…*"

"Poppy, if you let go of the wall, all you're going to do is swing back. I've got you." I watched her knuckles go white with the grip she had on the wall and just when I thought I'd have to get a ladder, trying my best not to be disheartened by this date going to shit, she spoke.

"Okay," she said quietly and I was half convinced I imagined it.

"Okay?" The question was mainly fueled by my own shock.

"Okay, I'm going to let go now, are you ready?"

Her voice shook with her nerves and all of a sudden this seemed a lot bigger than just letting her down slowly to the ground.

I knew she found it hard to lean on people. To let people look after her. I'd gleaned as much when she was incoherent on my couch, gripping her stomach and asking if she could do anything to help me look after her. She'd fallen back asleep before I had to deign that with a reply.

"I'm ready."

And then she let go. It was accompanied by an ear piercing scream, *but…* she let go and then her scream dissolved into laughter. This huge, incredible laughter that had to have come straight from her soul. I half expected all the lights around us to implode, unable to contain the energy that burst into the room. She paired that world changing sound with an expression that lit up her entire face in a blinding show of happiness and it did something to me.

It did *everything* to me and I couldn't help but begin to compile a list of ways that I could hear that sound all over again, every day for the rest of my life. There were lyrics and melodies and drum beats that had never existed before but now did, just for her.

She was bright eyed and rosy cheeked and then she was right in front of me.

Poppy's helmet had gone a little wonky from the way she'd pancaked herself to the wall. She peered up at looking like the world's biggest goofball. I knew I was staring, but it wasn't my fault. She was beautiful.

"Hey," she said, still beaming up at me.

"Hey," my voice was a rasp and my mouth was dry and all I wanted to do was kiss her.

"You had me." She reached out and looped a finger through my own harness. It wasn't a question, or a tentative statement. It was three little words that she spoke clear as day with not a single ounce of doubt.

"I did." I was still staring at her, trying to slow my own heart, to slow down my emotions and calm down but she was still looking at me in that way and I wasn't sure I could remember *not* feeling like this. Like any time before Poppy was just simply missing her until I met her.

Lifting up onto her tiptoes she slid her arms up my chest and around my shoulders pulling me down to her until she could press her lips to mine.

I snapped back into myself and reached for her, sliding my arms around her waist and then standing back up to my full height and bringing her with me so her feet were dangling in the air.

She laughed into our kiss and the feel of it drove me wild. I wanted to hear it again. To feel her laugh against my skin over and over until it was all I knew.

Poppy pulled back, her cheeks flushed and helmet still crooked, looking the happiest I'd seen her. She kissed me again gently and then spoke softly with her lips against my ear, "I want to do it again."

I'd seen Poppy almost every single day of the last week. We'd gone back and forth on meeting at her house for dinner and then deriving a very skilled and watertight plan of getting her up and into my penthouse even though new photos of us together and alone surfaced on the internet daily.

It was the Friday night before our wall climbing date, something I still hadn't told her the details about even though she'd pleaded a great number of times.

She'd been pulling a pasta bake she'd made out of the oven by the time I got home from the studio. The elevator doors opened to the lights on and dimmed, casting the living room into a warm glow where she'd already put two glasses of what looked like wine on the coffee table and lit a candle I was pretty sure I'd owned for like two years and hadn't lit once.

I could hear her around the corner in the kitchen and walking into her pulling the dish out of the oven, an episode of what sounded like *Queen Charlotte* playing from her laptop. She'd seen me right away and her face had lit up in an easy upward tug of her full lips. Those looks of genuine happiness were coming easier and easier from her.

I knew I was breaking down her walls. That whatever those 'rules' she'd mentioned that we'd broken were losing their grip on her. I'd half wanted her not to notice me right away, so that I could see her moving around, bringing so many of my wishes to life just by standing right where she was.

"I hope you like pasta bake!" she beamed, taking off the oven mitts and pausing her show.

What Poppy didn't know was that I was a die hard *Bridgerton* fan, and nothing made me cry like a baby quite like the final episode of *Queen Charlotte*, so I was familiar with the episode she had paused; right when Charlotte and George were about to dance together at the ball for their son. I walked over to her laptop and pressed play. '*You and me,*' George said, and then the instrumental music started.

I reached for Poppy and she came to me easily. I held one of her hands in mine against my chest and felt her other hand wrapped around my back, gripping my shirt.

We moved in slow circles and when Poppy looked up at me with a small, happy smile on her face, I moved down to kiss her knowing I had everything I'd ever wanted right then and there.

20

February 5th

Poppy

"Tell me again!" Leah squealed. We were FaceTiming while folding our laundry.

"Let the people note this will be the fourth time I've told this story." I rolled my eyes but it was all for show.

Something in me felt *lighter*. It happened gradually over the last week and I was struggling to recognize this version of myself.

"You're lucky that I love you so much that I'm willing to look over the fact that I'm hearing all this juicy goodness *months* after it actually happened. All I ask is for you to tell me your sexual escapades over and over again whenever I ask no matter the time of day."

"It hasn't been months," I counter, folding a sweater that wasn't mine. "Hey, this is yours!" I held it up to her.

"You're joking, I have been looking for that for *days.*" Leah had pulled the phone right to her face.

"Want me to mail it?" I set it off to the side.

"Nah, I'll grab it when I come to visit next." She kissed the camera of her phone and put it back down. "Now, please tell me again like this is the first time you're saying it."

"Leah–"

"*Please,* Poppy? I haven't had sex in so long my lady bits are pretty much filing me for divorce." She pouted, a facial expression that would now forever have me recalling Leah's 'dry spell'. Just for reference, it had been *maybe* a month since she'd seen any action.

I took a deep breath, "I have something to tell you."

She dropped the clothes she was folding, eyes widening comically, "What is it? Are you okay?"

"Aspen picked me up from work a couple weeks ago."

"I saw the photos, but do go on." She gave me a half hearted glare and I glared back, having not so soon forgotten how she aired my sexual history with vigor on loudspeaker while Aspen had been in the other room.

"I ended up having food poisoning and he took care of me for a while on the weekend."

"I'm swooning!" The back of Leah's hand shot to her brow and she disappeared from view.

"I threw up on myself so he bathed me."

"He bathed you?" She sounded overjoyed.

"He had to undress me and hold me upright in the shower and I was so incoherent I'm pretty sure I was speaking Klingon and he didn't even look. He just kept his eyes on my shoulder blades."

"Your shoulder blades?" Now she sounded in awe, regardless of this not being the first time she'd heard the story.

"You're just repeating everything I'm saying."

"Because the words coming out of your mouth are rocking my world." Leah popped back up into view with her own beaming grin.

"On another note, I think I'm going to make a real effort with Jess."

"The founder of the choking bell?"

"The very same."

"I have a wonderful feeling about her. I want to meet her," Leah said with an air of finality.

I wanted them to meet too, Jess and I had been spending more time together throughout the last week, not just because of the leaps and bounds we'd made on the friendship side of things, but because Winny had the capital idea of volun-telling us that we would be the soul organizers of the Say No To The January Blues party that was now supposed to be at the end of February.

We'd been permitted an hour every day to sit down and plan. It was far too much time for what needed to be done, but Jess and I had made the cafe just outside our building into our official meeting place and most of the time we spent there had been used to get to know one another more. We'd even tentatively put down this Thursday as our Wine Night because her boys would be with their dad.

"Speaking of me coming to visit," Leah said as a segway. She'd just taken a deep breath when my phone started to buzz with another incoming call. It was Aspen.

"Leah, Aspen's calling," I said, and because I was on FaceTime, I could see the way my own face lit up.

"Already ditching me for boys," she heaved a sigh that had absolutely no substance. She was just as happy as I was. "I'm so happy for you, Pen."

I knew if she'd been here she'd have wrapped me in one of her hugs that had acted like glue to all my cracks for so many years.

"Godspeed, sissy," she said as her farewell before stopping a second and doing her best to hold meaningful eye contact with me through the phone. "Hey, I really like seeing you like this."

"Like what?" I asked her even when I already knew the answer.

"Happy." With a little wave she ended the call and I picked up Aspen's incoming one.

"Hello?" I held the phone to my year, already smiling like an imbecile.

"I'm desperately sad and lonely, will you come have dinner with me?" His voice was muffled and it sounded like he was either talking directly into a pillow or he was super far away from his phone.

"Can we get take out from that Mexican place near your building? The one that's always playing Jamaican music?"

"Poppy, no one has ever said anything so perfectly perfect to me in all my twenty eight years of life."

"I'll order an Uber," I laughed, putting my folded laundry away and the unfolded stuff back in the basket to, let's be honest, never find its way out of there again until it was time to wear the articles in question.

"No need you sweet, sweet lady. I'm out front."

"Of where?"

"I can't be sure, but it looks like a huge boot."

"You're outside the house of the old lady that lives in a shoe?"

"I wouldn't say you're *old*, but–"

"You better watch your tone or I'll steal all your queso and hide your favorite apron."

"Now you're just being mean." I would bet my next paycheck he was pouting.

"I can't believe you drove here before I said yes," I said, pulling a sweater on and making my way downstairs.

"Call it quiet optimism. Oh, and pack a bag, I refuse to return you to your humble abode after our meal. It kills me a little every time." After a second he added, "If you want." Another second, "I'll take the couch if that's what you're worried about."

"I wasn't worried," I said, not meaning to make him freak out but I had been too stunned to speak. Stunned silly, actually.

Silly with oodles of excitement that I was trying really hard not to scream in delight. I'd taken the stairs two at a time back to my room and had already finished backing a bag by the time he'd spoken about the couch nonsense and my reply was accompanied with the solid click of my deadbolt.

Aspen still had the phone to his ear when I slipped into the car and for the first time I didn't let myself think about any of the repercussions when he leaned over the console and kissed me. And I mean, he *kissed* me. Like it had been years instead of hours since he'd last done it. Like, if that was the last kiss we ever had, he'd gone out with a bang.

"Hey," he smiled against my lips.

The sigh that left my body took with it all worries as I let myself fall into him, to kiss him again and with everything he made me feel, "Hey."

Aspen had parked his car and grabbed the bag of take out food from my lap before I'd realized he'd pulled the keys from the ignition. He was up shoving corn chips into his mouth before my shout of baffled displeasure had finished leaving my mouth.

"You're eating my corn chips!" I shouted at my lap while trying to get the seat belt to unclick.

He had replied with something but his mouth was so full of *my* chips that I didn't understand what he said.

In my haste to get out of the car, my phone dropped from my lap and disappeared under the seat, so far that I couldn't even remotely figure out where it had gone.

Aspen's laugh was bouncing around the basement garage in unbridled glee while I rolled my eyes and crouched down next to the car, sticking my head into the footwell to try and see where my phone had gone. It was only after I'd spotted the device, reached in and grabbed it did I notice out of the corner of my eye all the stickers that littered the underside of the dash.

"Asp–" I tried to say his name because my heart had started to beat too fast and I was half convinced I was seeing things.

Half the stickers have been peeled off, the ones closer to the part of the dash you might be able to see from the seat. The outlines of old glue still remained, an ode to a time and place long come to pass, to a whole separate life entirely. But further underneath, I could see them. The once white bubble stickers in shapes of unicorns and rainbows and flowers all yellowed with age.

"Aspen," I said his name again, but I wasn't sure any noise was coming from my mouth.

I remembered putting those stickers there.

I'd been small enough to sit in this very footwell, seven maybe. Casimir had stopped at his work because he'd forgotten his wallet and needed to grab it on our way to do something, I couldn't really remember. He'd just gotten me these stickers and I had been in an awful mood all day because I loved them so much and I hadn't been able to think of a special enough place to put them.

Somewhere that I felt was deserving of them.

But then I'd thought about how much my brother deserved my fancy new stickers. I climbed into the front, pushed the seat all the way back and started to decorate his car. Something *he* loved, with my stickers, something *I* loved.

Looking back now, there had been a moment of shock on his face when he opened the driver side door to see me, mid sticker-sticking, and anger had crossed his face. No doubt thinking that not a single thing in his life could be just his. It had to be covered in stickers, or hold little ballerina slippers or sparkle in some capacity. I hadn't seen it then though, I'd simply held a sticker out for him to pick where it would go and just like that, his face had softened. He'd walked around to my side of the car, opened the door and sat right on the ground next to me.

"You wanted to put your special stickers on my car?"

"You said it was our car, Cassy." I still held my little finger out to him, sticker and all. "So, these are our stickers too."

I would give anything now to know just a single thought that went through his head.

He plucked the sticker from me and placed it front and center on the glove box before leaning in to give me a kiss on the cheek and saying, "Thank you for sharing them with me."

The memory was so painfully vivid. It had thrown open that door in my mind where I kept it along with everything else that had to do with Casimir.

I was crying. A full, snotty, hiccuping mess. I'd even go so far as to say I was beside myself, half there in Aspen's garage and half with my brother, all those years ago.

"I got you," Ap said into my hair, hauling me up and into his chest. "You're okay, I've got you."

He just kept saying it over and over again. He didn't know why or what was happening, but he didn't need to. I knew with certainty that he'd always be there, just like this, knowing or not.

"I'm here," he murmured into the hair on the top of my head, "I'm right here."

I wasn't sure if it was being safe in that very knowledge, that I was being held up by hands that I knew wouldn't let me go no matter if all the jagged pieces of the grief I couldn't even express cut him as they exploded from me, but I knew for sure that I surprised us both with what came next.

When the crying had eventually subsided and my breathing returned to normal, I looked up at Ap who had nothing but helpless concern on his face and gave him a watery smile. Tears filling my eyes again and paving hot tracks down my face. I reached out and put my shaking hand on the top of his car, looking at it like I could see Casimir's hand there instead of mine.

"This was his car." I looked back to Aspen who was looking between me and my hand and then back to me before his face softened out in complete understanding.

"Your brother?" His voice was soft, but encompassing a hint of the awe that I knew was written all over my face.

I just nodded and gently pulled him back down to the ground where he followed me without hesitation. I pointed to the stickers that he had probably never noticed and watched as he reached out to trace what was left of them reverently.

"Those are my stickers, Ap," my voice cracked but I was still smiling. Caught in this weird limbo of heartbreak and happiness.

Aspen turned his attention back to me, reaching out to wipe the tears from my cheeks and then using the sleeve of his sweatshirt to wipe my nose which made me laugh and hiccup some form of the word, 'ew'.

He got up and came back with our take-out bag, resuming his previous position. Reaching into the bag he pulled out my corn chips, stopping only to give me a pointed look with a small eye roll, single-handedly making the moment that much easier to bear. He pulled out the queso dip next and dipped not one, not two, but three single chips. He handed one to me, kept one for himself and put another in the foot well of his car.

Aspen reached for my hand to cheers my chip and then the one he'd placed in the car, "To Casimir, and his car's safe return home."

He had no idea what he'd just done. Such simple words and he'd unpacked everything I'd always kept close to my heart about home, and that feeling you got when you were there. Of just *knowing*. Like he knew how it felt too. That it wasn't the house you lived in in the city you were born in, or the share house you paid too much rent for with your friends in your first lease after college. It was knowing that you could be anywhere in the world with the people that were on the other side of those doors and feel whole, simply from being safe in the knowledge that they were there with you.

I couldn't do anything except nod my head, tapping my chip to Aspen's and then to the one he'd set aside for my brother, feeling more complete in that moment than I had in the last thirteen years.

21

February 5th

I thought I'd be borderline catatonic after Aspen and I had sat in his cold basement, eating our Mexican food with my brother's car, but I wasn't. He hadn't treated my breakdown as a plague. He hadn't tried to say anything other than reassure me he was there and then he'd sat down and eaten with me like it had been perfectly okay for me to be both sad and happy.

Like it was okay that I was sitting in my grief almost thirteen years on from its moment of inception but also laughing at the way he had managed to smear guacamole onto his forehead and regardless of my detailed description and even *pointing* where it was, he hadn't been able to wipe it away.

It felt as though, until that moment, I hadn't realized that I could have both.

Aspen hadn't treated me like I was something in need of fixing. He'd just treated me like 'Poppy'. The same as he had at the bar, then on the hike and every day after. During all our phone calls and messages dates. Always the same.

He had retreated into himself a little since we'd made our way up to his apartment and I desperately wanted to know what was running through his head because whatever it was, it had taken him somewhere else. It wasn't so much that I thought I could help, or that it was even anything he might want my help with, but I wanted to sit in whatever troubled him *with* him, like he'd done for me.

If he could feel my blatant staring at his face while he watched the movie I picked but hadn't watched a single moment of, he didn't say anything about it. He didn't even look at me while all I did was catalog his features over and over again like he was all the answers to everything I'd ever be asked from this day forward and I needed to know it all.

One of his hands rested on the top of my legs which were draped over his lap, his thumb moving in a gentle path up and down.

I took a deep breath and moved before I could over think the entire situation. I grabbed the remote from where it lay discarded between us and paused the movie. Ap didn't look at me, didn't even seem to realize that anything had changed until I pulled my legs from his hold and made my way onto his lap, straddling him.

When I finally brought my eyes to his, he was already looking at me. Clarity coming back into his forest green gaze, his hands settling on my hips.

I didn't really need to say anything, not as I reached up to take off his hat, pushing my fingers through the thick, soft strands of his dark brown hair. So dark that in the dim light of his living room it looked black.

Aspen was striking. He was both beautiful and handsome all at the same time.

My fingers grazed the roughened edge of his jaw, a shadow of his stubble making itself known and I couldn't stop my smile from growing.

"What?" he said, the corner of his mouth pulling upward a fraction while he watched me watch him.

"You're very handsome, Aspen Killian," I whispered the simple fact into the space between us.

His features slipped into something serious and I watched, transfixed, as his throat worked on a swallow.

My own breath caught when he gripped my waist tighter and when I braved a glance back at his eyes, they were on my lips.

"I want to kiss you," he said, eyes unmoving.

"Okay," I nodded, really putting my self control to the test by not squirming in his lap.

He said those words, but he didn't move.

"But?" I prompted, my hands had settled onto his biceps and it was an actual effort to keep my grip on him soft.

"There are no 'buts' for me, Poppy." And I knew exactly what he meant. "Are there any for you?" His eyes were all seeing. Breaking down every wall I'd put up between us, making me want everything from him. Trusting me to trust him, to be able to navigate it all together, whatever 'it' was. No matter the fall out of the decisions we made.

"No," I said, and I meant it. Right then, I meant it more than I'd meant anything. "No 'buts'."

And then he kissed me.

Aspen's hands were in my hair, they were rough and soft, tugging and caressing all at the same time. His teeth grazed and then pulled at my bottom lip before he let go and we both looked at each other.

"Woah," I said, blinked at him like I was seeing him for the first time. My bottom lip tingled from the lingering sting of his bite.

"Woah good? Or woah bad?" His eyes were bright and his mouth already curving upwards.

"Good," I nodded. "Very good."

"I told you I could seduce the shit out of you." He was leaning back in, arms wrapping around my back and pulling me close to him. His hands were warm in the path they carved out, gliding over my shirt, but every single point of contact was lighting me up and I wondered how he'd react if I just spontaneously combusted.

"Never doubted you for a second." I crashed my mouth back to his, no longer wanting to be timid or careful. Only wanting every part of him pressed to every part of me.

I pulled back abruptly, "Wait, just to clarify, we are going to have sex right now, right?"

His smile was blinding. It was wide and carefree and existed solely for me, "Yes, Poppy. We're absolutely going to be having sex. Imminently."

I nodded in whole hearted agreement, "Okay. *Good.*"

Even if I'd wanted to get another word in, there was no space for it.

Aspen was incredibly thorough in the way he kissed me, just like the times before. His hand reached up to hold the side of my face, his thumb sliding along my jaw to angle it. Kissing me slowly, in ways that lingered and sent pulsing waves of heat through my body, starting at the base of my throat and pounding outward. The languid, lazy way his mouth moved made my body respond to him in a way I hadn't even known it could.

With the gentle roll of my hips against him, urged on by the way his hands gripped me, the way he helped me move, it was going to be the very thing that made me go insane.

I pulled back, however reluctantly, to tell him as much, that I needed *more* but he dragged his mouth down to my jaw. To the place behind my ear, to my neck and my collarbones and I realized if I had lived all the days of my life without being touched like this, by this man, it wouldn't have been a life I much wanted at all.

"Aspen." I was perhaps the most impressive woman alive to still be able to speak under my current circumstance.

"Mm?" He reached for my shirt and pulled it up and over my head, leaving me in front of him in my best bra (thank God for laundry day and leaving my best if not arguably most uncomfortable bra to the end of my rotation).

I knew what he'd see the moment the shirt came off and I steadied myself for it. For whatever was going to happen, the questions. He'd seen the scar before but he hadn't said a thing about it.

This felt different now and I realized if he asked, I'd tell him. I'd tell him anything he wanted to know.

His eyes moved from my face to the scar of the bullet wound on my left shoulder. I saw the way his throat worked, the way his jaw flexed, but nothing happened the way I had thought it would. I should have known that.

Nothing with Aspen had ever played out the way I thought it would.

His thumb moved across the scar, causing me to shiver before he pressed a kiss to it once then leaned his forehead on my shoulder like another puzzle piece of me had slid into place for him.

Like those pieces were things worth collecting. He made me *believe* they were.

I let my hands move into his hair and pressed a kiss of my own to the top of his head.

"You said imminently." I could have just run through the finish line of a marathon for the way I practically panted the words.

"Poppy," Aspen was talking to the place where his hands touched the skin of my waist.

I looked down, just to see what he was seeing and was almost rendered unconscious by the sight of his hands splayed over my rib cage. "You're in no way allowed to rush me in this moment." He stood up in one fluid motion, doing wonders for my self-esteem. His mouth didn't leave my skin, walking the memorized path all the way to his bedroom.

He set me on his bed with a gentleness that no one had ever shown me, not even myself and, with a quick look up at me for quiet permission, unbuttoned my jeans. He tugged them off along with my underwear in one fell swoop. The entire visual was wildly impressive.

I reached up to unclasp my bra and then I was just there, completely and totally naked. Aspen's eyes unabashedly roamed over me. His appraisal was slow and unhurried and only when he finally looked back up to my eyes did he speak, "I think this is the best moment of my entire life." He delivered the words in a quiet reverence that made me immediately laugh.

"You're such a dork!" I reached for a pillow behind me and threw it right at his head.

When it dropped to the floor he was grinning at me in complete and total satisfaction. I knew my expression matched his own as I moved to kneel on the bed in front of him and reached for his shirt.

"My turn," I whispered. I took my time undressing him, making sure I cataloged every part of his body. Reveling in the way the muscles on his back, his arms, his stomach tightened at the slightest brush of my fingertips. Infatuated with the goosebumps that erupted along his thighs when I pulled his own jeans down his legs.

Then it all came to a crashing halt.

I couldn't breathe. Breath wouldn't enter my lungs and my eyelids were paralyzed.

"Poppy?" he whispered.

"Holy Toledo," I blurted. "That's—" I was, in fact, staring right at his penis.

"You have to know, my ego will never, ever, recover from this." He was beaming at me so big his eyes crinkled and his dimples had nowhere to hide. I wanted to flick his nose.

"No, Aspen, I've never–" My mouth was completely dry.

"Had sex?"

I gave him a look that could have wilted flowers, "I've had sex."

"I know, three and a half times." He wagged his eyebrows at me and I shoved his chest lightly.

"I've never had sex with anything remotely close to your…caliber." I couldn't look away from it. It was actually staring me down.

"Caliber?"

"As far as I'm concerned that's a weapon. I'm not sure I'll…that it'll…" I couldn't get the word 'fit' out because that would mean potentially a. Not having sex with Aspen and b. Reinforcing just how likely the reality that I'd regrown my own hymen actually was.

He didn't say anything for a while and I was still…well, I was still staring at his *weapon.*

"Poppy," Ap spoke softly, only the barest hint of amusement still tracing his words, "do you trust me?"

"Yes," I said, right to his penis. "I trust you."

He pinched my chin to tilt my face up so I could see the exact way his face looked when he spoke again.

He looked ravenous.

"Then it'll fit." He ducked down, capturing my lips with his.

He moved into me, urging me back up his bed until he was above me, and all I could focus on was how I had imagined what it would feel like to have his skin against mine a hundred different ways, but it hadn't measured up to the reality of it all.

I saw us from outside of my own body. Saw the way his hand glided up my thigh, the way he looked at me from above, how my mouth opened in a silent moan. It did something to me. Made me wildly, insanely needy for him in a matter of seconds. More than I had been before, if that was even possible. It inflated my confidence beyond measure and I didn't even recognize myself when I reached between our bodies and took him in my hand.

"Oh my holy *fuck,*" Ap's breath hitched and his hips gave an involuntary thrust, "Poppy."

My name on his lips, in that very moment, was like being picked first. Like winning gold in the Olympics. I was getting a Nobel Prize. Being handed an Oscar. Like waking up every morning for the rest of my life and the first thing I get to see are eyes of brilliant forest green.

"Yes?" My voice was husky and I was morphing into a butterfly. I could feel it.

"Your hand is cold." His eyes were half lidded with lust but they still glinted with amusement and I knew that sex with Aspen would never be anything but fun and easy and comfortable. Because *Aspen* was all those things.

He made absolutely everything better.

I pulled my hands up and breathed into them, rubbing my palms together, "Better?" I raised an eyebrow at him, letting my hands travel down the length of his chest, feeling the dips and hollows of the muscles beneath his warm golden skin until he was in my hand again.

"Uh-huh." Aspen's mouth had gone slack, eyes almost closing. He swallowed once, twice, "Thank you."

I had no idea who I became when Aspen's lips found mine again, when I continued to touch him and capture his sounds in my mouth, desperate to keep every single one of them forever.

"Poppy," Aspen said into the crook of my neck, "I just need to see something." He spoke the words against my neck, continuing his descent until he pulled himself from my grip and a small, displeased whimper left me. I felt the curve of his mouth on the skin of my stomach, leaving a trail of nips and kisses on his way down.

"What are you doing?" That was my voice, but also not. It was the voice of someone who was currently way more turned on than I'd ever been in my whole entire life.

Aspen looked up at me, eyes dark and hair falling in front of them, "I want to taste you."

"You do?" I squeaked.

He nodded, still moving down, "I've thought about it more than you could comprehend."

"You have?" *Holy cow.*

"A lot," he confirmed, settling down between my legs. *Ohmygod.*

I had little to no warning before his mouth was on me. Licking and tasting and devouring me until I wasn't *me* anymore. I was light as fairy dust. I'd completed my metamorphosis and had become a butterfly that was the only one its kind.

My hand reached down to thread into his hair while the other gripped the sheets beneath me.

Aspen splayed a hand across my stomach and locked the other around my thigh, keeping me still when my back was determined to bow off the bed. Every movement he made was a match striking, a flame igniting. I didn't think I could keep existing when I heard him groan in pleasure of his own and I opened my eyes to find his shadowed gaze already looking up at me. It was picture frames falling from walls and houses crumbling and planets colliding as everything I'd ever thought I'd known collapsed so that room could be made just for him.

His name was the only thing I knew. Over and over again. Shudder after mind altering shudder I knew nothing but the feel of his mouth on me. Nothing but his hands keeping me anchored to the bed instead of letting me disappear straight through it.

"That was the sexiest thing I've ever seen," he spoke against my skin. "And I'm positive I've never loved my name as much as I love it right now." He settled himself back against me, my thighs shaking and vision blurred and fingers still tangled in his hair.

"Poppy," he said into the skin of my neck, as he dragged his mouth along my jaw, his hands roaming my body. My stomach, my breasts. "Poppy. *Poppy,*" his voice cracked and I lifted my eyes to meet his. He kissed the corner of my mouth and said, "I think I knew you before I met you."

I couldn't speak. I had no idea what he was doing to me but I never wanted him to stop.

Ap gently pulled my wrists from him one at a time and guided them away from their happy place around his neck and in his hair. "I try to remember everything before you and all I can think of is how much I missed you until you showed up." He pulled my arms up above my head and firmly held both wrists in one hand. His other hand tracked back down the length of my body along with his eyes, like he was unconvinced this wasn't just a dream.

"I have wanted you *everywhere*. All the time. I've dreamed about this, did you know that?"

I just shook my head.

"How you'd sound, how you'd taste, how you'd *feel.*" He kissed me and I could taste myself on his tongue. The feel of him everywhere except where I was most desperate for him made me whimper, pushing me to my own absolute breaking point. "Aspen, *please.*"

That's what did it, I could see his restraint break but then he moved to get off me and I hadn't anticipated that at all.

"Wh–where are you going?" I hooked my legs around his waist to keep him against me, frowning up at him.

"Condom?" His voice was raspy and his eye were hooded like battling through the fog of

lust that covered us both was maybe the hardest thing he'd ever done.

"It's okay," I shook my head. "I'm on the pill and I…you'd be the first person I've done this with."

He knew exactly what I meant and if I thought he was ravenous before, he was vibrating with it now.

"Me too." He nodded, his grip on my wrists tightening again. "Are you sure?"

"*Yes.* Aspen, plea–"

The words died on my tongue as he lined himself up with my entrance and pushed into me slowly. *Completely*. A hand coming to my leg, hiking it higher up on his hip as he pressed in and in and *in.*

"Are you…is this…*Fuck.*" His jaw was clenched, every muscle in his body taught as we both watched the way he moved into me, until there was no space left between us.

"Poppy?" he gasped, dragging his eyes up to settle on my face.

I'd never in my entire life felt so perfectly, excruciatingly full. I was convinced that what was happening between us was altering the chemistry of my brain forever. How could anyone ever be the same after this?

"We're having sex." *Real profound, Poppy.*

"Mostly, yeah," Aspen said, his body still tense even as his face softened, the side of his mouth twitching upward.

"Ap," I whispered, wanting to reach for him but his grip on my wrists was absolute. *"More."*

"You want more?" he rasped, grip tightening as he lifted my leg higher, eyes frantically trying to read my face. To make sure I meant what I said.

"I want everything." And *God* did I mean it.

There's no other way to explain the way Aspen felt but extraordinary. Mind bendingly, body meltingly, marvelous. He moved in strong, even strokes. His lips were always on my skin, sometimes murmuring things I couldn't hear, and sometimes saying things I could.

"You're not real, Poppy. How are you *real?"* He released my wrists and moved his hand down to my waist. Broad and strong and beautiful.

"Aspen," I gasped, and he knew what I meant, knew he could feel the way my body was tightening around him. "I'm…"

Losing my mind?

Not sure of my own name?

Inspired by your athleticism?

All the above.

"Fuck. *Poppy.*" It was all he had time to say before I was exploding around him into tiny fragments of every incredible feeling that ever existed. Until he came back into focus and greeted me with the start of a smile that was lazy and satisfied and *happy*. A reflection of what I knew was on my own face.

I reached for him, just as he rolled us onto our sides. I couldn't even open my eyes fully but I tried, desperate to remember him, just like this, for the rest of my life.

"Well, we'll certainly be doing that again." He sunk his fingers into my hair, capturing my mouth in a smiling kiss and taking every note of laughter that tumbled along after it for himself.

As if they could have ever belonged to anyone else but him.

22

February 9th

Poppy had been soft and warm in my arms. I'd felt her fall to pieces around me twice more after that first time, and I cataloged every sound she had made. Every spot she liked to be touched. *How* she liked to be touched. It was my name on her tongue over and over.

That's all I was thinking about.

How this woman who'd been in my arms wanted me in the very same way I wanted her. It was *all* I could think about while I held her to me, a new rhythm filtering into my head and tapping along the surface of her skin while she ran her fingers through my hair.

Those were all the things running through my mind through every interview I had. It wasn't that I didn't like talking about the band. I loved telling people about the new album, the new tour, sharing dates for the first time and seeing our fans go absolutely insane about the upcoming shows and reading their theories on the theme of our next record. Taking photos with as many people as I could and signing so many autographs my hand started to cramp.

The fans weren't the problem. It was that I was terrified that I'd say the wrong thing. Blurt an important date wrong, release a secret I'd forgotten was a secret.

My phone rang showing Dax's name and I picked up on the first ring, "Yo."

"How's it going?" He had stayed home with the rest of the guys. None of us coped particularly well with the press stuff which sounded kind of stupid considering we were a bunch of kids that actively chased this life. But we just wanted to play music, that was all the motivation we needed. When all of us going to anything media related could be avoided they usually just volunteered me. "Just happy to be home. If I was there with you right now I actually think I'd cry. Thank you for going, by the way."

"Well, we can't have a crying rock star."

"Crying would be bad for my image." If you could hear someone wagging their eyebrows, that's exactly how Dax sounded.

Not a second later I heard Allie yell from somewhere next to him, "We just watched Spider-Man 2 and he cried!"

"Which Spider-Man?" I held the phone between my shoulder and ear while I got into the back of my waiting SUV and buckled in.

"The one with Andrew Garfield." Dax sounded distraught just recounting the actors name.

"Oh, he's my favorite. Was it that scene? With Gwen?"

"Yeah." His voice was thick with emotion. "Look, I gotta go. Thanks again, Ap. Love you."

"Alright, hi to Allie for me. Love you guys."

"How's your brother?" Jane asked from the seat next to me.

"Crying." I shrugged, giving her a big grin.

"That sounds about right. Alright, you have two interviews tomorrow, a free day on Sunday, then two more Monday and then we'll fly you home the day after."

"I can't just leave on Monday?" My heart sank.

"The second one is the *Late Late Show* so I figured you'd want to crash and I'd get you home early the next morning." Jane was already putting her phone to her ear letting the hotel know we were on our way.

The group chat we had as a band that usually went dormant when we were all in the same place had suddenly sprung back to life.

Rip:
Aspen, we miss you

Rip:
Aspen, come back

Me:
You assholes wouldn't miss me if you just came to these WORK events like you're supposed to

Luke:
Pls, we all know ud be the only 1 not having a mental breakdown

Dax:
You looked sexy in that interview last night.

Angus:
So sexy, Ap.

Me:
Fuck off

Me:
But thank you.

Rip:
Did your girlfriend see you on TV like
the famous rock star you are?

Angus:
Oh my god, did she?

Dax:

That article that just went up about you guys was cute

Luke:

Your names sound so nice together, Ap

Luke:

When do we get to meet her? Why are you keeping her from us?

Angus:

Why are you keeping her from us??

Luke:

I just said that…

Angus:

I was emphasizing your point. Will you bring her to family night?

Aspen:

I'm going to mute this chat.

Rip:

So you can call your girlfriend?

Angus:

GIRLFRIEND!

Angus:

What's your couple name?

Dax:
Paspen?

Luke:
Popspen?

Rip:
Aspoppy?

Angus:
Aspenelope?

Aspen has left the chat
Angus added Aspen to the chat
Aspen has left the chat
Dax added Aspen to the chat

As soon as the door to my room closed behind me, my phone started to ring. The irritation I had at myself knowing I'd pick it up when all I really wanted to do was hurl it out the window sent a flare of anger through me until I realized it was Poppy.

She'd called me Tuesday evening after I flew out and told me all about how she and Jess had been asked (forced) to do the coordinating for their office party to help with morale on account of Todd, who apparently started coming to work again but stopped harassing Poppy in the kitchen. She'd talked the entire time which had been sort of amusing because it had been totally *not* like her. I knew it was because she was trying to help me take my mind off the trip.

When Jane had called to confirm all the details for this press trip which I'd completely forgotten about on the night before, Poppy had been dozing on and off in my arms. I'd only just begun my mission of trying to wake her up for a fourth time because keeping my hands to myself now was probably going to be borderline impossible. I'd gotten off the phone and saw the little frown that had scrunched her brow because I knew she heard me tell Jane how excited I was and that I couldn't wait, when Poppy knew for a fact that couldn't have been farther from the truth.

"What I'm specifically after is your opinion on the color combination of magenta, dark brown and mustard yellow," she said as her greeting.

"I'm struggling to visualize it without getting this really horrified look on my face."

"So you see the dilemma Jess and I are facing."

"I'm actually wishing I could unsee it entirely," I said while pulling a pillow under my head from where I landed in the middle of the bed.

"Well, too bad. You're in this with me now. You were all 'trust me, Poppy. Let's do that fun thing that adults do again and again and again'."

Somewhere in the background of her phone call I heard someone, I assumed Jess, say, "Poppy, that was not at all discreet."

The rumbling laughter that she pulled out of me at her attempt at mimicking my voice even shocked me, "Okay, point taken. Let me see, it can't be that bad."

She was mumbling something about how it *was* that bad while she swapped our regular phone call into a FaceTime and…that's when I saw it. Poppy had taped three different colored balloons together and stuck them to the wall in what looked like a kitchen.

"Oh, wow." I could see my face, which meant she could see my face. I did my best to control my facial expression.

"You look constipated." She sounded wildly amused.

"Constipated with pride at what you've achieved here with your limited resources?"

"That was very smooth." She flipped the phone back around and the moment I saw her I just wanted to reach through the screen and pull her to me.

"Hey," I said, feeling like I could breathe properly for the first time all day.

"Hey," she said back, a little grin on her face. "How's your trip?"

"About how you'd expect."

"So you really are excited and having the best time ever?"

"You're a brat, you know that?"

"I am merely repeating your own words back to you." She walked out of the kitchen and now sat in what looked like a little cubical.

"You're working late," I said, trying to change the topic.

She gave me one of those looks that made me want to hide under the covers of my bed and never come out, but relented.

"The party's on Monday so this is it as far as time frames to set up and Winny wanted us to wait until everyone had left." And because it was Poppy she didn't even wait a whole second before she asked, "Why do you do things you don't want to do?"

I'd known she would ask me that question again. Knew that the lack of answer I gave the first time she asked on our hike would eat at her until she built up to ask again.

"Poppy –"

"No, I know. It's definitely none of my business it's just…you did it when I asked you about the singing too, I just..it makes me sad. I know the press stuff is something you *have* to do. But…you doing it on your own because everyone else likes it as little as you do? That doesn't make sense to me.."

"I'd love to sing for you," I said, and I meant it too.

"Ap, you know that's not what I mean." She frowned a little harder.

I was tired from the day, yes, but also tired of lying all the time. *All the fucking time.* I didn't want that with Poppy, I wanted her to know me for the person I was, not the person that I tried to be for everyone else. When I thought about it that way, telling her the truth was exceptionally easy. "They think I like it. Love it, actually. Because I told them I did."

"Why?" Her frown morphed from something sad to something confused.

"I wanted to help out. I was stressed about them being stressed. I thought, what if one of them went without me and something happened to them that I could have stopped? A freak accident, maybe an unhinged fan. What if something happened because I didn't want to go? So, right at the start when the band was just taking off I told everyone I actually loved doing press and I'd do it all when everyone else could get out of it."

I had never felt more seen as I did when Poppy's face softened and it was as if I'd become a little bit clearer to see in her eyes.

"Aspen." Her voice was quiet and full to the brim with all the thoughts that must have been swirling around in her head. It was the closest I'd come to telling anyone about my past and, actually, it was a relief. It was a fucking *relief.*

"Well, I wish I was there with you." That was all she said on the matter. She didn't push me, just sat with me without even knowing fully what my reality was.

A reality that maybe who I had been, maybe the way I had decided to cope with things, wasn't working for me anymore.

I knew nothing at that moment except the fact that there'd never been anything that made me want to break free of the shackles I'd put on myself over the last decade. That I'd become who I was because I'd been the cause of something awful once, and I felt like I owed it to the people in my life to never be that again.

But I hadn't accounted for Poppy.

Now there was her, this person in my life that made me want things for myself when I never had before. I'd never cared to want anything more than to play music with my friends and do everything I could to keep the people I loved safe. By doing everything I could to make sure that I was there for them.

I was happy to be second. *Needed* to come second. But I wasn't the only one now that would be impacted by the ghosts of my past and if I wanted to keep Poppy, I knew I'd have to learn to let them go.

"Poppy?" I said.

"Yes?" She looked at me like she wanted to reach through our phones too.

I decided that she made me brave enough to do that, to want this for myself. "When I think about coming home, I don't picture my apartment."

She looked like I'd reached right into her chest and held her beating heart in the palm of my hand. "What do you picture?" she asked, sounding devastatingly vulnerable.

"I picture you," I whispered.

23

February 11th

Poppy

Jess and I hadn't been able to have our wine night on Thursday. So, instead, she asked if I wanted to go over for dinner on Sunday with her and her boys and after a quick pep-talk from Leah, I did it.

Turned out her kids were the actual best and we all sat together and played board games after dinner. When monopoly got too heated between the twins they went off for an hour to put together a choreographed routine to a song Jess had picked by Taylor Swift.

They then came back and performed their routine for us. We laughed so much that Jess had to crawl to the bathroom, all the while yelling "I'm peeing! I'm peeing!" and I caught the wine that shot out of my nose in the palm of my hand.

I'd left with a permanent look of contented happiness on my face and called Aspen on the way home to tell him all about it. He told me about his day off and that he had tried meditating and when that didn't work he spent pretty much the whole day in the gym because he was filled with all this restless energy and no drum kit.

"No drum kit, or girlfriend." He said it so casually that it took me a second to realize that it was the first time he had, in fact, said it.

The reality was that I could only see one way out of this, and it wasn't a fairy tale ending. It would mean getting hurt, *Aspen* getting hurt, because of me. But I'd compromised with myself, hadn't I? That I'd give into him even though I hadn't really had a choice. Everything about falling for Aspen Smith was as inevitable as me leaving.

It was wrong to take everything he was willing to give me while I could, but I did it anyway.

"Okay," I said, my heart thrashing in my ears.

"Okay?" He said the word in a way that I knew, without a shadow of a doubt he was smiling so big his dimples would be on full display.

"Yeah, no 'buts' right?" If I hadn't been sitting on a train right at that moment I think I probably would have screamed in delight. Shoving the debilitating guilt behind that door in my mind that was now bursting at the seams and trying to reassure myself that he knew what he was getting into.

Aspen knew that I was leaving and he wanted to do this with me anyway.

"Will you come to our Fun Friday Family Fiesta night next week? Everyone's been wanting to meet you for a while and I've held them off as long as I could."

"I have no idea what that means but the alliteration could have convinced me all on its own."

"That was Allie," he laughed.

"They know who I am?" Why did that make me nervous?

"Well, sort of. They know that I have a friend who is a girl. The only person I've actually spoken about you to is Allie because she told me to pretty much go and find you after that first time we met. Everyone else has been scouring the internet for every picture and article they could find."

"*Aspen!*" I whisper shouted and felt my blood pressure rise a fraction. I'd been actively *not* looking at the news but Leah had promised to let me know if anything alarming came up. So far it was a lot of speculation and photos of me coming and going from work. Aspen coming and going from his apartment, and one unflattering photo of Aspen driving his Jeep into the underground parking of his building with me in the front seat and his hand covering my entire face.

"What do you think?"

"I think Allie and I will get on swimmingly," I said, getting off the train at my station and starting the walk home.

"So you'll come?" He sounded so hopeful, it made me hopeful too.

"I'll come."

"I think this is a hit," Jess said, waving at two of our coworkers that walked into the Say No To The January Blues party.

"Jess, they're the first people to arrive." I forced my mouth into something that looked sort of pleasant and waved too, even though I felt about as comfortable as one might feel if they'd discovered an ants nest in their underwear. If there was one thing I would have been confident that I *wouldn't* do in my life, it was help to organize an office party.

"Yes, but they came. To me that's an instant success."

"Here's to hoping your optimism rubs off on me."

"Oh, speaking of rubbing, my cat has changed your blue sweater into a white sweater because I didn't realize you left it on the couch and she's absolutely demolished it with fur. Like, I didn't even know it was your sweater because it was so white." She cringed while telling me, not even making eye contact just staring directly at my boobs.

"Consider it a gift from me to your cat." I could actively feel my esophagus closing at the thought of that amount of cat hair.

"Are you sure?" She looked at me from under her dark rimmed glasses.

"Desperately."

"Ladies!" Winny said with the sort of enthusiasm you had to wonder where he got the energy to possess it.

"Winston! Welcome to the party!" Jess matched his enthusiasm completely.

"You guys have done a fantastic job, and I see you got the balloons I ordered!" He pointed right at the cluster of balloons that consisted of colors no one in their right mind would ever look at and think 'yes, that works. That really, really works'.

"It just works, doesn't it?" Winny said, reaching forward to give Jess a weird side hug that she half accepted and flushed into a serious shade of magenta. It must have been written all over my face because she reached out to subtly pinch my side.

"Hey!" I yelled, swatting her hand away and unintentionally gaining all of Winny's attention. "Hey *hey*!" I said, trying to cover my outburst and wanting to die a little at the way I sang those words out. "That…is a true statement. Thank you for the balloons."

"You're very welcome, Poppy. I think the rest of the office is really moving past the whole," he leaned in very close and all I could smell was peanut butter, "cousin thing."

Jess and I both looked at the two people who had arrived before Winny. Her face said 'I worked on a cheese board for a whole hour and the two people that came to this stinker of a party are dairy free'. My face said something that contained a few more cuss words and my smile was more of a wobbly showing of my teeth. "Thanks, Winny."

I clung to Jess for the rest of the evening and when Winny volunteered me to start a round of acapella karaoke, Jess, bless her literal soul, jumped up so fast her chair clattered to the ground before she announced, reluctantly, that she would actually like to go first. And second. *And third.*

Jess sang the entire evening and Winny had sat with impeccable posture, clapping along to every song she sang like it was the concert of a lifetime. The man had hearts in his eyes. When it was just us after Winny and the two other dairy free cheese board neglectors had left, I pulled her into the biggest, most grateful hug.

"Jess, I'm indebted to you."

"I will cash it in in the form of another Sunday night dinner, but you bring that cousin of yours." She hugged me back just as hard.

"Deal," I laughed knowing that Aspen would have the time of his life watching her boys perform. He'd probably get up with them.

I wish I'd realized earlier that that was going to be my last easy moment for a while; I would have held onto it a little longer.

24

February 14th

It was like the universe was demanding balance and I was just the closest person to provide the cause and effect.

Everything had been fine on the way to the airport. Jovial, even. I mean, sure it was a little wild on the roads, but I'd driven in heavy snow before. I was no stranger to the defensive maneuvers you needed to master, especially considering how lackluster the Taurus was (said with nothing but love), but it didn't really seem *that* bad.

Turns out, it was actually *that* bad and we had been in the midst of a blizzard. Jane kept on talking about how our driver, Garrett, was super human for getting us to the airport in one piece only to not blink an eye and drive us all the way back to the hotel when they canceled all the flights for the rest of the day. I think Jane just really liked Garrett.

Jason, my security guy, had sat up the front while Jane and I were in the back and I should have known, really, considering the way he held firm to the assist grip like his life depended on it.

"You okay, bud?" I did my best to hide all the amusement from my voice but it was impossible.

"I quit," he said, sounding like he was trying not to hyperventilate.

"You can't quit, Jason. You're the only security we've had that's managed not to get the slip," Jane said, a little smile on her face while her fingers moved at the speed of light across the screen of her phone. I wasn't entirely sure what she was doing seeing as no one had service because of the storm.

"That's not true." I sounded like a toddler but it took incredible skill to out maneuver one's security and I couldn't let her take that from me.

"I follow you to that bar and sit outside. I'm literally always with you, even when you don't see me. Please shut up now so I can concentrate on not dying," Jason groaned and I sat there feeling like I'd just been told my mom was in the row behind me at the movie theater the first time I took a girl on a date.

"What? Even Poppy's house?"

"Yes," he squeaked.

"I can't believe this." I didn't really mean to say it out loud.

"Believe it, Aspen," Jane said, her tone half chiding and half amused.

"I mean, I'm impressed, Jase. I've never once seen you."

"Thank you." The man sounded like he was about to shit himself.

We were back at the hotel and every time I tried to call Poppy the line dropped or crackled or just didn't connect at all. For my last attempt I'd been standing on a chair and half of my face was immersed into the curtains trying to keep the line. My messages were also refusing to send which was just the cherry on top of this incredibly awesome press trip.

That wasn't totally fair. It had been great, really. The response was exactly what we'd hoped for. More, even.

The double upside? We'd pretty much finished the album. There were a few drum tracks that we needed to rerecord. There was nothing wrong with the originals but after listening to what was supposed to be the final versions of the tracks, there were a couple songs that I wanted to tweak and I'd been buzzing all week to get behind a drum kit.

I wasn't entirely sure how it happened but I'd sent Poppy a message that I knew wouldn't get through until the storm passed and then, shockingly, fell asleep. I didn't even remember closing my eyes before I woke up with my fingers tapping and this insatiable itch to get to the studio.

For a long time, drumming was the only thing that had never lost its spark for me. I craved it consistently. Just doing it, getting better at it, finding new ways to record sounds I wanted to create and new things I could do while playing live that would blow the ever living minds off our fans. That hadn't changed, but now I felt that passion and want and *need* for something else.

Someone else.

Look, I wasn't one to make that big of a deal of Valentine's Day, but if I had been home I would have probably baked something in the shape of a heart and hand delivered it to Poppy. I didn't know if she loved the holiday particularly, but I picture the way she would have looked at it and then at me with her classic, unrestrained grin and launched herself at me. I could feel her body beneath my hands, feel her pressed against me and, holy *fuck,* did I miss her.

That first bit was a lie, I fucking *loved* Valentine's Day. I was now actively in a relationship on this very day for the first time in a very long time and I'd purposely played it casual over the last week when Poppy and I spoke.

I'd been very proud of the fact that I hadn't brought it up once. A task that had been like swimming against the current of my own mind. So, I knew the bouquet of roses that were due to land on Poppy's door step any minute now would not be something she expected but I hoped it would be something that might earn me one of those smiles she'd come to give me freely and I'd come to crave hopelessly. The second most exciting part was I knew for sure she wouldn't anticipate the bouquet of fish food canisters I had organized for Nat.

There had been no word from her at all, during the storm yesterday or since I'd woken up. Which usually I wouldn't have thought about twice. She probably ended up doing something with Leah through FaceTime and then fell asleep while still on the call. I'd seen it happen before and both their faces had been smooshed to their phones. I'd screenshotted the visual of Leah before I had ended the call on Poppy's end and when she woke up to see it she laughed so hard she fell off the bed.

I was practically bouncing in my seat with excitement to hear from her now though. And usually I was patient. Okay, *sometimes* I was patient.

This was not one of those times.

Me:
Happy Valentine's Day Poompaloompa x

I sent off the message just before shutting off my phone and settling into my seat on the jet. Thankfully, the storm had passed and the roads had been cleared by the time Jane knocked on my door. I'd been up for hours when her wake up call had come in at 5 AM.

I was desperate to get home. Back to the band.

Back to Poppy.

When the plane landed I checked my phone, vibrating with fucking excitement at the very idea of what sort of message she'd have sent through, what she might think of Nats Valentines day present, but…nothing. There was nothing.

I watched the screen of my phone the entire drive to the studio, waiting for her three dots to show up but a message from her never came.

I knew the storm had come through Blazewood too, though nowhere near as bad, so it was still possible that she had no service on her phone. Or, she was at work probably learning something increasingly random like facts on emus from a zoology seminar that was specific to flightless birds. Poppy was relatively diligent about replying, but when she got stuck into something that fascinated her, she got lost in it.

I pocketed my phone and moved my mind from one obsession to the other.

My brother came for me in a bear hug that the rest of the guys piled.

"Is everyone's feet off the ground?" Luke's muffled shout came from somewhere behind me and was answered with a swarm of equally muffled confirmations.

"He's not budging," Dax said, his mouth closest to my face. I could feel his body shaking with laughter more than I could hear it.

"Ap this is by far your best pile yet," Angus said from where he clung to my waist. "But I'm letting go because I'm looking right at your crotch."

"Lucky you." I was laughing and the more I laughed the harder it was to stay standing, before any of them could jump off I went down and almost pissed my pants at the sound that came out of Luke from taking the brunt of my fall.

"It was like," Rip wheezed, "*a yodeling donkey*!"

That was all it took before we were off again, laughing so hard no sound was coming out of anyone's mouth except for Luke and his never ending yodeling-donkey noises.

"I leave you guys for like, two seconds," Adrian said, coming back into the room with the biggest coffee cup I'd ever seen and just like always, the ability to bring us back on track and focus on what we were there to do.

"You're up, Ap." He extended his hand to help me up and gave me a one armed hug. "Nice to have you back, our little drummer boy." He ruffled my hair.

"Thanks, band-daddy." I blew him a kiss and he held up the middle finger of his free hand.

"Alright, boys get up." Adrian sat down and rubbed his hands together. "Let's finish this album."

I took off my shirt and dropped it on the couch that Rip had settled into before setting my phone on the coffee table just in front of it, zoning out completely and letting myself find that place I could exist in forever. Where it was just me and the drum kit in front of me and the singular focus that was to be the backbone of the song. To pave the road for all the other parts of the song to drive on, to get from where it all started to where it ended.

That's how I'd been the entire day until we were done with the very last song. The album was done. It was *done.*

I took the headphone off, feeling the thrum of excitement watching the boys celebrate and hug and pile on top of one another until something got Rip's attention on the coffee table, a howling Luke still clinging to his back. Rip leaned forward and picked up my phone and I watched as he looked from it to me. With what had to be the most mischievous, cheekiest and shit-stirring grin I'd ever seen on his face he brought the phone up to his ear and I saw his mouth say the words, "Aspen's phone, this is Rip speaking."

"I didn't do anything! I swear!" Rip's hands were up in front of him in full surrender mode and my phone was now face down across the room.

"He threw your phone across the room." Angus said, looking down and focused completely on the guitar in his hands, still playing the baseline for the song I'd been drumming to without the guitar plugged into an amp.

"There was a woman," Rip's face was the perfect picture of fear. "She asked me to hold on a second and then she *screamed*." His eyes were now looking at the phone and he was pointing at it like it was possessed. "Aspen, she screamed *right into the phone*! Who *does* that?"

I looked from Rip to Dax who was actively trying not to laugh and take our friends' clear terror seriously, sparing only a second to grab and pull on my shirt. I didn't need to check the screen before I put the phone to my ear.

"Leah?" I felt the frown on my brow start to form. Leah hadn't called me before but we did swap numbers the night of our FaceTime dinner at Poppy's. She said it was in case of emergency but Poppy was sure it was because she liked walking around knowing she had the number of a famous person in her phone for the first time in her life. Apparently, it was a bucket list item.

"You mean to say you *know* that woman?!" Rip sounded genuinely affronted.

"Aspen, this is Leah McDonaugh, Poppy's best friend. Did I just speak to Rip Reynolds?" Leah was audibly hyperventilating.

"I know who you are Leah, and I mean, technically you screamed at him, but yes, that was him." Now *I* was trying to be sympathetic to Leah's mental breakdown without laughing.

"This might be the best day of my whole life," she said, sounding like her eyes were full of stars and she might just be clutching her heart.

"Leah," I said, trying to get her back on track.

"What?" She still sounded out of breath.

"Is everything okay?" As soon as I asked the question my stomach dropped and I had no idea why.

"Oh, yeah I just wanted to see how Poppy was today? She usually goes pretty quiet over the next couple of days and I know things can get dark for her. I know I'm being nosy but she's never wanted me around for it and I always worry about her."

"Poppy?" Everything she said immediately confused me.

"Well, yeah? I just assumed you'd be with her today considering… everything."

"Everything? What's everything?" I could hear the element of mild hysteria creeping into my voice and felt the stares of five pairs of eyes on my back.

"Aspen…you mean she didn't tell you?" Leah sounded devastated. "She's always been way too private about her grief. Right from when we were kids."

"Leah." My voice was sharper than I intended it to be. "Why are you calling me asking if Poppy is okay?"

"Today's the fourteenth of February." She delivered it like it should have been this light-at-the-end-of-the-tunnel kind of answer.

"I don't know what that means, Leah." There was no doubt about the panic in my voice now.

"It's her brother's birthday today."

"I—" I didn't have anything to say. I was trying to work out why she hadn't told me that. This huge part of herself that she was still figuring out how to navigate. Why she hadn't trusted me enough to be there for her through it.

"Sometimes she won't talk to me for a week except for random messages here and there so I know she's alive. She falls into these…I don't really know what else to call them but endless emotional pits? And she's always forced herself to brave it alone."

I nodded even though Leah couldn't see me, nodded in a little understanding of all the 'why's' racing through my mind before replying, "Not anymore."

"No," her voice was thoughtful and grateful all at once, "I don't think so either."

I hung up without saying goodbye, turning around to see my brother already standing there, my hat and jacket in his outstretched hands. His face was set into an expression of worry. His mouth a slash across his face and brows drawn down.

Dax knew what it was like to love someone who was hurting. He didn't have to say a single thing for me to know that he got it, in however broad a sense it might be, he still got it.

"Ap," he called out and I turned just in time to catch the keys to his car before I was out the door.

I will say something for Wyatt's car, it was very fast.

He'd bought the Porsche a year ago as a present to himself for literally no reason and now constantly referred to it as his 'bestie'. It had absolutely nothing on the Taurus but I promised myself I'd never say another bad thing about it. It got me to Poppy in a very timely manner.

I was standing out front of her house, the flowers that were delivered this morning already wilted from the cold with Nat's canister bouquet right next to it.

Poppy didn't have a car, but I knew she was home.

I knocked on the door, "Poppy?"

There was no answer. Not the first, the second or the tenth time I called her. No matter which version of her name I used, there was nothing but silence on the other end.

"Fuck it," I said, walking around the side of her house to where the first of the downstairs windows began. The first one didn't budge, but the second one did and though I was stoked about a way to get to her I would need to explain at some point the importance of locking all the windows and doors when you lived alone.

Poppy's house was dark and quiet. The bubbling of Nat's tank made the space feel homey even amid the still packed boxes and pale walls.

"Poppy?" I called out again, but didn't hear a single thing back. Walking over to Nat, I bent down to her level. "Hey Queenie," I said, pressing the pad of my index finger to her tank lightly before giving her a bit of food.

This might have been the most stalkerish thing I'd ever done but I would think about that later and use this very moment as an example in my 'for' points on locking all points of entry. Right now though, I made my way up the stairs towards Poppy's bedroom.

She was where I thought she would be.

I only hesitated for a second before I stepped into her bedroom, my chest going tight and heavy all at once, filled with a breath I'd been holding for way too long. Like my lungs had forgotten how to work entirely from the moment Leah called me to this very second.

Poppy didn't move, but I knew she knew I was there.

I didn't know what to do.

I wanted to do everything, *anything*, and I had no fucking idea where to start.

Toeing off my sneakers I walked to the end of her bed and stood there for a second, watching the rapid way her chest rose and fell.

I lay down facing her, my heart clenching and breaking a little at every detail I took in; her swollen eyes, the dampness of her pillow. The salty tear tracks that had dried on her cheeks and the new once being made by the rivulets still falling.

Poppy opened her eyes then, bloodshot with moisture clumping her eyelashes together and I'd realized I'd do anything, *anything*, to stop her from feeling the need to carry her pain all on her own. Of thinking that she had to sit in it by herself.

Her lips were cracked and dry like all the water in her body had made an escape, her voice husky like she'd used it all up.

"It's my brother's birthday today." Her eyes were sad and her face was drawn.

She took another breath before she spoke again and I didn't expect the next words that came out of her mouth, "I killed him."

Poppy's first line of defense was to push people away. She'd done it to me more times than I could count. I'd had to actively chip away at the armor she'd practically sewn into her own skin.

"You don't believe me?" she asked, her voice almost angry, like she was reaching for anything to feel other than what she already was. I knew what that was like, because I'd done it too.

"No." I didn't need to think about it. I knew the woman in front of me. I knew her mind and her heart and her soul because she'd let me close enough to see them all.

Her chest hadn't stopped its rapid rise and fall. I could see it building, whatever it was she needed to do to be able to tell this story that she'd kept so close she'd forgotten what it was like to live without it. That was another thing I knew, because I'd done the same thing with my own.

I didn't particularly care if the reason she was telling me was because she hoped it would scare me away. If she was hoping I'd look at her and see a monster, someone who deserved to suffer all on their own. It just mattered to me that she told me.

She took a final deep breath and started, "I was raised by my older brother."

25

February 14th

Poppy

"I was raised by my older brother," I started talking and didn't let myself stop. "He was quite a bit older than me when I was born. I was a surprise for the entire family after my parents thought Casimir was their one and only miracle baby. He was fourteen when I came along.

My mom, she died giving birth to me. My parents both traveled a lot for work so she missed a lot of appointments so all these things that could have been avoided, weren't. That's what I was told, anyway. After she died, my dad had to work more. Longer hours, a second job. He traveled more and more and then one day, he just didn't come home. He's actually still alive, but after my mom...anyway, he has a new family now. I'm not sure where he is."

Aspen just lay there listening to every word, barely breathing, his eyes never leaving mine, determined to live this with me.

"Eventually it was just the two of us." I swallowed, letting myself drop Aspen's gaze. I focused on the rise and fall of his chest and let myself be pulled into the memory.

"It was my sixteenth birthday. We'd been planning it for a long time. We went back and forth on a party. Doing something with some of my friends, maybe just Leah, but in the end I decided I just wanted it to be the two of us. He had started to work more to pay for school. He wanted to do more for himself – more for us – than to be a mechanic in someone else's shop. He wanted to be a mechanic in his *own* shop. So, he started studying while working and his classes were at night so we hadn't really been spending as much time together over the last six months he was alive. I missed him." I clutched at my shirt, wishing I could stifle the ache where it ricocheted off every broken piece of my heart.

"I'd picked a take out menu from our little pile in the kitchen and ordered right at 6 PM so that it would just be arriving when he got home." I felt a smile tug at my lips for the briefest second at the memory before it fell away.

"But he was late. They were understaffed and I knew he usually had to work through his lunch. They had a last minute drive in and he was there so he stayed to help out. He said he tried to call me, but I never heard the phone ring. I must have been in the shower maybe, I guess. I was *so mad."* My voice broke and it took me a second but I pushed on. I still felt Aspen's eyes on me even though I couldn't meet them.

"He tried and *tried* to speak to me when he got home, he explained everything through the door but I closed myself in my room. I wouldn't even *look* at him. He stood outside my bedroom door for over an hour. We had no locks but he had this rule that if you weren't invited in, you weren't allowed in. So he just *stood* there. Apologizing over and over and over again." I felt the tears as they fell down my face and did nothing to stop them. They were hot and angry and full of the hatred I felt for myself every single fucking day.

"It was like this light bulb lit up in his head and he said he knew what would fix it, what always fixed it. There was a place seven blocks from our apartment that made this frozen custard I was obsessed with. I used to say it was the best in the world even though I'd never been out of the country. Cas had worked a full day, including overtime. He hadn't even changed out of his work coveralls because he'd been standing at my door and then dashed out the house to make up for the fact that he was bending over backwards for us and had been a little late to my birthday plans." I couldn't even say the words out loud properly. They fell from my mouth in a strangled whisper and when I finally looked back up at Aspen, my vision blurred from the tears that had continued to fall. I knew that he could see the shame I felt, that I carried with me every single day. Refused to let go of because of what I'd caused.

Aspen reached for me across the bed, leaving his hand halfway between us, his own eyes glittering with the sheen of unshed tears, but I didn't take it.

I didn't reach back for him, for his embrace that I knew would help to soothe all the wounds that had never really healed and forced myself to tell him the rest of the story.

"He'd only been gone for ten minutes, that was all. It took ten minutes for my stupid sixteen year old tears to go from hurt and angry to ones of guilt and shame. I ran out after him, not even bothering to lock the door."

I closed my eyes, reliving it all in my own head as I finally told Aspen the truth of who I was.

What I'd done.

"Casimir!" I yelled his name while I ran, not stopping until eventually his jacket clad form came into view just a block away from the dessert shop. "Cas!" I could barely see him, my vision blurred and chest heaving from the six blocks I'd run, pushing my legs to move as fast as they could. I collided with him at full speed, wrapping my arms around him, sobbing into his chest.

"I'm sorry," I cried, voice muffled by his coat, immediately enveloped in his grease and tobacco scent that I would know anywhere. "I'm sorry, I'm sorry."

His hand came up to rest against the back of my head. I could still feel the ghost of it.

His voice soft and calm, "Penny, hey—"

"I'm such a bitch, a huge bitch."

"You're not a bitch. Also, don't say bitch."

"I am."

"Pen–"

"I am." I cried harder.

"Okay, fine. You are." There was only humor in his voice and I scowled into his

now tear stained jacket, pinching his side.

He'd been too focused on me, on my tears. On trying to stop them from falling and keeping me calm that neither of us had seen the three men that approached us.

"Well, isn't this sweet."

As long as I lived, I'd never forget the sound of that voice. Like rusted nails.

My stomach dropped out of my body right when Casimir pushed me behind him. I could see the eyes of the two men behind the one holding the gun. I knew what that look meant. What people like them thought of when they looked at sixteen year old girls.

There wasn't a version of me, in any other version of reality that wouldn't know the intent behind their eyes. The first guy came close enough that Casimir tried to go for the gun.

In the struggle it went off, going right through Cas's heart before lodging itself in my shoulder.

There was a moment of silence before a scream involuntarily ripped from my throat, and my brother stumbled back. I didn't register the pain lancing through my own body; my entire purpose became catching him.

A sound of shock escaped him as he stumbled back into me, his weight too much to hold as I fell back with him, his body crushing mine.

My hands were frantic before they settled on the wound in the middle of his chest.

"HELP!" My throat had burned with that scream. "Somebody, Some– HELP!"

"Pen-" Cas blinked up at me rapidly, like he was trying to clear his vision, to clear his eyes. "Penelope."

"I'm here, you're okay, help is coming," I sobbed while I kept my hands on his chest. Desperate to stop the blood from leaving his body.

"Penny, I—" Blood trickled out the side of his mouth and I knew another scream ripped from me. I could hear it then, the sound of my soul fracturing.

"Don't go." I pushed harder on the wound in his chest, my hands covered in red and trembling. "Don't leave me, don't you dare leave me. Please, please."

"It's okay." His words were weak, but when I looked at him again his eyes were on me, clear and focused. "It's okay," he said again, and I could see the goodbye in his eyes. See the love on his face.

Then I watched as it faded from his body.

His life, his soul, his love for me. It was there one moment, and then it was gone the next.

I woke up in the hospital with faces looking at me that belonged to people I didn't know speaking words I couldn't understand but knowing in my heart one undeniable truth; my brother was gone and for the first time in my entire life I was all alone in the world.

"So, you see," I rasped, lifting my heavy, swollen lids to find that Aspen was now right in front of me, tears streaming down his own beautiful face. "Hurting you is inevitable. And I refuse," my voice broke, "*refuse* to do that to you."

Aspen's hands shook as he moved into me, one sliding beneath my waist and the other around the back of my neck. I couldn't stop myself from leaning into his touch. I couldn't stop myself for hating how I did it, even as I'd just ripped myself apart to show him *why*—

"Poppy," his voice was quiet. A reflection of the pain I felt. "Poppy, you were sixteen."

I didn't know what to do, so I just shook my head. I shook it over and over refusing to hear what he was saying, but he held me firm, bringing his forehead to mine. "It wasn't your fault, do you hear me?"

No, I shook my head. *You don't understand.*

I didn't have to speak for him to know what I was saying.

"You were a *child,* Penelope. It was not your fault," he said again. He said it again and again and *again.* Until I was clinging to Aspen like he was the only solid ground I could find. Until the gentle repetition of his words against my temple, broken only by the gentle kisses he placed there, started to break their way through the walls I had rebuilt in his absence.

I'd been told those things before, many times, but never like this. Like I might believe them.

Aspen was silent for a long time before he spoke again, "I didn't have a lot of friends growing up. I was insanely attached to my brother and my parents weren't around a lot, it was sort of like they had kids to just tick it off on this list of things you did in life. Once we were there and old enough to manage on our own they…it was like having two old roommates."

I huffed a laugh despite everything and leaned into him more, reveling in the feel of the vibrations of his voice and the beat of his heart beneath my cheek.

"I had a panic attack on my first day of school, and this girl, Trixie, calmed me down. She was my only friend and I wouldn't even call her that, really. She lived on the same street as us so she was the only other person at my school that I ever really spoke to and when I started driving to school, sometimes I would give her rides. I'd always have to drive past her house and if she was there, I'd ask if she wanted a lift."

"That's a very Ap thing to do," I whispered, more to myself than to him.

His only answer was a soft kiss to my head.

"When Dax moved to college I fell into this intense sort of depression. I'd never been without him and I didn't want to bother him with calls or visits because he was at college, you know? But I started sleeping through the day, missing school…that sort of thing. Days would just blur into one another and I didn't have the energy to do anything.

"My phone buzzing woke me up one time and it was Trixie, which was weird because she never called me. I didn't know what the time was or the day but I looked right at my phone and watched as it rang out. She texted after asking if I was free, and I said no." Aspen's voice had gotten progressively more strained and I realized what he was doing.

A story for a story.

"It turned out to be a Saturday night and her mom forgot to pick her up from her job across town. She was calling to see if I could give her a lift, I found out after."

"After what?" I whispered back, my heart in my throat as he pulled me into his secret the way I'd pulled him into mine.

"She was walking along the highway making her way home. A drunk driver had passed out at the wheel and she was—"

Oh my God. "Aspen–" I moved away from him to look at him, the tears in my eyes now a reflection of his.

"Dax came home the next weekend, took one look at me and turned around and walked out." Aspen sniffed and wiped at his face, "I thought he hated me, thought he knew what I did and what I caused."

He shook his head, "It turned out my school had called him after Trixie. My parents hadn't been taking their calls, and so they called Dax and told them about the change in my behavior. The drop in my grades. As soon as he saw me I think he knew how bad I was." Aspen looked down at where my hand lay over his heart, and his hand lay over mine. "He moved home that afternoon, walked right back into my room and said, 'So, how about we start that band?'" Aspen laughed, wiping at his eyes again.

"I promised myself that I'd never do anything like that again. That I would make sure I picked up the damn phone when someone I cared about called. That I would do anything and everything I could to make sure the people I loved were safe. That Dax's sacrifice to move back home would be worth it, that when I was needed I would show up. I'd be that person between them and danger, no matter what. That I would always, *always,* put them first before myself, no matter the cost."

I stared at him and felt the shift in my body as the whole picture of who he was clicked into place. It felt like I was meeting him all over again for the first time. I wanted to say back to him the very things he'd said to me, that I'd shook my head at and refused to believe.

You were a child.

It was not your fault.

He looked at me the same way and I knew why he'd told me his story too.

Sharing the hardest parts of myself had always been easiest to do in the quiet darkness, but. I don't think that was the case for Aspen. I knew that Aspen didn't like the quiet, he didn't like the dark, but he'd done it anyway for me. To show me that he was like me. Living a life that had grown around grief.

"I've realized, though," Ap said, his eyes cleared now of the story he'd shared, and completely focused on me, "that what I've been doing, how I've been living, might not be working for me anymore. That I've got to learn to be a little selfish, to put what I want first."

I could feel the way his heart sped up beneath my palm, "How's that going?"

The side of his mouth quirked up, "You tell me?"

I heard what he was saying in the same way I had when he'd made me his chicken soup. Seeing through the words he said to the ones he hadn't.

I'm letting go of my ghost, so I can hold onto you.

Hold onto me, Poppy.

My bottom lip trembled as I nodded my head, "Pretty good."

He reached out to swipe a final falling tear, "Yeah?"

I nodded again. "Yeah," I said, knowing he'd hear the hidden words there too.

I am.

I felt it as I melted into the kiss he pressed into my lips. From days of being apart, from the relief at knowing I had all of Aspen right there before me and he had all of me.

I am.

I thought it over and over again as he peeled the clothes off my body, leaving a lingering kiss to my scar. While I peeled all his clothes off too.

I am.

I chanted it in my own head as he whispered more secrets just for us two into my skin and pulled his name from my lips. Pushing into me, again and again, until there was no way of knowing where his soul started and where mine ended, only that there were two of them where there used to be just one.

I am.

Aspen held me in the quiet of my bedroom. The blankets tangled up in our legs and the

steady sound of his breath the focus of all my attention. Neither of us slept and just when the sun began to rise it occurred to me that I hadn't actually let him inside my house.

"Ap?"

"Mm?" he hummed from where he was nestled against my neck.

"How did you get into my house?"

Aspen pulled back, his hair mussed and expression lazy, "Your window. That reminds me, we'll be having a discussion on locking all points of entry as a person who lives on their own."

I ignored him in favor of the first part of his sentence, "You mean, like Edward Cullen?" I was laughing already at my own personal joke. Of being totally in love with that fictional character right beside Leah, though she was also partial to Team Jacob.

"I have no idea why you're laughing," he said, his face so serious it only made me laugh more. Aspen gestured down the length of his body, "This is the skin of a killer, Poppy."

That sent me so far into a laughing spiral I started to laugh *backwards*. My body was only able to make noise when trying to drag air into my lungs instead of out and then Aspen finally broke character, trying to mouth something through his wheezing laughter that looked like 'yodeling donkey' but I couldn't be sure.

I was sure, though, that I don't think I'd ever felt like this before. Maybe once, but it was different. This feeling I had now was new and old. Like the way wine only gets better with time, that's what this feeling was like. It was a hand holding mine in a crowded place. A seat saved at a table just for me. It was making me soup when I was sick and leaving the house just to feed my goldfish.

It made me want to run nowhere else but straight towards it.

26

March 1st

Poppy

The day after Aspen stayed over, it was sort of like I'd never seen clearly before. Like my prescription had been wrong for years and I just learned to live with seeing things with fuzzy edges.

The two weeks that followed when I saw him with my brand new eyes, and he could see me with his, were this blur of incomparable happiness. I found myself feeling guilty from time to time before I pulled myself back into it.

You knew what you were getting yourself into.

That had become my mantra. That and, well, it seemed Aspen's name had also become a mantra of sorts. One that I said out loud rather than in my own head.

Was this what it was like to date someone? Because it was fucking *fun*.

Aspen had been working long days and late nights, filled with finalizing all the songs for the new album, some he even shared with me. One he let me FaceTime Leah so she could hear it too. As you might have suspected, she excused herself off frame and screamed in terrified happiness.

Now that the album was done, it was time to start on the tour prep. Named after their new album, the *Salvation Tour* was going to be their biggest yet.

Every arena they were playing was the biggest the cities had to offer, more dates than before had been added to every city and they were going to be on the road for longer than ever before. They were doing photo shoots to prepare for their new tour merch and actually started to practice for their shows. It was so incredibly exciting to be able to watch the way the band worked up close. It made total sense to me that they were as successful as they were.

The mini press tour Ap had done was to announce the sale dates for their tour which officially started in June, but *Lady Luck* had always done things a little different and loved to play a stream of shows in their home city of Blazewood. Those would all be done at the start of April so the boys were completely immersed in set lists and rehearsals.

I asked him about it and he gave me one of his dimpled sunshine smiles when he replied, "We owe it all to this city. It only seems right that they get their very own pre-tour tour."

And that's literally what they did. There were a bunch of venues in the city and I learned that Allie's best friend Savannah managed them all.

Actually, that's not true. That was my best guess.

"She's a big-wig," Aspen said one of our many evenings together. He was in the kitchen making blueberry sourdough bagels he'd started to prepare earlier in the week and I was sitting at the island counter chopping up strawberries for the homemade jam he was going to make with them.

I saw a video online of this lady who had made her own bagels, all I said was 'yum'. I may have groaned it gutturally, sure, but it was still only a single word. Next thing I knew, I arrived at his penthouse thinking he'd still be with the band to find him shirtless in the kitchen wearing one of his many random aprons, this one said '*Check Out My Bakers Dozen*', with flour on his nose.

"Ap, that doesn't actually tell me anything." I rolled my eyes, putting all the strawberries I'd already chopped into a bowl and getting more.

"Yes it does, sweet Poppy. It means she's a *big*-wig."

"Okay, but what are you saying? Am I meant to take it literally? Like, she has big hair?"

"I guess you could, but that's not what I mean in this instance."

"What's her job title?"

"B-"

"If you say 'big-wig', so help me I'll spank you with a spatula."

He gave me the goofiest eyebrow raise, "Hey now, don't threaten me with a good time."

I did my very best at following through on my threat. It resulted in flour on almost every part of my body and the vigorous christening of his kitchen floor.

The paparazzi were still outside my work, but they pretty much just left me alone except for a picture here and there. No one had followed me home from what I knew and I hadn't seen any photos of my house online. I knew I probably had Jane to thank for whatever she had managed to do. And I would thank her profusely if I ever go to meet her.

Sometimes I'd get to Aspen's place and he wouldn't be there. It never really bothered me though and it never felt weird to be there without him. Walking into Ap's apartment was like being surrounded by the very essence of him. On those nights, I would cook something or order in enough for him to eat if he was hungry when he got back, shower and then read on his couch. Sometimes I'd fall asleep there and wake up to the gentle rhythm of his fingers combing through my hair, and sometimes I'd make it to his bed and be woken up by his lips on me. My throat. My stomach. Between my legs.

Then there were the nights when we were at my place. He'd come over early enough for us to have an evening together and we fell into that version of our routine.

In one of the posts that went up on Nat's instagram about her new bedazzled tank, Aspen's elbow was in it and that post now had over two thousand comments requesting (demanding) a face reveal of me and 'the guy with the hot elbow'.

"You do have hot elbows," I said, scrolling through the comments while Ap rested his chin on my shoulder.

"Mm." I felt the rumble of his chest against my back and it made my entire body shiver. "Your compliments are so erotic, love."

We'd ended up christening the floor of *my* kitchen that evening.

It was the end of the week now and I was exhausted. Todd now left me alone at work, but he stared at me unblinkingly whenever we crossed paths in the office. I won't admit it to anyone else, but at the start of the week when he stared for way too long I flipped him off.

I didn't say a word, just held up both my middle fingers in what felt like the most impressive power move I'd ever made and got into the elevator. The doors closed before he gathered himself enough to try and get in with me.

I wanted to wait up for Aspen, but the week had caught up with me and my eyes were sealed shut with the heaviness of sleep before I even registered my head hitting the pillow. I was cocooned in his bed when I came to from the mattress dipping behind me. It only felt like it had been minutes, but the digital clock next to his bed read 2 AM.

"I didn't mean to wake you up," he whispered, smelling like minty toothpaste and his woodsy body wash. His body was still hot from his shower when he pulled me against him and kissed the very back of my neck.

My sigh was a tangible thing.

"I've decided I'm taking you out on a date, Poppy." He sounded so awake and resolved, like he'd been thinking this for a while. I turned in his arms to face him, stealing a kiss before I spoke.

"What about Fiesta Night?" My sleepy mumbles against his chest were barely coherent.

"That will come after. I'm warming you up first."

"People will see you." I tucked myself in closer to him and he wrapped his arms around me, settling his chin on the top of my head.

"I have a plan, don't worry."

"Alright," I said around a yawn. I wondered if maybe he'd gotten us a table at that restaurant *Clover* his sister-in-law mentioned to him a few times. I'd heard only the best things about it but it was fine dining and I'd never done fine dining a day in my life. The idea that I might not know the right spoon to use gave me a little heartburn and I tried to make a mental note to watch a YouTube video on how to eat at a fine dining restaurant.

"So, that's a yes?" Aspen's question roused me awake again. I was pretty sure I had started to dream about spoons.

"That's a yes." I placed a kiss to the base of his throat. He might have said something else, but I'd already fallen back into a dreamless sleep where there were no spoons at all, only the smell of freshly cooked bagels and jam and violets.

27

March 3rd

I opened the door to Aspen already striding in. He was the epitome of a man on a mission and he was also wearing…overalls?

Linen overalls. They looked like a bigger version of a pair I'd seen Jess wear.

"Aspen, what –"

"It will all make sense." He waved away my confused concern with a flourishing hand before he tacked on a reassuring, "And I'm wearing two sets of thermals."

He turned on his heels to face me from the middle of my kitchen, "There are a couple things we need to do first." He walked up to me and, contradictory to his firm strides, he held my face gently between his hands and kissed me, "Hey."

I wrapped my arms around him and just as I was going to say hey back, to complete the circle of our usual greeting, my hand came across…drumsticks?

"Um," I pulled back and took them with me, holding them out between us. "Can't separate the man from his craft, huh?"

"I know you're being silly, sweet Poppy, but no. You cannot. I realized I didn't have any here. Can I, uh, put them near Nat? Just in case."

"You want to leave a pair of drumsticks here?" I was trying not to swallow my own tongue.

He gave me a double take, "I mean, yeah? But not if you don't–"

"No, I— Yes, of course." I set them right next to Nat's tank and took a photo of the pair together.

"I'm thinking the caption for this one will be *'Dad's going to teach me how to play the drums'.*" I was too busy laughing to myself while I typed it out that I didn't register right away that Aspen hadn't laughed too.

He just looked dazed and I couldn't figure out if I'd said something right or wrong.

"Sorry, that was a bad joke." I started to delete the words, but then Aspen was there, taking my phone.

"No, I just…what about a family photo?" I saw his throat move as he swallowed.

"You want to post a photo of me, you and Nat on her Instagram?"

"That would be correct."

"But they've never seen my face before. They don't even know my name. They'd see *your* face."

Was I excited or horrified by his suggestion? Maybe both. Excited for sure on the whole 'family photo' suggestion. And horrified because that was over two hundred and fifty thousand people seeing my face.

"First time for everything." Aspen could see the horror on my face and I knew this just amused him to no end.

"There are people in the world that think I'm your cousin, though."

"Oh, well that's easily rectified." Aspen pulled out his phone, held it out in front of us and looked down at me. It all happened so fast because one second he was looking down at me like he'd won something important then he was kissing me until my knees began to wobble.

"Done!"

"What?" I was still trying to remember my own name.

He just held his phone out to me.

It was a photo of him grinning down at me and me with a small smile looking back up at him, one I didn't even realize I'd been wearing. He swiped over to the second photo and my breath caught in my throat. He was kissing me. And yes, I'd experienced it in real life, but it was a whole other thing to see it in photographic evidence.

We looked good together.

The thought was small and fleeting and completely overshadowed when I noticed the caption.

"Aspen!" I grabbed his phone, pulling it closer to my face until the words were blurry like somehow that would make any difference.

He'd written, '*Managed to get @queen.nat.the.first's mom to eat my bagels. What a woman. #definitelynotmycousin #ihavenocousins #poompaloompa #sweetpoppy*'.

"You didn't," I gasped in mock outrage. It was just for show, to see that twinkle in his eye that flickered anytime he did anything mischievous. I was actually trying very hard not to laugh, to maintain my serious disposition.

"Oh, yes I did." He grinned, pulling me back into him. "Now, about that date."

We did not, in fact, do to *Clover.*

"Aspen, you cannot be serious about this," I whisper shouted while I walk-ran next to him, trying to keep up with his long strides. He held one of my hands and the other was trying desperately to keep the bright purple wig with a bob cut from flying off my head.

"I am absolutely serious." He walked with the confidence of a man who's wig was staying where it was supposed to. He'd explained his date idea to me in detail. I, of course, decided to humor him. Fully expecting the towel to be thrown in once he got a look at me in his chosen getup.

I was wearing the aforementioned purple wig paired with an oversized sweater that had in extremely large font across the front, 'my grandmother knitted this' and a pair of those jean-leggings in a light acid wash color paired with my black boots. It was all topped off with a pair of thick, black rimmed glasses that reminded me of Jess.

Aspen…well, he was another story entirely. He was wearing the aforementioned linen overalls. He'd paired them with his regular black boots but added a jacket that someone had clearly painted on the back of saying 'honk if you're horny'.

"Where did you even find these clothes?!" I was still whisper-yelling while intermittently laughing every time a car drove past us and honked.

"The thrift store near my apartment." His voice was so full of pride I knew I'd never be able to get rid of a single thing I was wearing. Ever.

The best part of this entire date-mission was his face. Aspen was wearing a blond wig styled into a long, curly mullet, with big aviator sunglasses and a handlebar mustache.

He had no reservations at all when he pushed open the glass door to the ax throwing establishment called *'Let's Get Axey'* that resided in a town an hour out of Blazewood and dragged me right up to the help desk.

He turned to me and quickly threw over his shoulder, "Your name is Darla, by the way."

"What's your name?" How had we not covered this before embarking on this exercise?

"The reservation is under Cletus." He was peering at me over the top of his glasses.

I suddenly got the full body image of what it was he looked like and a laugh erupted out of my mouth, pushing past my clamped lips, making me splutter.

"You've got to be kidding me…" I clamped a hand over my mouth to try and stifle the way my body was desperate to release all the pent up laughter.

"Poppy, if you make me laugh, my mustache *will* come off," he spoke quickly before turning back to the receptionist guy who looked about fourteen and frightened for his life.

"We've got a reservation under Cletus." Aspen delivered it with a southern drawl that had also not been in any of his verbal briefing notes.

I gave up and pressed my face into the back of his musty, thrift store pervy jacket, the laughter wracking my body in silent tremors.

"Last name, sir?" The kid's voice trembled as his eyes darted from us to the computer, unsure where he should be actively looking.

"You mean there's more than one Cletus with a reservation here today?" Aspen dropped his accent entirely and the same noise from the other night that he'd referred to as a 'yodeling donkey' launched out of me and assaulted the air. That's all it took for Aspen to break character. He clutched the edge of the reception desk in a white knuckled grip while he tried to keep it together.

We eventually let the poor boy know that there was no last name on our booking, and he showed us to our ax throwing cage. The longer he was with us, the more troubled his face became. It wasn't until he'd left after explaining to us what we were supposed to be doing with the *rubber* axes and how they lodged into the special bullseye made out of rubber pegs did Ap and I actually turn to face one another.

That was when I realized that Aspen's handlebar mustache was hanging half off his face.

My face hurt from smiling and my arm hurt from throwing but I'd never laughed so much in my life. It had been both the best and most challenging experience. The best because Aspen turned it into a game of who could do the most bizarre leadup to their throw, and the most challenging because none of my axes lodged into the bullseye and stayed there.

And no one noticed him. Not a single person.

Sure, lots of people looked our way, but no one said a single thing. Not even the older couple who we asked to take a few photos of us, one of which was now the background of my phone; Aspen sticking his tongue out at the camera and me, looking up at him like I was determined to remember him just like that with my own two eyes.

We'd stopped for ice cream and decided to walk a little though it was still freezing outside, even at the start of March. It was also a very poor choice of food for maintaining our body heat but I wasn't complaining, and neither was he.

Aspen's hand around mine was anchoring. An anchor to the moment we were in, to everything I had felt through the entire day we'd spent together. I'd been staring at our joined hands when he stopped abruptly and turned to face me. His brows were furrowed and his eyes were focused on my mouth like maybe I'd be able to say whatever it was he was thinking for him.

"You're my best friend, Poppy." It was like he'd weighed each word for its importance before he spoke it out loud and then he finally looked up at me. His eyes flickering through different shades of green, all reflecting off the trees that surrounded us.

That's when it hit me.

Right then and there like a bolt of lightning striking me directly in the chest. Like an obscure fact that you just *knew*, without remembering when you'd absorbed the information. It was like I'd never known anything as completely as I did just then.

I didn't know how people didn't *know*. How you could look at someone and not immediately feel that overwhelming, earth shattering, breathtaking shift to the very foundations of who you were and not know that it was love. And I loved him. *God,* did I love him.

"You're mine too," I said, feeling the truth of it in every part of my body. "This was the best day, Ap."

"Not bad for a real first date, huh?" He leaned in to kiss me, forever imprinting the memory of today to the flavor of his mint choc-chip ice cream.

I shook my head, kissing him back, "Not bad at all."

28

March 8th

"This was the absolute wrong thing to bring." Poppy looked from the tray of carrots and hummus in her hands up to me with horror on her face. "How did you let me bring this?"

"Poppy, trust me, they will love it." I knew she could see the amusement in my eyes. She'd talked about how her boss, Winny, always gave people hummus and carrot sticks as a snack in high stress meetings and it was weird but sort of nice. For some reason, that inspired her to do the same.

"You're laughing at me." She pointed between my eyes.

"I'm not." I shook my head.

"You are, I can see it. That's it, Aspen, we need to –" and it was that exact moment that the front door opened.

Allie greeted us with a mildly insane look on her face that I assumed was meant to be not at all threatening and probably warm and welcoming.

I shot her a look of my own that I hoped said '*What's wrong with your face? Please, for the love of God, fix it*'. She rolled her eyes and stepped back to let us into her house. Dax was right behind her, an arm sliding into place like a band across her chest. Mainly (I was certain) to stop her from pouncing on Poppy.

It didn't work.

Allie gripped Poppy by the shoulders and pulled her into a squeezing hug. I managed to grab the tray of food from between them and my heart started thudding at double time as I watched her slowly wrap her hands around Allie. Tentative and unsure and first, and then she really hugged her back.

"It's so, so nice to have you here, Poppy," Allie said, pulling back and looking over her shoulder to my brother who nodded his agreement.

"We've heard a *lot* about you," he said, and Poppy's face went white.

"*Wyatt!*" Allie hissed at her husband.

"Okay, that was a lie. Aspen has been annoyingly tight-lipped about your existence and so, please prepare for what will likely be a very inquisitive evening." He grinned at her before giving her a hug of his own.

"I can handle inquisitiveness," Poppy said with a lift of her eyebrows before turning back to Allie. "Thank you for having me. I brought carrot sticks and hummus. I have no other excuse except that I've been super nervous for Fun Friday Family Fiesta night that I blacked out when deciding on my contribution."

"Sweet *maple bacon*!" Allie's face lit up. "It sounds even better when someone else says it!" She looked at my brother, "See! I told you it would catch on."

He just rolled his eyes and led Allie back down the hallway to the living room where the classical music was already playing. He called out over his shoulder, "Come back when you're ready!"

"I thought that was the name of the evening?" Poppy asked while taking off her coat.

"It is, but besides me, Allie and Sav are the only ones that use it. They're trying to get it to catch on so you probably just made her whole week."

"One point for Poppy then," she said, rubbing her hands together.

I couldn't help but tip my head back in shocked laughter.

"What?" She raised an eyebrow at me and I just shook my head.

"Nothing," I said, taking off my own coat and hanging it next to hers. "Just that I think you guys will get on great."

Everyone started on their best behavior and I dare say it had something to do with Savannah threatening their balls with some sort of painful repercussion. The good behavior lasted about an hour before everyone returned to their normal selves. Poppy sat right next to me in the spot that had always been empty, a glass of wine in her hand and a look on her face that said she wanted to be nowhere else but where she was.

She was talking to Rip about how she and I first met and he was in tears at the part where she asked me if it was a felony to have come up to me.

"God, I hope you said yes." He looked at me with hope in his eyes.

"I didn't say yes, you dick." I pushed him back onto the couch with a hand on his face.

Allie brought out the grazing board, Poppy's hummus and carrot sticks included, and when it was finally time for charades, the girls had the audacity to try and change the teams to girls versus boys versus boys.

"No fucking way!" I set my beer down on the table. "The one time I finally have a partner and you try to take her from me." I grabbed Poppy and pulled her closer to me.

"I'm confused," she whispered.

"Don't worry, Poompaloompa, I've got this," I whispered back.

"Did he just call her…*Poompaloompa*?" Luke whispered to Angus sounding befuddled and I did my best to ignore them both in favor of the more important matter at hand.

"No, I'm putting my foot down. Poppy and I are on the same team and everyone else stays in their couples."

"Luke and I are not a couple," Rip said, earning a somewhat hurt look from Luke.

"You may as well be," Sav mumbled and the rest of us sort of shrugged our agreement.

"Fine," Allie conceded, looking a little sad, but her puppy dog eyes would not work on me this time.

"Fix your face, Alice Smith, I'm not falling for it." I pointed right at her and she just leaned further into it.

"Oh, this is a good one," Sav said.

"Nope." I held my ground.

"You sure?" Allie asked, a final attempt, a mischievous little grin growing on her face.

"I have never been more sure of anything pertaining to Fiesta Night. Get the fresh deck out, we're going to win the shit out of this."

"Ap, what are we agreeing to?" Poppy sounded a little frightened.

"The new deck?" Luke guffawed. "We've been saving it for like a year."

"Ap's right," Allie said, her face now back to normal if not a little proud. "It's time for the new deck."

Poppy and I were winning.

We were winning...kind of.

It was down to the wire. Dax and Allie had eleven points and so did we. Sav and Angus were on eight and Luke and Rip were on three.

"You're not interpreting any of my movements properly," Luke said, sitting down in defeat after Rip guessed his attempt at a rocket ship was 'someone texting'.

"I am, you just suck," Rip said back, equally as unimpressed.

Allie was up and, in all honesty, it was a valiant effort. Dax thought she was doing hopscotch, Allie was in fact trying to portray someone walking through the house with mud on their shoes."

"Close, babe," Dax said, pulling his wife down onto his lap and kissing her on the cheek.

"This is it," Sav said, rubbing her hands together in delight. "If Ap and Poppy get this one, they win. If not, we have a draw for winners this time around."

"You ready?" I asked Poppy, who had settled into this game like a champ. Her game face was on and she hadn't shied away at all when the game was announced. She simply stated that it was something her and her brother used to do.

"Oh, does he live close?" Dax asked, not knowing any better because I hadn't said anything. Poppy's hand gripped mine a little tighter but that was all. Her voice was strong and even when she answered him. "No, no. He–Casimir died when I was sixteen."

"Oh, I'm sorry, Poppy. I didn't –"

"No, it's okay. Really." She gave him a smile that made her words feel true.

I leaned over and placed a kiss behind her ear which she leaned into. My silent support for this incredible woman.

"Wait, sorry, you said your brother's name was Casimir?" Dax had this look on his face that was a mix of shock and disbelief.

"Yeah, not super common I know." She nodded and it was something completely other to see her so at ease talking about this part of her life that had caused her pain for so long. "Penelope and Casimir. We were quite the pair." She laughed and so did my brother.

"Hey, you know what's wild?" I chimed in, "He actually owned the Taurus."

That little nugget was met with a chorus of baffled '*Woah's!*' and one very exuberant "No fucking way!" From Savannah.

"Yeah, Poppy saw something that confirmed it and I asked Jane to help pull up the old records of the car. Last person to own it before Wyatt was Casimir Hart."

"I thought the car was yours now?" Poppy asked, leaning into me.

"It is, but it's still in Wyatt's name. Never had a reason to change it."

Everyone had moved on easily from what was by default a heavy conversation but Dax got up and left the room for a bit, not coming back for a good ten minutes. When he did though, he was back to himself and I just played it off as being unprepared to learn about Poppy's loss.

Her experience in this game turned out to be invaluable. She looked at me with determination in her eyes, "Oh, I was born ready."

She got up and took the 'stage'. It was just the middle of the living room with the coffee table pushed off to the side, but it was a stage for all intents and purposes now.

Poppy picked up a card and the moment she read whatever was on the other side her face lit up like a fucking Christmas tree.

She slapped the card down on the coffee table and held up one finger to me.

"One word," I said, and she nodded.

Poppy didn't break eye contact as she tucked her arms close to her sides, stuck her hands out and started fluttering them like her life depended on it while jumping up and down in a squiggly sort of way. She looked like…like…

I stood up and pointed right at her, "NATALIE!"

She nodded with a big grin on her face and did the motion that told me to keep going, but that I was on the right track.

"MATING CALL!" I was yelling. I was yelling so loud but I couldn't help it.

"How the fuck is he getting that from–" Angus started.

"*Shut up*!" Savannah hissed at her boyfriend.

Poppy made the same motion to keep going and I knew it with certainty. "GOLDFISH!"

"YES!" She yelled back. Laughing with her head tipped back before jumping into my arms and wrapping her legs around my waist.

"That was the weirdest thing I have ever witnessed," Rip said, staring at us like we'd lost our minds.

And maybe we had, I didn't really care. I just knew without a shadow of a doubt that I was madly in love with Penelope Elizabeth Hart and there wasn't a damn thing I could do about it.

29

March 10th

Poppy

Waking up on Saturday was like being dipped in honey.

The warmth of Aspen's body wrapped around mine kept pulling me back under and I could only assume the same for him. Every time I swam to the surface of our honey pool of sleep and into consciousness he was breathing evenly. Mouth slightly lax and face absent of any traces of worry.

He was so completely peaceful.

On one of our many nights together at his place, when we'd both been half pulled into the fog of sleep, he mumbled that he now finally 'got' the allure of sleep.

"What do you mean?" His question had woken me up enough to be determined to get my answer.

"It was too loud in here," he lifted up one of his strong, broad hands and pointed right at his temple. "I hated it. Every time I closed my eyes it was a constant stream of; did I do enough today for the band? Or, did I miss any calls? Or, was I everything everyone needed?"

"But it's not like that anymore." My response was a statement because I knew it was true. I could see it with my own eyes.

"No." He opened his eyes and looked right at me.

I was completely captivated by his bright green eyes. With no trees around us for them to reflect in their color I could see them clearly. They had a dark ring of green on the edges that got lighter the closer the color got to his pupils and they were nothing less than absolutely beautiful.

He kissed me before speaking again, "No, it's not like that anymore."

We spent the day in bed, some of it quietly memorizing one another's bodies. Some of it *loudly* memorizing one another's bodies and all of it with this inescapable happiness that moved through every moment. Like a vein right from the heart. Happiness was an undeniable part of what was between us. It was this thing we were both acutely aware of and instead of tiptoeing around it, we dove straight in. Covered ourselves with it completely. Reminded one another of it consistently in touches and looks and laughter.

That was how every day with him had been since we'd met. Bright and full of color. Like moving into the sunshine and, little by little, removing the layers of clothing you'd put on to keep away the cold. Feeling your fingers tingle as they started to defrost.

It was uncomfortable at first. I had wanted to pull away from the burn, from the unfamiliar sensation, but now the thought of eventually having to put my layers back on and go inside was almost too much to bear.

It was now Sunday night and Aspen drove us back to my house. We both shuffled in out of the cold, both yelling out greetings to Natalie.

I jumped into the shower and Ap made us a couple of teas. I was drying off and getting dressed, listening to how he was playing out a drum beat with the sticks he'd left here on the kitchen counter while he waited for the tea to steep.

We passed each other on the stairs with a kiss while he went up to shower and I got out some cookies for us to share.

Without even realizing it we had started to live life *together.*

There were so many routines that had just formed. Naturally and all on their own. It made my heart pang while I sat at the kitchen counter and waited for Aspen to come back down stairs.

He pressed a kiss to my temple just as he took his seat beside me.

One of the best things about Aspen was the silence we could sit in together. It was this comfortable safety blanket.

The same night he told me his secret about sleep, he'd also shared that he had never been a fan of the quiet, but when we were together he could stay in it forever. That had felt pivotal to me. Another secret he had let me in on, just like I continued to let him in on mine whenever one made itself known.

I wish that we would have had enough time for me to share them all with him.

"You know," I said quietly while we sat with Nat and drank our tea. I could feel him looking at me but kept my eyes on the bubbles from the water filter in the fish tank as I spoke. "Sometimes I'll let myself imagine what it would be like to have you forever."

I reached for a cookie as something to do but just held it in my hand and kept talking. "I imagine game nights with your friends and family, but maybe Leah is there too sometimes and she screams every time she sees everyone. Maybe Jess too. I picture my clothes next to yours in your closet and a bigger tank for Natalie. Going to that Mexican place near your house so often they know our names and all the different people we would become on all the different dates we would go on."

Aspen reached across to tuck some hair behind my ear, "We can have all of those things." He sounded so sure. So certain it broke my heart a little bit.

"I don't see how." I put the cookie down, my sweet tooth gone.

"Those are the things our lives would be full of anyway, my love."

I looked at him then, my heart aching with every beat, "Aspen, come on. That's not funny."

He just frowned at me, "Why can't we?" We were standing on two opposite ends of a river and both just waiting for the other to jump in and swim to their side.

"Aspen, I'm—" I frowned back. "I'm leaving? April fifth, I told you when we met."

"When we met, sure, but things have changed since then." His frown was made up of all the things that I knew would break my heart.

I'd already begun to hurt him and it killed me.

He was right and wrong. Not just 'things' but *everything.* Absolutely everything had changed and now it was all careening around my head without any order or sense. That door to the part of my mind I had closed off had been ripped off its hinges the night we exchanged secrets in the dark quiet of my room. I had meant everything I'd said to him, meant everything I'd felt but it had never crossed my mind that I would stay.

Never crossed my mind because the possibility of it wasn't something I could conceptualize. This version of myself I was with Aspen was not the real version. Who didn't hide the darkest parts of herself from the world, who let her sadness coexist with her happiness.

This person who'd been forgiven for everything that she'd done. Who'd forgiven herself.

No, none of that was real, and I didn't see how it ever could be when the only person who could fix it all, who'd always fixed it all, had been gone for almost as long as I'd had him.

I knew that no matter how much I loved Aspen, I would still hurt him and it was better to control when it happened than to have no say in it at all. It was the only way I could manage the damage inflicted.

"Aspen," I said it again more firmly, refusing to think about what I was about to do in more detail than the surface level. More than the simple truth I'd always known; I was leaving. He *knew* I was leaving. *He knew I was leaving.*

I said the words I knew would hurt him and refused to acknowledge the way my voice shook. "I'm leaving. I was never going to stay. I…I thought you understood that. Right from the beginning. *Aspen,*" my voice hitched, now barely more than a whisper. "I was honest with you right from the start. I was never going to stay."

The words were bitter. They tasted foul on my tongue as I took that version of myself I'd been with Ap and led her back into me. Right into that room in my mind where she stood and watched while I fixed the hinges of the door that he'd helped me blow right off. The moment it was sealed shut I could feel that part of me banging on the other side. Scraping and scratching at that door, her throat being ripped apart by pleas not to do this. That version of myself who had only started to get her color back. Skin golden from the sun that was Aspen, fingers warm and tingly from being in his orbit.

I knew once the memory of it all faded, when the color from her skin paled with each passing day and the feeling in her hands dissipated that it would be easier to look back on the decisions I'd made and feel fondness instead of devastating loss.

Ap looked like he'd been winded, but I also knew that Aspen Smith had been putting the people he loved before himself for as long as he could remember. I was sure there was a special place in hell for people like me. Who knew the secrets of the people they loved and used them *against,* instead of *for*.

So, I knew that there would be no other option for him but to nod his head. To tell me that he understood and that it was okay.

That night when we went to bed and Aspen hovered above me before sliding into me, slowly, deeply, I didn't think about the ways that it was different than before. How every touch of his lingered longer than normal, just like mine. How he held me tighter, closer. Watched the way our bodies met with fierce determination, like he was making sure he'd never forget it.

He held me close and only when I felt his breathing even out did I let myself cry and hold him tighter, knowing with world fracturing certainty that we had just said goodbye to one another.

It had been the only right way forward, and I knew It had to be right because it was painful.

In the moments of my life when I had been sure nothing could be worse than it was. When I was positive there was no room left to hurt the people I loved, the thing I remember most was unfathomable pain.

It was physical at the time, in part. But I'd learned the day I turned sixteen that pain manifested itself in many different ways, and the worst of which was the way no one could see. Lacerations on your soul, your mind.

Your heart.

It had been selfish of me to give into Ap, but it was always going to be okay because it was never meant to be forever. That's why this momentary happiness, this joy and freedom, had been okay. But when I felt like that, it meant there was a very long way to fall and I always seemed to soften my own landing with the people closest to me. Leaving them to take the brunt of the fall.

If I kept on moving then I'd never be in one place long enough to make a mark. You might know I'd been there but like everything, with time, the traces of me would fade away and it would have been like I'd never been there at all.

So, I told myself I needed to go. To keep moving because I was looking for something important and refused to admit that maybe what I'd been looking for, I'd already found.

30

March 11th

Ap:
You wanna come over tonight?

Poppy:
Hey, I don't think I can make it.

Poppy:
Rain check? x

Ap:
Okay, rain check x

31

March 14th

Aspen

"Aspen?" Dax came into focus right in front of me.

I'd been looking at him the whole time but I hadn't been in the room. Hadn't really been there with the band working through one of our many remaining rehearsals.

"Sorry," I said, taking my hat off and running my hand through my hair before putting it back and rubbing my eyes. "Sorry."

"You said that already, but I'm not sure what I'm supposed to be accepting your apology over?"

"Probably for having his head in a sex crazed cloud instead of in the rehearsal like he's supposed to be," Rip contributed unhelpfully with a stupidly happy expression on his face and a wag of his eyebrows.

I pointed at him with a lackluster expression on my face, "Stop thinking about my dick."

Rip's expression dropped and he lifted his hands before dropping them in defeat.

We'd been here all day but only started to actually play in the last hour or so. Up

until then we'd mostly been finalizing our discussion from the last session where we'd decided to scrap the original set list and start again. Though we'd been rehearsing for the *Salvation Tour* since February it didn't mean as much now that we'd shifted our approach.

The way we played our live shows had always been with the same goal: be able to give our fans the experience of listening to our recorded album live, yes, but also to make it a whole new experience.

It was exactly what I needed to pour myself into because if I didn't, I would focus on how I was watching as Poppy pulled away from me day after day. I would focus on how she had gone from being someone who I'd had all of and face the reality that that was changing.

And I had.

I had every single part of her and it had been the single best thing I'd ever experienced. Being trusted by someone like that? Being *loved* by someone like that?

She hadn't said the words to me but I didn't need to hear them. She didn't need to hear them either to know I felt the same. I felt it in the way she looked at me when she thought I wouldn't notice. The way her head tilted to the side when she was listening to what I was saying, absorbing every single word like each one spoken was a revelation. A secret of the universe that she wanted to covet.

I knew she loved me in the way she fit herself into my side, as close as possible while we were watching an episode of *Friends* on her couch, in the photos on my phone that I began collecting. Of her sitting at my kitchen island helping me bake, of her on the balcony of my apartment, hands on the railings and face raised towards the sun. Her, rumpled from sleep wearing one of my shirts and messy bun hanging off to the side with a small but mischievous look on her face and the photo after of her that very next moment, running straight for me, her smile big and her eyes bright.

It was in every single photo that told the story of us. This story that had only just fucking started and somehow I'd convinced myself would never end.

"Aspen?" Dax called my name again. He hadn't moved from where he was in front of me, and I'd been looking through him again.

"Sorry, just tired." I waved him off and all he did was frown deeper. It wasn't a lie, I was tired. I hadn't been sleeping and after getting used to the longer hours of rest with Poppy beside me, the soft and gentle curves of her beneath my hands, my return to my previous way of living had been…well, it had been fucked.

"Maybe we should call it —" he started but I cut him off.

"No. *No*." My voice was louder than intended, catching the attention of the other guys, but calling it early meant going home. To my apartment that had learned what it was like to host a life better than the one I'd been living and now in the absence of it I found myself completely unwilling to face that reality. "Let's keep going."

Dax stared at me for a while longer and only after putting every single ounce of energy I had into convincing him through the expression on my face did he nod. The moment he turned away, I dropped my smile, picked up my drum sticks and fell into the comfort of putting them to use.

That's how it went on.

Day after day.

Night after night.

I would wake up and head straight for my drum kit. If it was a day that something else was on for the band like doing stuff with our label, or meeting with our tour manager, or flying across the country to do more press, or approving designs for the new tour merch, then I did that instead. But, I always came home to sit right behind my drum kit.

I couldn't remember when I'd practiced this much. Maybe when I was first learning. I knew I had been borderline obsessive before but I knew I was particularly bad when I woke up with blisters on my hands. It was tough to keep playing like that, tougher than the time I'd dislocated two of my fingers on tour a couple years ago when Angus and I were throwing a ball back and forth during the day before a show. I had been distressed to the point of throwing up at the idea of not being able to play the show that night, of letting down the fans and the band.

I'd asked the doctor to wrap them in a way so that I could still play. He'd advised against it of course and it took twice as long for them to return to normal, but I'd done it.

I'd put everyone else first, just like I always did.

I'd tried being selfish, putting what I wanted first. Chasing after it with both hands but it hadn't done me any real good in the end.

I put the people I loved before myself and that's why instead of picking up my phone to call Poppy, I picked up my drumsticks and started to play again.

32

March 17th

Me:
Poppy?

Poppy:
Yeah?

Me:
I miss you.

Poppy:
I miss you too.

33

March 18th

The new routine I'd settled into was like a familiar balm on an open wound. We rearranged the set list *again* and added another date to what we'd dubbed the '*Salvation Pre-Tour Tour: City of Blazewood*'. It had sold out in minutes.

We were now doing four nights, all of them had a day in between and the first date was April fifth.

That felt painfully poetic to me.

I'd decided somewhere in the last week – fuck me, *longer* than a week – that I hadn't seen Poppy that this old version of myself felt about as good as the sleep routine I'd reverted back to.

It didn't *fit* anymore. It was like wearing clothes that were too tight. I couldn't breathe right in them. This ghost of mine I'd let go of and forced back to my side looked at me with pity. With a very obvious sense of displeasure at being chained back to me the same way I'd chained myself back to it. So, I turned off my phone.

I turned off my fucking phone.

I would have thrown the thing right off the balcony if I hadn't actually needed it for whenever I needed to call someone. Mainly the pizza joint across the street for delivery.

I turned off my phone and I didn't go to Fiesta Night.

What was the point? Actually, that's not true. Or fair. I loved Fiesta Night, but I hadn't wanted to walk in and carry the weight of all the people I loved until I buckled beneath it all. I hadn't wanted to sit down and stare at the spot Poppy had once been. I knew they would worry and that was never my intention, so I had turned my phone on to let Dax know I wasn't going and then I turned it back off.

My brother was a smart man, who'd married an even smarter woman who was best friends with an equally smart woman and the rest of them would catch on eventually. I knew that they'd figure out something had happened with Poppy. I'm sure they'd be confused and wouldn't be able to understand *why*.

Why?

I hadn't had the mental capacity to try and explain it to them, at least I let myself put it off until tomorrow.

There was only one real explanation for the 'why' that they'd ask, and it started long before I started losing Poppy.

I'd just wiped the sweat from my eyes when I heard the knock at my door. I couldn't tell you if that was the first time they'd knocked or the twentieth. My heart immediately started hammering because there were only a small number of people it could have been and I'd immediately let myself hope for one in particular.

I opened the door drenched in sweat, still holding my drumsticks and came face to face with my brother.

"Dax?" I stepped back and let him in.

He was on his own which was the first indication that something was amiss. Where he went, Allie went and vice versa (unless you count Allie and Savannah's weekly wine and Italian night which was strictly no boys allowed - I'd tried).

I turned to find him standing in my living room, one hand rubbing the back of his neck the other clutching something.

An envelope.

"What's up?" I stepped closer to him on instinct. Immediately wanting to help him, to make sure he was okay. Not because of some fucked up idea that by doing that I'd make up for not being there for someone when I should have been. For being unable to pull myself out of the pit of loneliness I'd fallen into, but because he was my brother and I loved him.

He held the hand out to me that was clutching the envelope. Now that I could see it clearly, it had a business logo on the top left that I'd never seen before and the paper had yellowed with time. Black marks dotted the sides like someone had gripped it with hands covered in grease.

It wasn't those things that all but stopped my heart.

My drumsticks clattered to the tiled floor beneath me.

No, it was none of those things. Rather it was the writing on the front. Written in neat, clear letters.

Penelope,
Happy 16th Birthday.
Love, Casimir

34

March 20th

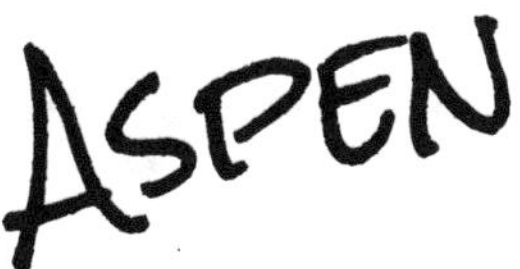

Me:
Poppy?

35

March 24th

I realized it had nothing to do with putting Poppy first that stopped me from driving to her house. From banging on her front door and telling her no.

No, I don't *accept* that you have to leave.

I accept it a whole fucking zero percent because I know for a fact that everything you need is here. With me. I knew it in every bone in my body. In every thought in my head. Knew it as confidently as I knew the drum pattern for a new song we'd only begun to write.

It just *was*.

I didn't go to her because no matter how much I wanted her to stay, no matter how much I wanted to keep her with me, it would mean nothing if she didn't want to stay for herself too.

I knew she was it for me. Knew it the first time I saw her, probably. I knew now too that it had nothing to do with letting go of my own ghosts.

Poppy had to come back to me all on her own.

I *needed* her to come back to me all on her own, otherwise there would always be a part of her wishing she'd kept on running.

36

March 30th

I had been ignoring all the calls from Leah to the best of my ability. I had successfully managed to not talk to my best friend for a total of twenty days.

That's two followed by a zero, and in doing so I'd broken one of my three golden rules. There was a list, a really fucking *long* list, of rules that lived under the 'Poppy's Life Rules' title, but speaking to Leah no less than three times a week had been one I'd never broken.

My phone was ringing in my hand and I was terrified to pick it up. It was 6 AM and I was sitting on the floor of my bedroom, slowly packing up my stuff in boxes and making detailed notes on the sides of all of them. I picked up the call.

Leah's face came into view. As usual, she was so close to the camera I mainly just saw her nose. It occurred to me that for a millennial she had really no idea how to use a phone.

"Sissy?! What," she screamed and it made me jump, "the *actual* flaming motherfucking *fuck* is wrong with you?!"

I deserved that.

"Do you have *any* idea how worried I've been? What the hell is wrong with you, Penelope?"

I deserved that too.

"You think that just because you found this perfect man, with that perfect face and brain and heart and ass that you can suddenly forget about your *best fucking friend?"*

And that's when I started crying.

I hadn't cried since I was sixteen. Right up until Aspen, and now? Well it was like my tear ducts woke up from the world's longest hibernation and were working overtime in a real big F U to the layer of dust they no doubt had to make their way through to start operating correctly.

"Wh— I—" Leah's whole face came into view when she pulled back the phone and looked at me like I was an alien. Looked at me like the world was ending and all she had to hold it together was craft glue and painters tape.

"I didn't mean it!" she yelled. And now she was crying. Big, huge tears that tracked her mascara down her face. "I didn't mean it, but you fell off the face of the earth and I thought you had *died,* Penelope. You scared me really fucking bad." Her voice got higher and higher as she spoke and it wasn't funny but a little bubble of laughter mixed in between my sobs sputtered out of me.

"I need you." It was all I managed to get out.

The moment the words hit Leah's ears she stopped crying. Just...*stopped,* just like that. Wiped her face and gave me one, solid nod. That one movement flipped a switch in my brain, catapulting me back to a different time in my life. A time when I was younger, made of glass with fissures running through every part of me. My arm was looped into the arm of a sixteen year old Leah's. She was talking a million miles an hour about something I couldn't recall, but I did remember the way she held onto me tightly as she had started to do. Clutching me to her like maybe she was scared something might snatch me away right there in broad daylight.

We had been in the sun but I hadn't felt its warmth, I'd merely wondered how it could still shine when my whole entire world had been ripped apart. No single part of it remaining whole.

Except for Leah.

I remember her looking over at me, her sentence stopping halfway through its existence. I was looking right at her and watched her face change. Like this mask slid into place and then she nodded at me. Just once.

Just one solemn nod and I could see it now for what it was. It was this silent acknowledgment that she'd made for the both of us that she'd carry my weight right along with her own until I could learn to bear it myself again.

And it had been *heavy*. It had been so heavy it was crushing me beneath it and I hadn't realized then like I realized right now that yes, I lost my brother, but Leah had lost her best friend.

That I changed in order to figure out what navigating life was without Casimir, but she had changed too. She'd had to learn how to navigate life with enough will to live not for just one soul, but for two.

Leah had had other friends besides me, but day after day, night after night, she'd been *right there*.

That was all I thought about while I waited through all the hours of the day. Until evening came and my doorbell rang and I flung myself into the arms of my best friend and told her truthfully, *honestly*, for the first time in my life the very thing I should have said at sixteen.

"Thank you."

Leah and I lay on my couch, my feet near her head and her head near my feet. It was the same way we'd always settled into any couch, made infinitely better by the way we rubbed each other's feet.

I told her everything.

It had been frighteningly difficult to push past this bizarre notion that I'd somehow managed to shield this woman from the most fragile and broken parts of myself for the last twelve years when in reality she'd been there, woven basket in hand picking up the shards as they dropped. Pieces of myself I had disregarded and deemed to have no value while she picked them up, held it up to the light and thought *'yes, you'll do just fine'*.

"I love him," I told her, feeling the pressure behind my eyes increase again. "I love him and I'm terrified I'll hurt him."

"Do you think it's fair to make this decision for the both of you?" she asked plainly.

"No," I said honestly, "but I've done it anyway."

"You'll regret it, Poppy." Her words were sad and resigned, like she knew even as she tried that I couldn't be swayed in this.

"I know." She'd find no argument from me.

"You'll live the rest of your life regretting it," she said.

"I know," I said. "But I already know how to live like that."

Leah sat up, legs tucked to her chest where she sat on the other end of the couch, me on the other side, her mirror image.

It was dark outside but the room around us was bright, and I owed it to her to share this secret where there was nowhere for it to hide. "I'll never forgive myself, Leah. I can't." I shook my head. "I don't know *how*. I tried. I've tried. With Aspen, *I tried.*" I swiped at the tears furiously as they fell, sick of their constant presence. "I'll never be able to forgive myself," I repeated, knowing with my whole heart that was the real reason. I couldn't forgive my sixteen year old self, for how I'd failed the one person who had never failed me. I'd never be able to love Aspen like he deserved. There would always be this shadow, this dark cloud that would follow us and eventually, it would completely overtake every bit of sunshine that he was made of.

"You're punishing him too, you know." Her words hit a pain point, one I'd thought of and conveniently ignored.

"Maybe, for now," I nodded, "But with time, he'll forget me."

"I think you underestimate how much that man loves you."

We were at an impasse. I think I might've underestimated how much he loved me too, but it didn't change the truth of it all.

She stared at me and I stared at her and then there was that nod again, the one that I'd always thought meant 'I don't know what to say. I don't know how to help you.' but really had always meant 'I've got you, do you hear me?

I've got you'.

"Alright. I'll get the wine, you call Jess." Leah was up and in the kitchen between one blink and the next, just like that. Shifting gears like she always had.

I picked up my phone, my heart panging as I scrolled past Aspen where he sat right at the very top and tapped Jess's name.

"Poppy?"

"Aspen and I broke up and Leah is here and would you like to come over?" The words tripped on one another as they all but fell out of my mouth.

"I'm malfunctioning. I have the boys, Poppy –"

"Leah, she's got the boys!" I called out to her in the kitchen.

"Then we're going over there!" Leah called back.

"We're coming over, see you in twenty?" I asked.

"I'll make a cheese board."

37

April 3rd

Poppy

Winny had tried to organize a surprise farewell for me and it all panned out in a way that seemed almost fitting to the way that I felt.

I'd managed to walk into the staff kitchen (the same one Todd had tainted with his overbearing cologne) just in time for Jess and Winny to sing "Surprise!" and then to see one of the brown colored balloons unstick from the wall and slowly flutter to the floor.

"This is..." I was smiling, or at least trying to smile.

"Average at best?" Jess supplied helpfully.

"Jessica!" Winny admonished from his spot beside her. What caught me off guard was the fact that instead of rolling her eyes and walking over to me, she rolled her eyes and gave the man a kiss. *Right on the mouth.*

Winny went beet red, Jess's whole face was practically twinkling in a manic sort of delight and I was gaping like a bigmouth buffalo fish.

"I've missed something crucial here." I was waving my hand between the two of them, and set my gaze right on Jess. "*Jessica?*" I quirked an eyebrow and all she did was walk over and throw her arms around me. I hugged her back without question. It was the same way she'd greeted Leah and I when we rocked up and her house.

Leah had six bottles of wine in her hands all of which she'd packed in her luggage before flying in.

Jess had hugged me, pulled back and held my face between her hands. "The boys have put together a small performance for you in hopes it might cheer you up."

With that, she sent me into the living room where Leo and Aiden were wearing pots on their heads and matching pajamas. I was still close enough to the front door to overhear what Leah said though.

"She loves you, so I do too."

"Words from my own mouth. I Ubered another four bottles of wine too, they're in the kitchen."

I turned in time to see the two women hugging and wondered if maybe we'd all been friends before, in another life.

"Also I'm a big fan of the choking bell concept," Leah was breathless in her awe, still hugging Jess tight.

"That means a lot to me, thank you." Jess replied with her face pressed against Leah's chest. Their height difference was polarizing.

Mostly, I think it was Leah and Jess who were one soul split into two because Leah needed to excuse herself halfway through the boys routine, walking pigeon legged to the lavatory screaming something about how she'd already started peeing.

Leah had to leave Sunday night but we now had a three way chat she'd called '*Sistaz*'.

Jess pulled back and looked at Winny who'd busied himself taking photos of the cheeseboard she'd had put together with copious amounts of pride.

"You didn't say a single thing on Saturday," I grumbled to her with a pout.

"It didn't feel like the right time to tell you I was in love with our boss."

"A younger man, huh?" I waggled my eyebrows at her and tried desperately to shove the sadness that sprouted at her words down deep into my body and just be happy for her. Like, deep down into my feet somewhere.

"I know," she said, looking at him again where he was still snapping photos but from a different angle. "He's a good man and he loves the boys. And I think he might love me too."

"Oh, he loves you," Winny said without an ounce of hesitation, not even moving his attention away from his phone. Jess turned back to me with a crimson blush creeping up her neck.

I lost control of my features then, unable to help the way my mind reached down into my feet and pulled up image after image of Aspen. Unable to ignore the feel of his unanswered text that was burning a hole in my heart.

"Oh, Poppy." Jess wrapped her hands around my waist, squeezed tight. When I looked up again, Winny had left the little kitchen.

"I'm so happy for you, Jess." I wrapped my hands around her and hoped she knew I meant every word.

"You really have to go?" She asked, her face pretty firmly pressed into my boobs. She hadn't asked me that question yet. Her questions and comments all through Saturday had been fiercely non-invasive and I loved her for it. All she did was nod during the moments I was steadfast in my resolve and hold my hand in the moments when that resolve had crumbled a little.

I just nodded, because I didn't want to, but it was the only thing I knew how to do.

38

April 5th

Poppy

I'd descended into this state of pure movement and no thoughts. There wasn't a single thought in my head except for just a narration of the things I was doing. A step by step monotone recount of the things I did, as I did them.

Wake up.

Shower.

Make sure Nat's travel tank was secure.

Make sure the lock on the back of the U-Haul was secure.

Force myself to eat something.

Message Leah.

Message Jess.

That's all I could do, just one thing after the other, knowing the steps because it was pure muscle memory. I'd done it all more times than I could count.

The last couple of days had been a blur. I'd finished packing up my stuff, most of the boxes I'd never unpacked at all still left me wondering what was even in them. I'd been tempted to leave everything behind. The things I would unpack when I got to my new apartment and would look at only to remember Aspen.

But I wanted to remember him. I wanted to never forget him for as long as I lived. This man who had settled into my bones, who deserved so much more than to be loved by someone like me.

So I kept everything, made sure to spend extra care keeping safe the things I knew would hurt the most to unpack and lugged everything out to the U-Haul I'd parked in my drive. My next door neighbor was a burly man I'd only ever seen twice. Once because he had accidentally gotten my mail and once because I'd accidentally gotten his. He helped me move my couch, my coffee table and my mattress.

When he asked me how I managed to get them into the house and even up the stairs in the first place I said, "It's surprising what you can achieve when you're not afraid of getting a hernia."

He'd looked at me like I'd responded in the form of interpretive dance. I decided there was no love lost there on account of the fact I'd made no effort to get to know him at all in the year I'd been there.

Have you ever woken up with that feeling of dread right in the very center of your body? Like you knew without a shadow of a doubt that something was wrong. Very, *very* wrong, and you didn't know what or why or how to fix it?

I was covered in that feeling.

It clogged my pores and coated every part of my body like invisible tar. The worst part was, I knew why. I knew *what.* I even knew what would fix it.

I sat there in the middle of my empty house and let myself think of him. Of strong hands and green eyes. Dimples and trail walk narrations. Of being able to see my whole life in one person.

I sat there, holding the hand of the version of myself I'd been with him and meant it when I whispered the words 'I'm sorry'. But there was no other way I could protect him but leave.

I stood up, swiped the tears from my cheeks and wrenched open the front door to find probably the last person I'd ever thought would be on my porch.

Wyatt Maddox Smith.

APRIL 5TH

I stood in my empty living room now, standing across from the front man of the biggest rock band in the entire world.

His black hair was shaggy and flicked off to the side. Like he'd pushed it up and back and it had just slowly fallen back down. He was dressed the way I'd always seen him dressed; a leather jacket, though this one seemed to be a little more lax on the buckles, a pair of black skinny jeans and, ah, converse. I sort of thought he always just wore those black Doc Martens with the harness across the front.

The only thing that had changed in the years the world had watched him from afar was his rings. Wyatt used to wear all these silver rings on both hands. Now, he only wore one, and it sat on his left hand.

If you're wondering if I'm cataloging everything he was wearing in order to not think about the fact that Aspen's brother was in my living room, then you'd be correct.

My heart was fucking *galloping*. "Is–" I cleared my throat, "Is he okay?"

"Mm," Wyatt hummed contemplative, sliding his hands into the pockets of his jacket. "Define 'okay'." He didn't say the words like he'd wanted them to hurt me, but they did anyway.

I was exhausted. Just so fucking tired. I walked over to the wall where my T.V. had been and slumped against it.

I hadn't really expected Wyatt to follow me, but he did. He released a weary sigh that spoke volumes. More than any words could.

"I'm sorry," I whispered to him, too tired to do more than that. "Believe it or not, I'm doing this so I *don't* hurt him."

I braved a look at Wyatt and he sat looking straight ahead, his head resting back against the wall and legs splayed out in front of him, hand still in his jacket pockets. I'd wager a bet this guy just always looked cool.

I stared a little longer than I should have, probably. But I could see a bit of Aspen in his side profile. The slope of his nose and the height of his cheekbones. I looked away quickly, wiping the tears that had escaped in their silent journey down my face quickly. But Wyatt wasn't stupid, he saw.

"My brother," his voice was deep and thoughtful and I stared straight ahead where Natalie sat on the floor near the front door and did my best to listen to each word he said, "he's always been secretive. I think that *he* thinks I'm completely unaware of his...certain way of coping with things, but I know. Maybe I didn't realize it at first, but I eventually figured it out."

He took a deep breath, pushed his hair back from his face and kept going. "I will be the first to admit I could have done more to help him. Done more that made him feel like he didn't need to keep doing things for everybody else the way he started doing.

"I don't know if he told you about Trixie –"

"He did." My voice cracked and I cleared it.

He just nodded and kept talking, "When I came home I didn't even recognise him. He'd lost so much weight and his eyes were sunken into his face. I was looking at my brother but I had no idea *who* I was looking at. I was furious at my parents for not noticing, but that wasn't fair. They had never noticed much. Good people," Wyatt said, looking at me, "just, absent."

"Ap said it was like living with two old roommates."

Wyatt huffed a laugh, "Yeah, that's pretty accurate." He pulled a hand out to rub at the back of his neck before he kept talking, "All that to say, I kept a pretty close eye on him after that. So, when he started to change, to become this version of himself I hadn't seen since we were kids, I noticed." He looked back to me for a beat and I knew what he was saying; *that's where you came in.*

"There were times I wish I'd done better. Not called him as much even though I knew he'd answer. Not asked him to go and do something just so I knew he was getting out of the house. Put him up for press events just to get him out of his routine. I even pulled him into doing this half marathon with me one time even though he hates running. Even though *I* hate running." I couldn't help but smile at that. Mainly thinking about how Aspen would throw his head back in howling laughter, too. At the pair of them grinning and bearing it, all while cursing one another out on the inside.

"I think I got really close to losing him at one point in my life, and I'm haunted by the face of this seventeen year old boy looking back at me with…with these *lifeless* eyes. Every day. Every single day I see him. I wish I could go back and see the things I missed, say the things I thought of too late. Protect him a little better than what I did. But, I can't. I can only help him now, and I'd do anything for my brother. So, I guess that's why I'm here."

"You're going to ask me to stay?" I kept my eyes on my shoes, because I wasn't sure I'd be able to say no.

"No," Wyatt said, pulling out an envelope that was folded in half from his pocket, "I don't think he'd want me to do that. But I do want to try and help you heal."

Wyatt handed me the envelope and I just looked at it hovering between us.

"Take it," he said. With a final look at his face I reached for the envelope and unfolded it.

My whole, entire world just stopped. Everything, *everything,* it all just stopped.

"I was eighteen when I bought my first car," Wyatt spoke to me softly and I could feel his eyes on my face. "It was the start of my senior year of high school and I saved up enough over the summer to buy something. Not particularly fancy or safe, but I saw it in the lot and pointed right at it, 'That one' I said."

I saw Wyatt hold his finger out in front of him from my peripheral vision, but I was still looking at the envelope in my hands.

"This guy had bought it cheap for his car lot from the other side of the country. There was something about being shown the wrong photos and he got something he didn't want so he wanted to get rid of it fast. It still had a bunch of stuff in it and so he gave it to me for cheaper than what he'd had it listed. I loved that car. It was my ticket to freedom. Aspen's too."

I didn't expect it, but Wyatt turned to face me, cross legged and hands out of his pockets folded in his lap.

I tore my eyes from the letter and looked at him. His face blurring in my vision, then clearing, then blurring again.

"I didn't mind the stuff. There were some clothes in the back, a whole cardboard box of pine and vanilla air fresheners in the boot."

Wyatt stopped on account of the sob that escaped my throat. I hadn't meant it too, I was determined to hear every word out of his mouth but I could see it all. Everything he was describing. He waited a second more before he kept talking.

"The most peculiar thing that I found though," he pointed at my hands, "was that letter."

I looked back down at my hands to see the envelope with Casimir's old mechanics logo in the top left. I could make out his fingerprints imprinted in grease stains on the edges and his handwriting in the very middle of it all, looking right back at me after thirteen whole years of not being able to see it. Not being able to recall it.

"He died on my birthday," I told Wyatt. I hadn't thought about him yet today. I always tried not to, but I wanted to tell someone. Because at that moment, there wasn't just one person who knew my brother in my house, there were two.

"When's your birthday?" he asked.

"Today."

I felt my eyes on the envelope as Wyatt stood up. "I'm sorry I read it before you, Poppy. I didn't ever think I'd meet the person who it was intended for, but I'd also never managed to throw it away. I guess I felt like I understood a lot of what he said. How he felt about you is how I feel about Aspen."

I just nodded, the letter getting heavier and heavier.

"Happy birthday, Poppy."

I heard Wyatt say the words, but I didn't notice when he left. Didn't hear my front door open or close, but right where he was standing now sat one single car key and a ticket for the first show of the *Lady Luck Salvation Tour.*

With shaking hands, I pulled the letter out of the envelope and started to read.

39

April 5th

Penny,
Today is your sixteenth birthday and that blows my mind. How did you grow up so fast?
I thought a lot about today, and how I could make it a day you would remember forever because I know how important turning sixteen is. You're not a kid anymore. That's wild. My baby sister isn't a baby anymore.

I know that it hasn't always been easy, with it just being the two of us.
I know sometimes you have questions that I can't really answer. I hadn't really thought that far ahead and I'll admit there have been times I've wished we could go back to a time where the hardest thing I was going to have to explain to you was that Santa Claus wasn't real. (...or is he?)

The first thing I want to tell you is; Ask your questions, Pen. Even if they're hard. Even if it hurts. Ask them. If they're for me then I'll always do my best to answer them, but if they're questions you ask of the world, don't be frightened.

You're probably wondering why I'm writing you this letter. I could have just said this stuff to you, but it felt important to write it down. I wanted you to have it just in case you ever needed to read these words back. In case one day when you set off and out into the world and we're miles apart that you might need to read them again. That you might miss your big, goofy brother and hear my voice while you read them.

Poppy, I'm so proud of you.
Sixteen is when you really start to grow up and I'm so proud of how you're growing up. I think a lot of the time people say that how kids grow up is really a reflection of the people who raise them, but they couldn't be more wrong.
This person you're becoming, it's all you. It's you who is teaching me, Pop.

Last week you told me you auditioned for the lead role in your school play. I remember the week before that when you were moping on the couch, down and out about how you didn't think you were good enough to get it. That you were scared.
When I got home today you told me you got the part. I wasn't even half way in the door and you were barreling into me.

I want you to remember that feeling, Poppy.
I hope you always run right towards the things that scare you.
I hope you remember how brave you are, how good and kind and generous you are. Because in the end those are the things that matter most and you have them in spades, Poppy Girl.

You can still be scared of things in life and want to grab onto them with both hands. That's sometimes the thing that makes it harder, wanting something so much and the knowledge that there will be times where it's just out of your reach.

I want you to ask yourself in those moments, whatever it is that scares you, do you want it with both hands? Is it worth that final jump?
If the answer is yes, then you do it. No question about it.

I thought to myself, 'how can I help her with that? To feel brave in running towards the things that scare her? How do I help her run towards them?' and then I thought of my car.

That car you always give me shit for was the first thing I bought for myself.
You were five and after everything…it was finally just me and you.
It's the very thing that drove me right towards the things that scared me most.
Job interviews, your first day of school, your first school dance, the first call I got from your principal after you kicked that kid in the nuts for cutting your ponytail with scissors in class (still super proud of you for that).

So, now it's yours. (This is a good 16th birthday present, right?)

The world is scary, Penelope. There is no way to sugar coat that.
You will make mistakes. You will find yourself in situations that scare you. You'll find yourself in situations where you'll have to forgive people and sometimes, might even need to forgive yourself. I've found that last one to be the hardest of them all.
I know that all sounds scary, but I also know you can do it. You just do what you do best, you run hell for leather at everything life throws at you and grab it with both hands.
That's what your big brother would do, anyway!

I don't remember the day I was born, but I remember the day you were.
It will forever be one of the best days of my life.

You're my whole world, kid. It hasn't always been easy but it's always been worth it.
I wouldn't change a thing about our story, Pop. It's my favorite one that's ever existed.

Happy Birthday.

Love Always. Your brother,
Cas

40

April 5th

I read the letter over and over.

I read it until I knew every word by heart. Until the curve of Casimir's gentle, clear scroll was embedded into my mind again. Tattooed anew with fresh ink.

By the time I snapped out of the trance I'd been in, the sun had set, and my feet couldn't move fast enough.

I had driven like a bat out of hell. The ticket Wyatt had left me clutched tightly in my hand, the rumble of the Taurus beneath me, eating up the miles that spanned between me and the arena. I was almost positive that I'd run a number of red lights, so much so, I probably gave Ina Minit a run for her money.

Lady Luck was meant to walk on stage at 9 PM, and I pulled the Taurus into what I was sure was an illegal park outside the main doors of the venue at 9:01.

My whole body was thrumming with a deranged sort of panic. It was feral in the way it buzzed beneath my skin, clawed at my stomach and took over complete control of my body. It made my feet slap the pavement under my boots harder, *faster*.

I still wasn't moving fast enough.

The thunderous applause of a completely sold-out arena of a hundred and fifty thousand people cracked like a whip through the air around me. *Lady Luck*'s logo was all around the exterior of the stadium. The tour name just beneath looked like it had been written in red paint that was dripping down the building. All five members of the band were plastered there, watching me with unmoving gazes as I crashed into the glass doors that led inside.

I guess I thought I would have been able to just run straight in.

That was a very stupid thought to have had.

I was stopped no fewer than five different times going through different security points and body scanners. Wyatt had given me a VIP ticket, which gave me access to the mosh right at the front of the stage where there were no assigned seats, as well as access to the band after the show.

An older woman scanned my ticket no faster than a sloth might, completely oblivious to the fact that my heart was beating so fast that I was starting to see spots dance along the sides of my vision. She handed me back my ticket and a lanyard with a pass attached to it that I assumed gave me clearance of some kind and then I was off again with absolutely no idea where I was going.

The venue the band was playing at was one of the largest in the entire world. It was astonishingly impressive if I let myself think about the structure around me, but I didn't. I kept trying to look at my ticket, to find the right door to enter, but I couldn't focus on it long enough to actually understand what I was looking at. Not with the roaring of the crowd on the other side of the doors that I kept running past.

Running and running and *running.*

"Blazewood!" Wyatt's voice pierced through the booming screams and I couldn't help the sob that clawed its way up and out of my throat. I was *so close*.

"My name is Wyatt Smith!"

The screaming got even louder that I was tempted to cover my ears with my hands. "And it's my fucking pleasure to welcome you all to the first night of the *Salvation Tour.*"

Never say never, because the sound of the screaming sky rocketed and I had no choice but to cover my ears then. I wanted to stop, to ask someone for help because this entire building had been built way too big, but my legs wouldn't stop moving. It was like they literally just *couldn't stop.* There was only one destination they needed to get to, and until I was right before him they refused to let up.

The doors I ran by started to blur, my heart rate was picking up and I was breathing so hard I wondered if I was really getting any air in at all.

Aspen was *right there.*

"I'm a little lonely up here all on my own, I have to tell you," Wyatt said, his voice carrying so clearly it was like he was right next to me. I was certain they heard him across the entire city. "How about we get the boys out here?"

Another panicked sob started to make its way up my throat right when I smacked into someone. I half thought it was a wall and I wouldn't have been all that surprised considering that I'd run the perimeter of the stadium at least a couple times by this point and I was both exhausted and honestly a little dizzy. The shock of the collision landed me right on my ass, snapping me momentarily out of my frenzied panic.

"I'm so sorry," I stammered. Wiping at my eyes and scrambling back to my feet. "Are you alr–"

"Poppy?" Savannah was still sprawled on the ground in front of me looking for all the world like she'd just been slapped. I suppose it probably wasn't far off, considering I'd run into her traveling at what I assumed was a million fucking miles an hour.

"Savannah?" I was stunned for a second, just long enough for my head to clear and remember that Savannah was a big-wig at this exact venue and likely knew the layout like the back of her hand.

"Are you okay?" She got to her feet quickly, already reaching for me like we hadn't just met once. Like we were the sort of friends that spanned far beyond a single encounter. "Hey, what—are you here with the guys?"

I just shook my head, but changed half way through to nodding and then stopped completely. I didn't actually have an answer to her question.

"Come on," she said, taking my hand and starting to lead me back the way she'd just come. "We can wait in the green room until they're done."

No. My feet refused to move another step in her direction. I couldn't wait until after. *This* couldn't wait.

"No, I need to get in now." It was my first full sentence to her and it wasn't particularly kind or gracious. Usually I'd follow that right up with an apology but there was no room to be sorry for anything right now, all I needed was to get in there to *see*–

"I want to hear how loud you can *scream* for me, Blazewood!" Wyatt's voice cut me off again, my heart beating a frantic rhythm, the organ making its finest effort in trying to escape from my chest.

"Let me hear you scream for the one, the only, Rip Reynolds!" Wyatt yelled and you could tell the moment Rip walked onto the stage because the actual ground beneath our feet *shook*.

"Savannah, I need to get in there now." I repeated, handing her my ticket. She didn't miss the way my hand shook as I held it out to her. Her eyes flicked to the ticket in my hand then back to my face before a little smirk curved her bright red painted lips. She grabbed my ticket from me and stepped forward, reaching around to slide it into the back pocket of my jeans.

Grabbing me by my shoulders she looked at me, her eyes scanning me from head to toe. Savannah swiped her thumbs under my eyes and reached up to run her fingers through my hair, no doubt fixing any pieces that had gone haywire in my frantic attempts to get into the concert.

"Let's see if we can do better than that, shall we? I know just how loud you can be, Blazewood." Wyatt's voice pulsed around us again. The noise from the audience started to change, instead of clapping it turned into the rumbling stomps of a hundred and fifty thousand pairs of legs. There was only one member of *Lady Luck* that got that sort of reaction from the crowd and Savannah's eyes sparkled knowingly.

"Make some fucking noise for the bass guitarist of *Lady Luck,*" Wyatt screamed. *"Angus Dravin!"*

I couldn't even hear myself think, but Savannah's grip on my shoulders kept me right there with her. She turned me to my left to face a huge set of black double doors with a sign above it that read *'Floor Entrance K-1'*. Walking right over to grab the handle of the door, she looked at me before pulling it open.

"Go get your man, girl." With a wink in my direction Savannah opened the door, letting the euphoric sounds of the fans of *Lady Luck* pour out and over us.

I didn't even give her a second look as I walked straight into the arena, my legs taking me straight towards the stage.

41

April 5th

There were so many people.

So many people.

Packed together and screaming and sweaty and desperate to be noticed by the band on the stage.

I kept moving, just one foot in front of the other, step after step. It was like being stuck in quicksand; the more I tried to squeeze my way through, the less I seemed to move.

I was half way through to the front of the stage when Wyatt spoke up again.

Now that he was joined by both Rip and Angus on stage, all three of them had begun to play their instruments, filling the air around us with the addictive lilt of their guitars. There were people around me screaming like they were dying. Crying like nothing in their lives would ever beat this moment.

The song they were playing wasn't one I'd ever heard before but the mere notion of them creating music right in front of their eyes was sending everyone into a frenzy.

It wasn't Wyatt's voice that crackled through the air next, but rather Luke's.

"Blazewood," he sang the name of the city tauntingly and the lights swapped from white to red. Rip changed what he was playing to the haunting introduction to a song I knew was from their last album called '*The World is Ugly*'.

Wyatt stopped playing his guitar as the song shifted and started to clap above his head. The loss of whatever he was playing didn't last long before it was picked up by Luke. I watched him walk on stage just as the guy next to me started to scream, *"Oh my fucking God!"*

"I believe you all know Lucas Blake, rhythm guitarist for *Lady Luck!"* Wyatt said into the microphone and Luke walked over and planted a kiss right on his cheek. The screaming increased and I started to move again. I was still too far from the stage.

I was *too fucking far.*

No one was moving, if anything people were pushing me back and the frustration of it all made my nose start to string. I wanted to scream, because no one was fucking *moving*. A sob shook out of me, exhaustion starting to settle in from the press of bodies around me.

It was right then that I looked back up at the stage and locked eyes with the front man of *Lady Luck.*

Wyatt was staring right at me, his hands frozen above his head and nothing but shocked elation on his face, slashing into existence in the form of the most genuine smile I'd ever seen.

I kept on fighting against the people around me to get to the front of the stage. Pushing and pulling against the bodies of fans that were desperately trying to claw their way closer to the stage too.

The kick of a bass drum permeated the space around me and my whole body just froze.

Thump, thump, thump, thump, thump, thump, thump, thump.

Wyatt grabbed the mic off the stand and walked along the stage, right over to the far left and held the microphone up to the people on that side of the stadium. "Do you know who's next?" He asked the crowd. The response was thunderous.

"Well...if you *do* know who's next, I want you to yell his name on the count of three. One…two…*three.*"

"Aspen-Fucking-Smith!" The fifty thousand people on the left side of the arena screamed his name so loud I could feel every syllable vibrate through my body.

"Hmm," Wyatt said, pushing his jet black hair back off his face and walking all the way to the right side of the stage. "I didn't catch that. Did you guys catch that at all?"

"Who?" Rip said into his mic.

"Nope!" Angus said.

"Not even a little" Luke said before jumping up onto an amp at the front of the stage.

"Let me try over here," Wyatt said to the right side of the arena. "Do *you* know who's missing?"

He held his mic out to them and I was still frozen where I stood, looking from Wyatt to the other guys in the band, across the whole stage to find the source of that drum beat.

"Aspen-Fucking-Smith!" They screamed and screamed and *screamed.*

Wyatt walked to the front of the stage and looked right at me as he announced the last member of the band. "There's no *Lady Luck* without him."

The drums started to pick up even more and I was positive someone to my left had just passed out but I refused to take my eyes off the stage.

"He's actually been here the whole time." Wyatt grinned at the crowd before his eyes fell back to me, like he didn't want to lose where I was standing. "Blazewood…let me hear you lose your goddamn minds for Aspen *fucking* Smith!"

The lights on the back of the stage ignited, casting the previously shadowed space into blinding light. Aspen sat behind the most impressive drum kit I'd ever seen, raised on a podium set above the stage. He had a black singlet on with his hat on backwards and the drum beat he'd been playing kept constant even as he stood up, twirling a drumstick in one hand and pointing the other out at the crowd.

I couldn't take my eyes off him and the fact he was *right there* made me start to move again with a desperation that I didn't have before. I had to get to him. He had to *know.*

Even if he'd changed his mind, even if I'd already lost him for good, he had to know.

My eyes hadn't been on the stage, instead they had been focused in front of me. Focused on the people around me, on how I could get through them, so I didn't see Wyatt move from his spot at the front of the stage, and walk towards his brother. Didn't see how he took the mic and stopped right in front of Aspen until I heard the words projected across the stadium.

"Ap," Wyatt's voice echoed. "Poppy's here."

The drum beat just stopped. It just cut out completely.

"What?" Aspen's voice was picked up by the mic his brother held and I finally pulled my eyes up from the people in front of me towards the stage.

"Aspen," his name tumbled from my mouth, getting lost in the chants of everyone around me even though their confusion was clear and the noise of the stadium had started to drop.

"Where?" Aspen hopped off the platform his drums were on and walked around to his brother. I watched on as Wyatt turned to the crowd and pointed right at me. I locked eyes with Aspen at the same time that roughly a hundred and fifty thousand people turned their attention on me.

"Aspen!" I called out his name again, louder this time, determined to get to him. He was stunned in place for maybe five seconds and then he started to move. Aspen walked to the edge of the stage, stopping at the very front to find me in the crowd again before he jumped down.

The stadium let out a collective gasp as Aspen walked to the guard rail at the front of the mosh and stood on it. Security swarmed him, the hands of huge, burly men reached up to hold onto him as the frantic hands of fans reached for him.

"That's Poppy." I heard someone say from beside me, but I refused to pull my eyes from his.

"Hey, look! There she is."

"Help her through." Someone else said.

"Move aside, let her through!" And slowly, people started to move. They

finally started to *move.*

I kept my eyes on Aspen, clung to my name that I could see on his lips even though I couldn't hear him and I fought my way towards him until he was right there. Until he was so close all I needed to do was reach out my hand.

The feeling of his palm sliding into mine tore a sob from my throat so brutal I felt my legs finally give out. Finally, they stopped after fighting to get me where I needed to be.

Aspen hauled me up and into him, my arms wrapped around him, my face buried into his neck. The roar of the stadium seemed so inconsequential to the feeling of the strong band of his arms wrap around me, holding onto me so tight it hurt to breathe.

I didn't care, not as I kept repeating in my head that this was him, it was *him.*

I hardly registered it as he hauled me up and over the barricade. He just kept holding onto me fiercely as he walked us back towards the stage, clinging to me like if he didn't I might just disapear all over again.

The stadium erupted like a fucking volcano and I couldn't even hear the words in my own head.

"Guys!" Wyatt called out, trying to get the crowd under control and little by little they started to quiet.

"Poppy," Aspen's lips were at my ear, his hand on the back of my head. "You're here. I can't believe you're *here.*"

He set me down and the stadium continued to settle, every single pair of eyes on us, including the rest of the band on stage.

"I feel like I've interrupted something important here," I said against his neck and felt the rumble of his laughter against every part of my body that was pressed against his.

"It's okay," he laughed, pulling back to look at me. Aspen set me down and I realized that it wasn't just that I'd blocked out the screams of the stadium, but that every single person in the arena had gone quiet. I looked away from Aspen for the first time to see the view he usually had, to see hundreds of thousands of people with their phone lights up in the air.

I looked back at Aspen who hadn't taken his eyes or hands off me for even a second. There were far more than twenty pairs of eyes on me now, but I couldn't find it in myself to care even the tiniest bit. Not a single person mattered more than the man in front of me.

"I probably should have waited, but I couldn't. This couldn't wait." I reached for his shirt and gripped it tightly. There was so much I wanted to tell him, so much I wanted to explain, but in the end, there was only one thing that really seemed to matter.

"You once told me that when you pictured going home, you didn't think of your apartment. Do you remember what you said?" I thought I heard my own voice echo around me.

"Yes," he said, nodding his head like it was still a fundamental, crucial truth. There was no mistaking it that time; Aspen's voice reverberated around us.

"Tell me again?" I asked, knowing full well the entire world was listening to every word we were saying. I didn't care, I wanted them to know. I wanted every single person alive to *know.*

"I said, I pictured you." His eyes were glassy as he looked at me, his grip on me tightening even more. I reached up to wipe away a silent tear that had fallen down his beautiful face.

I nodded my head, letting myself say the words I'd wanted to tell him for the moment I saw him standing in my living room. "I picture you too."

I knew in the very soul of me that nothing could have ever felt as right or true or perfect as those words. Aspen crushed his mouth to mine before the last word left my mouth. The moment he did I wrapped my arms around his neck, pulling him into me, keeping him close, all while the entire stadium went fucking *wild.* There wasn't a corner of the world that wouldn't have heard the screaming chants of the people around us.

I felt the sound through the soles of my shoes. In the tips of my fingers.

I laughed against his lips that had curved into one of his most beautiful smiles as he kissed me, vowing never to take for granted the way his skin felt beneath the palms of my hands again. The warmth of it, the roughness. Like a song I could go years without hearing but I'd never forget a single word.

"I love you," he said, and I couldn't hear it, but I *felt* it. I felt every word he said against my lips, felt the truth of them.

An undeniable and unwavering fact. Not something fragile and made of glass but of stone and steel. They would never break. They would *always* last. Again and again he said it against my eyelids, my cheeks, the base of my throat.

I pulled back to look at him, reaching up to hold his face between my hands. "To your *bones,* Aspen," I raised my voice so I could be sure he heard it over the crowd. Even as it shook, I shared the words I had thought I would have to carry on my own forever. Not because I was scared, but from the unbelievable *joy* of letting myself say them to him.

My tears made him blurry but not blurry enough for me to miss the look on his face. A look that I didn't think I'd ever forget as long as I lived. I only needed a glance at the small furrow of his brow, the widening of his eyes, the way his lips parted slightly to know that no one in my whole life had ever looked at me like he was looking at me right then, like he couldn't live without me either.

I wiped his cheeks with the sleeves of my sweater and pressed my forehead to his, "I love you to your very bones."

"He got the *fucking girl, Blazewood!"* Wyatt screamed into the microphone just as Rip howled at the audience in the way he always did and Aspen started to laugh again, his face pressed to the curve of my neck. I tried to pull away but he refused to let me go. Instead, he jumped back on the stage and reached down to haul me up after him. I thought he would just lead me off to the side but instead he reached for his brother's microphone and I watched him yell right out to the sold-out stadium, to the whole world, *"I got the fucking girl!"*

Aspen reached for me, pulling me in for another kiss that was not at all appropriate to be doing on stage before finally leading me off to the side and away from the applause of his fans. He handed me a set of noise canceling headphones and with a final kiss he turned to head back on stage. He took two steps before stopped abruptly and walked back to me so we were toe to toe.

"Stay, Poppy." His eyes were pleading and I knew he was asking from more than just right now.

I nodded, meaning it with every single piece of me. With every piece that was broken and the bits that were not starting to heal. Knowing that even if I'd gotten into that moving truck, I would have only ever ended up here, with him. Since the moment I saw him, there was never going to be anywhere else for me to go.

"Always."

42

Epilogue

1 Year 6 Months Later

Poppy

Aspen was on the couch when I'd gotten home, forearms settled onto his knees and head in his hands. The visual lasted only a second before he bolted up straight to his feet and yelled right across the penthouse a very high pitched, "I've done something!"

He'd cleared his throat and tried again but I was already in a fit of laughter.

"Poppy, I've done something," he said for the third time once I arrived in front of him, dropped my bag to the floor and melted right into him.

Aspen's hands came up and around me, warming me immediately despite the balmy day outside. It was like now that I was home, after the sun had mostly finished it's shining for the day, *my* day was only just beginning. My sun was only now coming into view.

He reached up to tuck a strand of hair behind my ear and I caught his hand before he could wrap his arm back around me, placing a kiss to the little fish tattoo on the inside of his wrist. The twin to my own.

The day I had run towards him, when I battled my way through a crowd of thousands to reach him, the day I'd decided to finally stay still, we'd gone back to my empty house after that first show of the *Salvation Tour* to collect Natalie only to find her floating on the surface of the water.

Her little fins still, her little heart silent.

Aspen had sat with me as I held her tank in my lap until the sun had risen. Our backs pressed against an empty wall of my empty house. My head on his shoulder and one of my hands clutched tightly in both of his. It had taken some time for the shock to wear off, but by the time we had gotten back to his apartment all that was left was this feeling of complete and total peace.

Like she finally moved on because I had too.

It was later that day Aspen had come home to the penthouse and shown me his wrist. "It's not a spider web or fuzzy dice, but I still think it's pretty badass," he said, taking my hand and kissing the middle of my palm.

When I told him I wanted one too, we went back to the tattoo parlor that very hour and Nat had been with us both ever since.

"That sounds precarious," I mumbled against his warm, worn cotton shirt, shifting to peer up at him. That's when I noticed that he was biting the inside of his cheek and that his brows were pinched.

Aspen was nervous.

I knew he'd essentially been a 'yes man' with his friends for the last fourteen years but it baffled me how none of them had picked up any of his tells. Well, except for Allie, she'd been onto him right from the get go. Of course Dax had known but that had been different. Allie had seen him when the others hadn't. Always doing her best to support him when she could, to soften any exchange that she thought might have sent Ap spiraling. Aspen and I had been dating for a while when I'd realized the extent of her silent guarding of the man I loved and when I took her to the side and wrapped my arms around her with a whispered 'Thank you', all she did was hug me back. We'd pulled back to find one another with watery eyes which of course made us both laugh, then made us both cry.

"You're nervous," I said to him, resting my chin right on his chest.

He didn't say anything, just took me by the hand and led me into the small recording room that resided in our penthouse. It turned out that Aspen hadn't just been partial to the drums, he was a wonderful piano player, something Allie had taught him.

He pulled me down to sit on the piano bench right next to him, and with a final look at me, he started to play. I could *feel* my mouth hanging open wide, my eyes completely unable to look away from his hands. The way they moved; strong and sure.

Every single note he played pushed its way into me and stayed there. I was completely unable to let it go. The way he played was gentle, every note that came into existence rose and fell to meet one another in crescendos and decrescendos and it became clear to me why he'd written this song. He played and played until it came to a beautiful end, his fingers staying on the notes until the sound rang out.

The silence that pressed in on us was one of our usual kind. The kind we loved to sit in together when I could hear his quiet breathing and he could hear mine, when the world beyond the space around us didn't matter half as much as the one we'd built together.

"The first time you laughed it made me think of a small melody. Your actual laugh, it sounded like four notes strung together." He played those notes now, the same ones that started the song. "I used all the best notes," he went on, eyes still on the keys in front of him, "that's how you sound to me."

Those exact four notes played into the space around me as I watched Aspen turn around from his spot at the end of the aisle. His suit was all black, of course, and his hair was pushed off his forehead, looking for all the world like he woke up just like that. Like he'd maybe never even gone to bed but rather stood right there though the hours of the evening, waiting for me.

The song Ap had composed built in the air around us, this beautiful, soul grabbing melody.

I stood at the start of the aisle alone. I hadn't wanted to be walked down by anyone, even though every single one of Aspen's friends had offered, including his older brother who stood next to him with shining eyes, not as he looked at me, but as he looked at the man I was about to marry.

I hadn't wanted anyone to walk me down because even though I couldn't see him, I felt Casimir in the space beside me. I felt the ghost of his arm looping through mine. How he would look down at me, tears in his eyes the same way Wyatt had and he'd bump my chin with his rough and worn knuckles. His grease and tobacco smell lingering even though he'd have cleaned up nicely in his suit.

He'd say, 'we can still leave, I can hold them off so you can get a head start'. He'd be joking and serious all at once and I'd laugh and cry at the same time while I stared back at him. He'd keep me steady as I placed one foot in front of the other until he shook Aspen's hand before placing mine in it.

I opened my eyes, coming back into the present knowing that maybe in another version of this life my brother would have been beside me, but knowing for certain that no matter what, in every version of life that ever existed, I would marry Aspen Killian Smith.

In every single one.

So, I did what I'd been doing every day since I was eighteen; I picked up the front of my dress and ran.

Right down the aisle, straight towards the only thing I'd ever wanted.

I ran to Aspen.

I ran home.

About the Author

Celine L. A. Simpson is an Australian romance and fantasy author, a dog mum, Punk Rock enthusiast, and owns at least 6 dungarees that she consistently pairs with Converse.

Most commonly known for her Romance publication Just My Luck (2023) and Music to my Ears (2021), she was raised on the Mid-North Coast of Australia and graduated from La Trobe University with a Bachelors Degree in Creative Arts, majoring in Creative and Professional Writing. Growing up with a passion for reading, she began writing at an early age, moving into content creation as a career path before writing and publishing her own novels.

Also by Celine L.A. Simpson

Just My Luck

An 'enemies-to-lovers' romance by Celine L.A. Simpson. Dark, dirty, witty and steaming hot. Perfect for fans of ***Ana Huang, Emily Henry, Tessa Bailey and Emily McIntire.***

"The tension, the story, THE TENSION!" - Emma (Goodreads review)

"Fantastic plot, brilliant story, characters you will fall in love with" - BooksWithBanter (Goodreads Review)

Lucky.

Cole Thompson used to wish for my downfall.

He took every opportunity to break me, to best me. But this man? This was not the Cole I remember from my youth. Not the kind kid that played with me in my backyard, and certainly not the infuriating boy who had eventually realised that he had only been born with one to challenge me in every aspect of my life.

This man was self-made, dripping with the proof of how he climbed that ladder of success. And he was beautiful. *Too* beautiful.

It was really too bad he was still hell bent on breaking me. He thinks he can, now that I'm the lucky girl without her luck, now that I'm at the bottom while he looks on from above.

What he doesn't know is that, luck or no, I'll break him first.

Cole.

It was clear and clean before, what I'd wanted from Lucky Peters. I'd wanted her to suffer. I wanted her to see me standing at the top of the world she had insisted on taking from me time and time again, and I wanted her to *beg* me for mercy. I wanted to hold every single part of her in my hands. Her happiness, her freedoms, her career, her life. I wanted her to look at me and *know* what it was like to be powerless.

That was all I had wanted.
But that was then.
This is now.

Convincing Florence

Florence wasn't a people person.

Flossy learnt right from the get-go that to expect anything from anyone (apart from her grandmother) would only ever lead to disappointment. That all the minutes and seconds of her life constantly intersected with the hard and tough minutes of everyone else's, right from the moment she entered this world and let loose a wail of arrival.

It was the friends who couldn't be bothered to return the friendship, the dates that were only ever interested in one thing, and the general strangers who were never interested in returning her smile.

Florence loved two things. Her job at the library and her grandmother, Dot.

Apart from them?

People sucked.

Nathaniel Connors loved a challenge.

Tall, dark, and handsome; Nathaniel Connors sailed through life on a dimpled smile and buckets of charm. But when Florence finds him in the library, breaking more than one rule, she might have been the first person who didn't give him the time of day.

If there's one thing that Nathaniel needed to do now, it was to convince Florence that he was worth her time, and that there were people who were worth her while.

She was sure he'd fail.

He knew he wouldn't.

Challenge Accepted.

Music To My Ears

He had one of those side, half smiles that you read about...I always thought that was absolute nonsense - no single smile could make you want to cry out for mercy, but there you have it.

I did manage to, however, maintain enough of my dignity to cry on the inside.

Allie could sum up her entire life in two whole minutes. She lived walking distance to everything; work, her best friend's place and perhaps most importantly, the 24-hour corner store that was only a 1-minute walk away. Allie frequently sought comfort from the bottom of premixed brownie boxes at all times of the evening when she perused the baking aisle alone, until one night...

Wyatt Smith was the front man of the most popular modern rock band to date. Lady Luck travelled the world, their look and their music was recognised by everyone, everywhere. That was until he found himself the midnight errand boy for a runaway baking ingredient where he met Allie. And she had absolutely no idea who he was...

It's true that when someone catches your eye you start to see them everywhere.

But what happens when you do see them again?

Sometimes it's easier to put feelings in boxes, and sometimes it's easier to run away when the going gets tough. But sometimes you find someone to help you unpack, someone who will stand beside you, feel the fear, and take that leap of faith with you.

Terraleise (The Lost Child of the Crown #1)

Terraleise turns 18, only to discover she is now gifted with the elemental power of Earth. The thing about elemental gifts is that only those with royal blood possess them.

Terraleise is thrown into a life she never dreamed to be a part of, discovering all of the secrets entwined with her past, and her future. The heir to a kingdom overthrown by a corrupt branch of her own bloodline, Terra will see what it means to have courage and be brave, learning that the fate of the four kingdoms of Vaashaa rests on her shoulders.

Finding a life to fight for only to be faced with sacrificing it all, Terraleise will have to risk her love and her life to keep the world from falling into darkness. Will the Lost Child of the Crown find her rightful place?

Heir of Vaashaa (The Lost Child of the Crown #2)

The land is dying and the promise of war is thick in the air. With Terraleise still held captive by the enemy, Silas is forced out of his grief to move forward, to march on and ensure Terra's sacrifice, her life for his, doesn't go to waste.

The threat to the World of Vaashaa is more horrific than anyone could have ever anticipated. A long-forgotten darkness has crept back into the hands of the wrong person and time is running out to stop it. The Kingdoms of Vaashaa will have to come together to save their world from the bleak future it is heading towards, all while hoping for aid to come from the truths laced within myths and legends.

There is only one who stands to be a force between the darkness and the light, only one who can save them all. Will the Heir of Vaashaa rise from the ashes?

www.ingramcontent.com/pod-product-compliance
Lightning Source LLC
Chambersburg PA
CBHW070551310726
48982CB00011B/1546/J

* 9 7 8 1 7 6 3 5 6 5 9 2 0 *